Congratulations Sarah!

Here is the copy of Origin – Season One you won through my Goodreads giveaway.

I hope you enjoy reading it. As I mentioned in the giveaway, this has been primarily an effort at garnering some much-needed reviews for my book. You are, of course, under no obligation to write one and I assure you that I will make no effort beyond this one to encourage it. The truth is, reviews are hard to come by, and that goes double for new authors. I guess you could call it a classic Catch-22. Reviews are vital because aside from informing potential readers about the book and its merits, they also form a base for other important marketing efforts. So if you do like the book and choose to share your thoughts, be it at Goodreads or Amazon, you have my undying gratitude.

Sincerely,

Nathaniel

# ORIGIN

## SEASON ONE

A NOVEL BY

**NATHANIEL DEAN JAMES**

MILLENNIUM BIRDHOUSE
Digital Press

First published in the Republic of Ireland in 2014 by Millennium Birdhouse Ltd.



1st Print Edition

ISBN: 978-0-992844639

Millennium Birdhouse Ltd
75 Steeplechase Green
Ratoath
Co. Meath
Ireland

www.millenniumbirdhouse.com

For Nichola

# NOTE TO READERS

This book contains several pieces of artwork commissioned for the novel by the publisher. To view them in their original uncropped size and in color, visit: www.pinterest.com/mbirdhouseltd. At our Pinterest page you can also browse additional artwork currently in production for the launch of Origin Online, the dedicated website that will accompany the series, due to be launched in early 2015.

# CHAPTER 1

**Federal Reserve Bank**
**New York, New York**
**Friday 14 July 2006**
**1600 EDT**

Gert Dekker wiped the sweat from his brow with the palm of one hand and took another step toward the curb. The nervous tic in his right eye gave him the odd appearance of a man staring at a flashing disco ball. His attention was fixed on the intersection of Nassau and Liberty Street, where the motley parade of afternoon traffic continued to inch forward under the pitiless sun of a Manhattan summer. Now slowly suffocating inside his wool suit, he had resolved to turn and go back inside when he saw the car.

It was hard to miss.

Unlike most embassies in post 9/11 New York, the Zambians still thought it was a good idea to fly the national flag on their cars. The white S-Class Mercedes pulled to a stop at the curb, and a young man in a chauffeur's uniform got out to open the door for his passenger.

The man who emerged from the car was blacker than the history of Europe and towered a full eight inches above Dekker. He wore a navy suit and a white shirt with a blood-red tie. His hair was cropped in a flattop that made him look more like an action figure than a diplomat.

"Mr. Ambassador, it's a pleasure to see you again," Dekker said.

The ambassador flashed him a shark's grin, but ignored Dekker's outstretched hand. He stepped aside to let his assistant out, a thin, bespectacled man carrying a dark brown alligator-skin briefcase.

"Right this way, Ambassador," Dekker said.

Two guards joined them inside the lobby and Dekker led the small procession toward a row of polished brass elevator doors at the end of the hall. One of the guards took a key-card from his breast pocket and inserted it into the slot below the buttons on the panel. A moment later the radio on his hip squawked. "You're clear for Sub Two."

"Gentlemen," Dekker said, "I'll have to ask you to wait here until we've opened the vault. I'll be back to escort you down as soon as we're ready."

The ambassador clearly didn't like the idea of waiting but voiced no protest.

The sublevel antechamber was a narrow room about twenty feet wide. Four marble pillars ran up the corners to a domed ceiling decorated in a series of murals of Greek or Roman origin. It gave the room the eerie feel of a mausoleum. In contrast, the vault doors were modern. Not the round steel doors you might expect to find in one of the oldest banks in the country, but square and made of brushed titanium. The seam between the frame and the doors was barely a millimeter wide, and there were no visible hinges.

Dekker removed a chain from his neck and inserted a small toothless key into the panel beside the door.

"Allied Bishop Control, go ahead."

"Vice President Gert Dekker. I need access to 2-A, please," Dekker said.

"Please scan in, sir."

Dekker placed his thumb onto the small rectangle next to the screen.

"Thank you, Mr. Dekker."

Somewhere inside the wall an electric motor began to turn, and the entire door moved out of its frame as if levitating. It extended about a foot, then began to rise, revealing two large hydraulic arms that pushed the heavy door up from the inside.

As both men watched the door rise the indifference on their faces gave way to a look of stupid incomprehension. They leaned forward like a well-practiced double act, then rose again as the door ascended to eye level and finally came to a stop several inches above the opening.

Dekker walked toward the open door the way a man might approach a sleeping creature of unknown temperament. He glanced back at the guard. "Get the chairman down here."

When the guard didn't move, Dekker shouted, "Do it. Now! And get rid of the ambassador."

The guard ran back to the elevator. Dekker stepped into the vault, his eyes still fixed on the wall. Something toppled over beneath his foot and rolled across the room. Dekker's eyes followed it. It hit the far wall with a soft clang, and he saw it was a spray can. Several feet above it, written in two rows of large clumsy red letters were the words "*SED QUIS CUSTODIET IPOS CUSTODES*?" In some places the paint had run all the way down to the marble floor and formed small pools.

Dekker knelt and picked up the can. There was a sheet of paper fastened to it with a rubber band. When he unfolded it, a small memory card dropped to the floor. Dekker knelt to pick up the card. He recognized it as a standard SD card, the same one his own digital camera used. He scanned the safety deposit boxes along the wall, but saw no sign that any of them had been opened.

The paper was a printout of the vault's 120 deposit boxes, complete with the names of their owners. At the bottom someone had written the words "Back Off" followed by a long line of numbers that meant nothing to him.

Dekker was too shocked to hear the guard return.

"Sir, the chairman is on his way. What the hell is going on?"

Dekker turned to him, his eyes vacant, uncomprehending. "We're fucked, Andy. That's what's going on. We've just been fucked."

# CHAPTER 2

**The Pentagon**
**Washington DC**
**Friday 14 July 2006**
**1800 EDT**

The helicopter was bright red except for the words *Skyline Defense* painted across the tail boom in thick black letters. It hovered briefly over the landing pad before nosing up and gently settling onto the manicured lawn.

Carl Bosch, chairman and CEO of Skyline, stepped out into the bright afternoon sun and waved an impatient hand at the waiting navy lieutenant.

Dressed casually in a collared white shirt and tan slacks, Bosch made no effort to hide the gray in his hair, which was cut short and complemented by a thick salt-and-pepper mustache. As the head of one of the Pentagon's less advertised contractors he enjoyed a number of rare privileges and exuded a corresponding arrogance that endeared him to few.

"Good afternoon, Mr. Bosch," the officer said. "The admiral is waiting for you in his office."

"Where else would he be waiting?" Bosch said.

They made their way down the concrete path toward the north face of the building. Inside, a marine gunnery sergeant handed Bosch a photo ID and put the briefcase he was carrying through the x-ray scanner.

Five minutes later, he stepped into the office of Rear Admiral James O'Connor. O'Connor was a tall, thin man with gaunt features and a sharp nose. He was standing at the window overlooking the inner courtyard. He didn't turn around when Bosch entered, only looked down at the tumbler of scotch in his hand and stirred the ice cubes with a shake of the wrist.

"Thank you, Adam," the admiral said, and the aide promptly left the room.

Without waiting for an invitation, Carl sat down on one of the two leather chairs facing the admiral's desk. "I didn't realize inflation was running so high."

The admiral put his glass down and smiled. "Christ, Carl, you should be thanking me, not complaining. I had to call in a lot of favors on this one."

Bosch set his briefcase down on the desk blotter. "Happy retirement."

The admiral walked over, opened the case and ran an absentminded hand over the bills inside. "What's so important about this ship, anyway? Why not just sail her around the Cape?"

"She's on a tight schedule," Bosch said. "She also represents a sizable investment. The last thing we need is for her to be stuck off the coast of Somalia for three weeks while the insurance people haggle with the locals over ransom money."

The admiral opened the top drawer of his desk and handed Carl a sheet of paper. "The USS Princeton will be authorized to leave her patrol zone for twelve hours. That will get you into Egyptian waters. After that, you're on your own."

# CHAPTER 3

**Federal Reserve Bank**
**New York, New York**
**Saturday 15 July 2006**
**0900 EDT**

Special Agent Mike Banner pulled up to the loading-bay entrance on Liberty Street and stubbed out his half-smoked cigarette in an empty coffee cup on the passenger seat.

Both security guards in front of the door were carrying shotguns. To his bemusement, one of them retreated to a covering position as the other approached the car. Mike lowered the window. "Afternoon. Mike Banner, FBI. I should be on the guest list."

The guard wasn't amused. "I'll need to see your ID, sir."

Mike handed it over. The guard took it, then stepped back and conferred briefly with someone over his radio. When he handed it back, he said, "Sir, are you carrying a weapon?"

"Just my service issue," Mike said.

"I'll have to ask you to leave it here, sir."

Mike was about to ask why, but the look on the guard's face suggested it would be a waste of time. He reached over, pulled the Glock 23 from the glove box and handed it over. A moment later the doors began to open.

Mike recognized the black Chevy Suburban parked at the bottom of the ramp as one of their own. He got out and approached the woman at the top of the steps to the loading platform. "Afternoon, boss."

Mary Winters, the assistant director of the New York field office, looked tired. Her hair, normally her most striking feature, had been tied back in a simple ponytail, and Mike didn't think she was wearing any makeup.

"Thanks for coming in, Mike," she said. "I appreciate it."

"Not at all, I could use the overtime. Especially now that Susan wants us to find a place in Nassau."

When she didn't smile, he said, "What's going on?"

"Follow me," she said.

She led him through the door at the back of the loading bay into a small room filled with monitoring screens, then through another door at the back of the room into a long hallway that ended in a narrow flight of steps. At the top was yet another steel door that looked even thicker than the previous two.

The room was a larger version of the one downstairs. There were at least thirty screens mounted in an arc around a wide counter with two keyboards and a joystick built in.

Two people were waiting for them inside. The first was a portly, bald man with a thick gray beard. He wore no tie, had rolled his shirtsleeves up to his elbows, and looked to Mike as if he hadn't slept in a week. The assistant director introduced him as Paul Shaffer, chairman of the bank's board of directors.

Shaffer held out a hand. "Mary you know. This is Gert Dekker, our vice president. It's a pleasure to meet you, Agent Banner. Mary says you're her top guy. I sure hope she's right. Gert, show him the video."

Mike, who knew neither what was going on, nor why he was there, watched as Dekker walked to the control terminal. A loud burst of static issued from the wall-mounted speakers; then the video feed began to run on one of the two large screens above the counter. The picture was only a moving blur at first, then it settled. It took Mike a moment to understand that the camera had just been mounted somehow to the head of the person making the video.

When the picture came into focus Mike could just make out a door in the dark, grainy image. There was a click and the door opened. The view suddenly blurred again as it swung back to the door and a hand reached out to close it. As soon as it was closed, the image was suddenly flooded with light, presumably from a flashlight also mounted on the person's head. After that things moved fast.

Less than three minutes later, Mike, who was now dizzy from the constantly moving picture, saw the elevator doors open on the sublevel antechamber. The man (Mike assumed it was a man) turned right and approached the control panel next to the vault door. For several seconds the image was static; then the door began to open. Mike watched as the figure stepped inside and walked to the far wall. There was a loud rattle as he shook the spray can and began to write. When he was done, the view swung back to the door and the video stopped.

Mike turned to the assistant director, who turned to Shaffer.

"Agent Banner," Shaffer said, "What you've just seen is a recording of someone breaking into the New York Federal Reserve. I'd like to explain how it was done, but I don't have a clue. And neither does anybody else around here."

"Jesus Christ," Mike said. It was all he could think of.

Shaffer nodded to Dekker, who said, "This bank is protected by one of the most secure systems in the world. As you can see, they managed to somehow bypass it completely. As for the people that monitor the system from Boston, they don't even know it happened."

"When *did* it happen?" Mike said.

"Sometime between Wednesday afternoon and midnight last night. From what we can see, that was when all the camera feeds for the areas concerned were automatically erased by the system."

As he listened, the frown on Mike's face deepened. "How? I don't get it. There's no indication in the system that the doors were even opened?"

"None," Dekker said. "And everything appears to be running just fine now."

"Do you know what was stolen?" Mike said.

Dekker handed Mike a sheet of paper. "This was also left in the vault."

The sheet was a printed list numbered from 1 to 120. Each entry contained the name of an individual or company. Mike recognized quite a few of them, including several prominent members of the New York political elite. Below the list, written in the same clumsy handwriting as the Latin on the wall were two words: *Back Off.* Below this in even smaller letters there was a long string of what looked like some kind of code.

"Well, the message is clear enough, if nothing else is," Mike said handing back the sheet. "We go looking for these people and everyone on that list gets a copy of the video, along with the Times and the Journal, is that right?"

"Something like that," Shaffer said.

"But if this is just blackmail," Mike said, "where are the demands? It's hard to believe someone would go to all this trouble just to prove it can be done. Have you considered the possibility that they have taken something, and that you won't know what until the target does?"

"It's a possibility," Shaffer admitted. "But as you say, we have no way of knowing. What concerns us right now isn't who did this, but how. This bank is the cornerstone of the Federal Reserve System. We hold gold reserves here for over two dozen sovereign nations, the Israeli war chest, and enough cash to buy out Berkshire Hathaway several times over. I had to talk the secretary of the treasury out of bringing in the damn army to protect the building this morning. You can imagine what a can of worms that would have opened."

Mike only nodded.

"I hope you can," Shaffer said.

Mike turned to the assistant director. "Ma'am, are you sure I'm the person you need here?"

"You're my most senior agent, Mike," she said. "You've also got the most experience with cyber-crime. And if I'm honest, you're the only one I fully trust to keep his mouth shut. This needs to be handled under the radar. Director Gobain has made it clear that no one else is to come in on this."

Mike considered this for a moment. "All right, but I'm going to need you to make one concession."

"Go on," she said.

"I'll need Mitch Rainey up here from the Office of System Development."

"Who?" Shaffer asked.

"Kid I busted in Phoenix a couple of years ago. He's the best computer guy we have, trust me."

"No way," Shaffer said.

"Then you're wasting your time," Mike replied.

"You want me to let a convicted criminal in here? I'd have to be fucking insane to even consider it."

"Ma'am," Mike said, ignoring Shaffer, "from what I understand, someone just robbed this bank with a computer. Is that a fair summary of the situation?"

"That's what it looks like, yes."

"So we're not dealing with some local crime syndicate. And I think we can rule out terrorism. I have trouble sending e-mails, so veteran agent or not, I'm of no use to you there. Rainey's the best guy we have."

Mike turned to Shaffer. "And he's not a convicted criminal; he's an employee of the FBI."

"Sure," Shaffer said, "Because you wanted him. I'm guessing he was spared the interviews and the trip to Quantico, am I right?"

"You're missing the point," Mike said. "If I didn't know better, Mitch would probably be one of my first suspects. By which I mean, if anyone can figure out what happened here, it's him. When we tracked him down in Phoenix he was about twenty-four hours away from wiping out the credit card accounts of three of the largest issuers in the country. In fact, you've probably heard of him."

Shaffer frowned. "You're talking about the Bank of America thing? The kid from Seattle?"

Mike nodded. "That's the one. If it's any consolation, he's more than made up for it working with the Bureau. My point is, he'll be a lot more useful around here right now than I am."

"All right," the assistant director said. "I'll put it to the boss. But don't hold your breath."

"I'm telling you, I don't like this, Mary," Shaffer said.

"You have a better idea?" she asked.

He didn't.

# CHAPTER 4

**Federal Reserve Bank**
**New York, New York**
**Saturday 15 July 2006**
**2000 EDT**

Mike was standing outside the open vault when the assistant director stepped out of the elevator. He was holding the can of spray paint in one gloved hand and peering at it as if concentration alone might reveal the identity of the man who had left it behind.

"Anything?" she asked.

Mike shook his head. "No. The prints are Dekker's. What do you make of the cryptic clue?"

The assistant director walked to the open door of the vault and stood looking at the wall. "Who will watch the watchmen? That's what is says, right?"

"I think it's 'who will guard the guards themselves?'" Mike said. "It's a line from Juvenal's Satires about the dangers of corruption in high places. It certainly makes you wonder what this is all about."

Mike was about to say something else when the elevator doors opened and Dekker stepped out. "Agent Rainey has arrived. Should I bring him down?"

"No need," the assistant director said. "He'll need access to the security mainframe. Agent Banner will come up with you."

- - -

Mitch was standing by the counter in the main lobby when Mike arrived. He was dressed in his time-honored combination of faded jeans and a t-shirt. Mike didn't think he'd shaved since they last met.

"Hey, Mike," Mitch said when he saw him. "Long time, no see. You're not going to tell me someone actually robbed the New York Fed, are you? Because that *would* be funny."

Mike gave the guard behind the counter a nervous smile and ushered Mitch down the hall. "Jesus, Mitch. What part of discreet didn't you understand?"

"Someone *did* rob the Fed. Holy shit."

"Mitch, I'm not kidding."

"Yeah, yeah, I get it. I just can't believe it."

Dekker was waiting for them when they reached the security office.

Mitch walked straight to one of the terminals at the back of the room and pulled a laptop computer out of his bag. Every inch of it was covered in stickers depicting rock bands, cartoon characters and comic book superheroes. He took a USB memory stick from his pocket and put it in one of the slots in the terminal beneath the counter.

"You'll want my login details, I take it?" Dekker said.

Mitch moved aside to show Dekker he was already logged on. "Lesson number one, either replace your keyboards regularly, or clean them at least once a week. Lesson number two, never use a common name as your password. That goes double for terminals you don't use to type on very often."

Dekker turned to Mike, blushing slightly.

"It's okay," Mike said. "He does that to everybody."

Mitch turned back to the screen and started opening windows. Occasionally he would mutter something under his breath and open another, then close it again and murmur something else. This went on for about ten minutes. When he was done, Mitch pulled the USB stick out and put it back in his pocket.

"May I ask what it is you're doing?" Dekker said.

Mitch turned and looked at him as if he'd just suggested they all get high. "Mike, you know I do my best work when I'm left alone, right?"

"I believe the chairman was quite clear about anything being removed from the system," Dekker said. "You'll have to clear whatever it is you're taking with him first."

"I can't work like this," Mitch said and began to stand.

Mike stepped forward and put a hand on his shoulder. "Sit down, Mitch."

"I think it's best if I get Mr. Shaffer," Dekker said and left the room.

"Christ, Mitch," Mike said when he was gone. "Could you please keep that damn tongue of yours on a leash? Things are tense enough around here as it is."

"Fine. But could you please do the same with that fuck stick? He wears Old Spice, for god's sake!"

Dekker returned several minutes later with Shaffer and the assistant director in tow.

"Agent Banner," Shaffer said. "I've been told you're removing data from our system. Is that really necessary?"

Mike was about to answer him when Mitch said. "All I'm copying are system activity logs. I could write the information out into my notebook but I didn't bring enough of them, nor do we have the six months it would take to do it."

"How do we know that's all you're doing?" Shaffer asked.

Mitch sighed and turned to face the four of them. "That's just it, you don't know. Because you don't really know what any of this stuff does or how it works. Unless someone who does - and in this case that would be me - is left alone long enough to figure out what happened here, you will never know. Make sense?"

Shaffer could find no response. He turned to the assistant director, who only shrugged.

"Yes. I see your point," Shaffer said.

Mitch slapped both knees and stood up. "Good. I'm done here anyway."

"That's it?" Mike asked.

"Not quite."

Mitch connected the USB stick to his laptop. They all watched as he typed something into a simple command line interface, his fingers a blur above the keyboard. When he was done he ripped a Post-it note from the pad on the counter and wrote something down.

"Can I see that note again?" Mitch said to Mike. "The one with all the numbers at the bottom."

Shaffer nodded at Dekker, who handed it to Mitch.

"Bingo," Mitch said.

"What is it?" Mike asked.

"I need to get in there," Mitch said pointing at the door to the server room.

"What for?" Shaffer asked.

Mitch only looked at Mike and the assistant director, his eyes pleading.

"Let him in," she said.

Shaffer hesitated for a moment then nodded at Dekker again. Dekker pulled a small ring of keys from his pocket and unlocked the door. Mitch disappeared inside.

They watched through the small pane of safety glass as he pulled back one of the glass panels covering a stack of server modules and consulted the sheet of paper. When he pulled his arm back out he was holding a small circuit board. Mitch squinted, trying to read something on the label, consulted the sheet again, and nodded to himself.

"Here's your bank robber," Mitch said as he stepped through the door and handed the circuit board to Mike.

"What do you mean?" asked the assistant director. "What the hell is it?"

"Memory," Mitch said. "Standard one gigabyte ECC DIMM module. Only that one isn't exactly standard."

"Meaning?"

"Meaning I'd like to meet the guy who made it so I can get his autograph. Whoever it is, he or she is a genius."

"Mitch, this is serious," Mike said. "Are you saying they used that thing to hack the system?"

Mitch looked around the room and saw nothing but blank, expectant faces. "All right. Systems like this can't be hacked from the outside. That's just something the idiots in Hollywood came up with along with those ridiculous graphic interfaces they always use to do it. It can't be done. Not even from the control room in Boston. And it sure as hell can't be done over the Internet. Whoever did this either had a copy of the software or he was familiar enough with it not to need one. Either way, he knew the only way to get inside was by accessing the mainframe directly. So that's what he did. With that." Mitch pointed to the memory module in Mike's hand.

"I don't understand," Mike said. "You're saying he was here?"

Mitch shook his head. "No. He got a maintenance engineer to do it for him. Once this was installed it was just a case of waiting for the designated time, and off you go. The program would have done the rest. Opened the doors, wiped the camera footage, whatever they wanted."

"How the hell can it be that simple?" Shaffer asked, looking incredulous.

"It's not," Mitch replied. "For one, he would have had to do it twice. You'll find another one of these inside the server up in Boston. It's the only way it would have worked. And there's nothing simple about the way it was done. That memory module is a serious piece of engineering. It's not just a case of sticking a program on it and letting it run. To go unnoticed it would have been designed to mimic the real thing in every way. If it didn't, it would have crashed the system as soon as it was installed. Without getting too technical, the way this managed to override the system was almost certainly by manipulating the data stored in memory by the program itself. As for how they got around the error correction code, I could only guess."

Seeing he had lost them, Mitch said, "I don't know who's behind this, but I can tell you there aren't that many people capable of making something like that. Personally, I would suggest you start with the people who wrote the code in the first place."

Shaffer turned to Dekker. "But how the hell did it get in there?"

Before Dekker could reply, Mitch asked, "When was the last time the server was upgraded?"

"Last year," Dekker said. "In April of last year."

Mitch nodded thoughtfully. "If they knew who supplied your hardware, it wouldn't have been that big a deal. There's no way of checking the authenticity or integrity of a hardware component like this unless it fails. They would have made the switch somewhere in the delivery chain between the factory in China that produced it and the courier that dropped it off here. They simply switched it somewhere along the way. The guy who installed it would have had no idea it wasn't authentic. Pure genius."

"And this?" Dekker said pointing at the bottom of the sheet in Mitch's hand.

"That's the memory address location. Without it, it might have taken me all day to find the right module."

"You're saying they *wanted* us to know where it was?" Mike said.
Mitch nodded. "Yep."

# CHAPTER 5

**Skyline Defense**
**New York, New York**
**Saturday 15 July 2006**
**2300 EDT**

Carl Bosch stood looking down at Central Park from his office on the 78th floor. Jack Fielding, the company's corporate head of security, picked up a bottle of Glenfarclas 1955 from the small bar in the corner of the office and held it up to the light. "I didn't know you drank whiskey."

"I don't. Rosenberg sent a case of it over last week."

"How is the old Jew, anyway?" Jack asked.

"Considering he's almost eighty and still drinks that piss, I'd say he was fine," Carl said.

"He'll outlive us both, you know."

"Speak for yourself."

"Mind if I take a bottle?" Jack said.

"Take all of it. I can't tell that shit from motor oil."

Jack shook his head in mock disgust and put the bottle back down. Carl walked around his desk to a large glass display case sitting against the wall beside the door. Inside was a scale model of a large research vessel with a dark green hull and white superstructure. The small print on the stern read *Pandora - Busan.* He stood looking at the model for a moment, taking in the extraordinary detail.

"How did things go with the admiral?" Jack said.

"Greer's a son of a bitch. He asked for another twenty thousand. Can you believe that?"

"You want me to get it back?"

"And deny him his goat ranch in New Mexico, or whatever the hell it is? No, I quite like the idea of him shoveling shit for the rest of his life. Right now I'm more worried about finding someone to replace him. He may have been an asshole, but he was our asshole."

"You have anyone in mind?"

Carl shook his head. "No. But Marius will find someone. He always does."

# CHAPTER 6

**Federal Reserve Bank**
**New York, New York**
**Sunday 16 July 2006**
**0400 EDT**

Mike left with Mitch just after four in the morning. They drove to an all-night diner in Prospect Heights, not because it was the closest place to get a bite to eat, or even the best, but because aside from his small rented apartment in Manhattan, it was the only place Mike knew.

Aside from the pretty young waitress who had been using the downtime to give herself a manicure, and seemed anything but happy to see them, they had the place to themselves. They took a table in the corner. Mike ordered pancakes and Mitch asked for a cheeseburger, then changed his mind to the all-day breakfast, changed it back again, and was on the verge of another switch when the waitress put her pen back in her apron and left without another word.

"Remind me never to move here," Mitch said when she was gone.

"I don't know if you've noticed," Mike said, "but your people skills need some fine-tuning."

"Are you saying you don't like me anymore, Mike?"

"Oh, forget it."

When their food arrived Mike discovered he wasn't that hungry after all. He watched Mitch make short work of his breakfast and managed to eat one of his own pancakes. When Mitch was done he let out a loud belch, drank the rest of his Coke, and did it again.

"Charming," Mike said.

Mitch regarded him for a moment. "Mike, you do realize we'll never find these guys, don't you?"

"It's a hard pill to swallow," Mike said, "but I think you're right."

"And the Fed of all places. I mean the fucking Fed!"

"Jesus, Mitch. Keep your voice down."

Mitch looked around and leaned closer. "The home of the US greenback, which, incidentally, just happens to be the cornerstone of the global economy. Do you have any idea what would happen if this got out? I don't even want to think about it. Trust me, by this time next week they'll be reading us the riot act and we'll be signing confidentiality agreements thicker than the Bible."

"You're probably right," Mike said. "What's your point?"

"Nothing. I'm just thinking out loud. Aren't you curious why someone would do this? I mean, the hard-core fern sniffers get up to some pretty crazy shit, but there's no way this was some cabal of concerned citizens trying to stick it to 'The Man.' It's just hard to believe they haven't asked for anything."

"Like what?"

"I don't know. Pull our troops out of Iraq, cancel Third World debt, who knows?"

"What makes you think they haven't?" Mike said.

"Yeah, you've got a point there."

"Don't forget," Mike said, "we don't actually know they didn't take anything."

Mitch considered this. "Man, can you imagine the look on the face of the poor bastard that opens up his safety deposit box and finds it empty? I'd give anything to be there. Guy would probably drop a shit brick right there on the vault floor. He'd be like 'Ahh, which one of you doughnut vacuums helped yourself to my fucking porn stash, man!'"

"Jesus, Mitch, grow up, will you? This is serious."

"I know it is. I'm just saying. This whole thing is way out there in left field." Mitch squinted and raised a pinky to the corner of his mouth in an imitation of Doctor Evil. "Give up Austin Powers or the next time, we'll take one – billion – dollars."

Mike was shaking his head, but smiling. "Mitch, I worry about you."

When the waitress brought the bill Mike gave her a twenty and a ten and told her to keep the change.

"Come on," Mike said. "I need to get some sleep. You can crash on my couch if you want to."

"Gee whiz, Mike. I never thought you'd ask."

They left the diner and walked back to the car.

"What do you think about the message they left on the wall?" Mike asked.

Mitch shrugged. "Not everyone is a fan of the Federal Reserve System, you know. Some would even argue it's responsible for the economic mess we're in. Don't forget, the Fed is a private institution with a monopoly on our money supply. I'm not exactly a fan myself, if you must know."

"I'd keep that to myself if I were you," Mike said.

Mitch laughed. "I'm way ahead of you there, buddy. I pledge allegiance to the flag every time I have an unpatriotic thought."

Mike rolled his eyes. "Just get in."

# CHAPTER 7

**CIA Headquarters**
**Langley, Virginia**
**Sunday 16 July 2006**
**0600 EDT**

Richard Fairchild, the director of central intelligence, sat looking at the two pictures on the small coffee table in the corner of his office. The bearded man sitting across from him was in his early sixties. He wore an outdated brown wool suit with patches on the elbows over a shirt and knitted vest, the spitting image of a doting grandfather.

"Did George know about this, Norton?" Fairchild asked. "Because if he did, he forgot to pass it on when he left."

Norton shrugged. "Does it matter now? We know he has the information and we know what he wants."

"Does it matter? This agency is running a fucking assassination program off the books that I know nothing about, and you ask me if it matters? Yes, it matters a lot. And I have to find out about it from a man trying to blackmail us into shutting it down? A scandal like this would sink the fucking agency. You do realize that, don't you?"

"Read the letter, Dick. He's not going public."

"And you believe that?"

"We're still here, aren't we? I don't think this guy wants to see this spread across the broadsheets any more than we do."

"So now he's a patriot? Perhaps we should offer him a fucking job. He's clearly one step ahead of everyone else in this place."

Norton took off his glasses and rubbed his eyes. "What do you want me to say, Dick? We've been here before. These are the risks we take."

"Does the White House know?" Fairchild said.

Norton turned to the window and sat looking out for a moment, the lines on his face deepening as he considered the question. When he turned back to Fairchild, he put his glasses back on and picked up one of the photos. The man in the picture looked like he'd been dead for some time. His lifeless eyes seemed to stare back, as if accusing anyone who looked at it of his misfortune.

"They know, don't they?" Fairchild said.

Norton nodded. "They do. But it's not quite that simple."

"Meaning?"

"These pictures aren't from the Fed."

Fairchild frowned. "They're not?"

"I cleaned out that safety deposit box three months ago, Dick."

"I'm not following you. The guy says he's got the hard drive."

"I'm sure he does," Norton said. "But it's not ours. Nothing from Princip has ever been digitized."

"What the hell are you saying?"

"I'm saying that the safety deposit box isn't ours anymore. Whatever he's got, it belongs to someone else. If he hasn't figured that out yet, he will soon enough."

"And these," Fairchild said, pointing at the pictures. "You said it yourself; they're both your people."

"I'm not saying he doesn't know about the program, just that he doesn't have the files to prove anything."

Fairchild stood and began pacing the length of his office. "So who owns the box?"

"Some investment firm out in Ohio. Millennium Holdings."

"You're telling me some guy is going to walk in there in a week or a month, open his box and discover someone has taken a hard drive out of it?"

Norton nodded. "Yep."

"Christ! And we can't even tell them it's coming."

"Not unless you want to explain how we know. I wouldn't worry about it though. They know it's a possibility."

Norton pointed to the letter Fairchild was still holding. "What we need to discuss is what to do about him."

Fairchild ignored the remark and sat back down. He leaned across the table and fixed Norton with a cold stare. "First you're going to tell me about Princip and why the fuck I wasn't informed about it. Then I'll decide what to do about it."

When Norton spoke, it was in a tone of resignation. "What do you want to know?"

"How about everything. If it's not too much to ask, you can start at the beginning."

"All right, Dick. But you should know there were good reasons for not letting you in. Plausible deniability being just one of them."

"Start talking."

Norton sighed. "Princip was set up on Nixon's orders in '72. It was based inside the Special Forces Command in Saigon, and run out of the Pentagon. The idea was to infiltrate Hanoi and neutralize enough of the communist top brass to cripple the North and turn the tide of the war. It didn't work, of course. But then Nixon and Kissinger were both nuts, so that's hardly a surprise."

"Go on," Fairchild said.

"By the time Ford came along, Princip had been expanded. Nixon had them looking into all kinds of people, including the Pahlavis in Iran, King

Faisal, Isabel Perón, and a lot of other thorns in his side. He threatened to go public with the program after Watergate unless Ford promised to offer him a pardon when he resigned."

"So why didn't Ford shut it down?" Fairchild said, now looking almost as intrigued as he was angry.

"A lot was going on back then. I guess he came around to the idea. Being able to remove certain obstacles without jumping through too many hurdles has a way of growing on people under all that pressure."

"You're telling me Carter knew about the program, too? Reagan? All of them?"

"Not by name, no. And no details, of course. But they knew."

"And you? Where do you come in?"

"The program was originally run by a career infantry colonel named Reginald Styles. When he resigned, I was already the point of contact for the Oval Office. I guess you could say I was next in line. After 9/11 we had to move everything out of the Pentagon. The Chief of Staff wanted it run here under NCS, but I advised him against it."

"Why?"

"I wanted to make sure the White House didn't get a chance to fuck it up along with everything else. And believe me, I have no regrets."

"And why move the files?" Fairchild asked.

"I just wanted to tie up any loose ends," Norton said. "You know, tighten the reins. I don't know if you've noticed, but the NeoCon circus on Pennsylvania Avenue is beginning to make Nixon look like a saint. You know they're talking about Lebanon and Syria as the next two in line for a makeover, don't you?"

"I've seen the file," Fairchild said. "It's just talk."

"So was Iraq. You should go downstairs sometime and have a chat with Gabriel. Ask him for his paper on the projected budget deficit and what would happen if we commit to another war. I'm telling you, I don't sleep much anymore."

"You're changing the subject," Fairchild said. "We were talking about Princip. Remember?"

"I've shut it down, Dick. That's all that matters. We tie up this loose end, forget it happened and move on. If I'm being honest, I've had enough of this shit anyway. I'm looking forward to putting my feet up."

"What about the FBI investigation?" Fairchild asked.

"I spoke to Nathan Remark at State this morning. Director Gobain has been ordered to shut it down and hand everything over to Treasury. Like I said, we find this guy, take him out of the picture and move on."

Fairchild was shaking his head. "Have you even considered where the leak might be? He's killed two of your operators already. When he finds out he doesn't have quite as much of our balls in his hand as he thinks, what do you think he'll do? Roll over and play dead?"

"I doubt it."

"Besides, it doesn't even matter. He knows he doesn't need the files now that he has us all in a corner over the break-in. If you ask me, I think getting the files was just a bonus. Or maybe he was going to clean up the rest of your team if you dragged your feet. You've got to give it to him, he's one smart son of a bitch."

"I still think we should pursue the option of elimination," Norton said. "We'll just have to tread carefully. We can't afford a risk like this, Dick. Think about it."

"What about this Colonel Styles?" Fairchild said. "Have you considered him?"

"I've checked. He's clean. I've called everyone out of the field. I'll have more for you in a couple of days."

Norton stood up with an audible pop from somewhere in his lower back. When he reached the door, Fairchild said, "Norton?"

"What?"

"You don't move on this without my say-so. Is that clear?"

"Sure."

"I mean it. Nothing happens until I say it happens."

Norton nodded. "All right. I'll be back in a couple of days."

# CHAPTER 8

**Federal Reserve Bank**
**New York, New York**
**Monday 17 July 2006**
**0900 EDT**

Jack Fielding didn't quite shit a brick in the way Mitch Rainey had imagined it, but he came close. By the time he left the Fed and made his way down Liberty Street he was sweating profusely.

He remembered thinking the man who had taken him down to the vault was unusually tense. He also couldn't recall the security check having been anywhere near as stringent when he had first opened the account, or on the day he returned to deposit the drive. But none of these things had prepared him for what he found when he opened the safety deposit box. The money was still there, or most of it anyway. The hard drive wasn't. It had been replaced with two photographs of corpses: one of them little more than a charred skeleton, the other white and bloated. Written on the back of one was a message that meant absolutely nothing to him: *Shut down Princip! Last warning.*

In that moment he had felt as if the entire world had begun spinning around him. The voices of the men waiting outside the vault for him to finish had faded to distant echoes and he had found it hard to breathe. And there had been something else. A faint trace in the air of what he thought might have been fresh paint. But it was hard to know if that hadn't just been his imagination.

He felt a little better out here in the fresh air, but far from all right. When he reached the intersection of Liberty and Nassau, he almost stepped straight into the path of an oncoming bus. That brought him a little closer to the moment.

Jack hurried across the street and ducked into the first alley he reached. He pulled out his cell phone, dialed and waited. "Marius, get a message to Bruce Jessops right away. I need to speak to him."

# CHAPTER 9

**Morisson, Vermont**
**Monday 17 July 2006**
**1000 EDT**

By the time Jesse got to the offices of the Morisson Herald, it was five past nine. Mrs. Abernathy, a tall, thin woman in her early seventies who appeared far more frail than she actually was, glared at him as he came through the door. When she was satisfied her silence had produced just the right amount of tension, she said, "Jesse Corbin, have I ever told you what I said to your father the first and last time he ever asked me to change one of his ads after our print deadline?"

"No, ma'am," Jesse said.

"'You're too damn late, Corbin.' That's what I said. And here I am, saying it again all these years later."

Jesse's mind went blank. He looked down at Julia, the Herald's forty-something spinster receptionist, who offered him a sympathetic smile.

"I was running an errand, ma'am. I'm very sorry."

"Was it an urgent errand?" Mrs. Abernathy asked, sounding perfectly reasonable.

"It could have waited, ma'am."

"When you get to be my age, you'll discover that everything is urgent. But if you're going to work for me, I'll have to insist that you place my urgencies at the top of your list. Is that fair, Jesse?"

"Very fair, ma'am."

"Excellent. You can start by taking this to the post office."

She handed him a package wrapped in brown paper.

"It's not important, so don't let that old fart talk you into sending it express. Standard will do. When you get back, I want you to go down to the sheriff's office and get a picture of the new deputy for the appointments section. Maggie will give you the camera. It's one of those digital things, so you shouldn't have any trouble using it. Head and shoulders only. Make sure he's not wearing a hat and that his hair is combed."

"Yes, ma'am," Jesse said and turned to leave.

He was halfway out the door when Mrs. Abernathy coughed twice. He turned around and saw she was still holding the package. He walked back, took it, flashed her a fool's grin and left.

When he got to the sheriff's office at around half-past nine, Jesse found the man himself sitting behind his desk with both feet up, reading a copy of *Law and Order*. Sheriff Dale Trent peered over the edge of the magazine and said, "That you, Jesse Corbin?"

"Sure thing, Sheriff."

"My Betty tells me you got yourself a job working for that witch over at the Herald. I told her it couldn't possibly be true."

"Guilty as charged," Jesse said.

The sheriff put down the magazine, crossed his arms over his chest and looked at Jesse like a man contemplating what to say to a child who was obviously too dumb for reason.

"Did she send you over here to get a *scoop*?" he said.

"No, sir. She wants a picture of the new deputy for the paper."

"Oh. Well that's easy enough. He's in the locker room."

Jesse was waiting for the sheriff to say something else, but he only pointed to the door at the end of the counter.

"Just go on in, son. His name is Brendan. As far as I know, he doesn't bite."

At first, Jesse thought there must be someone else with the deputy. He could hear talking as soon as he opened the door. Then he saw him.

Deputy Brendan Mills was standing in front of a long mirror at the end of a row of lockers. He was wearing his uniform pants and his Sam Brown belt, but nothing above the waist. He had one hand on the butt of his gun and appeared to be speaking to himself.

"Yeah, that's not gonna happen, pal. Now you let her go or I'll have to introduce you to my friends Smith and Wesson."

The deputy drew the gun, but instead of getting it out of the holster, he succeeded only in pulling the belt, pants and all, right up to his rib cage. Jesse tried not to laugh, but it was futile. Deputy Mills spun around. "Who the hell are you?"

"Jesse Corbin, sir. I work for the Morisson Herald. Mrs. Abernathy sent me to get a picture of you for the paper."

"How long you been spying on me?"

"I just walked in," Jesse said.

"Well, then you missed the best part, kid. That last line was just one of my backups."

"Sounded all right to me," Jesse lied.

"So, you want this shot with or without my shirt on?" the deputy asked.

"It would probably be best if you had it on."

Jesse decided he liked the new deputy. The man was a little vain, to be sure, but not in an annoying way. He was also clearly a rookie, probably fresh out of the barracks down in Concord.

"I'll be outside," Jesse said and turned for the door.

"Be with ya in a sec, kid." Deputy Mills said and gave him a wink.

He got fifteen shots. Deputy Mills checked every one of them and had him delete all but five. By the time he got back to the Herald, he had deleted another three, believing, and rightly so, that Mrs. Abernathy would have had something to say if there had been more.

Jesse spent the rest of the day doing odd jobs around the office. When Julia left at half past four, he made a point of not noticing what time it was. Mrs. Abernathy, who always knew what time it was, played along for fifteen minutes, then sent him on his way.

When he got home, Jesse put on his best pair of jeans and the only shirt he owned with a collar. When he was ready to leave, his mom followed him out to the porch and handed him a fifty-dollar bill.

"Mom, I've got a job. I'm not broke, seriously!"

"You run errands. For what, ten bucks a day? I know that old cow. She won't be parting with more than that. Now take it."

She stuffed the bill into the pocket of his jeans.

"She doesn't pay me ten bucks a day. She gives me a hundred dollars a week. And she's not a cow."

By the time he passed the familiar town sign (Welcome to Morisson - Population: just right!), the first wave of nerves had started to come over him. He had spent the day deliberately not thinking about this evening on the understanding that the more he did, the more on edge he would become. Now it appeared the effort had been in vain.

When he reached Farmland, Morisson's premier and only farm machinery dealership, he pulled off the road and stopped.

- - -

Jesse had first met Amanda in second grade, on what had probably been the worst day of her life. At least up until then. In those days, he and Bill Perry had been Siamese twins, played in the same imaginary rock 'n' roll band and had developed the closest thing to telepathy that existed outside the Twilight Zone. On that particular day, Bill was in the hospital having his tonsils removed. Jesse had been on his way back to the locker room after PE when he heard someone crying behind the bleachers and went to investigate. He had found her sitting on the ground with her arms around her knees. When he had moved closer, she put her hands over her chest and he saw that the back of her T-shirt had been torn from neck to hem.

The sight of her sitting there, trying to cover herself up with arms that were shaking as if it had been January instead of one of the warmest days in June, had made him feel both sad and angry at the same time. Without thinking, he'd taken off his own T-shirt and held it out to her then walked back to the sports field. When she still hadn't emerged several minutes later, he'd gone back. She'd been standing just around the corner. His T-shirt ended just above her knees. With the lack of tact characteristic of most eight year olds, he'd said, "No one will believe that's yours. My mom sews name tags into all my clothes."

For a moment neither of them had said anything, then, as if on cue, they both burst out laughing. And by the invisible stroke of magic that is also characteristic of most eight-year-olds, they were friends.

In that instant, the two of them fit to split and unaware the world was still turning, Jesse's young mind formed a simple, yet very powerful, idea. He thought he loved her.

Like Jesse, Bill didn't have a sister. That meant neither boy had developed any serious fear of the cooties. Amanda had slipped almost seamlessly into their friendship, not tearing it apart, but adding a new dimension to it, like a good pitcher joining an already successful baseball team. Amanda never did give him his T-shirt back and for eleven years Jesse had kept his feelings to himself.

When he finally did get around to breaking the news to Bill, both Bill and Amanda were saying goodbye to the small town they had grown up in. Bill was going to State College in Lyndonville and Amanda had been accepted into Penn State. Jesse had the grades, but hadn't applied to anywhere, a fact that had the faculty, his parents, and his two best friends wondering out loud if he was all there. What none of them understood, and what he was loath to admit even to himself, was that he was afraid if they both left Morisson, he would never see her again.

"You're a fucking idiot," Bill had said. "After all this time, you break this to me *now*?"

By then Jesse had been on the verge of tears. Bill had put an arm around him and squeezed. "All right, it's okay. I get it, man. It would have fucked everything up."

"It's not just that."

But Bill, who had a knack for simplifying the complicated, had hit the nail squarely on the head. It *would* have fucked everything up. And whichever way it went, their friendship would have been over.

"Do you want me to talk to her?" Bill had asked.

"No. She would hate me. It would ruin things for her."

"I doubt she'd hate you, man. But you're right, it would be awkward the way things are now."

That had been the entirety of their conversation on the matter. Jesse had driven Amanda to the airport and said goodbye. She had cried and he had told her it would be cool. They'd get together whenever she came home. It would be just like old times.

Jesse had saved his own tears for the parking lot.

That had been almost two years ago. But sitting behind the wheel of his mother's Volvo and looking out at the tractors in the yard at Farmland, it might as well have been yesterday.

But Amanda had her own troubles. He'd known that from the moment he picked up the phone. She wasn't coming home, she was running home.

The thought both worried and angered him. Someone had hurt her. If she had made friends out there, they obviously didn't amount to much in a crisis. Jesse tried to focus on that, and it went a long way towards steadying his nerves. He would be the friend she needed, not another problem.

Feeling a little better, he shifted the car into drive and pulled back onto the road.

# CHAPTER 10

**FBI Field Office**
**New York, New York**
**Monday 17 July 2006**
**1200 EDT**

Mike left his office to get himself a cup of coffee in the staff canteen. Someone had left a copy of the Times on the table and he scanned the headlines as he sipped.

So far the blackout seemed to be working. After taking Mitch to the airport, he'd spent the rest of the morning tracking down names on the list they had gotten from Allied Bishop, the company that ran the Fed's security system. Then he had spent another hour dissecting the company's merger history. The idea was to put together a list of everyone who had worked on the security system both when it was written and during any subsequent modifications. The people who made the calls in Washington had thought this a good precautionary measure. Mike wasn't so sure.

Nova, the original security system, hadn't been designed by Allied Bishop, but by a German company called GSL Systems, which had been contracted to create it by a consortium of German banks in 1998. Allied Bishop had acquired GSL in 2001 and then licensed another company, a British firm called Titan, to use the Nova platform as the basis for an updated version. Only by the time it was completed, Allied Bishop had also acquired Titan and renamed the project, rather unimaginatively, Nova 2. In 2003, Allied Bishop won a contract to install the new system in six of the banks in Manhattan, including the Fed.

Unraveling the puzzle of people who had been involved with Nova and its successor since 1998 had proved more complicated than Mike had anticipated. Allied Bishop had bought up no fewer than eight smaller firms in that time, and the migration of personnel that had occurred as a result was enough to give anyone a headache.

His thoughts were interrupted by Gregory Johns, one of the field office's rookie agents, who appeared in the doorway and said, "The assistant director wants to see you, boss."

She was on the phone when he entered and gestured for him to take a seat. When she put the receiver down, she said, "Have we got anything stronger than coffee around here?"

"What's going on?" Mike said.

She looked at him for a moment, then closed her eyes and let out a deep breath. "Close the door."

Mike did.

"The White House is pulling the investigation. They're sending someone over to pick up the files."

"Why am I not surprised?" Mike said.

"How did you get on with the list?"

"I think I've tracked down most of the names."

"Good. Put everything you've got together. They should be here in the morning."

"That's it?" Mike asked.

"That's it."

When he reached the door Mike turned around. "I really hope they know what they're doing."

The assistant director nodded. "You're not the only one."

# CHAPTER 11

**New York, New York**
**Monday 17 July 2006**
**1300 EDT**

Jack handed the cab driver a fifty and got out before the man could count out his change. He walked the two blocks to Park Avenue and arrived in the parking lot just as the man he had come to see pulled in behind the wheel of a red Ford van with the words *Mitchell Plumbing and Heating* stenciled across the door. Jack followed the van to the end of the parking lot and got in.

Steve Rollins was in his mid-forties, at least six feet tall and well built. He wore faded jeans and a black t-shirt under an old green army parka with a peace symbol sewn onto the left breast.

"Jesus, Jack. You look like shit," Rollins said.

"I'm fine," Jack said.

"So what can I do for you?"

"What do you know about the New York Fed?"

"It's a bank?"

"I know it's a fucking bank, Steve. What I'm asking is, do you know if anyone's - you know - made a move on it recently?"

Rollins looked at him as if he'd lost his mind. "Made a move on it?"

"Robbed it! I'm asking you if anyone's robbed the god-damned place!"

"First of all, if someone had I wouldn't know," Rollins said. "As you're well aware, I'm not in that line of work anymore. But even if I was, the Fed is the last place anyone would try and break into."

"Why?"

"Why? Because it can't be done. That's why you wanted to see me? To ask me about the Fed?"

"It *can* be done," Jack said. "I know because I'm the fucking guy they did it to."

"You know, Jack, I've never taken you for a practical joker."

Rollins studied Jack's face for a moment and saw nothing remotely jovial in it. "You're serious?"

"The assistant director of the FBI field office got a call yesterday morning."

"How the hell do you know that?" Rollins asked.

"I have a contact inside the Bureau. But that's beside the point. I was there this morning. Something was taken out of my safety deposit box."

"What?" Rollins said.

"A hard drive. A very fucking important hard drive."

"If it was yours, you must have some idea who would want to steal it."

"I don't," Jack said and pulled the two photographs from his jacket. "But the asshole left these."

Rollins studied the photographs then read what was written on the back of one of them. "Jesus. What's Princip?"

"How the fuck should I know?"

"And you have no idea who these two people are?"

"Never seen them," Jack said.

"Maybe they hit the wrong box. How long have you been using it?"

"About two months."

Rollins nodded somberly. "If the feds are involved, they won't be for long. I can tell you that."

"They're not," Jack said. "The investigation was shut down by the White House this morning."

Rollins nodded again. "Of course it was. Imagine that, someone pulling a job at the Fed. I'd give my right arm to know how they did it."

"Well if it's all the same to you," Jack said. "I'd rather you kept it for now. Can you help me or not?"

"I don't know, Jack. You're asking me to put my ass on the line. This isn't some local street gang we're talking about."

Jack reached down between his legs and set the briefcase he had brought with him on the seat between them. "That's two hundred and fifty thousand. Get me the drive back and I'll make it half a million. I can get you names, maybe help find some of them, but that's it. This isn't a company job. If someone finds out what's going on, I'm fucked."

Rollins reached for the briefcase, then pulled his hand back. "Seven-fifty. And if I so much as suspect I'm stepping on someone else's toes, I'm gone."

"Done," Jack said.

# CHAPTER 12

**FBI Field Office**
**New York, New York**
**Monday 17 July 2006**
**1400 EDT**

Mike had only been asleep for half an hour when he was dragged back into the land of the living by a knock on the door. He sat up slowly and rubbed his neck. The couch in his office was comfortable enough, but at least a foot short. "Come in."

Mike's first impression of the man who stepped into his office was that he wasn't real. He was only a few inches over five feet and wore a tailored black pinstripe suit that looked like it might have cost at least a grand. His skin was a smooth, deep bronze, almost certainly the product of a daily routine involving a tanning bed and a cocktail of men's designer skin care products. His jet-black hair was combed back and held in place by some kind of gel that gave it a shine matched only by his shoes, which gleamed like polished glass. To Mike, he looked like he'd strayed off the set of a 1930s gangster movie.

"Agent Banner?" the man said, offering him a grin composed of teeth that were both too white and too symmetrical.

"That's me."

"Bruce Jessops, White House liaison. Mary said you might be hiding in here."

Mike stood up and straightened his jacket. He brought a hand to his mouth to stifle a yawn and realized he hadn't shaved since yesterday morning. "You'll have to excuse me. I'm roughing it at the moment."

"No apologies necessary," Jessops said, holding up his hands. "This is some shit storm, hey? I still can't quite believe it myself."

"That makes two of us," Mike said.

"Still, it's not every day you get to be part of something this big, right?"

"I can't say I've thought of it that way," Mike said and pointed at the seat in front of his desk. "Take a pew."

Jessops sat down. Mike offered to get him a cup of coffee.

"No, thanks. I never touch the stuff. Bad for the skin. I'd take a glass of guava juice though."

"Yeah, I think we're all out of that," Mike said. "Water?"

"No, I'm good. Listen, I'm only here to run interference when the boys from Treasury show up."

"Are you expecting trouble?" Mike said.

Jessops laughed. It was right on cue and hearty, but Mike thought it sounded practiced.

"I'm sorry," Mike said. "Did you say you were the White House *liaison*?"

"Sounds a lot grander than it is," Jessops said. "I'm more of a glorified errand boy, really."

"And you're here to do what, exactly?"

"The boss isn't happy about what's going on. If it were up to him we'd still be dealing with this ourselves. That said, if we don't have any choice in the matter, he wants to make sure the transition is as smooth as possible. I know these guys."

"You mean you're here to make sure I give them what they want."

Jessops shook his head. "Of course not. Why wouldn't you? Speaking of what they want, do you mind if I have a look?"

"Be my guest," Mike said and handed Jessops the folder on his desk. "I doubt you'll find it very interesting. If you'll excuse me, I need to step out for a minute."

Mike left and walked down the hall to the assistant director's office. For once, she wasn't on the phone. He walked in and closed the door behind him. She cut him off with a raised hand before he could say anything. "I know, I know. When he walked in here I almost burst out laughing. He looks like a twelve-year-old Al Capone."

Mike, who didn't feel remotely jovial, found himself laughing at the image.

"What do you want me to do, Mike? It's a brave new world."

As she said this, she glanced over at the picture of George W. Bush hanging on the wall by the window.

"He calls you Mary," Mike said.

"Mike, I get it. Believe me. As soon as our friends from Treasury are gone, I'll drive him to the airport myself. How about that?"

"And we're just going to forget this ever happened, right?" Mike said.

"Yep. That's exactly what we'll do. Forget it ever happened and go back to chasing our own bad guys. Does that really sound so bad?"

"When you put it that way, I guess not."

"Good. Then go back out there and play nice. I know Jane keeps a bag of marshmallows in one of her drawers. Perhaps he'd like one."

When Mike got back to his office Jessops was talking to someone on his cell phone with the folder open on the desk in front of him.

"Anyway, I've got to go," Jessops said. "I'll call you later."

He put the phone down and closed the folder. "Tell me, Agent Banner, you think it was just one guy?"

"Unlikely," Mike said.

Jessops stood and held out his hand. "For what it's worth, I think you did a good job. I'll make sure the director knows that."

Mike had to stifle what would have been a sarcastic laugh. "Thanks, I really appreciate it."

When Jessops was gone Mike closed the door and called Mitch in DC.

"Hey, Mitch, how's it going?"

"That depends on what you mean. If you're talking about my car, it's hardly going at all."

"Yeah, well I'm not talking about your car. Listen, we're off the job."

"The Fellowship of the Fed is breaking up already?"

"I'm afraid so. Have you finished your report?"

"Yeah, it's right here in front of me. You know, I've been thinking-"

"I'm going to stop you there, Mitch. One, because I haven't had a lot of sleep. But more importantly, I'm no longer the investigating officer on the case. Whatever you have, include it in the report. If someone else wants to pursue it, I'm sure they'll be in touch."

"Wow, you sound really pissed off," Mitch said.

"Well, I'm not. Relieved, maybe. And grateful to be getting back to my day job."

"All right, amigo. You're the boss. I guess I'll see you down here in about ten years then."

"Don't count on it. Actually, there is one thing you could do for me."

"Shoot."

Mike hesitated.

"I'm still listening," Mitch said.

"Could you run an internal personnel check for me?" Mike said.

"Sure. Although as you surely know, you're cleared to do that yourself."

"I know. It's just that-"

"You don't want a record of it showing up on your system. Now you're talking my language, Kemosabe. What's the name?"

"It's nothing like that. I-"

"Hey, say no more. Office politics, man. I get it."

Mike lowered his voice. "The name's Jessops. Apparently he's the White House liaison, whatever the hell that means."

"He's there? In New York?"

"Just arrived, yeah."

"I'm on it. I'll call you back in an hour."

Mitch called back fifteen minutes later. "Okay, I found him. Bruce Wayne Jessops. What did you want to know?"

"Bruce Wayne?"

"Yep, it appears we've found Batman. Born eleven March seventy-three in Sacramento, California. Joined the Bureau in '99. Mother deceased. Father is Jeffrey Wayne."

"The senator?"

"Yep. Jessops was his mother's maiden name. I'm guessing he took it to avoid the flak."

"That's it?"

"That's everything in the record, yeah. You want me to dig deeper?"

"What do you mean?"

"Oh, I don't know. Lift a few stones? That kind of thing."

"If you're talking about breaking the law, then no, definitely not. In fact, forget I ever mentioned it. Just send the report through."

"Solid copy. And if you need any more superheroes found, you know where I am, old buddy."

Mike put the phone down and made his way back to the couch. He needed a twenty-minute power nap to clear his thoughts. He was asleep within two.

# CHAPTER 13

**Skyline Defense**
**New York, New York**
**Monday 17 July 2006**
**1700 EDT**

Carl Bosch looked up when Jack entered. "Christ, Jack. When was the last time you got a full night's sleep?"

"I'm fine. Probably caught something on the subway."

"Well don't give it to me; I've got enough shit to deal with as it is. Some fucking hedge fund has decided to outbid us on the New Mexico site. Get Marius to find out who they are. If they want to play hardball, we'll give them what they want. And tell him I still haven't seen the profile on that guy in Omaha, what's his name?"

"Kesler."

"Yeah, him. Richelle has been chewing my ear off about it. If he's good to go we need to get him down to Houston as soon as possible."

"I'll get Marius on it," Jack said.

"Good."

Jack turned to leave.

"Hey, maybe you should take a couple of days off," Carl said.

"I'll think about it."

Jack's phone began to ring. "I need to take this."

"Just get me that profile."

"I'm on it."

It was Rollins. Jack let the phone ring until he was back in his office.

"Steve, what have you got?"

"Ever heard of a guy named Gerald Ross?"

"No. Who is he?"

"He's a security systems engineer. Retired a couple of years ago and moved to Massachusetts. He's not on the list you gave me, but his name's come up three times already. According to his former colleagues he was the best in the field."

"Where are you?"

"Still in Boston."

"Good. Check him out. Call me back if you find anything."

# CHAPTER 14

**Wellfleet Town Pier**
**Cape Cod Bay, Massachusetts**
**Monday 17 July 2006**
**1800 EDT**

Gerald Ross stood and raised his glass. "Gentlemen," he proclaimed in a voice that was not quite a slur yet, "As always, it's been a pleasure. To fair seas and the men who sail them!"

The rest of the men gathered at the table held up their own glasses and repeated the toast.

"Anyone heading back to the Cape this weekend?" One of them asked and the group quickly took up the discussion.

Gerald walked back to the bar and asked for the phone. The barman took the handset from the cradle behind the counter and handed it over.

"Darling, it's me," Gerald said when his wife picked up. "I'm leaving in a minute. Should be home before eight. Did you manage to get the car looked at?"

"No. The damn painters turned up an hour late," his wife said. "I haven't had time to go anywhere. I hope you've had dinner, because there won't be anything here when you get back. I've got to run down to the Jensens' at five and pick up the dog."

"I've already eaten."

"You mean you lost your appetite drinking."

"Christ, you know me well, woman."

"I know you well enough to be sure you'll sail that damn boat out into the open sea one day and that'll be the end of it."

"Oh, I don't think you'll ever get that lucky. Anyway, I'll see you this evening."

"Yes, dear. Two of me, I have no doubt."

Gerald hung up and handed back the phone.

"Another, sir?" The barman asked, pointing at the glass in Gerald's hand.

"No, thank you. I still have to sail home."

"I'm sure you'll do just fine," the barman said.

"If only my wife were as optimistic."

The young man gave him an understanding smile and walked to the end of the counter to serve another customer.

Gerald left the building and made his way across the yard to the foot of the main pier. His boat was moored at the end. She was a 48-foot Sunseeker Superhawk with a navy blue and white hull.

The boat had been his retirement present to himself and the fulfillment of a lifelong dream. Her name was *Felicity Gail* and she was sound to a fault. He had put in the hours, learning everything from navigation to engine maintenance. Eventually, even Cynthia had come to accept the boat, no small feat considering she had threatened to scuttle it herself when he first brought it home and showed her the stub in their checkbook. He had paid $115,000 for her.

He ran an absentminded hand over the sleek fiberglass hull and thought that perhaps, when he got old enough, and his head no longer dictated to his body, he *would* take her out and head into the sunset. It would be a hell of a way to go.

His daydreaming was interrupted by the ringing of his cell phone, which he had thoughtlessly left on the helmsman's seat. He climbed up the short rope ladder, walked around to the cockpit and picked it up.

When he saw the number, he dropped the phone and jumped down the short flight of steps into the cabin. He pulled the cushion off one of the seats, opened the hatch and pulled out a laptop. When the operating system had loaded, he found the pier's wireless network, opened the internet browser and typed *motherandbabystuff.com*. The web page had a pink and baby blue motif and contained a variety of prams, cots and other baby paraphernalia for sale. He clicked on one of the cribs and the screen displayed an error page to say the link had an invalid URL. Ignoring the message, he typed a sixteen-digit number on the keyboard that didn't appear on the screen. When he pushed *enter*, it turned blank for several seconds, then showed a simple command interface of green alphanumeric characters against a black background. He typed another password followed by the words *seek identify*, hit *enter* again and sat back. A moment later, text began to fill up the screen.

*pass-code accepted........*
*finding proxy 1...........*
*connected.................*
*finding proxy 2...........*
*connected.................*
*finding proxy 3...........*
*connected.................*
*finding proxy 4...........*
*connected.................*
*finding proxy 5...........*
*connected.................*
*satellite up-link..........*
*starting scrambler........*
*line secure...............*
*dialing...................*

The voice at the other end sounded worried. "Ross?"

"I'm here," Gerald said. "I thought we agreed we wouldn't use this line anymore."

"Where are you?"

"Cape Cod. On the Pier. Why?"

"I don't have time to explain, but you need to get out of there."

"Why?" Ross said.

"Because someone's looking for you, Gerald. And I'm not talking about the cops. Three of the engineers who worked on Nova have been contacted in the last twenty-four hours."

"Why the fuck are they looking for me, Walter? What happened to 'they'll never risk it because it would be suicide'?"

The line went silent for a moment.

"All I can tell you is that I don't think the hard drive I gave you has anything to do with what I was looking for. I don't think it even belongs to the CIA."

Gerald's face became a study in disbelief. "You told me no one would come looking. You promised me that!"

"I know. And for what it's worth, I'm sorry. Did you get a chance to see what was on the drive?"

"No!" Gerald said, his voice rising to a shout. "It's ten years old! I told you, I don't have the hardware. And it's in my house. Cynthia's at home, for Christ's sake."

"Listen to me. I'm going to help you, but first I need you to do something. Call Cynthia. Tell her whatever you need to, just get her out of the house and as far away as possible. She needs to take the hard drive with her."

"You're insane," Gerald said. "They can have the damn thing."

"It might not make any difference."

"It won't make any difference if we give them what they want?"

"I don't even know who they are right now, Gerald. Until I figure that out, we can't take any chances."

"Oh god!" Gerald said. "What am I supposed to do?"

The anger had gone out of him. Now he was just afraid.

"Call Cynthia. Get her to leave and take the drive with her. Tell her to put as many miles between herself and the house as possible."

"You know her," Gerald said. "She'll want to know why. She's sick, for Christ's sake. I can't just tell her to leave."

"You'll think of a way. You have to. As for yourself, just get out of there. Stay close to the shore. I'll contact you again as soon as I can."

"Where are you?" Gerald asked.

"Not far. Now go!"

The screen flashed and the new message read:

*line terminated...............*

Gerald pushed the laptop closed and ran back to the cockpit for his phone. Cynthia picked up on the first ring.

"Honey, it's me. I need you to listen to me very carefully."

"Gerald, are you drunk?" Cynthia asked.

Gerald took a deep breath and said the only thing he believed would get her attention. "Cynthia, shut your fucking mouth and listen to me. This is serious. I don't have time to explain, so you're going to have to trust me."

When she spoke again her voice was unsteady. "Gerald, you're scaring me."

"Cynthia, I need you to do what I tell you. Someone might be coming to the house to look for me. If they do, you can't be there. I want you to go into my office and open the safe."

There was silence, followed by a faint sob. And then, barely audible, "Okay."

He waited for her to get downstairs and heard the door opening. A moment later she was back.

"I don't know the code."

"It's two, eight, six, five, nine, five."

He heard the safe beeping as she typed in the numbers, then a click as the door opened.

"Take out the black bag and go to the garage."

"What is it, Gerald?"

"Never mind, darling. Just do it."

He could hear the initial shock beginning to wear off. Cynthia was unstable, but she was also stubborn. He was going to have her get some things together and take the gun from the drawer in his bedside table, but thought better of it.

"I'm in the garage," Cynthia said, her voice a little steadier now, a little more skeptical.

"Good. Get in the car and open the garage door."

It seemed to take an eternity, but eventually he heard the car door open and shut again. In the background the whir of the electric door opener started up.

"Now what do I do?" she asked.

"Put it in drive and go."

"Where?"

He knew that to tell her to just go anywhere would be too much. He decided to send her somewhere familiar. If Walter didn't like that, it was tough shit.

"I want you to go to Uncle Kyle's place in Mcindoe Falls. Drive to Chicopee, then cross the river and head up Interstate 91. I'll call you as soon as I can."

"Gerald?"

"What?"

"Please tell me you haven't sold the house."

The question was so unexpected, and yet so in tune with her over-cynical nature that despite everything, he almost laughed.

"No, darling. I haven't sold the house. Now I need you to get going."

"To Chicopee?"

"To Chicopee, then onto I-91. I'll call Kyle and let him know you're coming. Don't stop until you get there."

"You'll call me?"

"Yes. As soon as I can."

He hung up before she could say anything else and prayed that she wouldn't change her mind and go back into the house. It was by no means a sure thing that she wouldn't. If she went back now, it would be to the medicine cabinet upstairs. If she did that, whoever Walter thought might be coming could break into the house with a bulldozer and probably find her still asleep on the couch.

Gerald looked around, trying to decide what to do next. Walter had told him to get out of there. What he wanted to do was cross the bay, find a car and drive to meet Cynthia. Sailing down the coast while she was out there going out of her mind would be torture. What he decided to do was neither.

He started up the engine, walked to the bow and cast off the line. He did the same to the stern line, eased the boat back from the pier and turned her into the harbor. When he reached open water, he pushed the throttles all the way forward and set a course due north for the tip of Halibut Point and home.

# CHAPTER 15

**Boston, Massachusetts**
**Monday 17 July 2006**
**2000 EDT**

Francis Moore, who still thought of himself as Walter Scott or Harry Fisher, and sometimes Lee Baker, was sitting in the living room of a small rented apartment on the outskirts of Boston. There were eleven names and phone numbers written on the notepad in front of him.

He picked up the phone and dialed the next number on the list. The woman who answered sounded like she'd been asleep.

"Hello?"

"Good evening, ma'am. My name is Daren Hill; I'm with the Boston District Attorney's Office. I was hoping to speak to Mr. Parker if he's at home."

"Hold on."

He heard her shout something. A moment later, a man came to the phone. "Hello?"

"Mr. Parker, My name is Daren Hill; I'm with the Boston District Attorney's Office. I'm sorry to be calling at this hour."

"That's all right. How can I help you?"

"I believe you spoke to one of our investigators yesterday?"

"Yeah, Henry something."

"Harold Waxman."

"That's it, Harold. Nice guy."

"I just wanted to call and see if maybe you'd remembered something else. The case we're putting together is very important and we could really use all the help we can get."

"Like I said, I left Allied Bishop three years ago. I haven't really kept in touch with anyone in that time."

"I understand. Well, thank you anyway, Mr. Parker. And if you do think of anything, please give us a call."

"You got it."

Francis put the phone down and cursed.

Of all the possible problems the plan had presented, the one thing he had known for an absolute certainty was that they wouldn't dare retaliate. The danger of exposing the country's most clandestine assassination program might not have been enough to stop the CIA from trying to find him, but risking a leak to the press of the break-in would. The conclusion was obvious: the drive wasn't theirs. That led to two other very disturbing questions. Who the hell *did* it belong to? And what was it doing in a safety deposit box owned by the CIA?

To make matters worse, he had no idea what was on the drive. And if that wasn't bad enough, now he didn't even have it.

That Gerald could end up being a suspect had always been a possibility, and a risk he had been willing to take. Although never involved directly in the creation of Nova, Ross was the best in the field and had been consulted at one point or another by all three companies who had worked on it. Anyone questioned for long enough would eventually mention Ross. But Ross was also a genius. That much Francis had known from the start. It was the reason he had picked him in the first place. There really was no way to implicate him beyond the circumstantial. And even if the FBI had gotten around to asking him a few questions before they were shut down, a few questions was all it would ever be.

Francis thought Ross would be all right, at least for now. Cynthia was another matter. He had only met her twice, and then only briefly. But it had been enough to see that Cynthia Ross lived only a block or two away from her next nervous breakdown, an eventuality kept at bay only by a steady regimen of mother's little helpers. He would have to get to Cynthia, secure the drive and hide her. Ross would have to wait.

Francis opened the closet in the bedroom, pulled out a black leather motorcycle jacket and dressed quickly. There was a Walther P22 semi-automatic pistol and two magazines in a shoebox on the floor. He put these in the inside pockets of his jacket. When he was ready, he took a final look around, then moved to the door, turned off the lights, and left the apartment.

There was a black motorcycle leaning on its kickstand at one end of the underground parking lot. It was a GSX1300R turbocharged Suzuki Hayabusa, custom upgraded by a firm in Ohio that took on business by referral only and did not advertise. When he pushed the start button, the engine roared to life and quickly settled down to a soft purr.

As soon as he was outside, he pulled to the side of the road and unzipped the cover on the fuel tank bag to reveal a small GPS tracker. He turned it on and waited until the icon in the top corner of the screen showed four bars, then scrolled through a touch screen menu until the words *Gerald A4* appeared in a drop-down list and selected it. A moment later, the screen displayed a map showing the Vermont/New Hampshire border. A small green arrow showed the car traveling up Interstate 91 past the town of Bernardston on the Vermont side.

Francis pulled back onto the road and took a left at the next junction. Gambling that Gerald had been smart enough to send her all the way to the border, he headed for Interstate 93, intending to cut across and reach her before she got there.

# CHAPTER 16

**Ipswich Bay, Massachusetts**
**Monday 17 July 2006**
**2030 EDT**

When he was a quarter mile from the shore, Gerald eased the throttle back and let the bow of the boat sink into the water as she lost speed and began to drift. He had turned off all her lights when he rounded Halibut Point. Now, standing in the dark, he scanned the shoreline looking for the house. He picked it out quickly as the central property in a cluster of only three on that part of the shore. No lights were on and he was too far away to make out any signs of activity. For the second time, he prayed that Cynthia had not stayed.

It took less than a minute to inflate the lifeboat using the battery-powered pump. When the small dinghy was in the water, he tied it off and went back to the cockpit to drop anchor. Next, he went below and put on a sweater and a beanie, then packed his laptop into a watertight bag. In one of the drawers beneath the counter of the kitchenette he found a snub-nosed silver revolver. After a brief moment of hesitation, he added the box containing the flare gun.

Half an hour later he was cursing himself for not having stopped closer to the shore. His arms ached and every time he turned to gauge his progress, land seemed further away, not closer. Another half hour passed and this time he thought the shore *was* getting a little closer. He had to stop and rest twice, and when he finally felt the boat begin to bob in the swells beating at the coastline, he put the oars down and let nature take care of the rest.

Gerald stepped into the shallow water, letting the boat drift away as he walked the final few yards to dry land and dropped the bag. In front of him, a cliff face about eight feet high marked the end of his own backyard. He clambered up the wall of loose dirt and rock to get a better look at the house.

Something moved behind him and he spun his head around, lost his footing and slid down the slope on his backside. When he looked up, a man was standing in front of him. At his feet Gerald saw the open box of the flare gun. It was now in the man's hand and pointed at Gerald.

"This yours?" the man asked.

Gerald didn't answer.

"I'm glad you showed up, Mr. Ross. We've been wanting to speak to you."

"I don't have it!" Gerald found himself saying before the man could ask.

"You don't have what?"

"The hard drive. It's not here. If it was, I'd give it to you, I swear."

"Then who does?" the man asked.

"I don't know."

"I was afraid you might say that."

The man pulled the hammer back on the flare gun. "Ever been shot with one of these?"

"I don't have the drive," Gerald said again, pushing himself away until his back was against the bank.

"Yeah, you said that. What I need to know is, who does have it? And just so we're clear, Mr. Ross, I won't kill you. I'll tear your eyes out and break every bone in your body, but you'll still be alive and I'll still be asking."

Gerald believed him. Walter had been right, and coming back here had been the biggest mistake of his life. Although that wasn't entirely true. Trusting Walter had been the biggest mistake.

"I can tell you who took it," Gerald said.

"Go on."

"His name is Walter Scott. He's the one who broke into the Fed. It was his idea. His plan."

The man studied him as if trying to decide if this was the truth or just the ramblings of a desperate man. "Some fucking friend you turned out to be. Go on. I'm listening."

"We're not friends," Gerald said. "He paid me. I helped him get around the security system, that's all."

"Did he tell you why?"

"Something to do with the CIA. He was going to blackmail them. That's all I know."

"Where's your wife?" the man said.

"I don't know."

"There," the man said, as if he'd just spotted something interesting to Gerald's right.

"What?" Gerald said, looking around.

"You just started lying. Things were going so well, and then you had to go and fuck it all up by lying to me."

The man stepped forward and reached down with his free hand. Gerald rolled to one side, scrambled to his feet, then turned and ran down the beach. Something exploded behind him. An instant later, a bright light darted past the right side of his head. It sounded like a rocket and gave off an intense wave of heat, burning the right side of his face and singeing all the hair there. Gerald screamed out in pain. A second later, the flare erupted on the beach in front of him in a blinding explosion of red.

The bank to his right receded as Gerald ran until it was only about four feet high. He stopped and began to climb. As he reached the top and pulled himself over, a hand grabbed his foot and started to pull him back down. Gerald kicked out with his free foot, connecting with something soft that gave way under his heel. The man cursed and let go. Gerald stood up and ran toward the house. When he was halfway across the yard, he saw two men come running out of the patio doors.

Gerald dodged to his right, but his foot slipped on the wet grass and he hit the ground. His shoulder joint dislodged with a muffled wet pop and a white-hot bolt of pain ran from his neck to his elbow. He got to his knees and reached across to his right pocket with his left hand, nudging the pistol out with his thumb. Then he picked it up, pulled back the hammer and put the barrel into his mouth.

They saw him and stopped. Gerald heard the man from the beach shout something to them. His voice had a nasal quality that made him sound like he had a bad cold. They stood back, unsure what to do. One of the men who had been waiting in the house took a step forward. Gerald fixed his terrified eyes on him and shook his head.

"Hey, that's a really bad idea," the man said. "We don't want to hurt you, buddy. We just need to ask you a few questions."

He sounded perfectly reasonable, almost casual.

"What do you say, pal? You put the gun down and we'll just talk. You can keep it in your hand if you don't trust us."

If he hadn't been almost paralyzed with fear and in such severe pain, Gerald might have laughed. Instead, he closed his eyes and pictured Cynthia standing on the porch of their first home with their baby son in her arms and smiling at him. It was the way he wanted to remember her. Forgive me, he thought, and pulled the trigger.

# CHAPTER 17

**Skyline Defense**
**New York, New York**
**Monday 17 July 2006**
**2100 EDT**

"Gerald Ross is dead," Rollins said.

Jack walked to the door and locked his office. "What?"

"He'd been warned someone was looking for him."

"How do you know?"

"We caught him trying to sneak ashore at the back of the house. Rowed up in a little rubber boat. He knew about the break-in. Says he was paid to help a man named Walter Scott get into the Fed. He made a run for it and shot himself in his own backyard before we could stop him."

"And the drive?"

"He said he didn't know where it was, but I'm pretty sure he was lying. We searched the house and found the safe open in his office. One of the neighbors saw his wife leave before we arrived. I'm betting she's taken it with her. Why else would he have shot himself, if not to protect her?"

"Have you got a plate?"

"Massachusetts 1 3 X P 2 7. It's a black Audi A4 convertible."

"Give me twenty minutes," Jack said. "I'll call you back."

Jack left the office and walked to the lobby. When the elevator door was closed, he pressed not one button, but six in quick succession. There was a brief pause, then the elevator rose for a moment and the doors opened again.

He stepped out into a room that occupied the entire seventy-ninth floor. The four massive steel girders that supported the building stood exposed at the edges, and the floor-to-ceiling windows were all heavily tinted, giving it the look of an enormous and sparsely furnished studio apartment. The building's elevator shaft ran through the middle of the room. At one end, several wide office desks had been pushed together to form a long counter against the windows overlooking Central Park. It was littered from end to end with a haphazard collection of computers, screens and cables.

"Marius, I need you to find someone for me," Jack said.

Marius Botha was a white South African in his mid-thirties. His face was deeply tanned and covered with freckles. He wore a thick pair of black framed glasses, the type issued by the army and commonly referred to as *Rape Prevention Devices* for their distinguishing lack of style. His deep Afrikaans accent often made it difficult to understand a word he was saying.

Jack handed Marius a sheet of paper. "Black A4 convertible. Left Rockport Massachusetts about an hour and a half ago."

Marius took the sheet and Jack watched as he began to do what he did best.

"What's going on?" Marius asked finally.

"I'll tell you later."

It took him just over five minutes to find Cynthia's car.

"This was captured an hour ago on the Blue Star Memorial Highway," Marius said, pointing at a grainy image on one of the monitors.

"Bring it up on a map," Jack said.

Marius opened a window on another screen and brought up a map of Massachusetts. He zoomed in and pointed at Interstate 495 just below the town of Lowell. Something flashed up on a third screen and Marius turned to it. "That's it. Northbound on Interstate 91."

Jack took out his phone and called Rollins back. "She's making a run for the border up I-91. Call me as soon as you find her."

# CHAPTER 18

**Morisson, Vermont**
**Monday 17 July 2006**
**2100 EDT**

Amanda was in the driveway, leaning on the hood of her father's prized '68 Chevy Impala when Jesse arrived.

"I've missed you," she said as soon as he got out.

"I've missed you too, Mandy."

She pointed at the Volvo and raised her eyebrows. "Your mom's station wagon? Classy!"

When they reached the interstate, Jesse said, "So, you gonna tell me what brings you back to the Big M in the middle of the semester?"

"I will. But not until I've had a drink."

"You drink now?"

"Are you kidding? It's practically illegal not to in college."

The parking lot at Fryer's was almost empty. They walked through a pair of western-style saloon doors into a large room dotted with round wooden tables and mismatched chairs. Half a dozen people were sitting at the bar, most sipping bottles of beer and watching the game on TV. To the left of the door, an old jukebox was playing "Dixieland Delight" by Alabama.

They took a table at the back of the room. Amanda went straight to the bar and returned with two glasses and a pitcher of Coors Light.

"Bottoms up," she said and poured each of them a glass.

Jesse took a sip and grimaced.

"It gets easier," she laughed and took a long drink from her own glass.

"Wow! You're an alcoholic," he said.

The conversation began naturally enough. Reminiscences about life in what they had always called the "Big M". Jesse told her about his job at the Herald and his decision to become a journalist, and the flamboyant Mrs. Abernathy. Amanda described her life at Penn State with increasing contempt.

Her advice about drinking turned out to be accurate. After the first glass, Jesse found the acrid, metallic taste of the beer developing an odd appeal. He also discovered it worked wonders on the tongue. By the end of his second glass, the room had taken on a euphoric clarity in which every detail seemed to spring out at him. He felt as if the world around him had been coated in a thick layer of pure optimism. Amanda found the situation amusing; she kept looking at him with a knowing grin.

"Someone's in a good mood," she said as she poured him a third glass.

"So tell me," he said, picking up the glass and downing half of it in a single gulp. "Why did you come back? I'd like to think you just missed me, but I doubt that's the whole story."

Amanda's face turned serious for a moment as she considered the question. "I guess you could say I fell in with the wrong crowd. I know that sounds kind of lame, but you have to be there to see how things really are. There are people with money and people without, and all the progressive politics in the world won't change that. Behind the scenes, the class structure is as medieval as it's always been. I can't say nobody warned me, I just refused to believe it. I guess I'd just seen one too many bullshit movies."

"So what happened?"

"I started dating a guy. Real charmer. He played varsity football and drove a BMW. Enough to make you puke, right? Anyway, his dad was a state senator. He took me to Aspen for the weekend and bought me a Rolex. Can you believe that? A fucking Rolex. His dad came up to see him and we went out for lunch. I'd like to say the bastard at least made an effort, but he turned out to be the most obnoxious prick I've ever met."

When she didn't go on, he leaned forward and said, "What did you do?"

"Suffered through it. When we left, I actually started crying in the car. I thought he would take my side, but the spineless shit bag actually started making excuses for him. So I told him his dad was an asshole and he-"

She stopped and looked down at the table.

"He hit you," Jesse said. It wasn't a question. Every muscle in his body had gone rigid.

She reached over and put a hand over his. "It wasn't that bad. More of a slap, really. He was a bit of a pussy. I'm not making excuses out of guilt or anything. It stung a little, that's all."

"What did you do?" Jesse asked. He felt like picking up the nearest chair and throwing it across the room. The fact that he was a little drunk made the idea seem perfectly reasonable, if not compulsory.

"I got out and walked away. He followed me for a while trying to apologize. When I told him I'd be reporting him to the Dean if he didn't leave me alone, he took the hint and left."

"Where did you go?"

"Back to my room. I packed my bags and took off. My dad paid for the ticket and here I am."

"You should have called me," Jesse said.

She pulled her hand back. "I should have done a lot of things. Starting with minding my own damn business."

"Christ, Mandy. It's hardly your fault."

"I know. But like I said, I had fair warning. I even lost my only real friend when she tried to tell me what I was getting myself into."

Jesse reached over and took her hand again. He looked her straight in the eye and said, "But you'd seen all those movies!"

For a moment she only looked at him, then they both started laughing.

"You're right, Jesse," she said, "I should have called you."

Amanda offered to get another pitcher and Jesse almost agreed when he remembered he still had to drive back.

"I've got to get the car home," he said. "I don't think getting pulled over and hit with a DUI is such a hot idea, do you?"

"No, probably not," Amanda said. "Should we go?"

"Want to head down to Lake Morey?" Jesse asked.

"That's the best idea I've heard all week."

They pulled back onto the interstate and headed south. Mandy appeared unaffected by the four glasses of beer she'd had. Jesse, who'd only had three, looked almost stoned.

"You gonna be okay?" Amanda said.

"I'm fine," he said.

"You going back?" he asked after a moment.

She looked out the window, her eyes distant, as if the question hadn't really occurred to her until now.

"My dad would kill me if I didn't," she said at last.

Jesse was about to ask her what *she* wanted when he saw the car. It had pulled off the southbound interstate, moved across the central divide and stopped only a few feet from the road. Someone was standing at the back looking into the trunk. Jesse pulled over onto the side of the road and stopped.

"That was a woman, right?" Amanda said.

"Yeah, it was. Stay here, I'll go see if she's okay."

He got out and crossed the road. The woman saw him and moved to the side of the car.

"Ma'am. Are you all right?" Jesse asked.

"What do you want?"

"My name is Jesse Corbin, ma'am. I live just down the road. Do you need a hand changing that tire?"

The woman took a step toward him. She had a tire iron clenched in one fist. In the dim glow of the car's interior he could only see her face. She looked haggard, exhausted. Mascara had run from her eyes in two black lines that made her look a bit like a sad clown. There was something mad in those eyes. The look of someone whose gears have started to slip.

"You should leave," Cynthia Ross said.

"You sure you don't want me to give you a hand with that?" Jesse asked, pointing at the tire.

"You should leave," she said again, her voice taking on an edge of hysteria.

"Would you like me to call someone?"

"No, don't call anyone!"

"Okay," Jesse said holding up his hands, "I'll go."

He decided they would call the police as soon as he got back to the car. The woman was clearly *on* something and he didn't think pleading with her would do any good.

"Wait!" Cynthia said.

She opened the back door of the car and leaned inside. When she stood back up she was holding a small black bag. Jesse saw she was limping slightly.

"Ma'am, are you sure you don't want me to call an ambulance?" he said.

She ignored the question and held out the bag. "Take this."

"What is it?"

"I don't know, just take it. Please."

Jesse did and saw she had started crying again. If there had been any doubt in his mind that the woman was nuts, that dispelled it.

"Go!" Cynthia said. "You need to get out of here."

Jesse left. When he got back to the car, Amanda was standing by the side of the road. "Is she okay?"

"She's crazier than a shithouse rat."

"What's that?" Amanda pointed to the bag.

"No idea."

"Shouldn't we help her?"

"You can try. But I think we would be better off calling the cops. I don't have a cell; do you?"

Amanda took her phone from her pocket. "No signal."

"Come on," Jesse said, "there's a phone outside Seven-Eleven."

When they were back on the road Amanda turned to look at the bag in the backseat. "What the hell *is* that?"

"No idea," Jesse said. "But I plan on handing to the Sheriff as soon as I see him. She seemed to think it was dangerous."

"I think we should take a look first," Amanda said.

She reached back and prodded it with her finger, then picked it up and pulled back the zipper before Jesse could protest. "Oh my god!"

"What?" Jesse said.

Amanda pulled the bag open and tilted it toward him.

"Holy fuck!" Jesse said.

"Why would she give you this?" Amanda said.

"I told you, she was nuts."

She pulled one of the bundles out of the bag and fanned the bills with her thumb. "They're all hundreds. This must a hundred thousand dollars at least."

Amanda put the bundle on the seat beside her and reached into the bag again. This time she pulled out a small rectangular box made of some light gray metal.

"Should I open it?" she said.

Jesse didn't answer, just looked at her and shrugged.

She unhinged the small clasp on the box's side, lifted the lid, and cautiously held up the thing inside, as if it might explode if shaken. "What is it?"

"A hard drive," Jesse said.

"A what?"

"A disk drive for a computer. Looks ancient."

He took it from her and inspected it briefly. It was a lot heavier than he'd expected.

They reached Seven-Eleven a few minutes later and Jesse got out to use the payphone. He dialed the number to the sheriff's office printed on a large red sticker above the number pad.

"Sheriff's Department, Deputy Mills speaking."

"Good evening, Deputy. It's Jesse Corbin."

"Who?"

"The photographer from the Herald?"

"What can I do for you, son?"

"My friend and I passed a car on the interstate about ten minutes ago. It had a blowout. I tried to give the lady a hand, but she started acting real weird. Thought she was being followed or something. And she didn't look too good either."

"Bit of a nut job, was she?"

"Yeah, something like that."

"Well, you did the right thing. You get some pretty crazy folks on the roads these days. I'll get Heck out there to check it out. North or south?"

"North. She also-"

The line went dead. Jesse turned to see Amanda standing next to him with her index finger on the switchhook.

"What did you do that for?" Jesse said.

"Jesse, we should think about this."

"Think about what?"

"I'm just saying, that's a lot of money. What if she doesn't tell anyone? Hell, what if she doesn't even know? You said she was nuts, right?"

Jesse looked at her, astonished. "Doesn't tell anyone? For all we know, she'll say we robbed her."

They heard a car coming up the interstate and turned to see two black sedans fly past, heading back in the direction of Fryer's. They both had blue bubble lights flashing on the dashboard and must have been doing at least a hundred miles an hour.

"That was quick," Amanda said.

"That wasn't the sheriff's department," Jesse said.

"How do you know?" Amanda said.

"They don't have any unmarked cars. Come on, we need to hand that in."

When they were back in the car, Amanda took the bag and put it in her lap. "Let's run away, Jesse. We'll go to California and rent a house on the beach. Live like bums. It'll be great, I promise."

"Very funny."

Amanda pouted her lips and looked away. "Jesse, you're no fun."

"Trust me," he said. "You'll thank me. When that woman turns out to be some drug dealer's wife running away with his money, you'll be glad one of us kept our heads."

"Fine. But not right away," she said. "Pleeeasse, Jess. Let's go down to the lake first. At least let me count it so I'll always know how rich we could have been."

He considered this for a moment. "Fine. But I'm not leaving your house without that bag."

They got back from the lake at half-past-eleven. When Amanda finally fell asleep on the couch just after midnight, Jesse got up and gently pulled the bundle of hundred dollar bills from her hand. He put it back in the bag, zipped it up and stood watching her for a while, then turned off the TV and let himself out.

It wasn't until he got back in the car that he remembered how much he'd had to drink. Turning up at the sheriff's office smelling of beer and carrying a bag full of money didn't seem like such a shit-hot idea. He decided it was best to leave it until morning. Just turning the money in by itself would probably get him off the hook for leaving it a little longer than necessary.

He drove away at a cautious 25 miles per hour. When he was out of the town proper, he pushed the Volvo up to 30. He no longer felt drunk, but still found his vision blurring if he kept his eyes open for too long without blinking. As he came out of the final bend in the road and onto the straight that led out of town he saw something that made him slow down. Thinking he was still a little more intoxicated than he had suspected, Jesse rubbed his eyes and opened them again. The scene didn't change. There was a car half-buried beneath one of the tractors on the forecourt of Farmland.

Jesse pulled to the side of the road, got out and took a few steps toward the tractor. The car beneath it was peppered with tiny holes, like the ones you see on road signs someone has fired a shotgun at for fun. Just as he thought the evening had reached its pinnacle of unlikelihood, it got even stranger.

When he turned around, the sight that greeted him was so bizarre something in his subconscious dismissed it as a figment of his imagination. A man was standing about ten feet in front of him dressed in jeans and a biker's jacket. In each hand he was holding some kind of large rifle. To

Jesse they looked a bit like the weapons used by imperial storm troopers in the original Star Wars films. When the man spoke, what he said rounded the evening off with frightening finality.

"Son, you wouldn't have a hard drive on you by any chance, would you?"

# CHAPTER 19

**Interstate 91, Vermont**
**Tuesday 18 July 2006**
**0030 EDT**

Francis cursed when he saw the blue lights. Two black sedans had pulled off the road onto the central divide between the south and northbound lanes. He put the bike in neutral, killed the engine and the lights and let the momentum take him forward. Ross's black convertible was on the other side of the road, parked a few feet behind a white and brown police cruiser, its own strobes blinking red and blue.

He coasted another thirty yards and pulled off the road. Leaning the bike against a tree he pulled the pistol from his jacket and ran back toward the cars.

A gunshot rang out. Someone shouted and Francis turned to see four men running across the northbound interstate. They got back into their cars, crossed the divide and sped off in the direction he had come from. Francis watched them go, then ran to Cynthia's car.

It was empty.

The decal on the door of the police cruiser said *Orleans County Sheriff*. The man who had been driving it was lying facedown on the grass by the passenger door. A few yards down the slope lay a single white sneaker. Francis began walking in that direction and almost tripped over Cynthia before he saw her.

She had been shot. A line of blood ran from the small hole in her forehead into one open, staring eye. Her face was a ruin of running make-up and blood. Her bottom lip was badly swollen and her left cheek had been split open. He searched the body quickly, then ran back to her car.

The hard drive wasn't there.

Francis returned to his bike and almost lost it as the back wheel spun out on the grass.

He caught up to them just in time. When they passed a sign that said *Morisson – Population: Just Right*, one of the unmarked cars turned off its blue lights and left the interstate.

Francis followed it.

When it reached the intersection in the middle of town, the car turned left and parked outside a single-story brick building with a red tiled roof.

Francis pulled into the gap between a red Ford Bronco pickup and an old Buick Regal that looked like it was being held together with body filler.

From where he sat he could see the building through the cab of the Bronco. He was about to stand up when a man walked out the front door of the sheriff's office holding a phone to his ear. He was wearing jeans and a pair of cowboy boots. When he turned away Francis saw the navy blue windbreaker he wore had the words *US Marshal* printed on the back in big yellow letters. The caller was joined by a second man wearing an identical jacket. They talked for a moment, then the one who had been on the phone went back inside.

No more than five minutes had passed when the other unmarked car appeared. Two men dressed in the same jackets got out and walked inside. They came back out a minute later, got back into their car and headed toward the other end of town.

Francis left his lights off and kept his speed down to 30. The road wound through thick forest on both sides. Twice he almost missed a turn and drove straight off. He passed a tractor dealership; the illuminated sign above the barn-like structure said *Farmland.* Half a mile up the road he passed a sign saying *Hope you enjoyed your time in Morisson – Come back soon!* Beyond the town line the road began to wind again. At one point he thought he caught a glimpse of the car's taillights disappearing around a bend. A minute later he *did* see them as they passed a small barn and turned off the road.

There were three mailboxes on the corner with no names on them, only numbers. The car had stopped around a bend somewhere up ahead. Francis couldn't see the taillights but he could hear the idling engine. He pushed the bike off the road, set it down on the soft grass to hide it from view and followed on foot. When he was only a few feet behind the car he raised his head and looked inside. There was no one in it.

The road was little more than two ruts in the grass that sloped down to an open gravel yard in front of a single-story brick house. In the dim glow of the porch light, he could just make out two men descending the slope on opposite sides of the track. There was a pickup truck parked by the porch steps with a bicycle in the back. When they reached the yard, the man on the left ducked across the tracks and knelt beside his partner. They conferred briefly, then one of them stood up and walked back up the track. Francis ducked, moved around to the other side of the car and lowered himself onto his stomach. When the man reached the road he was talking to someone on his phone.

"Volvo's not here," he said.

There was a pause as he listened.

"Okay, we'll be there in five."

Francis timed his move carefully. He had picked up a rock about the size of a golf ball and the moment the call ended he threw it over the road into the trees. The man instantly dropped to one knee, his silenced pistol drawn and pointed in the direction of the sound. After a moment he stood up and began to walk forward slowly. Francis was hunched down in a squat with both heels pressed against the front tire. When the man stopped, Francis leaped forward, using the tire as a springboard. His feet only touched the ground once as he closed the distance and raised an arm. He brought the first two knuckles of his right fist down on the man's neck just above the final vertebra and swung his left arm around in a chokehold. He kept squeezing until the man dropped his gun. Francis picked it up, pushed the silencer into the soft tissue beneath the man's chin and whispered, "Who are you looking for?"

When the man didn't respond, Francis pushed the silencer deeper until he could feel it pressing the man's tongue into the roof of his mouth.

"A boy," the man croaked.

"Name?"

"Jesse Corbin."

"Does he have the hard drive?"

The man nodded.

"Are there more than four of you?" Francis asked raising his head to look back over his shoulder. He felt the man try to shake his head. Francis dropped the gun and grabbed his left elbow with his right hand. He squeezed until the veins in his own neck bulged and felt something give behind the man's Adam's apple. The body twitched several times, then stilled. Francis checked the jugular for a pulse. When he found one he stood up and brought his right boot down on the windpipe. There was a crack followed by a squelching sound, like someone kneading an egg into raw hamburger. He didn't bother checking again.

The other man was still crouched at the bottom of the track. Francis considered waiting for him to come back up and shooting him, then had a better idea. In his mind he kept seeing Cynthia, one eye filling up with blood, the other staring sightlessly at him, as if accusing him of getting her killed.

He stood up and motioned the man to come back up, hoping he would fall for it, ready to shoot him if he didn't.

Francis got in behind the wheel of the car and waited. When the man reached the road Francis turned on the lights and drove forward slowly, veering left just enough to give the impression he was going to pull alongside and let him get in. Then he floored the accelerator and straightened the wheel.

The impact pushed the man to the ground and beneath the car. Francis stopped and reversed a few yards. The scene in the headlights was gruesome.

The man was lying on his side, his legs twisted back at impossible angles. One side of his face had been literally scraped off. The white of his exposed cheekbone was brilliant against the maroon mask that covered the rest of his face. He was moving, but that was about all he had going for him. Whatever consciousness he had left would be wandering in a fog of unbearable pain.

Francis got out. "Hey there, you piece of shit. Didn't see that one coming, did you?"

The man didn't appear to hear him. His one good eye was moving around in little jerking motions. It made him look like one of those cheap horror movie zombies that were as likely to make you laugh as cringe. Francis knelt beside him and pointed the silencer of the pistol at the side of his head.

"When I find out who you people are I'm going to kill every last fucking one of you," he said and pulled the trigger.

He checked the trunk of the car and wasn't surprised to find it contained a small arsenal. What *did* surprise him were the two Pancor Jackhammer fully automatic shotguns sitting on top of the pile. The Jackhammer was an experimental weapon that had never been put into production as far as Francis knew.

There was also a Special Forces-issue Colt M4A1 carbine, a silenced MP5 compact submachine gun, and an M40A3 Marine Corps sniper rifle, as well as two bulletproof vests and several handguns.

When he reached the end of the dirt road Francis stopped and picked up the cell phone he had taken from the first of his victims. He was turning it over in his hand when it began to vibrate. Francis answered it.

"Where the fuck are you guys?" the caller shouted.

"Did you know it's a federal offense to impersonate a US marshal?" Francis said.

There was a long pause. "Who is this?"

When Francis made no reply the man said, "Walter? Walter Scott?"

Francis flinched at the mention of the name.

"That's right, Mr. Scott. We found your friend. He sold you out. Then he shot himself to protect his wife, for all the fucking good that did him."

The caller's voice was amused now, mocking. "Why not just give us the drive and save me the trouble of finding you? I'll kill you quickly, I promise. I might even spare the boy."

Francis laughed. "Why not save *me* the trouble and kill yourself, you sick fuck? Because I promise I *won't* make it quick."

Francis heard the man speaking to someone, then the sound of an engine starting.

"Walter? You still there, pal?" the caller said. "Maybe we could make a deal."

Francis hung up.

He got out of the car and threw the phone into the trees, then walked to the trunk and picked up one of the Jackhammers. He pulled off the heavy cylinder and checked the loads. There were ten twelve-gauge shells in the cylinder. He reloaded it and checked the other one, then picked them both up, looped one strap over each shoulder and set off at a near-sprint in the direction of town.

He had just reached the forecourt of the tractor dealership when he saw the headlights. Veering to his right, he ran to the end of the forecourt where a big John Deere tractor was parked only a few feet from the road, and crouched behind the front wheel.

Francis watched the car approach. When it was no more than ten yards away, he broke cover and ran toward it. He swung the Jackhammers around, pointed them straight at the driver's door and squeezed both triggers. The barrels began spitting flame and buckshot at 240 rounds per minute. The windshield and driver's side window disappeared in a sparkling red mist of glass, blood and dashboard. A second later the rear tire exploded and the car veered onto the forecourt, hitting one of the tractors and coming to a sudden stop.

Francis staggered back from the recoil and regained his balance. He dropped the Jackhammers, walked to the car and pulled open the passenger door. The driver was still alive. Both his legs had been crushed beneath the dashboard and it looked like one of his arms was broken, but his eyes were aware. He tried to reach into his jacket, only to find the hand at the end of his right arm was no longer taking orders.

"Who sent you?" Francis said.

The man only smiled, revealing two rows of even, bloodstained teeth. "Fuck you!"

"Are you with Princip? Did Norton send you?"

The man only looked at him.

Francis pulled the gun out of the man's shoulder holster, pointed it at his temple then moved it down and pushed it into his groin. "If you want to die with your balls intact you'll tell me who sent you."

The man raised his good hand and motioned for Francis to come closer. "Eat shit"

Francis, his patience at an end, twisted the man's broken arm. "Who the hell sent you?"

The man let out a shriek of pain, then his eyes closed and his head fell forward onto the steering wheel. Francis put two fingers to his jugular and felt the pulse first weaken, then stop.

Francis had walked back to pick up the Jackhammers when he heard the sound of an approaching car. He turned around just in time to see another set of headlights rounding the corner at the end of the straight.

The car, a gray Volvo station wagon, stopped several yards from the forecourt. The boy who got out looked about nineteen and was well built, with long black hair that almost reached his shoulders. When he was only a few yards away Francis stepped into the light and said the only thing that seemed to matter.

"Son, you wouldn't have a hard drive on you by any chance, would you?"

Jesse didn't reply. He closed his eyes for a moment, and when he opened them again, the look on his face suggested he was disappointed Francis hadn't vanished. He studied Francis for a moment then mumbled something under his breath.

"What was that?" Francis said.

"I said she wasn't crazy."

"Who wasn't crazy?"

"The woman."

"Was the woman driving a black convertible?" Francis asked.

Jesse nodded.

"This woman, did she give you a hard drive?"

He nodded again.

"What's your name, kid?"

"Jesse."

"Okay, Jesse," Francis said. "Listen to me. Have you got the drive?"

Francis spoke as if the boy might have been slightly brain damaged, which for all he knew, he was. Jesse nodded again.

"In the car?"

Another nod.

"Can you show it to me?" Francis asked.

Jesse didn't move.

"Kid, I need you to snap out of it."

Jesse took a step back and seemed to really see Francis for the first time. "Who are you?"

"Listen," Francis said. "There's no time. If we stay here, we're both dead. I need you to show me the drive."

Jesse walked back to the car and got the bag. He unzipped it and rummaged inside for a moment. "It's not here. Mandy must have taken it out."

"Who?"

"My friend. She was with me when the woman gave me the this. I must have left it at her house."

Francis walked to the Volvo and got in behind the wheel. "Get in."

\- - -

When they pulled to a stop outside Amanda's house five minutes later, Francis turned to Jesse and said, "All right, how we gonna do this?"

Jesse, who up to this point had seemed too dumbfounded by events to do more than go along in silence, looked at Francis with a mixture of fear and curiosity. "What the hell is going on?"

"That's a great question," Francis said. "One I've been asking myself all day. All I can tell you right now is that we need to get that drive. The rest will have to wait. Is that going to be a problem?"

When Jesse didn't answer Francis snapped his fingers. "Hey, eyes on me, kid. Can you get the drive or am I going to have to do it myself?"

"It's all right," Jesse said. "Her parents are away. I'll go in and get it."

Francis put a hand on Jesse's shoulder. "You need to get the hard drive *and* the girl. You guys can't stay here."

Jesse looked down at the bag in his lap. "We didn't take any of the money. I was going to hand it in tomorrow."

"I don't care about the money. Now please go in there and get the drive, and don't forget the girl. We don't have a lot of time."

"Are you a cop?" Jesse asked.

"Are you going, or do I have to do it myself?"

Francis reached for his own door handle.

"I'll go," Jesse said.

- - -

"Are you all right?" Amanda said when she saw the look on Jesse's face.

"Mandy, we need to get out of here."

She took a step back and eyed him, amused. "Very funny, Jesse."

When the expression on his face didn't change, she frowned. "What is it?"

"I don't know. Something to do with the bag and the money. Someone's looking for it."

"Did you go to the sheriff?"

"No."

"Then what the hell are you talking about? How do you know someone's looking for it?"

Jesse sighed and turned to the door. "Look out the window."

She did.

"Who the fuck is that in your car?" Amanda said.

"He says we need to get out of here. He knows about the money and the hard drive."

"Okay, I'm being serious now, Jesse. There's a man in your car. If it's your dad then it's a little creepy, but I'm sure you can explain. If it's not someone from the sheriff's office, who the fuck is it? And what are they doing here?"

Jesse gave up. He walked to the door, opened it and signaled for Francis to come inside.

"Tell me you didn't just invite him in!" Amanda said and moved to close the door. Jesse held it open.

"Jess, this is my fucking house!"

Before Jesse could answer, Francis pushed his way in and closed the door.

"What's the goddamn hold up?"

Amanda ran into the kitchen. When she came back she was holding a steak knife. Francis looked at Jesse and held up his hands, palms up, in the age-old sign for *what the fuck*?

"You haven't told her?" Francis said.

"I've been trying."

Amanda raised the knife. "Hello? I'm standing right here! Could someone please tell me what the hell is going on?"

Francis looked her up and down. Amanda brought her arms up to her chest and crossed them above her breasts.

"Oh please!" Francis said. "I'm not that guy. Do I look like *that* guy?"

Amanda didn't say anything.

"Long story short," Francis said. "A woman gave you a hard drive. Some very nasty people want it back. She's now dead. I've killed four people this evening who came here looking for it. When the replacements arrive and find you, they'll kill you, too. Now can we please get the hell out of here?"

Amanda looked at Jesse, clearly unconvinced.

"He's right," Jesse said. "I saw two of them out at Farmland."

Amanda turned and walked down the hall. She came back holding the hard drive and handed it to Francis. "Now get out of my house!"

The look she gave Jesse suggested he was free to do the same.

"You don't get it," Francis said. "It won't matter that you don't have it. They'll ask you who you gave it to, you'll tell them, and then they'll kill you. It's that simple."

It took her a moment, but the look of stubborn determination finally left her eyes. "Okay, so if you're not from the sheriff's office, who are you? And why should we believe anything you say?"

Francis considered this. It was a fair question. "Let's just say I'm a concerned citizen who doesn't want to see anyone else get shot if they don't have to. As for trust, you're just going to have to take my word for it. Now if we're done playing twenty questions, we really need to go."

When Amanda came back into the living room for the second time, she was dressed in a pair of dark green combat trousers, a black North Face jacket and hiking boots. She stood looking at Francis for a moment, her skepticism clear for all to see. "I'm going to the sheriff's office. Try and stop me and I'll scream until the entire neighborhood is standing on the front lawn."

Francis sighed and raised his arms in exasperation. "Where do you think the men who came here looking for you went first?"

When she didn't answer Francis said, "That's right, the sheriff's office. For all we know there are people waiting for you there right now. They may even be cops themselves. Do you know what they would do if you showed up?"

"We could explain -" Amanda began to say, but Francis cut her off.

"You wouldn't get the chance. You'd be arrested and taken away. Only instead of putting you in jail they would find out what they needed to know and kill you before anyone around here knew what was really going on. You want to take that risk? Go ahead, the door's open."

Amanda only looked at him.

"I've got what I came for," Francis said. "I could just as easily leave you here and let you take your chances. But if you're coming with me, we need to leave right now."

It took her a moment, but the look of stubborn determination slowly left her eyes, giving way to something more akin to apprehension.

Jesse led the way. When Amanda reached the door, Francis stopped her. "There's one more thing."

"What?"

"We need the keys to the Impala."

Amanda went to the glass cabinet at the back of the living room, opened one of the doors and fished a set of keys out of a porcelain bowl. She threw them to Francis. "One scratch on that car and you won't have to worry about anyone trying to kill me. My dad will do it for them."

# CHAPTER 20

**Skyline Defense**
**New York, New York**
**Tuesday 18 July 2006**
**0230 EDT**

Jack picked up the phone and tried to call Rollins again, but there was still no answer.

"Boss, you going to tell me what's going on?" Marius said.

Jack had all but forgotten Marius was there. Now he looked at him and tried to think of something to say. Mindful that outright lies had a way of outrunning the people who tell them, he settled instead on a plausible half-truth. "The woman driving the car is Cynthia Ross. Her husband is a security systems engineer who helped someone at Albion steal several of our designs. I had Rollins looking for him."

"And you think she was headed for the border?"

"They have relatives in Canada," Jack lied.

"So where's Rollins now?" Marius asked.

"I don't know. He was supposed to call me when he found her."

Marius looked skeptical. "If there was a security breach at Albion why didn't you tell me?"

"I wasn't sure. I mean, I didn't know for sure until Rollins found Ross."

"Yeah, but if you suspected-"

"Marius, I'm having a bad fucking week. All right? You work for me, remember? Not the other way around. If I don't always remember to tell you everything, I don't expect to be questioned."

Marius shrugged. "Fine. I'm just saying. Site security's *my* job. If I don't know-"

"Marius, I get it. I'm going downstairs. I'll be back in a minute."

"You want me to try Rollins again?" Marius asked.

"No, I'll do it. I'll let you know what's going on as soon as I get a hold of him."

# CHAPTER 21

**Morisson, Vermont**
**Tuesday 18 July 2006**
**0230 EDT**

"You kids okay back there?" Francis asked.

"We'd be a lot better if we knew where we were going," Amanda said.

"Canada."

"I was afraid you might say that," Amanda said.

"Really? Why's that?"

"Isn't that where fugitives go? Hop over the border into good old Canada?"

"And for good reasons," Francis said.

"Name one," Amanda said.

"Well, for starters, it's not the United States. It's also a largely unpopulated country."

"So we're off to the middle of nowhere to shack up with the moose and Eskimos?" Amanda said.

"Can't promise you Eskimos," Francis said. "But I'm sure there will be plenty of elk. First we need to ditch this car though. Is there a truck stop around here?"

Amanda sat up and leaned forward. "You're going to leave my dad's Impala at a truck stop?"

"We can't cross the border in this," Francis said. "We'd have a better chance of getting across unnoticed on roller skates. They may assume we're leaving the country anyway, but assuming is not the same as knowing."

"Won't leaving the car in the same place we move on from just make it easier to find us?" Jesse asked.

"Yes" Francis said. "Being seen arriving and leaving the car there would be both dumb and dangerous. But that won't matter if there isn't a truck stop up ahead somewhere."

"Past Barton about a mile or so," Jesse said. "It's a small place with a diner. You usually get a couple of trucks parked up in there."

"Good. We'll pull off the road and hide the car before we get there. We'll have to walk the rest of the way."

"To Canada?" Amanda asked.

"Yes, to Canada. And then maybe Greenland if we're not too tired."

"I was joking," Amanda said.

"So was I," Francis said.

They drove on for a while in silence.

"That's Barton over there," Jesse said when they passed the flyover.

Francis slowed the car, checked the mirror to make sure nobody was behind them and pulled off the road. He crossed a small field and drove into the trees on the other side.

"This is the end of the line," Francis said and got out.

When Jesse and Amanda joined him Francis had already begun snapping off low-hanging branches from the surrounding trees and leaning them against the side of the car. They joined in and within ten minutes one side of the Impala looked more like a beaver dam than a vintage muscle car.

"It'll have to do," Francis said.

Jesse frowned. "I meant to ask, how *did* you get into town?"

"Motorbike," Francis said.

"Where did you leave it?" Amanda asked.

"If you really want to know, it's not far from your house," he said, looking at Jesse. "In the trees where your road meets the road into town."

"What'll happen when they find it?" Amanda asked.

"I'm not too worried about the bike, although it did cost me a small fortune. It's registered to a false address and a man who doesn't exist."

They set out parallel to the interstate, keeping out of sight among the trees. At one point they reached an open field with no cover from the road and Francis made them walk around it, adding ten minutes to the trip. They saw the truck stop twenty minutes later.

There were two trucks in the parking lot. One was a blue Peterbilt trailing a flatbed full of steel beams. Next to it sat a flat-nose Mack Ultraliner with a box trailer. Both The Mack and its trailer were decorated in the same detailed paint job, an airbrush painting of a long mountain range below a cloudy gray sky.

"You guys stay here," Francis said. "I'm going to take a look around."

"What's your plan?" Amanda asked. "Jump into the back of the trailer and hope for the best?"

"No. I don't think it'll come to that."

Francis walked to the parking lot, which was really just a large plot of unpaved dirt, and around to the front of the trucks. The Peterbilt had Canadian plates, but the Mack was registered in Tennessee. In the middle of the Mack's driver door the artist had written *John's MH Ultraliner* in red cursive letters.

Francis reached into his backpack, took out a black beanie and put it on before walking up to the front door of the diner and taking a look inside.

A thin man in a green and black plaid shirt and bright yellow cap sat at the counter eating. The other driver was sitting in the end booth with his back to the wall.

Francis guessed he weighed about 350 pounds. His stomach was partly folded onto the table. There were two empty plates in front of him and two with food on them, not including the one he was currently eating from. He wore a black T-shirt with the Harley Davidson logo on it, but Francis didn't think Harley made a bike that would be of any use to this man. He took one last look around and walked into the diner.

What greeted him was the smell of rich food and boiling oil. It made him realize how hungry he was. Francis walked forward along the faded line in the black and white checkered linoleum, past the man sitting at the counter and took a seat on a stool two places down. A man in his fifties wearing a stained chef's apron was standing in the doorway of the kitchen. He appeared to be fighting a losing battle to hang on to his few remaining teeth.

"I'll be right with you," he said and disappeared back into the kitchen.

Francis studied the two guests, trying to guess who was the American. He didn't want to offend either of them by getting it wrong, so he just said, "Which one of you boys is the proud owner of that doozy of an Ultraliner out there?"

The one at the table raised his hand. He pointed first to himself, then at his mouth to indicate he intended to talk when he'd finished chewing.

"That'll be me," he said, patting his stomach.

"That's one hell of a paint job," Francis said.

"Cousin's an artist," he said. "Took him two years on account of my bein' gone most of the time."

The big man had a heavy southern drawl. The other driver appeared either not to understand, or to be uninterested in the conversation. Francis thought he was probably French Canadian. Before Francis could say anything else the man beat him to it. "You lookin' to go somewhere, stranger?"

"As a matter of fact, I am," Francis said.

"Quebec's where I'm headed. You're welcome to share the load. But I warn you now, I like ZZ Top and Credence. If that disagrees with ya, you'll be better off waiting for the next bus."

"Green River was the first album I ever bought," Francis lied.

"Well, why didn't you say so?" the man said. "Take a seat. I like you already."

- - -

When Francis wasn't back after twenty minutes, Jesse and Amanda started getting worried.

"Jesse, what the hell are we doing?" Amanda said. "How do we even know what he's saying is true?"

"You think he's crazy?"

"I don't think he's *crazy*," Amanda said. "But he's definitely weird. Did he tell you who he is or how he knew about the money?"

"No. But I think he might have been following the woman. He doesn't even care about the money. He just wanted the hard drive."

"And the men he said he killed? Who were they?"

"I don't know. Maybe he was following *them*. But if we're in danger like he says, I think we're better off *with* him. He seems to know what he's doing."

"Yeah, that's what worries me," Amanda said. "He seems to know exactly what he's doing. You think he's a cop?"

"No way," Jesse said.

"Then what? Some kind of stray wandering hero?"

"Something like that."

"Jesse, I'm serious."

"So am I."

"You think he's one of those kick-your-ass-anytime army guys?" Amanda said.

"I'm pretty sure that's not what you call them, but yeah, I think he's a kick-your-ass-anytime army guy of some kind. Maybe a SEAL or something."

"He looks more like a human to me," Amanda said.

"Stop it. You know what I mean."

"No, Jesse. I'm pretty sure I don't."

"A Navy SEAL. They're like Special Forces. All that undercover, covert ops shit."

"You mean he'll get to be governor of California one day?"

"Mandy, stop kidding around, this is serious."

"That's how I deal with serious shit, Jesse." Amanda said. "Or have you forgotten?"

Jesse looked at her and saw she wasn't joking.

"Well I don't think *he's* kidding around," Jesse said and pointed towards the diner. Amanda moved forward to look.

"Wow," she said. "I think he's befriended the Stay Puft Marshmallow Man."

Jesse, who had once been an avid collector of comics, thought the man resembled more what the Kingpin might look like if he became five feet shorter without losing any weight. The man walking next to Francis was at least a foot taller and probably three times as heavy. They disappeared behind the trailer. A moment later they saw the cab of the truck with the paint job rock back and forth several times. Francis came around to the passenger's side, climbed up the steps and got in.

"Great. He's decided to go on without us," Amanda said.

"I don't think so," Jesse said. "He probably hasn't told him about us yet."

A minute later Francis opened the door and climbed down. "Guys. You can come out now."

His name turned out to be John Mathis, Big John to his friends. He was from Murfreesboro, Tennessee and owned a two-truck fleet that he ran with his cousin. They transported car seats made in Nashville to a Ford plant outside Quebec. The first thing he did when he met Amanda was make her feel guilty for calling him the Stay Puft Marshmallow Man by being one of the nicest people she had ever met. He showed them into the sleeping cabin behind the seats, which looked more like a small living room. There was a TV, fridge and microwave. The folding bed had been pushed up and turned into a couch complete with cushions and armrests. Big John offered them coffee then pointed to a cabinet mounted to one side of the cabin and told them to help themselves to his personal stash of Twinkies, Hostess Cupcakes and Oreos. Francis gave them each a Styrofoam box containing a freshly cooked cheeseburger and fries.

Big John started the truck and put it in first gear. No sooner had they set off than he turned and said, "I'm gonna kill the lights back there and pull the curtain now. Border's not far."

They sat listening in darkness as the truck rumbled to a stop and Big John rolled down his window.

"Hey there, Mike, how's life been treatin' ya?" Big John said.

The voice that answered him was jovial and familiar.

"Hey, Big J. Can't complain. Where you been? I haven't seen you in a week."

"Down Arkansas way visitin' Pauline's folks. You seen Ned?"

"Yeah, he passed through around six."

"Well, I'd better get goin'. Wanna try and get back myself by ten."

"See ya later. Drive safe."

"You betcha."

The truck started and began to move. A moment later they were stopping again. Big John leaned over and pulled the curtain aside. "Darlin', can you reach under the seat there and grab me them cartons of cigarettes?"

Amanda did. A moment later Big John rolled down his window again and said, "Hey, Karl. What's new?"

"Oh, nothing much. Quiet evening. Your cousin passed through here a while back."

"Yeah, I heard."

The door opened briefly and then shut again.

"Same old?" Big John asked.

"I don't know. The fellas say I should maybe try lights. I tell you what, get me a carton of lights and one of reds. I'll give it a shot."

"You got it," Big John said.

"All right John, I'll see ya later."

"Take care," Big John said and rolled up the window.

This time they moved off and picked up speed. A minute later the light came back on and Big John pulled back the curtain.

"Like stealin' candy from a baby, right?" he said, smiling.

"I'm impressed," Francis said.

"The fifty-five's about two and a half hours away," Big John said. "You folks might want to get some shut-eye."

"I'll join you up front," Francis said.

"I'll take you up on that, Big John," Amanda said and yawned, which got Jesse doing the same.

Francis climbed into the passenger's seat, then reached back and closed the curtain.

"Y'all want the light out back there?" Big John asked.

"Yes, please. So we can *sleep*," Amanda said.

"All right, little lady," Big John said laughing. "Ain't none of my beeswax either way."

Amanda leaned her head back on Jesse's shoulder. "I'm just resting my eyes."

She was asleep less than a minute later.

# CHAPTER 22

**Skyline Defense**
**New York, New York**
**Tuesday 18 July 2006**
**0500 EDT**

To a casual observer Jack Fielding would probably have looked dead. He had fallen asleep behind his desk with his head tilted back and his mouth ajar.

His eyes suddenly snapped open and he sat forward, looking around the office as if he'd never seen it before. He looked down at his phone slowly vibrating toward the edge of the desk and picked it up. "Rollins?"

"No, it's Marius."

"What time is it?"

"Five. I think you better get up here."

Jack, still half asleep, found Marius watching the CNN news feed on one of the monitors. The picture changed from the scene of a burnt-out car jammed beneath the undercarriage of a charred John Deere tractor to a woman standing in front of a single story brick building. A brown and white police cruiser with the words *Orleans County Sheriff* stenciled to the door was parked behind her.

"The local sheriff's office has yet to make a statement to the press," the reporter said. "This may be explained by the presence of both the FBI and the Department of Homeland Security, who we can only assume want more time to figure out exactly what happened here. All we know for now is that sometime in the early hours of the morning, this sleepy little New England town became the scene of several brutal murders, including that of an unidentified woman just outside the town on Interstate 91. A source at the local paper says some of the victims may have been federal officers, a claim that has yet to be confirmed or denied."

The picture changed again to the studio where the anchor appeared to be unaware he was back on camera. He was reading something from the screen on his desk when he suddenly looked up, flustered. "And we'll return to the town of Morisson shortly, but we've just received word that two local residents have also been reported missing. We're waiting for confirmation of the names, but this surely adds yet another mystery to what is already a very confused scene. We'll of course bring you more as soon as we get it."

Marius looked up at Jack. "We need to call Carl."

Jack seemed not to hear him. His eyes were fixed on the screen.

"Jack, we need to wake up Carl."

"What?"

"This is serious shit, Jack. Rollins is dead. And the Ross woman. What the hell happened?"

"I don't know," Jack said, still not quite able to comprehend what was going on. "I need a minute to think."

"I'm calling Carl," Marius said and reached for the phone.

Jack grabbed his arm. "Don't."

"Why not?"

All thoughts of lies and why you shouldn't tell them fled Jack's racing mind. He clutched at the first thing that came into his head. "Carl is the one behind this. I couldn't tell you before because we didn't know if you could be trusted."

"What are you talking about?"

Jack sat down in the chair next to Marius and did his best to look as grave as possible. "Caroline called me from Zurich a couple of weeks ago. She told me that a company had been buying technology from someone inside Skyline. Not just from Albion. She said it had to be someone here because everything was being downloaded from the mainframe and printed off. We thought it had to be you at first. But I began to follow Carl, you know, just in case. He's been meeting Gerald Ross."

Marius looked like he had suddenly developed Down's syndrome.

"Marius?" Jack said.

"What?"

"You okay?"

"I don't understand. How..."

"It's all right. I didn't believe it myself at first."

"What are we supposed to do?" Marius said.

"Nothing. We let him think he's gotten away with it. I'll deal with Carl. What I need you to do is carry on as usual. If I need your help, I'll ask. Can you do that?"

Marius nodded. "I don't know. I guess, yeah."

"Good. I need you to keep your shit together. Caroline is sending Titov. All we need to do is sit tight until he gets here."

# CHAPTER 23

**Sainte Eulalie, Quebec**
**Tuesday 18 July 2006**
**0745 EDT**

Big John turned on the hazard lights, downshifted and eased off the highway onto the escape lane. When the truck came to a stop, he held out a hand to Francis. "It's been a pleasure, sir."

"You're an all-American hero," Francis said.

Francis climbed out of the cab and stood stretching his legs. Amanda and Jesse climbed over the seat and followed him down.

"You kids take care," Big John said.

"Thanks for the ride," Amanda said.

"Nice truck," Jesse added. "Really awesome."

Francis climbed back up the steps and handed Big John five hundred-dollar bills.

"Not on your life," Big John said.

"It's not for the ride. I'm going to ask you not to tell anyone about this."

"I gathered you would. I can keep a secret, don't you worry."

"I'm sure you can but I'd feel a lot better knowing I'd made it worth your while."

Big John hesitated, then took the money. "I'll accept it as a contribution to my daughter's tuition fund."

"Glad to hear it," Francis said. "Drive safe."

"Always do."

They stood watching until the truck was out of sight. Amanda looked around at the desolate landscape and rubbed her eyes. "Great. Now what?"

"We walk," Francis said.

"Where?" Jesse said.

"There's a town about fifteen miles in that direction," Francis said, pointing across the highway at a two-lane road that marched straight as an arrow into the flat country beyond.

"Fifteen miles?" Amanda said.

"It sounds worse than it is," Francis said.

"Really? Because to my mind fifteen miles is where the earth ends in walking terms," Amanda said.

"Chances are someone will stop. People out here almost always do."

"I hope you're right," Amanda said.

"Come on," Francis said. "The sooner we get moving, the better."

Francis set off across the highway and Amanda fell in behind him, but Jesse didn't move.

"Okay, kid. Out with it," Francis said.

"I'm not going anywhere until we get some answers," Jesse said.

It was obvious Jesse had been planning this little mutiny. It was in the eyes and the way he tried to look calm despite clearly being anything but.

"Bearing in mind I don't know that much myself," Francis said, "what would you like to know?"

"Who are you? That would be a good start."

"Can this wait until we get off the highway at least? It's not a good place to have a conversation when you're on the run."

"Fine. But then you start talking."

"All right."

They crossed the highway and cut over a field to avoid the junction. When they reached the road Francis set the pace and positioned himself between Jesse and Amanda. "Okay, I'm all ears."

"What's your name?" Jesse asked

"I've got a few."

"Great. So what should we call you?"

"Call me whatever you want," Francis said.

Jesse stopped. For a second Francis thought the kid was going to take a swing at him. "I'm being serious! Do you understand the idea of empathy? Do you see how goddamned crazy all this is to me? To *us*?"

Amanda put a hand on Jesse's shoulder. "Take it easy, Jess. I'm sure he'll tell us."

She looked at Francis. "Right?"

Francis studied them for moment. "Okay, call me Eddie. It's what my mother wanted to name me."

Jesse shrugged as if to say he didn't care one way or the other. Francis began walking again. For a minute none of them spoke, then Jesse said, "Are my parents - our parents - in danger?"

"I'd like to promise you that they aren't," Francis said. "But I don't think you'd believe me. And calling them wouldn't change that, if that's what you're thinking. If you want my opinion though, I'd say they aren't."

"What makes you so sure?" Jesse asked.

"I didn't say I was sure. But harming your parents would achieve nothing as long as you don't contact them and they can't get hold of you. I'm assuming neither of you has spoken to them about the drive."

They both shook their heads.

"Good. Then I'd say they aren't in any danger. Does anyone else know?"

They shook their heads again.

"Well, that's a start. What else do you want to know?"

"Were you following the woman?" Jesse asked.

"Yes."

"How did you know she had the drive?" Amanda asked.

"Her husband was a friend of mine. He'd given it to her."

"Because the people looking for it knew he had it?" Jesse asked.

"That's right."

"Where did *he* get it?" Amanda asked.

Francis hesitated. "I gave it to him."

"That doesn't make any sense," Amanda said.

"He was going to look at it for me. See if he could find out what was on it."

"So you got her killed," Amanda said.

"Yes, I got her killed," Francis said. "For what it's worth, I had no idea they were in any danger when I gave it to her husband."

Jesse was about to ask another question when they heard the distant sound of an engine behind them.

"Don't turn around," Francis said. "If it stops, we'll accept the ride. If not, we keep walking."

They heard the car slow down. When it passed them they saw it was a pickup truck. It moved onto the side of the road and stopped.

"Jump on and wave to the driver," Francis said. "If he says anything, I'll do the talking."

They climbed in. Jesse and Amanda both gave the driver a wave. He waved back without looking around and pulled back onto the road. Fifteen minutes later they crossed a bridge and entered the town of Trois-Rivieres. Five minutes after that Francis leaned back and tapped the roof of the cab twice. The man pulled to the side of the road and stopped.

"Jump off and give him another wave," Francis said.

They did and the man waved back, no more interested in who they were than he had been when he picked them up.

"That was a bit of luck," Amanda said.

"Not as lucky as you'd think. This is rural Quebec, not Los Angeles. People in this part of the world are wired differently."

"You've been here before?" Amanda asked.

"Once or twice."

Francis led them down the road for another half-mile and stopped outside a fenced-in compound full of vehicles. There were several pickup trucks, a couple of vans and two flatbed trucks parked neatly in two rows. All were light green and had the provincial seal of Quebec decaled on the doors.

"This is the park warden's station," Francis said as they approached the gate. He pushed a button on the intercom and said something in French. Someone answered in the same language. A moment later a man stepped through the door of a small brick building in the corner of the lot. He wore green pants tucked into brown leather knee-high boots and a matching jacket with a furry collar. A crop of dark gray hair sprung from the rim of his baseball cap, and he had a short trimmed beard of the same color. As he approached he lifted a hand and waved.

"Bonjour, Maurice! Comment allez-vous?" the man said, smiling at Jesse and Amanda.

Francis replied in what sounded like fluent French and the two men chatted for a minute. Amanda turned to Jesse and whispered, "Maurice?"

Jesse shrugged. "The man with a hundred names. One for every place he visits, probably."

When they were done talking the man turned and walked back to the building.

"So, Maurice, what's the plan?" Amanda said.

Francis laughed and adjusted an invisible beret on his head. The gesture looked so stupid that even Jesse couldn't help laughing with him, despite his glum mood.

"Valerie is going to take us to Lake Commissaires. It's a three-and-a-half-hour ride, so you'll be able to get some more sleep if you need it."

"And who exactly is Valerie?" Amanda asked, looking amused.

"An old friend."

"And when we get to this lake, will your Mounty friends take us the rest of the way on horseback?" she asked.

"Very funny," Francis said.

"Just asking, *Maurice*." Amanda teased.

"I've told Valerie you're a niece and nephew of mine from the States. It would make things much easier if you played along."

"No problem, Maurice. Anything you say," Amanda said, unable to let it go.

Valerie returned behind the wheel of a passenger van and motioned for Jesse and Amanda to get into the back. Francis got in beside Valerie and said something that made his friend laugh and look back. Amanda stuck her tongue out at Francis and said, "I took a little French in high school, so don't think you two can sit there making fun of us."

"Perhaps you tell me a joke por Françoise?" Valerie said in heavily accented English.

"Maybe later," Amanda said and turned to look out the window, pretending to be more offended than she was.

Valerie turned out of the compound onto Route 155 and headed north. Amanda and Jesse, still exhausted, both fell asleep again within minutes. Francis, seemingly impervious to the effects of sleep deprivation, stayed awake and kept his friend company. As they drove, the towns along the route grew smaller and farther apart. For the first hundred miles the road followed the Sainte Maurice River, then veered northeast through the town of La Tuque toward Lake Saint Jean.

When they reached Lake Commissaires, Valerie pulled off the road about a mile from the small town of the same name and onto a dirt track that led to the lake's eastern shore. Francis had woken Jesse and Amanda fifteen minutes earlier and they had been gaping out at the wilderness, unable to take in the sheer size of the place. With the exception of the winding road, there were no signs out here that man had ever existed. No matter where you looked, all you could see were trees against the clear blue backdrop of endless sky.

"What's the opposite of claustrophobia?" Amanda asked.

"This!" Jesse said.

"Welcome to ze middel of nowhere," Valerie said. "Just bear and elk and beaucoup d'arbres."

"Don't let him scare you," Francis said. "This is one of the most beautiful places you'll ever see. Trust me."

They watched Valerie drive back to the road and turn left toward the town. When he was gone, Francis pulled his backpack over one shoulder and set off in the direction of the lake. "You guys coming?"

"Are we going to swim across?" Amanda asked.

"No need. I've got a boat."

Amanda thought he was kidding at first, but when they saw the small wooden shed nestled on the bank, her heart sank.

Jesse looked at Francis. "Amanda's not really a boat person. Are you, Mandy?"

"There's no *really* about it. I'm not a boat person, period. And you can thank this guy for that," she said pointing at Jesse.

"We'll make sure it doesn't have any holes in it," Jesse said.

"You better."

"I'm sure–" Jesse said, then paused, trying to remember what Francis had suggested they call him. "I'm sure Eddie has taken good care of it."

"Don't you mean Maurice?" Amanda asked.

"I'm sure *Maurice* has taken good care of it," Jesse corrected.

"Seriously, that's starting to get a little old," Francis said. "Now give me a hand getting this thing into the water."

When he finished mounting the small outboard motor, Francis stood up, leaned forward and yanked back the pull-start cord. The engine fired up immediately and spat out a thick cloud of black smoke.

When they reached the south side of the lake, Francis steered the boat to starboard, followed the shoreline for another hundred yards, then aimed it straight at the sandy bank and tilted back the outboard just as the bow scrapped the bottom.

"Anyone up for spaghetti?" Francis said.

Jesse and Amanda climbed out and walked up the beach to the tree line.

"You going back to town to find a Pizza Hut?" Jesse asked

"I was thinking more like Heinz," Francis said. "But you'll have to give me a hand with the boat first."

They pulled it out of the water and dragged it up the beach. Francis reached into a storage compartment in the bow, took out an old green tarpaulin and covered it.

"Follow me," Francis said.

Five minutes later they reached the cabin. It was about ten yards wide and made of dark gray stone covered in patches of thick moss. There was a small window to either side of the wooden door. The roof was covered in grass and the wall on the right extended up into a narrow chimney.

"Welcome to Canada," Francis said.

"This is your place?" Jesse said.

"Built it myself."

"I don't suppose you built a toilet around here while you were at it, did you?" Amanda said.

Francis pointed at the trees. "Toilet's out there somewhere. The ground for water and a shovel if you need to move your bowels."

"*Move* my bowels?" Amanda said.

"Take a shit," Jesse said.

"Yeah, I know what it means, Jesse," she said. "I just don't like the idea of doing it with the woodchucks watching."

The cabin was a single room about fifteen by twenty-five feet. In the wall to the right of the door there was a quaint little fireplace. Against the opposite wall there was a crudely built single bed made of rough boards. In the center of the room, a table and a single chair completed the cabin's inventory of furniture.

"Kill me now," Amanda said, looking around. But her tone suggested she was more intrigued than disappointed.

"Come on. It could be worse," Jesse said.

"Yeah," Amanda said, smiling, "it could have been a tipi."

Francis picked up three dry logs and staked them inside the fireplace. There was a rusty tin of lighter fluid and a box of long wooden matches on the narrow stone mantelpiece. He sprayed the logs, struck a match and threw it in. There was a whooshing sound as the fluid ignited and the logs began to burn.

"That's not how they showed us to do it in the Scouts," Jesse said.

"Some of that wood's ten years old," Francis said. "It would probably ignite if you rubbed your hands together and touched it."

They stood there for a moment in front of the fireplace, silently preoccupied with that most ancient of human pastimes.

"So," Amanda finally said. "Where's the kitchen? Now that we're back in the Stone Age, I'm guessing that's where you'll want me. Or maybe you have some pelts that need scraping."

"Is she always this charming?" Francis asked Jesse.

"No. This is her on a good day," he said, smiling at her.

"I'm just tired and hungry," Amanda said, leaning on Jesse. She yawned and stretched her arms. "Tired, hungry and still in denial."

Francis pulled the table to one side and pushed the chair out of the way. "I can help you with the first two," he said knelling down. "The third should come in time. I'm feeling a little weirded-out myself, if it's any comfort."

Francis knelt and brushed aside some of the dust on the floor, exposing the rough wooden boards beneath, then went outside and came back a minute later carrying a crowbar. The nails screeched as he pried one of the boards free, making all of them cringe. He pulled up four more and stacked them to one side.

"Holy shit!" Jesse said and motioned for Amanda to come over.

"My god, I think he really is a walrus," she said.

Francis looked up, puzzled.

"She means seal," Jesse said. "As in Navy SEAL."

For a moment Francis looked like a kid caught with his hand in the cookie jar.

"You are, aren't you?" Jesse said.

"I'm what?" Francis said.

"A SEAL, or Force Recon, or one of those Special Forces outfits."

"You've been playing too many video games, kid," Francis said.

"Yeah, I've played a few. I still think that's what you are, though. Why else would you have a damn arsenal under the floorboards?"

"They're for hunting."

"Really? Because I have a hunting rifle and it doesn't look anything like those. That one there? I know that's an M16 of some kind. What do you hunt with an M16?"

"Look, kid," Francis said. "Don't try growing up too fast. Let's just say I'm a guy who likes guns and leave it at that."

"Gun worship *is* the second biggest religion in the United States," Amanda said. "After fast food."

She stepped forward and held out her hands. "We need some spaghetti in this Western. Give me the Heinz and I'll see what I can rustle up. No beans, mind. This place is *way* too small for beans."

Francis looked up at Jesse and saw the topic was not going to be dropped that easily. He reached down and pulled a plastic sheet back to reveal a sizable selection of canned goods. He passed six cans of Heinz spaghetti to Amanda, then reached down and picked up a gallon-size milk jug full of water and held it out to Jesse. "Can you give me a hand with this?"

"Sure. Whatever," Jesse said.

Francis produced a Swiss army knife from his pocket, opened the cans and passed them to Amanda who lined them up next to the fire. Jesse was sitting on the bed and devoting his attention to a hole in the knee of his jeans. Amanda walked over to him and held out her hands. "What do you say, Bill? You want to join Calamity Jane and the gunslinger for a bite to eat?"

They sat and ate in a semicircle around the fireplace with Amanda in the middle. When she was done she turned and grinned at Francis. "Maurice the Seal! I like it, it's cute."

Jesse couldn't help laughing. Francis looked over at him, stone-faced for a moment, then caught the bug and joined in, which set Amanda off too.

They sat that way for a long time, caught in the grip of infectious laughter. And for a little while they weren't running for their lives but just three people enjoying the company of others. Outside, the thunderclouds were rolling in, painting the still surface of the lake a deep, ominous black.

# CHAPTER 24

**New York, New York**
**Tuesday 18 July 2006**
**1500 EDT**

Jack took the hotdog and handed the street vendor a five-dollar bill. "Keep the change."

"Thanks, pal."

He crossed Central Park West at 108th Street and found an empty bench along one of the footpaths leading into the park. He was acutely aware that stress was beginning to chip away at some fundamental part of the machinery between his ears. Thinking, something he had been managing perfectly well a few days ago, was beginning to get harder. He found himself having trouble remembering half the things he had told Marius. And he had a headache. Not the dull throb behind the forehead or temples that a couple of Excedrin would take care of, but a steady, piercing drumbeat behind his eyes, as if something with sharp teeth were chewing on his optic nerves.

On a good day he might have spotted them. But Jack hardly noticed the two men that approached the bench from opposite sides. Nor did he look up when a black Chevy van pulled to a stop not twenty yards away.

"Jack Fielding?"

Jack looked up. The man standing in front of him looked like he'd just walked off a construction site. He had a hard hat under one arm and a tool belt slung over his right shoulder. The man who stopped on the path several yards away was wearing a suit and carrying a briefcase.

"Who wants to know?" Jack said, looking around for the best direction to run.

"There's someone who'd like to meet you," the construction worker said, pointing at the van. "Right over there."

"Who?" Jack asked.

The man didn't answer.

"If it's all the same to you," Jack said, "I'm quite happy where I am."

"It's not," the man said. "And don't bother running."

Jack looked back toward Central Park West and saw two more men casually admiring the traffic.

Suit-man looked over at the van and nodded. The side door slid.

"What do you say, buddy?" construction man said, "you going to give us a minute or do we have to take it?"

Jack stood up. "I guess I can spare a minute."

"Wise choice."

When Jack got in, suit-man closed the door and tapped on it twice. There were no windows inside, only a small light in the roof. Jack tried the door, more out of reflex than any hope that it might be unlocked. He braced himself as the van began to move, accelerating and braking with the busy afternoon traffic.

It felt like they'd been driving for at least half an hour but it had probably been less. At this time of day that would still put them downtown somewhere, he figured. Jack squinted instinctively when the door opened, only to find it was just as dark outside. The man standing in the door was Asian. Japanese or maybe Korean, Jack thought.

"This way," the man said.

They were in an abandoned factory of some kind. Several rusting machines that looked like metal presses had been pushed against the wall at the back of the large room. Jack followed the man past these and up a flight of stairs that led to a small, elevated office overlooking the shop floor.

"Wait here," the man said.

Jack waited.

When he heard the sound of an approaching engine, he walked to the window and saw a white seven-series BMW pull up alongside the van. The man who got out looked well past retirement age. He had a thick beard and wore a brown suit with elbow patches.

When he entered the office a minute later the man sat down and nodded at the chair across the table. "Please, take a seat."

Jack did.

"You're a hard man to find, Mr. Fielding. Or should I say Albrecht? That *is* your given name, isn't it? Markus Albrecht?"

Jack couldn't quite hide his surprise, but didn't answer.

Norton Weaver sat down and opened the file in his hand. He took a pair of reading glasses from his inner coat pocket and perched them on the end of his nose. "Markus Albrecht. Born six August 1963 in Prenzlau. Your mother crossed the border in '66 and settled in Bonn. Father unknown. Have I missed anything so far?"

When Jack still made no reply, Norton went on. "Recruited out of the State Investigation Bureau in '93 by GMM Propulsion in Frankfurt. You changed your name to Jack Fielding a year later. Now a resident alien and the head of corporate security for Skyline Defense. Sound about right?"

"What do you want?" Jack said.

"That's not really the right question. If it were up to me you'd be sleeping with the fishes, as they say here in the Big Apple. My employer, however, sees things differently."

"Your employer?"

Norton ignored the question. "You've caused me a lot of trouble, Jack. Do you mind if I call you Jack? My German pronunciation is awful."

Jack said nothing.

"Your little stunt in Vermont is proving quite the headache. Did you know Rollins was Delta before he started robbing banks?"

Jack nodded. "I knew he was ex-army."

"Indeed. Anyway, there's nothing we can do about it now but grin, is there? I'm more curious to know what you were keeping at the Fed that was so important you're willing to hire a man like Rollins to find it."

"Why does it matter?" Jack said. "Whoever took it obviously thought it was yours or you wouldn't be here."

"You're brighter than you look, Jack," Norton said. "Luckily for you, the situation is one we might both be able to take advantage of."

"How?" Jack said.

"Let's just say we're limited in what we can do ourselves."

Jack relaxed a little and even managed a faint smile. "Because they have you by the balls, is that it? You go looking, they call CNN?"

"Something like that."

"And what can *I* do?" Jack said.

"You want your property back. We want our balls back. The man we're both looking for-"

"His name is Walter Scott," Jack interrupted. "Gerald Ross was his line into the Fed."

"I have no doubt Ross helped him, but I can assure you his name isn't Walter Scott. Not that it matters. What matters is that he's made a mistake. And he's smart enough to *know* he's made a mistake."

"And you want me to go after him for you," Jack said.

"You know, you really are a lot smarter than I thought you would be, Jack. Yes, we want you to find him. And kill him."

"And you think he'll keep his mouth shut because what, he's a man of honor? You saw what he did in Vermont. He's crazy."

"Oh, I don't know," Norton said. "You *did* kill Ross and his wife."

"We didn't kill Ross," Jack said. "He killed himself."

"And you had nothing to do with that, I'm sure. My point is, I don't think he'll go to the press because I don't think he wants to. He knows he's stolen something that belongs to you. He knows you want it back."

"In case you hadn't noticed," Jack said, "I've exhausted my resources."

"Which brings us to the point of all this."

Norton took a folded sheet of paper from the file and pushed it across the table. "That number is valid for another twenty-four hours. The money will be given to you when my men drop you off."

"Who am I calling?" Jack said.

"The best in the business."

"All right, and what happens when he's found?"

"You get your property back, I get my pound of flesh, and we part friends."

"That's it?"

"That's it. I'd tell you not to try and fuck me over, but I think you'd be insulted."

Jack stood and pushed the chair back. "The lease at the Fed isn't in my name."

"I know," Norton said.

"So how did you find me?"

"Your friend at the FBI."

"Jessops?"

Norton nodded. "Relax, the FBI is the least of your problems. But if you want my advice, you should find yourself another informant. Maybe one who isn't quite so stupid."

# CHAPTER 25

**FBI Field Office**
**New York, New York**
**Tuesday 18 July 2006**
**1600 EDT**

Mike was on his way out of the office when the assistant director caught up to him and asked him to follow her.

"What's going on?" Mike asked.

"I wanted you to hear this from me before you figure it out yourself and do something you'll regret."

"Hear what?"

"Five people were killed last night in a small town in upstate Vermont. Four of them were apparently pretending to be US marshals. The fifth was a woman named Cynthia Ross."

"Doesn't ring a bell," Mike said.

"Her husband's name is Gerald Ross. He wasn't on the list you drew up, but I think it would have been if you'd had a little more time to dig around. He's a retired security systems engineer. One of the best in the business."

"And where is he?" Mike asked.

"Missing. No one has seen him since yesterday afternoon."

Mike ran his hands through his hair and let out a long sigh. "Well, at least we know those crazy fucks haven't wasted any time screwing things up."

"Actually, from what I hear the White House is livid."

"You believe that? They lie, you know. It's what they do."

"Maybe. But I don't think so. What I need to know from you is that you're going to be professional about this."

"Oh, I know the routine well enough."

"Good. That's all I wanted to hear."

Mike stood. "I'm going home. I haven't slept in two days."

"That's a good idea. Tell me, is Rainey going to be a problem?"

"He's a smart kid. He'll put this together, you can count on that."

"Then I'm trusting you to make sure he understands the situation. Can I do that?"

"I'll call him."

"Good. I tell you what, take a couple of days off. Come back in on Thursday or Friday. We'll talk then."

"All right."

- - -

Mike got back to his apartment just after six. The light on his answering machine indicated he had two messages. He walked into the kitchen and hit the play button on his way by.

*"You have two new messages. Message one. Hey, Mike. It's Mitch. I just wanted to check in and make sure you're happy with my report. Give me a call when you get this. I'll be in the office till seven. - Message two. All right, Mike. What the hell is going on? I called and left three messages yesterday, which you obviously decided to ignore and now I'm asking myself if that's even the kind of person I want to be married to. Josh is fine, by the way, and so am I. Thanks for asking. I called the office and spoke to some woman, she gave me the usual 'out saving the world' bullshit and I told her to piss off. You can apologize to her, it was meant to be a message for you. She sounds really nice, by the way. Okay, well I've got to take Josh to baseball practice. Give me a call. I know that wasn't covered specifically in the vows you made, but I'm pretty sure love and honor covers phone calls. - You have no more messages."*

Mike found himself smiling. Susan was the queen of sarcasm when you got her back up. And there had been no mention of the 'D' word, so that was good at least. He debated which call to return first and decided that saving his marriage might afford him the clarity of vision to pursue the other big thing on his mind. He made himself a cup of coffee and sat down on the floor in the hallway with his back to the wall and dialed the number from memory.

"Banner residence."

"Hey, Suze."

"Mike, you bastard! Where have you been?"

"Actually, I've been out on a case."

"Don't tell me, you were investigating the mysterious disappearance of every phone in New York, right?"

"Very funny. Look, I walked straight into a big case. That's the truth."

"You better not be bullshitting me, Mike."

"Susan, I got home at midnight on Friday and was back downtown by noon on Saturday. It's been non-stop since then."

"Fine. But you still should have called."

"You're right, I should have. Although I did think we weren't speaking."

"And that's my fault?"

"No. It's mine."

"You see that it's bullshit now, right? All that crap you said about New York."

"Yes."

"Then say it."

"Okay. New York is a shithole. Are you happy?"

"So we're going to try and find a place in Nassau?"

"We're going to try, yes."

"You know my parents said they'd help."

"I know. Listen, Suze, I've got an idea. Ask Barbara if Josh can stay at Max's for the next couple of days and come over. I'll find a cheap flight. We'll have a look around together."

"Really?"

"Really."

"I didn't mean any of that stuff I left on your machine," Susan said.

"Sure you did. And I deserved it."

"I really did tell that woman in your office to piss off. I'm so embarrassed now."

"I'm sure she'll live."

"I do want this to work, Mike. I know Josh hates you right now, but he'll come around."

"He's a good kid. He'll be fine. Listen, Suze, I'm beat and I need to take a shower. I'll call you tomorrow and we'll arrange the weekend. What d'you say?"

"All right, darling. I'd better go upstairs and check on Josh. Max is spending the night and I've already caught them trying to change the content filter on the Internet connection."

Mike laughed. "All right, darling."

"Mike?"

"Yes?"

"I love you."

"I love you too, Suze. I'll speak to you tomorrow."

Mike checked his watch. It was half past six. He called the FBI's central switchboard in Washington and asked for the Office of System Development. A moment later Mitch picked up the phone.

"Rainey, OSD."

"Mitch, it's Mike."

"Hey, I thought you'd never call."

"Can you talk?"

"Sure, I'm the only one here."

"Listen, Mitch. I need to talk to you about the Fed investigation. I just spoke to the assistant director-"

"Mike, let me just stop you for a second. Before you say anything else, I need to tell you something."

"What?"

"You know you told me not to check on Jessops?"

"Yes, I was quite adamant as I recall."

"Mike?"

"Yes, Mitch."

"I did it anyway."

"Ah, Mitch! What the fuck did you do?"

"I just had a little look around, that's all. Banking records, DMV, maybe a few personal e-mails."

"I don't want to hear this."

"I think you do."

"Before you say anything, is this line even secure?" Mike asked. "I mean, is this being recorded by the Bureau? They can do that now, you know."

"Take it easy. We don't record our own calls. And I'm monitoring it anyway. It's called self-preservation, and I'm definitely a member of that society. If I see anything suspect, I'll run through the ingredients to my mom's famous meatloaf, starting in the middle. Happy?"

"No."

"Duly noted, boss. Here it goes. Jessops and his wife have three accounts with Citigroup and another with Bank of America-"

"Mitch, Mitch, stop. I can't listen to this."

"Mike, just bear with me for a moment. They're all fine. The accounts are nothing suspect. The wife's sitting on some money, but that could be inheritance or something, it's not a lot. But they also have a trust set up for the kids. Trusts are a pain in the ass from the IRS's point of view because it's almost impossible to get any information on them. And if they're sitting offshore, it's even harder. Unless you know what you're doing, of course, and then it's actually quite easy."

"Mitch, where is this going?"

"Hold on, I'm getting to the good part. So they have a trust set up for the kids and it's nestled offshore in the Caymans. It's a little odd, but not unusual. Anyway, it took me a while to untangle the thing, but the long and short of it is that it holds just over two million dollars."

"You're kidding."

"No. And that's not all. The bank has a cell phone contract with AT&T tied to the trust. I've never heard of anything like it, but it makes sense in a way. Anyway, I ran the phone records, and guess who Jessops called this morning?"

"Who?"

"Well, in addition to receiving two calls from a number in New York, he also called the CIA station chief in Vermont, who happened to be in the town of Morisson."

"The shootings," Mike said.

"That's what I thought. Now get this. The name of the woman who was killed is Cynthia Ross."

"I know, Mitch. It's why I'm calling."

"Then you'll know that her husband hasn't been seen since yesterday afternoon. The cops have been looking everywhere for him."

"Yeah, I know. What's your point?"

"He's a retired security systems engineer, one of the best in the business."

"Mitch, I know."

"Fine. But what you don't know is that the money in Jessop's trust is arriving in monthly installments through a British biotech research company called Avalon."

"And?"

"Avalon is owned by a fund in Zurich called the Karl Gustav Foundation. To find the connection I had to use two eggs. It just makes it so much more succulent. And dice the onions, don't just chop them up."

For a moment Mike had a total brain freeze and the line went silent for several seconds. Then he said, "Hold on. I'm just writing all this down. It says here I shouldn't use tinfoil."

"No, definitely use tinfoil!" Mitch said. "Bake it uncovered and you'll just end up with something that looks and tastes more like a giant dog turd."

"Listen, I really appreciate your help, Mitch. Maybe one of these days you can take a trip back up here and show me how it's really done."

"I'm looking forward to it already."

"All right buddy, I'll catch you later."

"Night, Mike."

When Mike put the phone down his heart was beating so fast he could feel his pulse in his ears. He looked at the receiver in his hand as if he'd never seen it before. Mitch's change of subject had been so seamless and unexpected, he'd very nearly fucked the whole thing up for both of them.

He went into the hall and locked the front door, thought about going to the window and looking down, then considered how that would look from the outside. He hoped like hell that Mitch had just misread something on whatever he had been using to monitor the call. Or someone might have walked in on him while he was talking. But it was hard to believe after what he had just heard.

Mike tried to call Mitch on his cell phone, but it went straight to voicemail. Unsure what to do, he turned the TV on and spent the next ten minutes watching the NBC news feed. The shootings in Vermont were the top story. He thought about calling the assistant director and then cursed Mitch for not listening to him.

What he settled on was the bottle of Johnny Walker Red Label in the cupboard beneath the sink. He found a teacup and took the bottle into the living room, filled it to the brim and drank half of it down in one gulp. It ran down his throat like liquid fire and quickly spread to his limbs.

His nerves a little steadier, he picked up his cell phone and scrolled down to the assistant director's number, almost hit dial, then didn't. What the hell was he going to say? That he had uncovered evidence a member of the FBI was a paid informant? All he knew for sure was that whatever he said would most likely cost both him and Mitch their jobs. That made him think of Susan and Josh.

In the end, he did nothing. An hour later, exhausted and still no closer to figuring out what to do, he fell asleep on the couch with the TV remote in one hand and his service weapon in the other.

- - -

Half a block from the apartment building, sitting behind the wheel of a semi-retired Chevy Blazer, a local private detective by the name of Shaun Denton picked up the cellphone on the dashboard and dialed the number written on the back of his hand. "It's Denton. He's still inside. You want me to stay on him?"

# CHAPTER 26

**Washington DC**
**Tuesday 18 July 2006**
**1830 EDT**

Mitch put the phone down and looked around the room like a kid who'd just been caught doing the nasty, as his mother had been fond of saying. He turned back to the monitor, moved the mouse pointer over a button marked *trace intercept* and double-clicked. Row after row of numbers began to move down the screen. When it stopped, the final line read:

*Intercept trace failed. Line contains multiple source values*

He opened a command line interface and typed:

*List all source values*

When he pushed enter four lines appeared:

*1: 22034-09774-09884*
*2: 48895-83793-83739*
*3: 47838-37398-39838*
*4: 45084-39893-30838*

He typed:

*Trace 1*

The response read:

*22034-09774-09884 – Invalid source value*

He repeated the process for the second line and got the same result. When he ran the third the line that appeared said:

*47838-37398-39838 – Valid source value*

He typed:

*Identify*

The line that followed read:

*47838-37396-39838 source value is classification 2 restricted*

Mitch wrote down the number, closed the program and locked the terminal.

He walked out of the office and down the hall to the elevator. When it arrived he got in and pushed the button for the basement archive. By the time the doors opened again he was sweating.

The archive was little more than a large bare room with a cage wall running end-to-end in front of several hundred square yards of government-issue shelving. Mitch approached the rectangular window in the wall and leaned in.

A casually dressed young man was sitting with his feet up on a desk and his back to Mitch, bobbing his head to the music in his earphones. Mitch took a sheet from the notepad on the counter, rolled it up and threw it at him. The man jumped and turned around. "Jesus, buddy, use the buzzer. I almost shit myself."

"Sorry," Mitch said. "It's my first time down here."

"What department you with?"

"OSD."

"That'll be why, then. You lost?"

"No. I wanted to pull something from the archive."

"I don't have anyone from OSD on the clearance list."

"So I can't look at anything?"

"Afraid not."

"You get Internet access down here?" Mitch asked.

"You're joking, right? The only thing I have down here is iPod access, and I'll probably lose that when the cameras go in."

"You want it?" Mitch asked.

The man looked at Mitch doubtfully. "You can do that?"

"In return for a favor, yeah."

"What's so important you're willing to risk getting us both fired?" the clerk said.

"Look," Mitch said. "I've got to get a report to the deputy director before I go home. I've already been here for twelve hours. What I need is on the system, but the host server is down and won't be back up till the morning. There's a backup in the archive, that's all I need. Just a quick look."

"What archive is it?" Kevin asked.

"A satellite registry. Anything published before '03."

"And you just need to look at it?"

"One minute and I'm out of here."

"All right, pal. But if someone comes down while you're here, you better act lost and split."

"Deal," Mitch said.

The clerk stood up and walked down one of the aisles. By the time he came back, Mitch could barely stand still. He dropped a giant volume onto the counter and looked over Mitch's shoulder at the elevator. "You got two minutes, pal. Then it's going back on the shelf."

Mitch flipped the book open and began thumbing through the pages. It took him a minute to find what he was looking for. The entry read:

*Darkstar CommSat 443*
*Launch: 3.9.1995*
*Altitude Class: Low Earth Orbit (LEO)*
*Inclination: Polar Sun Synchronous*
*NID: DSCS443-0098-887HG*
*Operator: Skyline Defense*
*License: IKL-77654-99 (expired)*

*Signal ID Tag: 47838-37398-39838*
*Retired: 23.5.1998*

When he got to the end Mitch looked up, frowning. "Are these records accurate? It says here this satellite has been retired."

The clerk laughed and shrugged his shoulders. "I'm on eighteen grand a year, buddy. People want something off the shelves, I go get it for them. If you need help with satellites, I suggest you call NASA."

Mitch took a pen from his shirt, scribbled the details down on the notepad and tore off the page. He closed the book and handed it back.

"Thanks a lot, I really appreciate it."

Mitch walked back to the elevator.

"Hey, pal. What happened to my Internet access?" the clerk asked.

"I'll have to come back and do it later," Mitch said and stepped into the elevator.

He returned to his office only long enough to pick up his backpack, then left the building. He found his old Volkswagen Rabbit sitting alone in the giant parking lot. When he got in he rested his head on the steering wheel. "Come on Mitch, think! Who uses satellites that don't exist to intercept secure phone calls on the FBI switchboard? Dead cosmonauts? Fucking Martians?"

He needed to get hold of Mike.

Tapping a domestic line was one thing, but an encrypted one, one that he had helped set up, was another. For one, it couldn't be anybody inside the FBI because he sat at the top of that particular intellectual food chain himself.

Whoever had done it was using a satellite-based system that deliberately made it impossible to trace. Unless you had a program to de-scramble the mixed ID values being thrown at your own intercept software, you couldn't even establish what satellite was being used. Mitch had one because he had made one, in the same way he had made a hundred other programs to deal with just about any problem he could dream up. And it had led back to a satellite that, according to official records, dropped into the Pacific eight years ago. A satellite owned by a company called Skyline Defense.

Mitch started the car and headed out of DC along Interstate 66 until he reached the junction at Meadow Mills, then turned onto Interstate 81 in the direction of Hagerstown and the Maryland-Pennsylvania state line. There was no reasoning to his choice of direction. What he felt was a need to move for the sake of it, to keep going until something or someone stopped him with a good enough reason. At least until he could clear his head and figure out what to do.

# CHAPTER 27

**Lake Commissaires, Quebec**
**Tuesday 18 July 2006**
**2200 EDT**

"You're leaving?" Amanda said.

"I have to," Francis said. "We can't just sit here and hope things blow over. And the longer we stay here, the greater the chances are that someone will find us."

"Out here?" Jesse asked.

"If I can find it, so can they. When enough people start looking, not even the dark side of the moon is a good hiding place for long. We need to know who is looking for the drive. Until I can answer that question, the only safe assumption is that everyone is."

"And you just want us to hang tight here until you get back?" Amanda asked.

"Yes."

"What if someone does find us?" she said.

Francis stood up from where he was leaning over the hole in the floor and pointed at the bed.

"Take a seat," he said.

They did.

"The chances of someone finding you here in the next few days are slim. But I'm not leaving anything to chance. Give me a minute to get my stuff together and I'll show you what you need to do while I'm gone."

Jesse looked suspicious. "You never got a chance to finish what you were saying about the hard drive."

"Didn't I?" Francis said, looking nonplussed.

"You said you gave it to that man to have a look at. But you never explained how you got it in the first place."

Francis looked down at the floor and scratched his head. "You're not going to leave this alone, are you?"

"Why should we?" Amanda cut in. "It's a pretty fair question."

"Okay," Francis said. "I took it. It seemed like a really good idea at the time and I regret doing it, believe me. But there you have it."

"You mean you *stole* it," Jesse said.

"Took it, stole it, what's the difference? We've got it and we're stuck with it."

"No. You're stuck with it and we're stuck with you," Jesse corrected.

"Whatever you say. But it doesn't change anything."

"If you took it, you must know who's looking for it." Amanda said.

"It's not that simple," Francis said. "I thought I knew who it belonged to; now I'm not so sure."

"That doesn't make any sense," Jesse said.

Francis ran a hand through his hair and closed his eyes. When he looked at them again the expression on his face was resigned.

"Fine. You want to hear it, I guess I owe it to you."

Amanda and Jesse both leaned forward like a couple of kids at bedtime about to hear their mother read their favorite story. Francis rested his elbows on his knees and looked down at the floor.

"I met a man two years ago on a plane," he began. "He was an American security systems engineer and consultant living in Belgium. One of the best in his field, as it turns out. I'd been looking for someone like him for a long time. We became friends. Not close, but we stayed in touch. I don't have time to get into too much detail, so let's just say that in a former life I ran with a bad crowd. When I left I decided to put an end to it one way or another. It took me a few years, but I eventually figured out a way it could be done. Gerald was the key. One thing led to another, and I offered him a lot of money to help me break into a safe where the people I was after kept all their dirty little secrets. We spent a year planning it. He helped me shut down the security system, and I broke in and took what I needed. Gerald was going to get the files off the drive for me. That was supposed to be the end of it. As it turns out, I either got my numbers wrong or something had changed. Now the people the drive belongs to want it back."

Both Amanda and Jesse looked dumbfounded.

"What did you think was on it?" Amanda asked.

"Files. Stuff I could use to force the CIA into shutting down one of its biggest blunders."

"When did you realize you'd made a mistake?" Jesse asked.

"When we planned the job, Gerald made a list of people who might become suspects if the break-in was investigated because of their connection to the security system. Three of them were contacted shortly after I broke in, and not by the FBI. I called Gerald and told him to run. He wasn't at home when I called, so I told him to get his wife to take the drive and leave the house. She made it as far as Morisson. The rest you know."

Amanda sat back, looking at him in a way that suggested she had never heard so much bullshit in her life and said, "I don't believe you."

"Believe me, don't believe me. That's what happened," Francis said, standing up.

"You said *if* there was an investigation," Jesse said. "Yet you just admitted to breaking into a government building. Why wouldn't there be?"

"Listen", Francis said. "It's a bit more complicated than that. Maybe when I get back I'll fill in the blanks."

"Try us," Jesse said. "How complicated can it be?"

Francis walked to the fireplace and pushed one of the logs back into the fire with the toe of his boot. "The place I broke into was the Federal Reserve Bank of New York."

"No way!" Amanda said. "You're kidding, right?"

"No, I'm not. In fact I recorded the whole thing. So you can see why there wasn't going to be an investigation."

"So if they tried to find you, you were going to what," Jesse said, "bring down the Fed, create panic on Wall Street?"

"Ever heard of poker, kid?" Francis said. "I made them believe I would so I didn't have to. It's how the game is played."

Jesse was looking at him, or maybe through him, and appeared to be deep in thought. Amanda was about to say something else when Jesse asked, "How did you know where she was going, the Ross woman? Did your friend tell you?"

"I had a tracker on their car."

"That's convenient," Jesse said.

Francis gave him a cold look. "Before I asked Gerald to help me, I spent a month following him. I had to make sure he could be trusted. I put a GPS tracker on his car. I know you're just a kid, but these things happen."

"Okay, fine," Jesse said. "And how did the other people looking for the drive find her, the ones who showed up in town?"

"They found Gerald."

"He's dead, too?" Amanda asked.

"Yes, I think so."

"Where *was* she heading?" Jesse asked.

"My guess is the border. I'm not even sure she knew herself. She was probably close to a nervous breakdown by then."

"Close?" Jesse said. "She'd *had* it. When we stopped to help her, I thought she might have escaped from the nearest lunatic asylum."

Francis turned around, the guilt clear and naked on his face. "It should never have happened. If I'd known who I was dealing with I would never have asked Gerald to send her anywhere."

"So," Jesse said, "They killed her. But before they did, she told them she had given the drive to me - to us."

Francis nodded.

"And they were looking for me when you showed up?"

"I caught up to her while they were still by her car. I heard them shoot her and saw them drive back into town."

Jesse nodded. "Were they in two unmarked cars?"

"That was them, yes," Francis agreed.

"We saw them drive past just after I called the sheriff's office," Jesse said.

Francis had gone back to the hole in the floorboards and begun taking things out and stacking them on the floor. Now he looked up. "You called the sheriff?"

"Yeah," Jesse said. "To tell them about the woman. We were worried about her."

"And did you tell them she had given you a bag full of money?"

"No."

"Why not?" Francis asked. There was a hint of smugness in the question.

"Hey," Jesse said shaking his head. "It's not the same thing. You stole it. The woman *gave* it to me."

"The woman on the side of the road who you thought was crazy?" Francis said.

"Okay, fine. But it's still not the same. I was going to give it to the sheriff."

Francis held his hands up to indicate he wasn't the one on the defensive. He smiled at Jesse and said, "I'm not blaming you."

"So were they cops, these people?" Jesse asked

"No," Francis said. "They definitely weren't cops. They were pretending to be US marshals. One of the cars went looking for you at your house. Which begs the question, if you weren't at home, where did you go?"

"We went down to the lake," Jesse said. "And then to Amanda's house."

"Well it's a damned good thing you did," Francis said.

Jesse looked troubled. "They were actually at our house?"

"Down at the end of the drive," Francis said. "There was a white pickup with a bike in the back parked outside."

"Yeah. That's it."

After another long moment of reflective silence, Jesse asked, "What did you do?"

"What do you think I did?"

"You killed them? Right there in front of my house?"

"On the road at the top of the drive, yes," Francis said, as if killing people were the most natural thing in the world.

Jesse tried to imagine it and found he couldn't. The feeling of unreality, which had seemed to be passing a little, was back, and stronger than ever. Amanda looked at him with a blank expression that suggested she was having similar problems. Jesse put an arm around her and tried to think of the right thing to say, but there were no words that seemed even vaguely appropriate.

Francis had to raise his voice to get their attention. "Guys! Everything okay?"

Amanda looked at him, the color in her face beginning to rise. "Why would you even ask a question like that? How the fuck could anything possibly be okay? We're stuck here while our parents go out of their minds. They probably think we're dead."

"I understand that," Francis said, trying to sound less annoyed than he felt. "But you guys are going to have to pull it together. I have to leave soon and there are some things I need to show you before I go."

Amanda held his gaze for a moment, then looked away. Jesse said something to her that Francis couldn't hear and stood up. "Show *me*. Mandy can wait here."

They left her sitting on the bed and Jesse followed Francis outside and around the corner of the cabin. As they walked Francis began to explain what they would need to do.

"There are sensors all the way around this place about twenty yards out. Anything that moves near the cabin will set them off. There are also four cameras in the chimney that cover the whole perimeter and one inside the cabin. If the sensors are triggered, you'll be able to see what's out there. You'll see what I mean because the local wildlife sets them off occasionally. I highly doubt you'll see people, though. There are hunting parties out here sometimes and I know they've been to the cabin before, but it's rare. Hunting is illegal on this side of the lake. If someone *does* find this place, he or they may be dressed to look like hunters. Don't be tempted to speak to anyone."

"What if they come into the cabin?" Jesse said. "We can't exactly hide in there."

"No. That's very true. But you won't be in the cabin."

Francis stopped in front of a log pile sitting partially buried in dead leaves. It covered a rectangular area about three feet by five. He knelt down and put his hands beneath the end of the log closest to Jesse.

"Grab the other end of this," Francis said.

Jesse did.

"Now pull."

The whole pile moved. The logs were all fixed together and mounted on a door of some kind with hinges at the other end. When the board was level with his chest, Francis asked Jesse to hold it and used a stick to prop the hatch open.

"After you," Francis said.

A crude wooden ladder led down to an earthen floor about six feet down. Jesse looked at Francis doubtfully, then turned and climbed down. He found himself standing in a small room about ten feet square. The walls and ceiling were made of rough boards still covered in bark and dry moss. Francis came down behind him and walked past him into the room. He fumbled with something in the corner and a dim clear bulb in the middle of the ceiling flickered and began to glow. Shelving containing canned goods, bottles of water and packages that looked like boil-in-the-bag meals covered one wall. Against another wall there was a single bed that looked identical to the one in the cabin. There were two wooden crates beneath it. A stack of similar crates was piled from floor to ceiling in the opposite corner. Next to them there was a little table and a stool. Below the table lay a bank of four truck batteries. On it there was a small TV monitor standing on a box that looked a bit like an amplifier in a hi-fi stack system. Both the amp and the screen were encased in green painted metal.

"It's not the Ritz," Francis said. "But you can get quite comfy in here."

"Were you expecting a nuclear war to break out or something?" Jesse asked, looking around the room in wonder.

Francis laughed. "I never know *what* to expect."

"It looks like one of those underground tunnels the Vietcong used to win the war."

"This is the alarm panel," Francis said, pointing to the table. "I'll show you how to turn it on. The cameras use sensors to switch between standard and night vision. To save power you should leave them off unless you hear the alarm. There's enough food in here to last two people a month. Those brown packs are Army issue MREs. Over there you've got Flameless Ration Heaters. You pour in water and it heats up whatever you want, so no need to light a fire. There are extra blankets in one of those crates if you get cold."

"Is there any way we can get hold of you if we need to?" Jesse asked.

"I'll get to that."

Francis knelt in front of the bed and pulled out one of the crates. He picked up a small machine gun and handed it to Jesse.

"It's heavy," Jesse said, turning the weapon around in his hands.

"That's an MP5 nine millimeter submachine gun. I wish I had time to show you how to use it, but I'll just have to run you through the basics. You said you had a rifle, what was it?"

"A Winchester Model 70 classic," Jesse said.

"Nice rifle. The single shot recoil will be slighter on that thing," Francis said. "But it's automatic, so it's progressive. Meaning -"

"I know what it means," Jesse interrupted, "I played a lot of video games when I was a kid."

"Good," Francis said, looking dubious. "So you know you need to compensate by holding it down. Keep it switched to burst fire, which means -"

"Three rounds every time you pull the trigger," Jesse said.

Francis held up his hands. "Hell, kid. I'll just leave you to it then. If I'd known video games were so good at churning out fighting men, I wouldn't have bothered…"

"Wouldn't have signed up for the Navy SEALs?" Jesse suggested.

"Wouldn't have bothered saying anything." Francis corrected.

Francis took something else from the box and held it up. It looked like a combination radio and telephone with a thick rubber antenna folded down on one side.

"This is a satellite phone," Francis said. "Did you use any of these in your video games?"

Jesse smiled. "No, Master Chief, I didn't."

"Okay, it's simple. You need a clear line of sight, so it won't work under the tree canopy. If you need to use it go back to the lake. When you turn it on it will automatically begin looking for a satellite. Once it's found one, the panel turns green and you're good to go. I'm going to write down a number but it won't get you straight through to me. Just let it ring a couple of times and end the call. I will call you back as soon as I can."

Jesse nodded and took the phone. Francis pushed the crate back under the bed and stood. "There's a spare battery for the phone and three more clips for the MP5 in there. If you pull it out, you'll also see I've got a couple of hand grenades. I strongly suggest you don't play with them."

"What? You mean like pull the pin and see what happens?" Jesse said, clearly annoyed at being treated like a child.

Francis gave him a stern look, then pointed at a board lodged between the bed and the wall. "One last thing. Behind that board there is a very narrow tunnel. It runs about thirty yards to the east. At the end there is about four feet of clearance with a metal plate in the top. Give it a good shove and it'll open. I'm not trying to scare you, but I want to cover every option. You have any questions?"

Jesse thought about it for a moment. "How long will you be gone?"

"I'd say five days. A week at most."

"And if you don't come back at all? What then?"

"Seriously kid, I don't know. I'd most likely be dead and you'd be on your own."

"So what? Go hunting with a submachine gun? Or maybe we could go fishing in the lake with your hand grenades?"

"The town's just across the lake. You know where the boat is. Or you could go on foot, but it would be a long walk. As for hunting, there's plenty of game out here and you'll find a ten thousand dollar hunting rifle under the floor in the cabin. Practically shoots stuff by itself. But it won't come to that."

"How can you be so sure?" Jesse asked.

"Because I've been doing this for a long time, and at the risk of sounding arrogant, I'm pretty good at it."

Jesse began to snigger. A second later he was flat on the floor with one of Francis's knees on his throat and the blade of a knife pressed against the skin on the back of his neck. Francis bent closer until Jesse could feel his breath on his ear. "Do you know why I resented you calling me a SEAL earlier?" Francis asked.

Jesse tried to say he didn't, but the knee was pushing down on his windpipe so he shook his head instead.

"Because the four men I killed back in your home town *were* SEALs, or something a lot like them, and frankly, I didn't rate them very fucking highly."

Francis stood up and Jesse brought his hands to his neck. Francis held out a hand. "No hard feelings, kid. I was just trying to make a point."

But Jesse was in no mood for charity. The look on his face was one Francis had seen many times – the look of murder. Jesse rolled over and got to his knees then stood and glanced at the MP5 sitting on the bed.

"You'd get maybe halfway there, maybe only a quarter," Francis said. There was no menace in the words, just certainty.

"What about later?" Jesse said, his face now turning red. "When your back's turned?"

Francis felt a little sorry for him. It had been a shitty thing to do, but he needed Jesse to understand that while his life might have been turned upside down yesterday, Francis hadn't been born then. He thought his chances of doing something about the drive and the people who wanted it back were at least as good as they were bad. He needed Jesse to believe that or the two of them might go nuts out here while he was gone.

"If you're determined to kill me," Francis said. "I'm sure you'll find a way sooner or later. But maybe you'll give me a chance to try and help you first. I can assure you of one thing, if I don't come back, it'll be because I'm already dead. Think of it as a win-win situation, if you like."

Francis saw Jesse relax a little and deliberately turned his back and walked to the ladder. If the gamble didn't pay off, the gun wasn't loaded anyway. But it would make things a little awkward, to say the least. Jesse made no move for the weapon. He followed Francis and looked up at the entrance. "We should get back. Amanda will be getting worried."

"I was meaning to ask you about that," Francis said. "Do you think she'll be okay out here?"

"Are you kidding? She'll be a lot more okay than me, that's for sure."

"She's a tough one, isn't she?"

Jesse nodded.

"You've known her for a long time then?" Francis said.

"Since second grade."

"It's just that I thought you guys were, you know, an item."

Jesse looked down at the floor and Francis patted him on the arm. "It's none of my business."

Jesse suddenly looked defeated. "It's complicated."

"It always is," Francis said and climbed the ladder.

They closed the hatch and returned to the cabin.

"You'll need to brief Amanda on everything I showed you," Francis said. "You can leave out the drop-kick and the stand-off though. That's just between us fellas."

"I could have kicked your ass," Jesse said. "I just didn't want to embarrass you."

Francis laughed. "Gee, thanks. You're a real sport."

They found Amanda asleep on the bed. She had found a candle and fixed it to the middle of the table. Next to it there was an empty can of tinned peaches.

"What did I tell you?" Jesse said. "If you'd left me here, I would've been *under* the bed by now."

"Amazing," Francis agreed.

"Better go while she's asleep or you might get another earful on your way out the door," Jesse said. "I'll wake her up and we'll go back to the Batcave when you're gone."

"Smart thinking. Let me just get my stuff together."

Francis put the things he had stacked up by the floorboards into an old canvas bag, then picked up some clothes and began to change by the fireplace. He put on a pair of tattered dark brown corduroy pants and a faded green sweater with the letters *USMC* still just about visible on the front. Then he pulled on a pair of steel-toed boots that would never be mistaken for anything else. Over the sweater he put on a black and white plaid zip-up jacket and topped the look off with a beanie that might or might not have been white at some point in the distant past. When he was done, Francis lifted his arms and posed. "How do I look?"

"Like a bum."

"Good. The look I'm going for is really more tramp-cum-hitchhiker, but bum will do."

"Why?" Jesse asked. "Have you run out of quarters or something?"

"Let's just say I don't want to attract more attention than I have to."

"America's invisible poor?"

"Yeah. Something like that. You all set?"

"We'll be fine," Jesse said, sounding a lot more confident than he felt.

Francis picked up the pistol he'd put down on the table, checked the breach and put it in the pocket of his jacket. He put two more clips in the other pocket, then threw his backpack over one shoulder.

"Wish me luck," Francis said and held out his free hand.

Jesse shook it. "I hope you find what you're looking for."

"I will. Don't you worry."

\- - -

As soon as Francis was gone, Jesse felt his heart sink. He looked over at Amanda, who was still sleeping the sleep of the dead. He had never been a great believer in divine intervention, but he thought that might soon change. If she hadn't been here with him, there was no way in hell he'd survive a day without going mad, much less a week. He sat down at the table and watched her sleep for a long time. When the silence was suddenly broken by a piercing shriek from somewhere outside, he stood up and walked to the bed.

# CHAPTER 28

**Skyline Defense**
**New York, New York**
**Wednesday 19 July 2006**
**0100 EDT**

When he returned to his office, Marius was sitting in front of Jack's desk with a small digital recorder in one hand.

"What's going on?" Jack asked.

"You were right about Jessops. I put an intercept on Mike Banner's home phone line. But I think we have a bigger problem."

"What?"

"It looks like we may have a security breach."

"What kind of security breach?" Jack asked.

Marius set the recorder down on the desk and pushed play. Jack listened to the conversation between Mike Banner and his wife.

"That's the first call to his wife in Phoenix," Marius said. "The second is to a colleague of his in DC named Mitch Rainey."

Jack felt his stomach tighten as he listened to Mitch detail what he had found out about Bruce Jessops. Then Mitch changed topic in mid-sentence and the call abruptly ended.

Marius stopped the recorder. "I ran back through the recording several times, looking for some sign of a trace. Whatever he used to intercept it, it wasn't anything the FBI have. He must have had some kind of pulse sensor or signal delay tracking device. It's the only way he would have been able to pick it up. If he managed to decipher the source values from the readings, he could trace them back to Darkstar."

"To Darkstar?" Jack said. "I thought that was impossible."

"Improbable, but not impossible," Marius said. "I'm not saying he could follow the line back here. But if he knows Darkstar is still in orbit, we could have a major problem."

"Do we know where he is now?" Jack asked.

"Sitting in a jail cell in Penn Hills. Local police brought him in last night on a DUI charge."

"I'll deal with it," Jack said.

"You going to bring him in?" Marius said. "That's what we're supposed to do, right?"

"Like I said, I'll deal with it."

Marius picked up the recorder but made no effort to leave.

"What is it?" Jack sighed.

"When's Titov getting here? I'm so fucking nervous I can hardly think.

Carl came upstairs yesterday to ask me about something and I thought I was going to have a goddamned nervous breakdown. I'm no good with shit like this, Jack."

"He'll be here tomorrow."

"I just don't get what's going on. First Carl, and now the FBI? And what does the Fed have to do with all this? They were talking about some kind of investigation."

"It'll all makes sense in a couple of days, Marius, believe me. Just hold it together a little longer."

Jack put a hand on his shoulder and gently escorted him to the door.

# CHAPTER 29

**Chemin des Gagnon, Quebec**
**Wednesday 19 July 2006**
**0115 EDT**

Francis reached the road shortly after one in the morning. When his feet hit the tarmac, he stopped, put down his backpack and spent the next few minutes going through a vigorous stretching routine to cleanse his muscle tissue of lactic acid.

He had left the cabin and headed not for the lake, but away to the east, toward the smaller road which rejoined Route 155 a few miles to the south. It had been a steady series of peaks and valleys across uneven ground and thick woodland. Several times he had come across a logging track or hiking path, and once he had scared himself half to death when he almost ran into an elk calf.

Satisfied there would be no backlash from his limbs somewhere down the road, he walked south at a pace just below jogging speed. He reached a junction twenty minutes later with a small dirt road leading downhill through a break in the trees. He followed it, studying the ground as he went, then climbed the bank at the edge of the road, picked up a stick and began to tap the grass around him.

He found what he was looking for a moment later. It was on old, rusting ammunition container with a length of thick rope inside that disappeared into the ground through a hole in the bottom. As he pulled it, the rope sprang from the ground in a straight line for several yards before going taught. He walked down the bank, planted both feet firmly on the ground, and pulled.

At first, nothing happened. Francis pulled until the veins in his neck bulged and his feet began to sink into the soft ground. There was a series of ripping sounds as roots snapped, then a large rectangular section of the bank simply gave way and slid forward, revealing what looked like a square mineshaft.

Sitting inside it was a black Land Rover Defender with balloon tires and two giant spotlights mounted to the grill. The license plate was Canadian. Francis squeezed himself into the narrow gap, climbed in and started the engine.

Twenty minutes later he pulled back onto Route 155 and headed in the direction they had come from the day before. By five in the morning he was nearing Three Rivers. An hour after that, he reached Quebec City.

\- - -

The man behind the counter at the Radio Shack repair desk studied the drive for a moment then handed it back. "I'm afraid we don't sell anything old enough to read ESDI drives, sir. This interface was phased out years ago. You know what computers are like, old by the time you get them home and all that."

Francis thanked him and was about to leave when a younger man stepped out from behind the partition wall at the back of the room and said, "Can I have a look at that, sir?"

Francis handed him the hard drive and the man inspected it briefly.

"My dad's got a pawn shop down in Beauport. Last time I was in there he had an old IBM PC that would read this. I doubt he's sold it."

Forty-five minutes later Francis was standing in a room that appeared to have been overlooked by time itself. The long, narrow shop had shelves running all the way to the high ceiling along both walls. Nothing he could see looked as if it had been made before 1990. There was nobody behind the counter, but someone was having a coughing fit out back. He waited for another minute, then rang the bell above the front door again.

The man who emerged from behind the curtain at the back of the shop was red in the face from strain. He looked about eighty and his clothes could have come off one of the store's many shelves.

"Bonjour," he said.

Francis returned the greeting, explained his predicament and asked him about the IBM PC. The man, who introduced himself as Mr. Mouliner, considered the question as if it bore a great deal of importance. After a moment he walked back through the curtain, calling for Francis to join him. They unburied the old machine together and Francis carried it out to the counter.

When it came to money, it seemed the man had no more joined the human race in ushering in the new millennium than his shop had. He wanted 350 Canadian dollars for the relic and made it clear that he would go no lower. Francis considered trying to explain that it was all but worthless, and put the idea aside. It wasn't exactly true anyway, when you considered what he needed it for in the first place.

- - -

He found a small motel off Highway 40 outside the town of Pont-Rouge and wasted no time setting the computer up. Using his laptop to access the motel's wireless Internet service, he spent two hours navigating various "how-to" guides online before he finally managed to get the drive to register.

He had been expecting to find any of a number of things on it. What he did find had not been one of them. It contained about two hundred files in twenty-one folders with names that meant nothing to him. A few of the files had *zip* and *rar* extensions to identify them as compressed archives. These were no good as the computer had no decompression software. The rest were image files, and these he *could* open.

The first few he tried resulted in an error message to say that the resolution of the monitor was too low to display them. When an image *did* finally appear on the screen it was a grainy black-and-white photograph of a submarine in drydock. Francis knew exactly what it was, a Russian Viktor-class nuclear powered attack sub. He found several other images of the same submarine, pictures of satellites, rockets, space probes, mining equipment, several dock cranes, a Caterpillar diesel generator and one of a building in Zurich with Fraumünster Abbey in the background. Nothing classified, nothing secret and nothing that meant anything to him. One of the folders was named "DPFCS images" and contained four picture files, but according to the computer, these required a password to open.

The last folder on the drive was named "notes." It contained about fifty plain text files. Francis doubled-clicked on the first and waited for it to load. What appeared on the screen was this:

*August 1 1988 – Preliminary inquiries confirm the unsuitability of western-based launching platforms on grounds of security. The political situation also discounts Russian facilities. This leaves only the Chinese, who present a number of other problems, primarily technical reliability.*

He closed the file and opened another at random:

*August 7 1994 – Third test of receiver array completed with mixed results. Decoding is causing the buildup of excess heat. This may be overcome by conditions in orbit, but the risk is too great. Will have to get Bonn to re-design the board using additional processors.*

He read two dozen more of the short diary-like entries looking for anything that might provide a clue: a name, a location, or just a reference to something he understood, but it was pointless. As fascinating as the entries were, none of it made any sense. At least not to Francis.

Exasperated, he shut the computer down and took a seat on the bed. He couldn't remember the last time he had slept, but it must have been days. His mind racing, his body exhausted, he fell into a dreamless sleep.

# CHAPTER 30

**Penn Hills, Pennsylvania**
**Wednesday 19 July 2006**
**0400 EDT**

"Sir, I need you to hold the board below your chin."

Mitch swayed slightly and closed his eyes again. The lights in the room were far too bright, making his already-pounding head feel like it might actually explode. He had to focus all his attention on not throwing up, which meant one steady breath after another. Everything else was a distraction.

"Mr. Rainey, you need to hold the board a little higher!"

The woman was losing patience with him. She stepped forward and the board in his hands rose until it bumped his chin. The stirring began somewhere in his bowels and worked its way up to his stomach. His mouth was suddenly flooded with warm saliva. He took a deep breath in a last-ditch effort to hold it down - then his torso contracted and he keeled over and dropped the board as he fell to his knees.

The policewoman realized what was happening, but she was a couple of seconds too late. The first salvo hit the floor a foot in front of her polished, black rider boots and covered everything below her knees in a thick slimy coating of partially digested Big Mac and chocolate milkshake. She took a step back, slipped, and almost sat down in the mess before pinwheeling her arms and recovering.

"Jesus Christ!" she said and moved toward the door.

Mitch raised his head and looked at her through wet, bloodshot eyes. Before he could say anything he was firing a second salvo. This one went straight into his lap. The sudden stench of stomach acid and vodka hit him like a prizefighter's southpaw and he began to dry heave. It felt like someone had poured lighter fluid over his abdomen, set it on fire and then kicked him there a few times for good measure. The policewoman was shouting to someone through the open door but he couldn't make out what she was saying. Someone else came into the room, but Mitch made no attempt to look up. A large hand grabbed his left arm and pulled him upright. "Sir, you need to sit up and lift your head."

It was a man's voice and the tone was one of concern, not anger. Mitch opened his eyes and raised one hand toward the ceiling.

"Lights," he said. "Turn off the lights."

A moment later the strip lights in the ceiling went out.

"Is that better? You think you can keep it down?"

Mitch nodded. The man put one foot to either side of him, one hand under each of Mitch's arms and pushed him along the floor until his back was resting against the wall.

"I'm going to leave you in here until we can get a doctor to have a look at you," the man said. Mitch raised a hand in a gesture of thanks, then leaned his head back against the wall and closed his eyes again.

He could remember everything right up to the blue lights in the rear-view mirror, and then the film went blank. He remembered stopping at a McDonald's somewhere near Hancock, crossing the border into Pennsylvania; he remembered the liquor store in Somerset and the woman behind the counter. She had tried to sell him an extra bottle at a twenty-five percent discount. If she had tried just a little bit harder, he thought, he might be dead now instead of just wanting to be.

Once he had decided to get drunk, and damn the consequences, it had been the advice of his friend, and now partner in crime, that he had taken. Mike had once joked that, God forbid, should he ever become an alcoholic it was going to be vodka or nothing because vodka was all kick and no hangover. If Mitch ever saw Mike again, he would have to ask him where that unhelpful piece of total bullshit had originated.

The plan had been to call Mike back at some point. Mitch had stopped at a rest area just off the interstate somewhere in the Kooser State Park to make the call. But his nerves had failed him and he had gone back to the car for the bottle and started drinking, which had really been 'Plan B' all along. And it had worked. Only when he finally *did* try to call, there hadn't been a single bar of reception on his phone.

That most useless of all tricks, hindsight, strongly suggested that that was where he should have called it a day. Instead, he had gotten back in the car, put the bottle between his legs and set off to meet his destiny in the town of Penn Hills. By the time he saw the blue lights of the highway patrol motorcycle, the bottle was empty, his head was somewhere in the upper stratosphere and his Volkswagen was doing about twenty miles an hour with two wheels on the road and two in the dirt.

It might have been five minutes later, or it might have been five hours, when the door opened and the lights came back on. Mitch guessed it must have been somewhere in between because his head still ached like a bitch, but his stomach had settled and the lights no longer felt like laser beams. A man was standing in front of him with a black case in one hand, dressed in the orange coveralls of a paramedic. He walked around the mess in the middle of the room and knelt beside Mitch. "Sir, how are you feeling?"

"Like an idiot," Mitch said.

"Sure. And how about physically? Are you having any trouble breathing?"

"No."

The man took a pen light from his breast pocket and pointed the beam into both of Mitch's eyes. He produced a syringe and before Mitch could protest, stuck the needle into his upper left arm and pressed the plunger.

"That should make you feel a little better," the medic said.

"About myself?"

"No; that's something you'll have to deal with on your own," the medic said. "If you want my advice, try speaking to the families of any of the 17 thousand people that died last year in this country from DUI-related accidents."

Mitch had no answer to that. He'd been too busy feeling sorry for himself to consider that side of it. It was a sobering thought.

The medic stood and closed the case. "The good news is you're fine. You'll probably feel like shit for another day or two, but that's par for the course when you drink yourself stupid."

The paramedic turned to the police officer standing in the doorway. "He's good to go."

Mitch looked at the cop and did his best to appear ashamed of himself. It wasn't hard. Aside from once or twice in his early college days, he didn't drink as a rule and had never been in trouble for it in his life. He'd been too busy saving up for much-needed hardware to have either the time or money to indulge in much else. Of course, that was probably the case with half the child-murdering drunk drivers this guy had arrested, Mitch thought.

"I guess you'll want that mug shot now," Mitch said. He felt a little lightheaded, but when he stood up the feeling passed. Whatever the medic had given him, it was doing wonders for his headache, which had settled down to a dull throb.

"We'll need to get you cleaned up first," the cop said and handed him a pair of folded light blue coveralls. There was also a pair of pull-on slippers with a zip-lock bag on top. "I need you to put your personal possessions in the bag. The shower's downstairs."

Mitch followed the man out the door to the end of the hall, through a set of double doors and down two flights of stairs. They walked past a block of cells which were all empty and the cop pointed to a door at the end of the room. Mitch took out his wallet and put it in the bag, then fished a handful of loose change from his pocket and threw that in, too. The cop pointed to his watch, and Mitch took it off and handed it over.

Half an hour later he was showered, dry and sporting a whole new look. He knew what he had done was bad but the jail suit made him feel like a convicted felon. Every eye that glanced his way seemed to suggest they knew he was either a rapist or a pedophile, but couldn't quite work out which. A woman sitting on a chair against the far side of the large open-plan office - she looked like a prostitute at the tail end of a long and fruitless career - winked at him and held up her cuffed hands. She was dressed in a pair of leopard-skin Spandex bottoms and a dirty white T-shirt that made her shoulders look like a coat hanger.

"Hey, honeybunch, I'm doing blow jobs for dime bags if you're interested," she said and began to laugh, exposing dry, white gums with only two or three teeth left. Mitch looked away. The cop behind him laughed. The woman seemed to take that as a cue and stood. She began grinding her bony hips and stuck out her tongue.

"I'll fuck everyone here for a buck a pop," she said and cawed with laughter, which quickly turned into a coughing fit. A man in jeans and a black T-shirt with the letters *PHPD* printed on the front turned to her and said, "All right, Wanda, that's enough. Sit down."

She sat and pouted her lips to suggest she was hurt by this rebuke, but when Mitch looked over at her she winked at him again.

"Take a seat right here," the cop said. "Detective Lawson will be in in a minute."

Detective Lawson turned out to be *Miss* Lawson, a squat, stocky, square-jawed woman with short, brown hair who was either busy infiltrating a lesbian crime syndicate or gay herself. Mitch thought the latter was more likely. She sat down at the desk and opened the file in her hands.

"Says here you're with the Bureau," she said and looked at him with raised eyebrows. "Were you on some kind of sting operation?"

The sarcasm in her voice was unmistakable. Mitch guessed that Miss Lawson was not just a woman-lover, but also a man-hater. Her eyes seemed to accuse him not of drunk driving, but of having the audacity to be alive.

"I'm a technician," he said. "Down in DC."

"And you're what? On vacation?"

"Not exactly."

"Sort of on vacation?"

"I don't know," Mitch said. "I had a bad day at the office. I needed to get away for a bit. It's hard to explain."

"So you thought you'd come up here and drown your sorrows on the interstate. That about the size of it, Mr. Rainey? I suppose you're going to tell me you're bipolar."

"Look, I'm not going to justify myself. It was an idiotic thing to do and I'm sorry."

"You're sorry? Well, that's all right then," she said. "I'm guessing your people down in Washington will want a slightly better explanation, though."

"I'm sure you're right."

She was about to say something else when a man stepped out of the office at the back of the room and said, "Brenda, can you come in here for a minute?"

She looked back at Mitch and stood up.

"Don't go anywhere," she said and gave him a smile that suggested she would love it if he tried.

A minute later she was back with two uniformed officers. One of them produced a set of handcuffs. "I need you to stand up and put your hands behind your back, sir."

Mitch got to his feet and did as he was told. The officer put the cuffs on and tightened them until Mitch felt the circulation to his hands stop.

"What the hell's going on?" Mitch said.

Neither officer said anything. They each grabbed one arm and led him back towards the door he had come through. Brenda gave them a wide berth and only took her hand off the butt of her pistol when they were gone.

They led him back down the stairs and into the cellblock. A third officer held the door open to one of the cells and Mitch was pushed inside.

"You going to take these things off?" Mitch said.

"Shut up," one of them said, and they both turned to leave.

"Hey! My hands are turning blue!" Mitch shouted after them.

He had no idea what had just happened, but whatever it was, it had clearly changed the mood. The idea that this was all leading back to what he and Mike had been up to hadn't even occurred to him. But it did now.

He sat down on the bunk, first trying to think, then trying not to. There was really nothing to think *about*. For all he knew, Mike was sitting in his own cell somewhere, arriving at the same conclusion.

At some point, overcome by mental and physical exhaustion, he managed to fall asleep.

When he opened his eyes again, there was a full-on argument going on outside his cell.

"I don't give a shit what he's been accused of," someone said. "He has rights."

Two uniformed officers were standing on the other side of the bars. One of them was carrying a tray of food.

"He's a damn terrorist," the officer holding the tray said.

"Suspected terrorist. This isn't Guantanamo. Take the damn cuffs off him and give him the tray. If you have a problem with that, you can take it up with the captain."

The officer with the tray turned to Mitch and said, "Turn around and approach the bars."

Mitch did and the man removed the handcuffs. Mitch walked straight to the toilet. His hands felt like two lumps of lead and he ended up getting as much piss on the floor as in the bowl. When he was done he turned around and said, "Thank you."

"Don't thank me," the cop said and dropped the tray onto the floor just inside the cell. Mitch walked to the bars. The other officer was sitting at the desk reading something.

"What have I been accused of?" Mitch asked.

The man looked up and frowned. "You'll know soon enough."

Mitch had no idea how long he had been going out of his mind when two uniformed officers he hadn't seen before opened the door to his cell and stepped inside. One of them was holding a Taser.

"I don't know what you've been told about me," Mitch said. "But I used to get beat up by girls at school."

The stony expressions on their faces didn't change.

"Stand up," one of them said.

"Where are we going?" Mitch said.

The man grabbed his arm, forced Mitch to his feet and ushered him to the door. When he passed the officer with the Taser, Mitch opened his mouth to ask again. He only managed a single word before something pinched his stomach just above the navel and his body began to spasm. His knees buckled under him and he collapsed to the floor. The fillings in his teeth felt like they were vibrating and his field of vision shrank until he was seeing the world through the wrong end of a telescope.

He was vaguely aware of being picked up by the arms and dragged, first across the room, then out a door and into fresh air. Somewhere about a million miles away a car door opened, and he was pushed inside face-first. There were voices but they were muffled and impossible to understand. His legs were pushed into the car and the door slammed behind him. He twisted his head round and saw the blurry image of someone getting in behind the wheel. Again, he tried to ask where they were going but his mouth refused to open. The last thing he heard was the engine starting. Then his eyelids grew heavy and he felt as if he were falling down a deep well, perhaps into Wonderland, or maybe into hell.

# CHAPTER 31

**New York, New York**
**Wednesday 19 July 2006**
**1200 EDT**

Mike woke up in his bed around noon with no recollection of how he'd gotten there. He reached below the covers, found his service pistol and was relieved to see he'd at least had the sense to engage the safety.

All the news networks were busy with the killings in Vermont. Nobody knew where Gerald Ross was, but it was being assumed that he had either been kidnapped or committed suicide on learning of his wife's death. At least that was what the thinking heads were telling their talking counterparts. Mike, thanks to the assistant director, and now Mitch and his illegal fact-finding mission, knew better.

He tried to call Mitch twice, once at his office and once on his cell. The woman who picked up the phone at OSD said he hadn't called in, but might have just overslept. Apparently Mitch did that a lot. His cell went straight to voicemail.

He made his way to the kitchen and found a loaf of Wonderbread, so named presumably because it was four days old already and still looked fresh. He was doing a test run with an unbuttered slice when the phone rang in the hall. It was the assistant director.

"Mike, how you feeling?"

"Fine. Everything all right?"

"Actually, I was calling to ask if you'd heard from Mitch Rainey today. No one's seen him at OSD and his cell seems to be turned off."

"I haven't spoken to him since yesterday," Mike said. "Anyone been to his home?"

"Someone's on their way there now. I just wanted to check with you. I know you guys are friends."

"No, I haven't spoken to him since yesterday," Mike said.

"Okay. I've got to scoot. You take care."

"Sure."

Mike put the phone down and finished the slice of bread. He returned to the TV to find a young Ivy League professional being interviewed on CNN. According to the presenter, he was a "counter-terrorism expert" with one of the big think tanks on Capitol Hill. Mike watched for a minute, musing at the way the man leaped from one absurdity to the next with characteristic lack of humility. He turned off the TV, cursing under his breath.

\- - -

On the street below, a red Buick had pulled up behind the Chevy Blazer. The man behind the wheel of the Buick gave his colleague a thumbs-up. A moment later, the Chevy pulled out onto the road and disappeared into the afternoon traffic.

# CHAPTER 32

**Pont-Rouge, Quebec**
**Wednesday 19 July 2006**
**1300 EDT**

Francis heard the door handle move and reached for the gun under his pillow. The maid saw him, muttered an unintelligible apology and quickly closed it again. He heard her murmur something as she pushed her trolley on to the next room. Francis checked his watch and saw he'd been asleep for several hours.

He sat up and glanced at the computer sitting on the small table by the window; then headed to the bathroom, intending to take a shower. One look at himself in the mirror changed his mind. He found his wallet on the bedside table, saw he still had a hundred and fifty Canadian dollars left, and decided he needed a change of clothes first.

He left the truck in the parking lot and made his way into town on foot. He found a UNICEF hospice shop at the end of the main drag and picked out a pair of jeans that looked about the right size, an old plain black T-shirt and a red sweater with the Canadian national ice hockey team logo embroidered on the breast.

Francis gave the woman at the counter a twenty-dollar bill and told her to keep the change. On his way out the door he saw something in the window that made him stop. Laid out in a row on top of a dusty box containing a Nintendo game console were several compact disc cases with the letters CD-RW printed on the sleeves. Francis picked up all six and took them back to the counter. There was no price tag on any of them, so he handed the woman another twenty and left the shop.

When he got back to the hotel he looked at the CD drive on the old PC and felt his heart jump when he saw the same four letters on the optical drive tray: CD-RW. He turned the computer on and waited with growing impatience for the lumbering old machine to load the operating system. When the churning inside the case settled down and the pointer began to respond to the movement of the mouse, he quickly opened the first file he came to and right-clicked.

And there it was, an option to *burn to disc using Nero Burning ROM*. He took one of the discs out of its case and put it in the tray, then selected the option and followed the prompts until he heard the drive spin up and saw the red light begin to flash. When it was done and the drive tray spat out the disc, he took it and put it in his laptop.

The file was there.

It took him almost half an hour to figure out how to add multiple files to a single disc but in the end he managed to burn everything, a total of 285 megabytes. It took another half hour for the disc to burn. By the time it was finished, Francis was all but jumping out of his skin with anticipation.

The first of the files the older computer had been unable to display turned out to be a scanned blueprint of a door-opening mechanism drawn by a German company called Arman Tenner. From what he could tell, the door was a proposed retrofit to a submarine of some kind. The fact that the drive also contained pictures of a Soviet Victor-class sub seemed to lend this credence. He sat staring at the bizarre image for a long time. Far from shedding any light on the problem, the more he looked, the more unclear things seemed to become. The next file he opened was a drawing by the same company of a space probe design labelled *SC-1135 Siren Call.* He opened the next drawing. It was another satellite, but this one looked like any other. It too had a name. In a box in the bottom right hand corner someone had typed: *Darkstar CommSat 443*, and below that, *Skyline Defense.*

He closed the folder, opened the Internet browser and typed *Skyline.* The first few results were all related to the Nissan sports car of the same name, followed by the definition of the word itself on several dictionary websites. At the bottom of the page there was an entry for the homepage of Skyline Defense Inc., and below that, a Wikipedia entry for the same company. He ignored the homepage, opened Wikipedia and began to read:

*Skyline Defense is an unlisted American multinational defense and engineering contractor headquartered in New York, New York. It was established in 1986 by the Karl Gustav Foundation (KGF). The company does not actually produce weapons systems, but is primarily a research and engineering body and consultant to various organizations including NASA, the ESA and the Pentagon. Skyline Defense is unique in that it is one of only two private companies in the world protected under US Federal Secrecy Laws, making it a de facto subsidiary of the US Defense Department. Owing to its highly secretive nature, little is known about the company's actual research activities and programs.*

Francis scrolled back to the top of the page and clicked on the words *Karl Gustav Foundation*:

*The Karl Gustav Foundation (KGF) is a private fund registered and headquartered in Zurich, Switzerland. It was established by the last will and testament of Swedish steel magnate Karl Ludvig Gustav after his death in December 1984 at the age of 92. The stated aims of the foundation are unusually vague, stipulating only that the board of trustees direct the fund's wealth into the establishment and funding of companies, organizations and educational bodies devoted to the pursuit of scientific progress in the fields of space travel and exploration. It is widely rumored that one of the largest beneficiaries of the fund is the Massachusetts Institute of Technology (MIT).*

*Activities – The foundation owns several companies, including British-based Biolab Technologies (BTN) and the American defense contractor Skyline Defense. The fund also holds a vast investment portfolio and is a major shareholder in some of the world's biggest energy and power infrastructure companies, as well as remaining a majority stakeholder in Gustav Steel (GS) now renamed Scandinavian Steel AB (SSAB) after the company was floated on the New York Stock Exchange (NYSE) in 1985. Very little information is available on the foundation's activities and it remains guarded about publishing details of its investments and grants. Some rumors even suggest that anonymity is a condition for such grants.*

*Board – The foundation's statutes are a matter of public record and stipulate that a board consisting of a chairman and four members govern the fund. The chairman may dismiss and appoint members as he sees fit, making him or her the de facto head and sole arbiter of the foundation's activities. While unusual, there is nothing in Swiss law that makes such an arrangement illegal. It is perhaps easier to understand when you consider Gustav himself ran the company he inherited from his father without a board until the day he died. The first chairman of the foundation was named as Peter Bershadsky, a computer engineer at Massachusetts Institute of Technology (MIT), a fact largely responsible for the rumors surrounding the foundation's patronage of the university. Professor Bershadsky died in April 1990 at the age of sixty-three in a boating accident. He was succeeded by his eldest daughter, Caroline de Villepin, who remains the chairman to this day. The identities of the remaining board members have never been publicized.*

Francis felt goose bumps rising on his forearms as he read on. He moved the cursor over the name *Karl Ludvig Gustav* and the page changed again:

*Karl Ludvig Gustav (June 5, 1892 – December 18, 1984) was the only son and heir of Swedish steel magnate Karl Leif Erik Gustav, founder and owner of Gustav Steel, the largest privately owned steel producer in Europe until 1984, when much of the company was sold and the remainder floated on the New York Stock Exchange (NYSE) and renamed Scandinavian Steel AB (SSAB). Karl inherited Gustav Steel (GS) at the age of thirty-two following his father's death from cancer in 1924. He married the exiled Russian princess Helena Barakirev in 1925. Helena was shot outside the Stockholm opera house in 1927 by a Bolshevik gunman. According to historic records and accounts, the young widower became a prominent and often controversial member of Swedish high society for a decade, fueling rumors of illegitimate children and a number of court cases, the most famous of which was brought by the daughter of an American diplomat in 1932. The rumors persisted until 1948 when it was revealed the billionaire was congenitally unable to sire children. He became a virtual recluse from 1937 when rumors of his ties to the German Nazi party were widely circulated. The speculation was fueled further when Sweden maintained its neutrality at the outset of the Second World War (WW2), allowing Gustav Steel, among others, to ship iron ore to Germany for the duration of the war. By the time of his death in 1984, Karl was rumored to be worth almost one and a half billion dollars, giving rise to an increasingly speculative argument in the press about the destiny of his vast wealth. Shortly after his death it was announced that he had left his entire fortune to a foundation to be established in his name under the stewardship of a little-known American computer engineer from MIT by the name of Peter Bershadsky, described as a long-time friend and confidant (see Karl Gustav Foundation).*

Francis sat back and stared at the screen, his mind racing in several different directions at once. He kept coming back to the name Skyline Defense. Did *they* own the hard drive? It made sense.

He opened the folder named *DPFCS Images* but when he tried to open one of the four files inside, a small window appeared demanding a password.

He spent another fruitless hour looking over the files he could access on the disc and finally shut the laptop down, feeling even more confused than when he had started.

- - -

Twenty minutes later Francis had packed everything back into his truck, checked out of the hotel and was back on highway 40. He passed Three Rivers and found a payphone outside a gas station on the outskirts of Montreal.

The number he dialed was at least six digits too long and contained no recognizable area code, other than the international dialing code for the United States at the front. It rang for several seconds before it was picked up. There was no greeting at the other end, only a curt request for a four-digit pass code. Francis read the numbers off the card in his hand and waited.

"Director Fairchild's office. How may I help you?" the woman said.

"May I speak to the director, please?" Francis said. "This is Senator Cleveland."

"The director is on the phone at the moment, Senator. Can I ask him to call you back or would you like to hold?"

"I'll hold."

Five minutes passed before the director of Central Intelligence came on the line. "Senator, to what do I owe the-"

"Who does the hard drive belong to?" Francis said.

There was a long a pause. "Who is this?"

"You know who it is. And you know why I'm asking."

This time the pause was shorter.

"You should come in. I can guarantee you protection."

"Wow, and they actually put you in charge, did they? I don't want your protection; I want to know what happened in Vermont. Was it Weaver?"

"I don't know what you're -"

"You can drop the act. I know he's involved."

"Weaver hasn't been authorized to do anything," Fairchild said. "And we had nothing to do with Vermont."

"Then you don't know Norton Weaver very well, Director. You might sign his checks, but Norton works for the Oval Office and always has. Now I want you to listen to me because I'm only going to ask once. I want the name of the lead investigator on the Fed break-in."

"I can't give you that kind-"

"Did you hear what I just said?" Francis interrupted. "I'm not going to ask twice. I have a CD here with a very interesting video on it. And I won't send it to your lapdogs at CNN, I'll send it to RT, Al Jazerra and every other hostile news network I can think of. So make up your mind."

Francis heard the long sigh on the other end.

"All right. Give me a minute," Fairchild said.

# CHAPTER 33

**Interstate 91, Vermont**
**Wednesday 19 July 2006**
**1800 EDT**

They reached the town of Orleans shortly after six in the afternoon and took a room at the Howard Johnson near the turnpike. Both men were dressed casually and attracted little attention from the locals, who saw only two more tourists on a road trip through New England - a sight as unspectacular at this time of year as a garden party.

Born Baruch and Daniel Zimmerman on the outskirts of Tel Aviv, they had long since traded both their Jewish faith and their Israeli identities for a more rewarding and less restrictive life in the private sector. Once agents for the pedagogic and overly Zionist Mosad, they had both risen quickly in that organization, a testament to their many and varied talents.

In the United States, the brothers had found the two essential components critical to a successful life of subterfuge in large supply: money and corruption. Their handler was a retired veteran of the CIA who would have been the envy of Hoover himself, had the man still been alive. In the eight years they had been operating as an independent cell, they had amassed a staggering sixty million dollars in fees. It was almost too easy.

The job at hand would add another million to the tally, half of which had already been deposited in one of their many accounts nestled in the web of the offshore banking system.

The local TV news was talking about almost nothing else. The entire town of Morisson had been designated a crime scene by the looks of it, and no one who wasn't a permanent resident was being allowed in. One of the local stations had a crew camped out close to the roadblock into town and was interviewing anyone who left or tried to enter.

Daniel, whose name was currently Lester Farley, would take point as the designated tracker. Baruch, now Eugene Sampras of Columbus, Ohio, would stay here and act as facilitator unless the track split.

When they were set up, Eugene drove them back onto I-91 and past the Morisson turn-off.

They were operating on two assumptions. The first was that the man they were looking for would head north toward the border rather than south. For a man who had just killed four people, getting out of the United States would be the only safe bet. The other was that he would never cross the border in the Impala he had taken from the girl's house. He would know it was only a matter of time before the car was discovered and called in. Unless he had made some prior arrangement. But that was unlikely, considering he had apparently only been following the woman who had been shot. He would be looking to cross the border unnoticed, and the innocuous little truck stop was the first place they found that might offer such a chance.

Eugene dropped Lester off beside the small gravel parking lot and returned to the motel. Lester ignored the diner and headed back down the interstate looking for signs of either the car or its occupants. When he had walked half a mile and found nothing, he moved into the woods.

It took him another ten minutes to find what he was looking for. The tracks were fresh. Three sets, two male, one female. The girl had been tired by this point. Her constant need to match the pace of the men made her strides inconsistent. He followed the tracks back until he found the Impala. A quick look inside was all the confirmation he needed. There was a faint trace of smoke and body odor. The man had been busy killing, and killing was hard work.

He had now returned to the diner and stood studying the dilapidated structure. There were no other cars in the parking lot and no guests inside.

Lester went in and ordered a hamburger and a glass of Coke. When the vile creature who served him walked back into the kitchen, he studied the room and tried to imagine his quarry sitting right here in this very seat. That was the trick; you couldn't guess what a target might do, you had to *be* the target. He would be looking for someone in the diner who might agree to give them a ride. Most likely a truck driver or a single male.

When the cook returned and set the hamburger down in front of him, Lester conjured up a mental image of the cook lying face down on the counter with a meat cleaver protruding from his back. He brushed the idea aside and forced himself to smile. In a flawless Southern accent he said, "Say there, Chef. You wouldn't know if there was any chance I might find myself a ride on up to the border around here, would you?"

The man looked at Lester and smiled back. His teeth, the few that had survived, were bent and tobacco-stained. "We get the odd trucker heading up that way now and then."

Lester forced himself to take a bite of the burger. With considerable effort, he commanded his features to ignite in appreciation. "I'll be damned! That's what I call a burger. Haven't had me one this nice since I left Texas, and that was more years ago than I care to remember."

He could almost smell the cook's sudden change of heart. Whereas before he had been politely cautious, now he began to positively ooze good cheer.

"Thank you very much," the cook said. "Now that I think about it, there's a man who does a run up to Quebec somewhere three days a week. Runs a little firm with his cousin delivering car parts or something. He came through here yesterday and gave a fella a ride up there. His cousin Ned does the Wednesday run. Usually stops in here around three in the morning for a bite. I reckon it'd be worth your while asking him if you can wait that long."

Lester gave the man an even wider grin and said, "Why that's real kind of you, Chef. You think he'd do it?"

"You won't know if you don't ask," the cook said.

Lester forced down the rest of the hamburger and had to exert his considerable willpower to stop himself throwing it back up. He picked up the plate and held it out to the cook, who now seemed to think they were best friends and was doing the talking to prove it.

"Chef," Lester said, cutting the man off mid-sentence, "If that hot plate back there is still sizzling, I'd give my throwing arm for another one of these."

Beaming, the cook took the plate and walked back into the kitchen. Lester was over the counter and behind him before the second hand on the clock above the door had a chance to move. He brought the sole of his right foot up and into the cook's lower back and sent him flying toward the far wall. The plate the cook was holding shattered on the tile floor. Lester sprang forward and grabbed one of the his hands. He pushed it back and the cook screamed. He increased the pressure until he could hear the ligaments in the wrist begin to tear. The cook's eyes vanished behind his eyelids and his body went limp.

Lester walked out to the counter and through the gap by the cash register to the front door. He flipped the "open" sign to "closed", found the panel of light switches and turned off all but the one in the kitchen. That done, he walked back, found a mop bucket full of brown water and poured it over the cook. The cook stirred and began to moan. When he opened his eyes, Lester was standing over him with a butcher's knife in one hand.

"Mister," the cook said, the words coming out in a slur, "What's in the register is all I got."

"The man. What did he look like?" Lester asked.

The cook only looked at him, his face blank.

"The man you said got a ride here yesterday. What did he look like?"

It took another moment for the question to register, then the cook said, "I don't know. Maybe five-ten, stocky, short hair."

"What color were his eyes?"

"I don't remember. Brown I think."

"Did he have any tattoos or scars?"

"I can't remember stuff like that. Are you going to kill me?"

"Yes," Lester said. "What was he wearing?"

The answer had been so matter-of-fact that the cook wasn't sure he'd heard it at all. "You *are* going to kill me?"

"Yes. I'm going to kill you. Now what was the man wearing?"

From the way Lester had said it, it sounded as if the cook had asked to be killed and was now annoying his would-be assassin by being impatient.

"I don't want to die," the cook said and began to sob.

"It would be a crime to let you live," Lester said and moved a step closer.

"You're crazy!" The cook screamed. "You're fucking crazy!"

Lester stepped forward and planted the heel of his right foot into the cook's stomach. The air rushed out of his lungs and for a moment he looked as if he was going to die right there and then. After a few long seconds, he managed to suck in just enough air to avoid fainting and began to hyperventilate.

"What was he wearing?" Lester asked again.

"I - can't – remember."

"You said his cousin usually gets here at around three. Does he ever get here before that?"

The cook shook his head.

"Was there anybody else with the man who got the ride?"

The cook continued to shake his head and Lester knew he wasn't lying. The creature was beyond that now. The kids would have been waiting somewhere outside. It was the obvious thing to have them do. Lester stepped forward and before the cook could utter another sound, he brought the knife down and buried it in the cook's gasping mouth.

That done, he sat down on a chair next to the grill and waited.

At precisely two-fifty in the morning he stood up, walked to the door, flipped the sign to "open" and turned on the lights. Fifteen minutes later a white Peterbilt truck towing a blue trailer pulled into the parking lot, spun around and lined itself up parallel to the diner. Lester turned the lights back off, flipped the sign again and walked out the door. He was standing beside the truck when Ned climbed down.

Cousin Ned was about six feet tall and very thin. He wore a pair of faded jeans pulled tight at the waist with a buckle so big it almost looked like a boxer's trophy belt. His white tank top exposed gaunt shoulders and scrawny arms. On his head he wore a huge, green John Deere cap that extended his height by another four inches. Any other man would almost certainly have laughed at the spectacle that was Ned the truck driver. Lester did not.

Ned looked at the diner and frowned. He turned, saw Lester and jumped. "Holy shit! Ya scared the livin' daylights outta me!"

"Are you Ned?" Lester asked.

Ned stood back and studied the stranger for a moment. "Might be. Who's askin'?"

"We're going to get back into your truck and drive to the border," Lester said.

"Easy there, big guy," Ned said. "Keep going like that and you'll be going no place. This may not be the glorious South, but manners is manners. Say, did you see the lights go out in the diner, I could have sworn-"

Lester punched Ned in the face. Ned's nose exploded like a piece of rotten fruit and he went flying back, bouncing off the side of his truck and landing a few feet away on the gravel.

"Get in the truck," Lester said.

Ned was quicker than the cook had been. He got to his feet slowly, holding one cupped hand over his nose. Lester stepped back to let him climb in, then he walked around and got in himself.

"Do you have ice in there?" Lester asked pointing back into the sleeper cab.

"Got a small fridge with a freezer compartment."

"Put some ice in a bag and hold it to your nose until the swelling goes down," Lester said. "If you are asked about it at the border, you will say that you refused a man a ride and he assaulted you."

Ned climbed over into the small compartment and pulled a tray of ice cubes from the freezer. He broke them into a small white trash bag and put the bag to his nose, flinching at the pain. Lester looked around and saw a roll of paper towels on the fridge. "Use those to clean the blood off your face."

When Ned was done he looked only slightly more presentable. He climbed back into the driver's seat and looked out at the road, not daring to speak.

"You have a cousin," Lester said.

Ned looked at him in surprise.

"He picked a man up here yesterday. The man was traveling with a boy and a girl. Where did he take them?"

Ned looked even more surprised. John had told him about the man and his two companions. Ned tried to remember where he said he had dropped them off.

"Junction of Highway 20 and the 55, I think. Runs over the Saint Lawrence into Three Rivers."

"Take me there," Lester said.

# CHAPTER 34

**Concord, New Hampshire**
**Thursday 20 July 2006**
**0245 EDT**

Francis woke to the sound of copulation in the room next door and cursed himself for not choosing a more up-market place to stay. The woman - he assumed it was a woman, but who knew these days - was earning her living in grand fashion. She began to moan louder as her patron picked up speed. Something on the other side of the wall began to clang, the man gave out a final triumphant groan of satisfaction and the room was quiet again. He could hear the murmur of conversation and pictured the woman pulling down her skirt and pocketing her fare. A door opened and closed followed by the sound of high heels on wood. Francis sat up and looked at the alarm clock.

He got up and dressed quickly, then pulled his backpack from under the bed, slung it over his shoulder and left the room. When he got downstairs a peroxide blonde in a pink miniskirt and black tank top was chatting with the man behind the desk. She gave Francis a glance as he walked by. "Hey, hon, you looking for some company?"

"Maybe later," Francis said and gave her a wink.

"If I'm not here, Bobby knows where to find me," she called after him.

Francis raised a hand behind his back in acknowledgment and turned left onto the sidewalk. He walked until he found a payphone next to a bus stop, pushed four quarters into the slot and dialed. It was answered on the second ring.

"Cassidy."

"What did you find?" Francis asked.

"Listen asshole, if you ever pull a stunt like that on me again, it will be the last time you and I do business. Is that clear?"

"What the hell are you talking about?" Francis said.

"Don't tell me you didn't know."

"Know what?"

"That the woman and the boy were being watched."

"Being watched? By who?"

"You really didn't know?"

"Cassidy," Francis said. "What kind of a fucking moron do you take me for?"

"Okay, all right, I believe you."

"Being watched by who?"

"Two guys. At the house."

"Serious?"

"Very."

"Did they talk?" Francis asked.

"They did. But it took me a while to get them in the right frame of mind."

"Hit men?"

"I don't know. They had no ID. The car they were driving was a rental."

"Did they give you a contact?" Francis asked.

"No contact. They were operating blind."

Francis closed his eyes for a moment and tried to think. He had only wanted a picture of Mike Banner's wife and son in case things got messy when they met.

"Am I good for the hits?" Francis asked.

"You were good for the capture and the interview," Cassidy said. "The hit's going to cost you."

"Go on."

"Twenty each."

"That's a little steep isn't it?"

"Times have changed. Besides, these guys are probably connected. Think of it as a risk premium."

"All right," Francis said. "Call it thirty-five for the two and give me an account number. And Cassidy, there's something else I'm going to need you to do."

# CHAPTER 35

**Vermont - Quebec Border**
**Thursday 20 July 2006**
**0330 EDT**

Lester sat on the bed in the sleeper cab watching Ned through a narrow slit in the curtains. Ned was sweating profusely. At some point he had also urinated into the seat beneath him.

Ned raised his right hand from the gear lever and turned, squinting into the darkness behind him. Whatever he thought he saw, it seemed to make up his mind. Ned reached over and picked up a cell phone from a tray in the center of the dashboard. He moved it to his left hand and put his right on the steering wheel.

"Don't be a fool," Lester said.

Ned jumped in his seat and dropped the phone.

"I was just – ah - just checking the time," he stuttered.

"Of course you were."

"I have to let John know when I reach the border. We're almost there."

"You can call him after our business is concluded," Lester said.

"You'll let me go?" Ned asked.

"That depends on you. Try something stupid and the knife I'm holding goes through the seat and into your spine. Get me where I need to go, and you're a free man."

Ned was visibly relieved. He sank back in the chair and ran the back of his left hand across his forehead.

"Mister, I won't tell a soul. You believe me, right?"

"I do."

"I can keep my mouth shut is what I mean. You're in a hurry. I get it. Whatever business you have, it's none of mine. I just–"

"Shut up," Lester said.

Ned did.

"Make a move to leave the vehicle or alert the officer to your predicament and you die. You, him and everybody else. Do you understand?"

Ned swallowed and nodded. He was about to say something else but Lester cut him off. "Stop talking and concentrate."

The fluorescent lights of the border station were growing brighter in the distance. Lester sat back and pulled the curtains closed.

When the truck stopped, Ned cut the engine and rolled down his window.

"Hey, Ned, How's life?"

For a long moment Ned didn't answer. Lester tensed and got ready to spring forward.

"You know. Same old, same old," Ned said in a voice that wasn't quite steady.

"That's a hell of a nose job you got there. You been brawling again?" the man asked.

"Damn hitcher. Tried to clean me out yesterday."

"I hope you showed him what time it was."

"Oh, he's regretting it, take my word," Ned said.

"Good on ya, man. What's the world coming to, right?"

"Nothing good."

"I'll let you get on, Ned. You look like you could use a good night's sleep."

"Been prayin' for one all day," Ned said. "I'll see you tomorrow."

Ned started the truck and rolled forward. Lester listened to a less informal exchange with another guard on the Canadian side; then they were on their way again, rolling down Highway 55.

"Hand me your phone," Lester said.

Ned reached down to the floor, picked up the phone and handed it over. Lester studied it for a moment, then reached over and placed it in the cradle next to the steering wheel.

"Make the call on the speakers. If the two of you have some arranged method of alerting each other to trouble, I will know. Use it and I kill both you and your cousin."

Ned reached forward with an unsteady hand, scrolled to the name *John* in the phone book and pressed dial.

"Hey, Ned. Everything all right?" Big John asked.

"Yeah. I had some trouble getting the phone to charge up."

"You over the border?"

"Yep. Should be dropping around eight if they're ready."

"You eaten?"

"Stopped off at Joe's place on the way up."

"All right. Give me a call when you've dropped. I might have something coming out of AB in Montreal for the return trip. It'll be a nice little earner if it comes through."

"Sounds good," Ned said. "I'll be in touch."

"Drive safe."

"You too."

Lester pulled the phone out of the cradle. He climbed into the passenger's seat, rolled down the window and threw it out.

When they reached the junction Ned downshifted and pulled the truck onto the verge of Highway 40, just ahead of the off ramp. Lester reached into his pocket and produced a small blue capsule. "Swallow this."

Ned took it but made no move to put it in his mouth. "What is it?"

"It's the alternative to me killing you right now."

"What will it do to me?"

"It will make you forget you ever saw me. Now take it before I change my mind."

Ned looked back down at the capsule and up again at Lester. His hand was trembling so badly he almost dropped it.

"Mister," Ned said, now on the verge of tears, "I promise I won't tell anyone I dropped you off here."

"And I promise that once you've swallowed that, you won't be able to. Now I'm in a hurry, so decide what you want to do."

Ned closed his eyes, placed the capsule on his tongue and swallowed it. When nothing happened he relaxed a little and slumped back into the seat. Lester reached over, grabbed the mic to the CB radio and pulled the spiral cord out of the receiver. He opened the door and climbed out without saying a word.

- - -

As soon as the door was closed, Ned thrust the gear lever forward and crunched the third gear before pulling it back and finding first. He popped the clutch and the truck jerked forward. In the rear-view mirror he could see Lester standing at the back of the trailer looking at him. Ned pushed the clutch down again and this time found fifth instead of third. When he finally got the truck back on the road and up to fifty, he began to sob, his whole body shaking like a man in the throws of hypothermia. He reached under his seat with one trembling hand and brought out a small waist pouch. When he finally got the zipper open and looked inside, he saw the spare phone he kept in there was gone. Ned grabbed the steering wheel with both hands and began to scream, rocking back and forth in the seat.

"Son of a bitch!" he yelled. "Son of a fucking bitch! You just fucking wait till I get to a phone you cocksucker!"

When his voice finally gave out and his shouts subsided into a series of hoarse whispers, he stopped.

The blood began to drain from his head and his anger gave way to an unexplained optimism. His head felt light. For a moment he couldn't even remember what he had been screaming about. When he looked down at the speedometer he saw the red needle bend slightly. Several of the numbers around the dial had fallen off and gathered in a pile at the bottom of the instrument panel. He closed his eyes. When he opened them again, the dial and the numbers were back in place. He looked back up and saw a spider the size of a Rottweiler scurrying across the highway. He tried screaming again but nothing came out. His heart stopped beating for several seconds, then it kicked back in and began to pound. Ned's breathing grew heavier and his body began to tingle as if he had pins and needles in every limb. Then voices began speaking in his head in what was either a foreign language he had never heard, or no language at all.

The vague idea that he needed to stop the truck was overshadowed by the sudden powerful certainty that he was either Jesus Christ or God himself, and the idea actually made him laugh, although what escaped his mouth was little more than a series of rasping croaks. His final vision was of a tall wooden cross standing in the middle of the road in front of him.

It was burning.

The truck breasted the top of a gentle slope and began to speed up under its own weight. When it reached seventy-five, Ned suddenly sat up and opened his eyes. In the dim light of the cab, they looked like the milky blind eyes of some deep-sea monstrosity. The man that no longer looked quite like Ned fumbled at the wheel, turning it sharply to the left. The big truck crossed the central divide before tipping over onto its side, sending a bright shower of sparks flying in all directions.

The cab hit the guardrail and came to a sudden stop, half the trailer still blocking both eastbound lanes. Ned was projected through the windshield like a rag doll into a field of timothy grass. Where his right arm had been, there was only a short stump of shredded flesh. One side of his chest looked like it had been crushed in a vise. He showed no sign of being in pain, but was actually smiling like a lunatic reflecting on some particularly pleasant memory. He turned his head up to the sky and began to speak, the words distorted by a steady stream of blood running from his mouth.

"I am the light of the world," he said, then his heart stopped beating and he collapsed face-first into the grass.

- - -

Several miles away Lester had turned his attention to the verge along the road and found what he was looking for. The tracks were unmistakable. He recognized the smaller footprints of the girl and the wavy tread pattern of her shoes. They had crossed the corner of the field and made their way along Highway 55 towards the Saint Lawrence and the city of Three Rivers.

Lester followed.

After less than a mile the tracks stopped. At the edge of the road a single tire track formed a narrow semicircle in the dirt. Lester studied the tread patterns for a moment before heading on. Five minutes later he heard sirens coming from up ahead and moved off the road. Three police cars and an ambulance flew past, heading back towards the junction. When they were out of sight he returned to the road and resumed his walk.

He reached the river and crossed the bridge shortly after ten and carried on along Highway 55. An hour later, he stopped. The tire track was less clear here, but the tracks of the three people who had gotten out of the vehicle were not. Lester mused at the stupidity of the man. He might be dangerous, but he was also careless.

They had carried on up the road for another mile and stopped outside a ranger station.

He surveyed the site. The gate was locked and there didn't appear to be anyone inside the small office building in the corner of the compound. Lester walked along the outside of the perimeter fence until he was shielded from the road by a truck, then scaled the fence and walked to the building. Neither of the two windows along the back wall was barred. He studied the one nearest to him and when he was satisfied the building did not have an alarm system, he picked up a stone and shattered the glass.

He found himself standing in a large white-tiled bathroom with two toilet cubicles on one end and a row of sinks and a single shower unit at the other. The first room he came to was a small lounge with a tattered couch along one wall and a flimsy table with a coffee machine piled high with old magazines.

The second door had a brass plaque on it with the word *Administrateur* etched in cursive letters. It was locked. He stepped back and kicked it. The bolt held, but both hinges broke and the door went flying into the room. There was a row of three filing cabinets standing against the far wall next to a large window that looked out onto the yard. Above these there were a number of framed pictures, each showing the smiling face of a man in the same uniform with a brass name-plaque underneath. He turned to the filing cabinets and surveyed the labels on the drawers, then opened the one marked *Registre de voyages* and pulled out the notebook tucked in front of the files. It showed a list of entries for trips made by the station's vehicles, including dates, destination and mileage. There was only one entry for Wednesday July 19. The destination listed was the ranger station at Lisotte and the name of the person making the trip was Valerie Tremblay. The round trip distance was listed as 547 kilometers.

Lester took out his phone and called his brother.

"Have you found them?" Eugene asked.

"No," Lester said. "But I'm close. They came through the city of Three Rivers yesterday. It looks like they were taken on from here by a local park ranger."

"Do you need him located?"

Lester moved over to the desk, picked up the Rolodex and flipped to the T's.

"I need a call made in French from the Three Rivers police to this number requesting he come to the ranger station at once. Tell him there's been a burglary. The name is Valerie Tremblay."

Lester gave him the phone number.

"Give me a minute," Eugene said and hung up.

Lester moved to the pictures on the wall. Valerie's was the first in the row. He studied the man's face, then sat down at the desk and waited. Two minutes later his phone rang.

"The call's been made. He'll be there in ten minutes."

Lester looked though the drawers of the desk until he found a set of keys. He unlocked the gate to the compound, returned to the office and found a road map of Quebec Province on the bookshelf behind the desk.

It took Valerie fifteen minutes. He was driving an old Saab that now looked more matte pink than red. He drove through the gate and skidded to a stop only five or six feet from the door to the office. Before Valerie could get out, Lester emerged from the building and rounded the front of the car.

Valerie lowered his window. He was about to say something when Lester reached in, put one hand behind his head and slammed his face into the steering wheel, breaking his nose. Lester kicked him into the passenger's seat then drove out of the gate and got out to close it again.

When he got back in the car, Valerie had come around enough to be fumbling for something inside the glove compartment. Lester reached past him and pulled out a black semi-automatic Colt 45. He pushed Valerie's head down onto the dashboard, brought the butt of the pistol down on the back of his neck and Valerie went limp.

\- - -

An hour later, they reached a bridge across the Saint Maurice River. Lester left the road and crossed it, then turned off onto the first road they came to on the other side. It was a dirt track that looped around and ended on the edge of a small clearing on the bank. Valerie was still unconscious. Lester reached over and slapped his face twice. Valerie stirred. When he opened his eyes and saw Lester, he pushed himself up against the door.

"Vous etes qui?" Valerie asked.

"Never mind," Lester said.

"Qu'est-ce que vous voulez?"

"You drove three people up this road yesterday. Where did you take them?"

The reaction was subtle, but Lester saw it as clearly as if the man had come right out and said it. Valerie shook his head and said, "Not me."

Lester produced the map. "Show me where you took them."

Valerie shook his head again. Lester picked up the gun in his lap and, without so much as an expression of warning, put a bullet in Valerie's right thigh. Valerie screamed and pushed himself harder against the door.

"Where did you take them?" Lester asked again. He sounded calm and perfectly reasonable, as if he thought Valerie might not have heard him the first time.

"Fuck you!" Valerie said through clenched teeth and Lester shot him in the other leg. This time Valerie shouted several profanities in French and closed his eyes. Lester lowered the barrel of the gun until it was pointed at Valerie's right kneecap. The man's face changed, defiance giving way to terror in a single blink of the eye. Lester pulled the trigger. The top half of Valerie's knee exploded in a shower of red meat and bone. Somehow he managed to stay conscious. He was crying and praying in both English and French. His pleas came in gasping spasms between sobs that sounded more like the howls of some wild animal. Lester moved the barrel to the other knee.

"Where did you take them?" he repeated.

In the end it was the calm, not the gun or the pain, that broke him. Valerie would never have believed that a man could be this violent and stay so serene. Through the fog of agony he considered his friend, whose name was almost certainly not Maurice, and how he might fare when this monster caught up with him. He didn't know who Maurice was – had never asked – but he knew the man could be dangerous. But he had also concluded long ago that Maurice was a good person doing good things. The kind of things, he had suspected, that couldn't be done in the light of day by people in official positions. The fact that this creature was after him seemed to vindicate that belief. He thanked God that he didn't know more than he did, because something told him the man in the seat next to him couldn't be lied to.

"Lake Commissaires," he said and pointed to the lake on the map.

"Where exactly?"

Valerie tried to focus on the map through his watering eyes and placed a finger on the shoreline where he had dropped them off.

"Good. Where were they going?"

Valerie shook his head and Lester confirmed his suspicions by not pursuing the matter. Instead he raised the barrel of the pistol to Valerie's abdomen.

"Consider yourself among the lucky," Lester said.

Valerie had no idea what he was talking about and he didn't care. He heaved in a final breath and spat a mouthful of blood into Lester's face. "Go to hell!"

For the first time in his adult life, Lester felt the iron grip on his emotions falter. The man was smiling at him through bloody red lips. And he was laughing. Lester raised the gun to Valerie's face and emptied the entire magazine into it. Valerie's features disappeared one at a time in a spray of blood, tissue, bone and gray matter. The window behind him shattered. Lester reached over, opened the door and kicked the body out onto the ground. He climbed across the seat and out of the car and began kicking the corpse until he was panting with effort. He stood over the body, his chest heaving, and looked up at the cloudless sky. Behind the rage, something unfamiliar was shining through a thin crack in his mind. A saner man would have known it for what it was; fear.

Lester looked at the gun in his hand and dropped it, as if the gun itself had been the source of his rage. He was suddenly overwhelmed by the certainty that the man lying at his feet had somehow infected him. It was the taste of Valerie's blood on his own tongue that had set him off. Was it not then possible that something in that bitter metallic substance was now spreading inside him? The very thought of it threatened to send him into another fit.

When he felt a little calmer, Lester dragged the body to the back of the car and piled it into the trunk. He got back in and used a strip of oily cloth he found in the glove compartment to wipe the blood from his own face, then picked up the map and pierced it with his finger at the point Valerie had shown him.

# CHAPTER 36

**Houston, Texas**
**Thursday 20 July 2006**
**0900 CDT**

Mitch came around for the third time at nine o'clock on the day following his arrest. The first time he woke he had been in the back of a car. That memory was vague. He thought it had been at night, although he couldn't be sure. The car had been moving fast and the motion had made him want to keel over and vomit again. When the car finally stopped, someone - he thought it had been the driver - had stuck something sharp into his leg and the lights had gone out again.

The second time was a little clearer. He had been strapped to a seat with a shoulder harness. The first thing he saw when he opened his eyes was bright green light coming from a narrow gap only a few feet in front of him. When his eyes regained their focus, he had seen it was an instrument panel flanked by two men wearing pilot's headsets. One of them had looked back and seen him, then said something into his mouthpiece. A moment later, the man sitting next to Mitch - Mitch hadn't even seen him raised a syringe over his thigh and the world had swum away again. That had definitely been at night. He could remember seeing stars through the windows.

This time at least he wasn't moving. He looked around the room, closed his eyes to make sure he really *was* awake, then opened them again.

He was sitting on a white leather couch in a room that looked like it might have been lifted off the set of a space opera. Everything was white, from the polished linoleum floor to the ceiling tiles. It hurt his eyes to look at it. It took him a minute to realize he didn't have a hangover any more, which was strange because the last time he'd gotten drunk it had lasted almost a week. Aside from being a little drowsy and extremely confused, he actually didn't feel too bad.

He was about to stand up when he heard footsteps approaching the door. It opened and two people entered the room. The first was a tall woman with long blonde hair tied back in a ponytail. The man who came in behind her was at least three inches shorter and looked no older than twenty-five. Both were wearing white lab coats. The woman had a stethoscope around her neck. She put her hand out and the man handed her a clipboard. She studied it briefly, and looked up at Mitch. "Mr. Rainey, how are we doing today?"

"I'd be doing a lot better if I knew what hospital this was," Mitch said.

"And how I got here."

She smiled. It was the kind of smile you might offer someone who was clearly insane, but not dangerous. She turned to the man beside her. "Where is his profile? I don't see it here."

"Doesn't have one," the man said.

"Then what's he doing here?" she asked.

"Security breach," the man said and pointed at the clipboard. "He's cleared. Authorization came through last night. They want him sedated all the way."

She studied Mitch for a moment then turned and left the room without another word. The man looked at Mitch apologetically, but said nothing.

"Okay," Mitch said. "Is someone going to tell me what's going on?"

The man only looked at him. He seemed as uncomfortable as Mitch himself. Mitch was about to ask again when the woman returned.

"I suppose it had to happen sooner or later," she said. "Still, it would have been nice of Brendan to let us know before he arrived."

She looked at Mitch. "I'm not sure keeping him sedated for the whole trip is a good idea. I want confirmation from Brendan before I authorize it."

"Hey," Mitch said. "Do you mind? I'm sitting right here. Now is someone going to tell me what the hell is going on?"

The woman regarded him for a moment and said, "Mr. Rainey, we're truly sorry about the manner in which you were apprehended. If you bear with us a little longer, I'll see what I can do about answering at least some of your questions."

"Okay," Mitch said. "That would be swell. In the meantime, could you at least tell me where I am?"

She looked from Mitch to the man beside her and back, apparently unsure how to proceed.

"I'll be right back," she said and left the room again.

Mitch stood up. The man by the door seemed to interpret this as an act of hostility and took a step back. "Mr. Rainey, please take a seat. She'll be back in a minute."

"Take it easy, pal," Mitch said. "I'm the guy who doesn't know where the hell he is, remember? The guy who just woke up on a couch in a fucking postmodern version of Narnia?"

The man took another step back and reached for the door handle. Mitch took another step forward.

"Oh no you don't," Mitch said and began walking toward the door. The man quickly shut it and Mitch heard the lock turn.

"Well, that's just fucking great," Mitch said, locking his hands together above his head.

A minute later he heard the lock turn in the door again. He was expecting the woman to return, but this time it was two men who must have weighed at least four hundred pounds put together. Both were wearing the same lab coats, although to Mitch they now looked more like the uniforms orderlies wear in mental hospitals. One of them had a syringe in his hand.

"Hey, back off," Mitch said. "I want to speak to the doctor. Where is she?"

"Mr. Rainey," the man with the syringe said, "This will be a lot easier if you cooperate."

"Yeah, not gonna happen," Mitch said.

He jumped over the couch and backed away until he reached the wall. The men split up, each moving to opposite sides of the room. Mitch made a dash forward, intending to jump back over the couch and head for the door. He had barely left the ground when a hand grabbed his arm and pulled him down. He hit the floor on his back and the air rushed from his lungs. A moment later, he felt the needle prick his left shoulder.

The last thing he saw as he raised his head was the doctor. She was standing in the doorway smiling at him sympathetically.

# CHAPTER 37

**Lake Commissaires, Quebec**
**Thursday 20 July 2006**
**1800 EDT**

Lester had been sitting behind the wheel of the Saab for over an hour trying to figure out what to do next.

He had found the road easily enough. The fresh tracks of the vehicle Valerie had taken them in could be seen coming and going. Finding *their* tracks had presented no challenge either. But then the trail had ended. He'd found the boathouse and cursed when he saw it was empty. Tire marks and footsteps were easy enough to follow, but a boat left no tracks and the lake was huge.

In all the time he had been sitting in the car, he had not seen a single boat on the water or another car on the road. This was dead country, a place *made* for hiding.

He considered calling Eugene to let him know what he had found but the idea insulted his pride. There had to be a way.

According to the map, the lake was almost fifteen miles long, making a blind search impossible. But the boathouse was located where it was for a reason, and unless it was simply to fool the likes of him, he thought what he was looking for would be somewhere directly across the lake and within walking distance of the shore. That meant a camp, or possibly even a dwelling of some kind.

He consulted the map again. There was a small town named after the lake several miles up the road. He started the car and drove back to the main road.

Two miles beyond the town, he found a narrow dirt road leading off into the trees in the direction of the lake. A slanted, rusting sign advertised a hunting shop a quarter mile on. Below the sign someone had tied a piece of cardboard with the word *BAR* written in black marker pen.

The hunting shop was closed, but the bar was open, if bar was really the right word. It was little more than a brick annex with a door and a window. A neon sign hung in it, advertising Molson Dry Beer, although half the letters were no longer illuminated. Above the door a small wooden board said *De Commissaires* in charred black letters. There were two old pickup trucks and a red ATV parked outside.

De Commissaires was as big a disappointment on the inside as it had been from the outside. Just an oblong room about twenty by forty feet. At the back, a makeshift counter made of unpainted plywood stood resting on two sawhorses. The walls had been painted white long ago, but were now yellow with smoke, except in a few places where a picture or poster had recently been taken down.

There were six men inside, seated around two mismatched tables that had been pulled together in the center of the room. A few Canadian one-dollar bills were piled in the middle and each man was holding several playing cards. All of them smoked the same cigarettes and all wore variants on the same basic theme: leather boots, jeans and thick woolen shirts in a colorful variety of scotch patterns. All but one of them had a beard.

When Lester entered, the conversation died and twelve eyes turned toward him in unison, each less welcoming than the next. They grew visibly uncomfortable as he approached the table. One even produced a knife and put it down in front of him with a deliberate clang.

"English?" Lester asked.

Their eyes all moved in the direction of the man sitting at the end of the table. He was the smallest of the group and looked about fifty, but that may just have been the beard. The man regarded Lester with dark-green malevolent eyes, then stood and pushed his chair back. "I speak English."

"Are you American?" Lester asked.

The man shook his head. "I'm from Vancouver. Is there something we can do for you, mister?"

"There is. I'm looking for someone hiding on the other side of the lake."

The man translated this for the rest of them. Two of the men laughed.

"Do you hunt over there?" Lester asked.

"Who's asking?"

"I am."

"And you are?"

Lester put one hand behind his back and reached into the waistband of his pants. The man with the knife stood up. When Lester brought his hand back around, he was holding a thick wad of American hundred-dollar bills.

"I'd make it worth your time," he said and threw the bills onto the pile already on the table.

A murmur went up among the men and Vancouver said something to them in French. He bent over, picked up the bills and leafed through them.

"My friends and I might be able to help you," he said.

"Good. Are there any dwellings over there?" Lester asked.

Vancouver frowned.

"Houses or cabins?"

He consulted two of the others and said, "This man says he knows of two cabins on the other side. He says one of them is in pretty good condition."

"I need you to take me to them," Lester said.

When Vancouver addressed them again, an argument erupted in French.

All eyes remained on the bills in the short man's hand. As the exchange grew more heated, Lester reached back and produced another wad. He threw it down on the table with deliberate effort and the group went quiet.

"Money is not an issue," Lester said. "Time is. That's ten thousand dollars. And this makes it twenty. Get me to where I need to go and there's another twenty in it for you."

This time there was no argument, just a lot of surprised faces. The men all stood up at once and headed for the door. Vancouver put on his jacket, picked up the money and stuffed it into his pockets. He held a hand out to Lester, who looked at it as if it were covered in shit.

"I don't want to know your name," Lester said. "And I don't want to be your friend."

Vancouver shrugged and said, "Suit yourself, pal. That your car?"

"Yes," Lester said. "I need you to get rid of it."

The man shrugged again, "Sure; why not?"

One of the men turned off the lights in the bar and locked the door. Vancouver asked Lester for the keys to the Saab and handed them to one of the others who got in and drove it away.

"You can ride with me," Vancouver said.

They moved out in a convoy, the quad bike taking up the rear. Within a few minutes the truck was bumping along a badly maintained set of ruts through thick woodland. When they broke through the trees into a clearing, Lester saw they were on the tip of a peninsula that ran some way into the lake.

From here the opposite shore was only half the distance it had been by the boathouse. The men began to assemble their hunting gear, looping knives to their belts - and in one case to a leg - checking flashlights and other equipment and stowing these away in any one of a hundred pockets. Each man had a rifle with a scope. Lester saw that two of them were equipped with night-vision.

When the group was ready, Vancouver handed Lester a Canadian Army-issue raincoat with a fleece lining. It had a strange pattern of camouflage that looked like a badly pixelated image of small green, black and brown squares. The men moved in single file toward the shore where a small wooden dock led out to two four-man, steel-hull fishing boats. Each had a large outboard. One of the men was in the process of starting one of these up when Lester shook his head "No motors!"

Vancouver didn't need to translate the message. The man held up his hands in exasperation and reached down to pick up the oars.

"We'll lose time if you're in a hurry," Vancouver said.

"Then I suggest we stop talking and get going," Lester said and pushed past him.

Lester climbed into the boat already occupied by two of the men and indicated for the one holding the oars to move aside and let him have them. When both boats were in open water, Lester began to row, first at a steady pace to keep up with the other boat, then faster. He increased the breadth of his strokes until the stern sank visibly and produced a steady series of small waves in their wake. Within minutes the other boat was at least a hundred yards behind them. The two men in the boat with him sat looking at Lester in a montage of horror and wonder. By the time they reached the far shore, the other boat was at least two hundred yards behind. Lester hadn't even broken a sweat.

"Where are the cabins?" he asked

Vancouver called to one of the men with a night-vision scope on his rifle.

"The closest one is a mile inland from here," he said. "The other is about three miles in that direction, a few hundred yards from the shore."

"Just the two of you," Lester said, pointing at Vancouver and the man beside him. "Tell the others to wait here."

"Can I ask who you are you looking for?" Vancouver said.

"That doesn't matter. If you see anyone, just stop and signal."

"I only ask because even forty grand doesn't cover being shot at if they have guns."

"They're not armed," Lester said.

The man with the night scope took the lead. Lester stayed ten yards behind Vancouver. It took them half an hour to cover the distance. Alone, Lester would have cut that down to ten minutes. But the men in front of him were both unfit and surprisingly clumsy for people who called themselves hunters.

By the time the lead man stopped and held up an arm, the light was growing poor. A storm front was moving into the area and it had begun to rain.

Lester saw the cabin. One of the walls had partially collapsed and half the roof had caved in. Most of what was left was covered in a thick growth of shrubs and vines.

"Doesn't look like anyone's here," Vancouver said and handed Lester his rifle. "Take a look."

The grass around the crumbling building was undisturbed. Two rusty tin cans sat in what had once been a window.

"They're not here," Lester said. "We're going back."

He let them walk ahead a few yards. When they reached a small patch of soft grass, Lester closed the distance quickly and grabbed Vancouver's head from behind. He put his right hand over the man's mouth and his left against the back of his head and snapped his neck in a single jerk.

The other man kept walking, oblivious to the carnage behind him. Lester pulled the knife from Vancouver's belt and ran forward. Instead of bringing it around to the man's throat, Lester lifted the knife and brought it down into the base of his neck in the fashion of a Roman execution. The man was dead before he hit the ground.

Lester picked up the rifle, checked the breach and the scope, then walked back to where Vancouver lay and removed the money from his jacket. He returned to the other body and searched it. What he found in the inside jacket pocket would have made any other man smile.

Lester pulled it out and examined it. It was a silencer for the rifle, about eight inches long and as thick as a coke can. When he had it on, he knelt and turned back toward the empty cabin.

He aimed at one of the cans in the window and pulled the trigger. A puff of dust and stone chips exploded in the wall about a foot to the left of the can and almost two feet below it. He lowered the rifle and adjusted the sight then tried again. The impact was level with the can, but still several inches to the left. He adjusted it again, and this time the can flew off the ledge. The only sound from the rifle was a dull thump, the sound a flat rock makes when dropped on soft ground.

He set off at a brisk jog, following his own tracks. When he saw the lake through the trees in the distance, he veered left to avoid approaching the others from the same direction they had set off in.

The rain had increased from a drizzle to a steady downpour and it had become too dark to make out anything but the silhouette of the three men a hundred yards ahead. Lester nestled the butt of the rifle into his shoulder and leveled the barrel. He spent a moment rehearsing the order of his shots. Two of the men were sitting side by side on the narrow strip of pebble beach. The third stood several yards behind them, looking out at the lake through the scope of his own rifle. Lester brought the crosshairs to a point just above the head of the standing man, exhaled slowly and pulled the trigger. A piece of the man's skull flew off and the head jerked back. Before his body hit the ground, Lester moved the cross hairs to the first of the seated men and fired. The aim was slightly off and the bullet hit him in the neck. The man beside him moved and his third shot missed, sending a spray of water up in the lake several yards from the shore. The man ran to one of the boats and jumped in. Lester aimed at the hull just above the water line and fired two shots.

When he reached the boat, the man was on his back, holding both hands over his ribs and groaning. Lester placed one foot inside the boat and brought the butt of the rifle down on his skull.

He found a handful of bullets for the rifle on one of the men, put them in his pocket and set off along the shore.

He had been walking for over an hour and didn't see the tarpaulin until he stepped on it. Lester reached down and pulled the tattered cover aside to reveal the bottom of a small wooden boat with a compact outboard lying underneath. He raised the rifle, turned on the scope and scanned the woods. When he saw no sign of the cabin, he began walking slowly inland.

# CHAPTER 38

**New York, New York**
**Thursday 20 July 2006**
**1830 EDT**

Mike woke to the sound of someone knocking on the door - three soft taps followed by three more. When had he fallen asleep? *How* had he fallen asleep?

The last thing he could remember was watching a segment on Fox News, a breaking story about Gerald Ross and his wife that suggested both had been up to their necks in some drug-trafficking scandal linked to Al Quaida.

There were another three taps on the door. Mike tiptoed into the hallway and pulled his service weapon from its holster on the side table. Someone was trying the doorknob. He moved closer and leaned forward to look through the peephole. All he could see was the top of a head covered in white hair.

"Who is it?" he asked

"Mr. Banner? It's Mrs. Jackson from down the hall."

Mike unlocked the bolt and opened the door. Mrs. Jackson was a black woman in her late seventies. She was wearing a yellow nightgown and leaning over a walker that looked as old as she was.

"Mr. Banner, you have a phone call," she said.

"I do?"

"Gentleman says it's real important."

She didn't seem remotely curious as to why the call had been made to *her* apartment instead of his, just lifted one hand off the walker and pointed a bony finger toward the end of the hall. "I thought it was my daughter. She always calls around this time. But the man said he was looking for a Mr. Banner in 845."

"Did he say who he was?" Mike asked.

She thought about it for a moment then shook her head. "Oh, he might have. I'm a little slow in remembering these days."

Mike stepped out into the hall and closed the door behind him. Mrs. Jackson pointed to her door again.

"You go ahead now. I'm going to be a while," she said and started turning the walker with small shuffling steps. He hesitated for a moment, but she lifted her hand again and waved it impatiently. "Go on. He'll have hung up and gone to bed by the time I get there."

The place reeked of mothballs and stale piss. An enormous black cat stood in the doorway to the kitchen regarding him with suspicion. About the only thing he could see that looked like it had been made in the current decade was the phone - a wireless handset sitting on top of a stack of phone books on a small table next to the door. Mike picked it up. "Hello?"

"Is this Special Agent Michael Banner?"

"It might be. Who's asking?"

"Agent Banner, I need you to listen to me very carefully. Your life may depend on it."

"Who the hell is this?"

"If it's all the same to you, I'd rather not say over the phone."

"Listen pal, you either tell me who you are or I'm hanging up and calling the cops."

"What do you think happened to Ross?" the man asked.

"If you think you can scare me, asshole, forget it!" Mike said. "I know what you people are up to. I know you've got Mitch and I know you traced our call. I also know you're responsible for what happened in Vermont. And you can tell Jessops he's history. I'm taking what I know to the top. Fuck you very much!"

"Wait!"

Mike almost put the phone down, then brought it slowly back to his ear

"I'm not who you think I am," the man said. "But I *am* the guy they're looking for."

"Why should I believe you?"

"Because like I said, your life may depend on it."

"All right. If you're him, tell me this, how did you get into the Fed?"

"We used two modified RAM modules. One at the Fed and one at Allied Bishop. I switched both replacement parts en-route from California at the UPS depot in Sacramento."

"That was all in the report," Mike said. "You'll have to do better."

"Okay, safety deposit box 107. That's what I broke in for. Was *that* in your report?"

"Go on," Mike said.

"The box was leased to a real estate investment fund called Millennium Holdings. The company is a front for the CIA."

"Assuming you're not full of shit," Mike said, "what do you want from me? If you think I can offer you protection, you can forget it. If I bring you in, you're probably a dead man. A smart guy like you must have figured that out by now."

"I don't need protection. And I have no intention of turning myself in."

"Then what do you want?"

"A simple trade. Whatever information you have in return for your own safety."

"How did you find me?"

There was a long pause. "We can discuss that in person."

"That's going to be difficult," Mike said.

"Because you're being watched?" the man asked.

"I think so, yes."

"I can help you with that."

"Did it occur to you that I might not want help?"

"If what you said about people tracing your calls is true, you *need* my help. You may not believe it, but I might be the only worthwhile friend you have."

When Mike didn't say anything, the man continued. "You're going to receive a package tomorrow morning. There'll be a phone inside it. Go to Times Square at noon. Make sure you can't be seen and dial the number in the phone book."

The man hung up before Mike could answer. He stood there for a long time, going over the conversation again. His thoughts were interrupted by Mrs. Jackson, who had made it back to the apartment and was lifting her walker over the doorjamb. Mike helped her inside.

"Not bad news, I hope," she said.

"Oh, nothing serious."

He was expecting her to start asking questions. If not, why had someone called her phone instead of his; then at least, how did they know her number? But she didn't. He reasoned that her memory problems might run a little deeper than just forgetting names.

"Son, could you help me into the living room?" Mrs. Jackson asked.

Mike took the walker and held out his hand. He escorted her into the small living room where the smell of cats was even stronger. There were two more of them sleeping on the sofa. She raised a hand and made a shooing gesture at them. "Go on, get off the couch, you two. We have a guest."

The cats looked up but made no effort to move.

"Just go ahead and kick them off," she said.

Mike did as he was told. One of the cats hissed and swiped a paw at him. The woman reached for the armrest and maneuvered herself onto the couch. "Would you mind bringing me my cigarettes? They're in the kitchen."

He found a half-empty pack of Winstons on the counter next to a red BIC lighter. He took one of the cigarettes out, handed it to her and lit it. She inhaled a long puff and blew it out slowly. "Started smoking on the advice of my doctor. Can you believe that?"

Mike could.

Mrs. Jackson reached forward, picked up the TV remote and handed it to him. "Don't know where I've left my glasses. Would you be a dear and turn the television on for me?"

Mike did and was about to make his excuses and leave when a clean-cut young reporter on CNN appeared on the screen, standing outside the doors of a small brick building. Mike turned up the volume.

"There are, of course, well-known links between terrorism and the drug trade," the reporter was saying. "As we know, the Taliban finances much of its activities with proceeds from the heroin produced in places like Afghanistan. There have been questions about the connection of these murders, and the Whitehouse has just made a statement to say they believe Mrs. Ross was killed by one of the men found just up the road here. Now it's still unclear exactly what happened after that, but the prevailing theory is that there was some kind of dispute within the cell operating here which may have led to the death of the four men. That explanation isn't going down so well with some of the local residents, however. I spoke to the owner and chief editor of the local paper earlier, and here is what she had to say."

The picture changed to an elderly woman standing next to the reporter outside a tall window with the words *Morisson Herald* stenciled on it.

"The idea that this town has been playing host to a terrorist cell is simply ludicrous," she said. "I have no doubt things transpire behind closed doors that no one would be proud of, but drug trafficking and plots to bomb Americans is not one of them. These men have never been seen in this town before, and the authorities have yet to explain where all of this is meant to have taken place. Nor, for that matter, have they been able to explain the disappearance of Jesse Corbin and Amanda Hinsdale, who have not been seen since Monday afternoon. Their families deserve to know the truth."

"Are you suggesting someone here is deliberately withholding information?" the reporter asked.

"Suggesting? I'm sure of it. I've run this paper for fifteen years, and in that time have never received so little cooperation. Even our own sheriff isn't being told much about what's going on."

The picture changed back to the reporter standing outside the police station. "As you can see, not everyone is happy with the way things are going. I tried getting an interview with the local sheriff earlier but was told he wouldn't comment. All we can do for now is wait and see what develops. From Morisson, Vermont, this is Peter Simms. Back to you, Gus."

Mike handed the remote back to misses Jackson. "Ma'am, thank you very much for taking the call. I'd better be getting back."

She waved it off as nothing. "If he calls again, tell him to make it earlier. My daughter usually calls around this time."

"I will. And thank you again."

When he got back to his apartment, he sat down in the living room and turned on his own TV. All the networks were covering the Vermont story.

It was going to be a long night.

# CHAPTER 39

**CIA Headquarters**
**Langley, Virginia**
**Thursday 20 July 2006**
**1900 CET**

Richard Fairchild was playing a dangerous game, and he knew it. Norton Weaver, for all his poison charm, was a not someone you crossed without thinking it through. In the shadowy hierarchy of power that both served and ruled over officialdom in Washington, Weaver was what the Mafia referred to as a "made man," an untouchable.

The phone call had confirmed what the letter had not explicitly stated: namely that the man behind it all had wasn't set on exposing the program or what had happened at the Fed as long as Princip was terminated. To Fairchild's surprise, he had come across not as maniacal or arrogant, but both levelheaded and even a little sympathetic to Fairchild's own position. If he was right – and Fairchild had no reason to think he would be lying Weaver had ignored his instructions to consult him before he did anything. It was this more than anything else that had settled the matter in Fairchild's mind.

He picked up the phone and called his secretary. "Jane, please send them in."

She opened the door a moment later and ushered in a young man and woman. Both were in their early thirties, lean, athletic and striking in their own ways. The man looked like he might have played college football; the woman, like the senior cheerleader he would almost certainly have dated. It wasn't hard to see why they would have been picked.

"Take a seat," Fairchild said.

They did.

He sat down and regarded them for a moment. Neither spoke or seemed remotely curious about the reason they were there. There was an indifference in their eyes that could easily be mistaken for a lack of aptitude. And what a mistake that would be. Fairchild felt a chill run up his spine at the thought of what Weaver must have done to these two to turn them into the cold methodical killers they now were.

"Effective immediately, I'm reinstating you both to active service," Fairchild said. "You'll be answerable to me only, not your former handler. Not Weaver, but me. Is that clear?"

They both nodded.

"Good. Now, here's what I need you to do…"

# CHAPTER 40

**Lake Commissaires, Quebec**
**Thursday 20 July 2006**
**2000 EDT**

"We should get back to the bunker," Jesse said.

"I hate it down there," Amanda said. "It feels like a tomb. Can't we stay in here tonight?"

He considered it for a moment and shook his head. "I don't think that's a good idea. I know I sleep a lot better knowing all those cameras and sensors are out there. Even if it's only animals that set them off."

During their previous night in the shelter the alarm had gone off three times. When Jesse had turned the monitor on the first time, a moose had been standing a few feet from the door of the cabin. On the second occasion, they hadn't seen anything but a blur that must have been a chipmunk or a rat scurrying back into the trees. Shortly after the sun had come up, the alarm had gone off again and this time the camera had been switched from the grainy green image of night vision to a clear color picture. The sight of two red foxes going at it like rabbits had sent them both into stitches.

"You're right," Amanda said. "I just hope he comes back, because I don't think I can do this for much longer."

"This will end," Jesse said. "I don't know when or how, but it will. When Eddie, or Maurice, or whatever his name is, gets back here, and I'm pretty sure he will come back, we'll get some answers."

She looked at him for a moment, then grinned. "I can't believe he called himself Maurice! It's the lamest thing I've ever heard."

"In this part of the world, it's probably like John or Paul," Jesse said.

"Or Peter?" she suggested, smiling.

"Yeah, or Peter. Now if Bible study's over, I suggest we make a move."

They tidied up the cabin to make it look as unoccupied as possible. Jesse put out the fire, then picked the machine gun off the table and slung it over his shoulder.

"That any good for hunting?" Amanda asked.

"Not really. But there's a proper hunting rifle under the floor if things get that bad."

"Moose burgers and fried bark? I think I'd rather starve to death."

When they reached the log pile they both knelt and pulled up the hatch. Amanda propped it up with the stick and went down first. She used the flashlight to connect the battery to the light bulb in the ceiling, and Jesse turned on the sensors.

"Hungry?" she asked

"Starving."

"Spaghetti and meatballs sound good?"

"Sounds more than good."

Amanda prepared the meals on one of the crates. It went considerably faster than the night before, when it had taken them almost an hour to figure out how to use the self-heating water bags. They ate the food and opened two cans of tinned peaches for dessert. When it was all gone, Amanda leaned back on the bed and sighed. "You sure you don't want the bed tonight? I don't mind sleeping on the floor."

Jesse shook his head. "No, you take it. I'm good. Besides, I want to stay close to the camera, just in case."

Amanda was asleep within five minutes. Jesse stayed up a little longer and sat watching her. He thought he could almost feel his own heart beginning to break. He had lost count of the number of times he had resolved to tell her how he felt. And every time he didn't, it seemed to get harder. Having reaffirmed his vow to do it the next day, he laid his head down.

Outside, the sun had gone down and a light rain had started to fall. Somewhere a wolf howled. Jesse pulled the machine gun a little closer and closed his eyes.

- - -

He was woken by the alarm.

Jesse opened his eyes and sat up, marveling at the sight of Amanda, who hadn't even stirred. He moved to the monitor and turned it on. The image on the screen was of the back of the cabin; there was nothing there but trees. He pushed the first of the four buttons on the panel, and the view switched to the log pile on top of the entrance to the bunker. There was nothing there either. He pushed the next button and froze.

What he was seeing didn't register at first. Perhaps because the idea of finding another person out here had seemed so unlikely. But there was no mistaking him. The man was hunched down and moving forward slowly in the direction of the cabin. He was holding up a rifle and looking through the scope as he went.

Jesse watched him.

It occurred to Jesse that it might be Eddie returning early and taking every precaution to avoid being shot by Jesse himself, but if that were true he should have made some signal to the camera by now to let them know it was him. It was impossible to make out the man's features in the grainy image. If he was a hunter just passing by, Jesse didn't think this is how he would approach a derelict cabin in the middle of the woods. There was something too methodical and calculating about the way he moved, as if he were expecting to find someone here, someone dangerous.

When the man reached the cabin, he leaned the rifle against the wall and walked to one of the windows. A moment later he moved back and slowly opened the door, looked around, then picked up the rifle and began to circle the cabin. Jesse changed the view back to the first picture and saw him slip around the corner. Every few yards he stopped, raised the rifle and looked around through the scope. When he reached the end of the wall he began moving away from the cabin and further into the woods. Jesse's heart started beating faster as he saw the man's course would take him straight to the log pile.

Amanda was still sound asleep. If he woke her now, she might do or say something that would alert the man to them. If he didn't, she still might. An agonizing minute passed in which he kept looking from Amanda to the monitor and back again. The man got within five feet of the log pile and stopped. Jesse could have sworn he was looking straight at it, but that might just have been his imagination, which was now in overdrive.

The man turned and walked back toward the cabin. Jesse switched the cameras again just in time to see him disappear inside, then switched it again to the internal view. The man took a flashlight from his jacket and scanned the room from floor to ceiling. He walked to the fireplace, put a hand over the ashes and his posture suddenly changed. He ran the flashlight across the ceiling and past the camera mounted there, turning the image on the screen a blinding white for a moment, then the light went out. The man ducked below the line of the window, shuffled across the floor to the door then took several steps back and pressed down on the board at his feet.

Jesse reached over and gently shook Amanda. Looking back to the screen, he saw the man now had a knife and was prying one of the boards out. Amanda stirred and turned over. He shook her a little harder and she opened her eyes. Jesse leaned over and whispered in her ear. "There's someone in the cabin."

Her eyes widened as she looked over at the screen. The man had removed three of the boards and was peering into the space under the floor with the flashlight.

By the time they got their shoes and jackets on, the man was putting the boards back. Jesse grabbed the machine gun.

"What do we do?" Amanda whispered.

"Nothing," Jesse said. "He might leave."

"How the hell did he find us?" Amanda said.

Jesse only shook his head. On the screen, the man was walking back out the door. Jesse leaned down and changed the camera view again. They watched him in silence as he closed the door behind him, then turned the flashlight on again and began scanning the ground at his feet. He turned left and continued walking with the light pointed down at the ground. Jesse felt the first signs of panic grip his stomach. The man was following their footprints around the corner of the house.

Jesse put the gun down and knelt in front of the board Francis had showed him. He gently pulled it back then picked it up and leaned it against the stack of crates. Amanda knelt beside him.

"What the hell is that?" she asked.

"I forgot to tell you. It's a tunnel. Comes up somewhere in the woods."

"It doesn't look wide enough."

"It's going to have to be because you're gonna use it."

She shook her head. "There's no fucking way I'm going in there."

Jesse took her face in his hands. "Amanda, listen to me. You need to get in that tunnel and keep going. There's a space at the end big enough to stand up in. You understand?"

She nodded. He could see she was on the verge of tears.

"I'm going to be right behind you. When you hear me coming, push up on the board as hard as you can. It will open and you can climb out – we can climb out."

A tear ran down her cheek. Jesse, who until now had only been scared to death, suddenly found himself getting angry at the man outside. It seemed to clear his mind.

"Go," he said.

She knelt down, got on her hands and knees and looked back up at him. He gestured for her to go on and she moved into the tunnel. When her feet disappeared inside, Jesse switched the camera to the log pile and saw the man was now only ten feet away. Jesse pulled the crate out from beneath the bed and took two of the three hand grenades out. He laid them on the bed, then he picked up the satellite phone and pushed it into the back pocket of his jeans.

He took one of the grenades and stuffed it into his left front pocket. Taking the machine gun in one hand and the remaining grenade in the other, he knelt against the wall with the tunnel to his back.

The man was now standing over the log pile, examining it with the flashlight. He kicked the pile with one foot. When the logs didn't topple over, he reached out and tried to pry one loose, and the entire hatch moved. Jesse curled his finger around the trigger and checked the safety. The man kicked the pile again. Something fell from the hatch cover and bounced off one of the rungs on the ladder. In the silence it sounded like a hammer blow. A second later the hatch opened a few inches and Jesse saw four fingers appear in the gap. Then it began to rise.

Jesse closed his eye and pulled the trigger.

Nothing happened.

For a moment his mind went blank, then he put the grenade down, pulled back the cocking handle and released it. The hatch fell back into place just as he squeezed the trigger again. In the confined space the chatter of the machine gun sounded like full-scale war. Splinters flew everywhere as the edge of the plywood board disintegrated. He forced the barrel down as it rose to keep the fire aimed at the hatch. On the screen, he saw the man jump clear of the woodpile and dive to the ground. Jesse felt the gun go still in his hand. The ringing in his ears was so loud he thought he might actually have gone deaf in the few seconds it had taken to empty the magazine. The top of the small room was shrouded in thick tendrils of gray smoke and the smell of cordite was overpowering.

He turned back to the screen and saw the man crawling out of view in the direction of the cabin. Jesse moved forward on his knees and switched the camera. The man was now running towards the cabin. Jesse had to change the view again and only just caught the man coming through the door. When he switched it again to the inside of the cabin, the man had already removed the floorboards and was pulling out the M16. A second later he was running back out. Jesse didn't bother following his progress on the screen, but switched it straight back to the woodpile.

It probably saved his life.

He saw the man raise the M16 just in time to drop his own gun, turn around and fall to the ground. He spun around and pushed himself into the tunnel feet first and was halfway in when the ground in front of him erupted in a series of small explosions. Dirt and fragments of stone peppered his face. He reached for the grenade on the ground in front of him and scrambled the rest of the way into the tunnel, beginning to push himself back with his elbows. The sound of gunfire stopped as abruptly as it had begun. When he was about six feet in Jesse realized there was no easy way to throw the grenade in the cramped space. He heard the hatch being opened and then thrown aside. The man didn't bother using the ladder. Jesse saw a pair of boots hit the ground less than twelve feet in front of him. He turned onto his left side and pushed himself as hard as he could against the tunnel wall. It gave him just enough room to bend his elbow. He pulled the pin with his teeth, released the safety lever and thrust the grenade forward. It was more of a punching motion than a throw. The grenade hit the ground and rolled towards the opening. It cleared the tunnel, but not by much. Jesse saw it roll to the right and out of his line of sight. Then it exploded.

The rush of hot air pushed him another three feet down the tunnel before the hole in front of him disappeared and the world turned black. It felt as if both his eardrums had burst this time, although he thought he could hear faint screaming coming from somewhere behind him. He started moving again, pushing himself back, first with his hands and then his elbows. After an awkward minute of this he figured out a way to use his knees to gain a little more momentum, but it was still slow going. His hands and elbows went numb as the skin turned raw in places. If Amanda hadn't been waiting for him at the other end, he thought he might have just given up. The ringing in his ears was so loud he didn't think he would be able to hear her, no matter how close he was getting. He was about to stop for breath despite his panic when his foot bumped something. A hand reached down and grabbed his ankle.

"Jesse?"

Her voice sounded as if it were coming from the other end of the tunnel. He moved a little farther until his legs were bent up against her feet and reached for her hand. She grabbed it and squeezed, sending a bolt of pain up his arm as the sweat on her palms soaked the raw exposed flesh on his palms.

"I can't open it," she said. "It's too heavy."

"I'm not even sure I can stand up unless you climb out," he said. *His* voice sounded like it was coming from inside his own head. He heard the groan of effort as she tried again to push the plate up.

"It's stuck," she said. He could hear that she was starting to really panic now. This was the claustrophobic's worst nightmare. Not just being trapped in a small space, but buried alive. The other end of the tunnel was closed off now, which meant it was this way or none at all.

"Try to squat," he said. "Hold your palms out and keep your arms straight. Then stand up quickly like you were going to jump."

It took her a moment to make sense of what he was saying, but then he felt her backside touch his knee. There was a thump and he felt her squat again. On the third attempt she let out a little yelp and Jesse felt a rush of cold air sweep past him. Her foot brushed his leg as she climbed out. He pushed himself the rest of the way into the small space and just managed to stand up by bending his neck and pushing his head out of the tunnel with one hand. When he turned his face up to see the entrance he felt cold rain on his face. Amanda reached down to help him. When he cleared the lip of the hole he dropped to the ground and lay face up staring at the blackening sky. After the heat in the tunnel it felt wonderful. Amanda had dropped to one knee beside him and was looking at him in horror, but he didn't notice.

"My God! What happened to your face and hands?" she said. She was crying, had probably never stopped, Jesse thought.

"I'm fine," he said. "Really."

"What happened?"

"I threw a grenade into the bunker."

"He's dead?"

"If he's not, he can't be killed," Jesse said and let out a hoarse bark of laughter that didn't sound entirely sane.

"Was he alone?" Amanda asked.

That made Jesse sit up. It was a pretty fucking good question. One he hadn't even considered.

"I don't know," he said. "But I don't think we should wait around to find out."

"Where do we go?"

Jesse thought about it and pointed east. "We should follow the lake around. It's a long way, but I don't think heading that way is a good idea."

He pointed into the forest. She looked in that direction and nodded.

"I'm pretty sure the cabin is that way," Jesse said, pointing east. "If we cut across to avoid it, we'll reach the lake eventually."

He got to his feet and helped her up despite the agony it caused his hands. She went to hold one of them and Jesse winced.

"Oh, shit. Sorry," she said grabbing his wrist instead. They set off at a slow walk. The moon had all but disappeared behind the clouds and visibility was close to zero. Within a minute they were both soaked to the bone.

"Jess, we're going to get hypothermia if we stay out here," Amanda said.

"I don't think you can catch hypothermia in July," Jesse said.

Amanda's reply was interrupted by a loud thump. A chunk of bark on the tree beside her exploded and peppered the side of her face with small fragments of wood. Jesse grabbed her arm and pulled her to the ground. Amanda looked at him, her eyes full of confusion.

"Rifle shot," Jesse said.

"How do they know where we are?" she said.

"He's using a night-vision scope," Jesse said, remembering the way the man had kept lifting the rifle to look through it.

He tried to think but it was hard. Too much was going on and he had no idea who was following them. If there were two of them, there could be three, or ten for all they knew. And if they had been expecting Eddie instead of a couple of scared kids, that made perfect sense.

But he wasn't going to just lie down and die. Not while Amanda was alive and there was a chance, no matter how slim, of saving her life.

Jesse reached down and felt the contour of the second grenade in his pocket. He pulled it out and held it up to Amanda.

"What is it?" she asked

"The other grenade. You're going to crawl over to that tree. I'm going to throw this thing as far as I can in that direction and run."

She shook her head. "I don't think that's a good idea, Jess."

He ignored her and began to crawl away. Mandy, get behind that tree and don't move."

Jesse got to his knees, pulled the pin on the grenade and imagined it was a football. He threw it high, using every bit of strength he could find, then set off at a run despite being almost blind in the darkness. He hit a tree with his shoulder, fell to the ground then got back up and kept going. A moment later the grenade exploded.

For several seconds the forest around him lit up as if someone had turned on a set of stadium floodlights and he saw the shooter. He was on his knees and leaning against a tree about thirty yards ahead and slightly to the left. Jesse turned toward him and started sprinting. The flash of the explosion faded as quickly as it had erupted, but the ground where it had landed was still burning. It was too far from the shooter to make him out in the faint glow, but it made it much easier to avoid running head on into a tree and braining himself.

He closed the distance quickly, but the man saw him when he was still several yards away. Jesse saw a very faint muzzle flash and something stung his left arm. He fixed his eyes on the point, took five long strides and jumped.

The first thing he felt was the scope of the rifle hitting him above the left eye, followed by a bright light on that side of his head. A second later he collided with something that felt almost as hard. Jesse bounced off the man and hit the ground on his back. Before he could get up a cold hand closed around his throat. The voice that spoke to him barely sounded human. It was a voice he associated with severely retarded people, or deaf people who had learned to talk. Jesse couldn't make out a word of what the man was trying to say. As the grip grew stronger Jesse felt his windpipe start to close.

Jesse reached out with his right arm - his left had gone numb - and felt for the man's face. What he found was a jawbone full of jagged teeth covered in warm liquid. He brought his hand up, feeling for the nose and found only a hole. One of his fingers traced the line to the man's left eye, but the socket was empty and oozing what felt like warm jelly. And yet somehow the man's grip on his throat kept tightening.

Knowing he would soon be unconscious if he didn't do something, Jesse lifted his right shoulder off the ground just far enough to extend his hand across the man's face to his other eye. He put four fingers on the temple and pressed his thumb into the eyeball. The response was a howl of rage, and then the hand let go of his throat. The man staggered back. Against the backdrop of the fire, Jesse saw he had no right arm. The man tried to stand up, got to one knee and fell back down again. Jesse was having too much trouble breathing to do anything but watch. The man began his incomprehensible mumbling and lashed out blindly with his remaining arm. How he could still be alive was something Jesse would never know.

The man began to crawl away. When Jesse could just about breathe, he got to his knees and reached for the rifle. He pulled back the bolt, saw a bullet sitting in the top of the magazine and pushed it into the chamber.

Jesse raised the barrel, making no effort to aim, and pulled the trigger. The bullet hit the man in the center of the back and he went toppling forward onto what was left of his face. To Jesse's astonishment the man was still mumbling. This time Jesse stood up. He reloaded the rifle, brought the silencer to the back of the man's head and pulled the trigger again.

Jesse stepped forward, not quite daring to believe the man was dead. If he had come from hell, as Jesse strongly suspected he had, it wasn't an unreasonable thing to think. He kicked the man in the side, then did something he wouldn't have believed himself capable. He lifted the butt of the rifle and brought it down on the side of the man's skull. He began to scream as he repeated the motion until there was nothing left but a stain on the ground above the man's shoulders, then sat down, threw the rifle aside and regarded the mutilated corpse though the eyes of a lunatic.

He might have sat there until the sun came up if he hadn't remembered Amanda. That got him back to his feet. He knelt beside the body and pulled off the waterproof jacket. It was shredded in places and missing an arm, but it would have to do. He set off in the direction he had come from. When he tried calling out, he discovered his vocal cords had stopped working. He made a conscious effort to retrace his path through the trees and found it impossible. The rain had almost put out the fire and everywhere he looked he saw only darkness and the vague outline of trees.

When several minutes had passed and there was still no sign of her, Jesse began to panic. He tried to shout her name again and began to cough instead. When he stopped to try and get his bearings, he found he had lost all sense of direction. Then he heard something behind him, or thought he did, and began to run in that direction. With the light from the fire all but gone, he was now effectively blind as well as dumb. He had time for one final thought before he hit the tree – please, god, let him be the only one they sent – then he was falling back, his vision a field of bright exploding stars.

\- - -

When the light from the exploding grenade began to fade, Amanda got to her feet. She moved cautiously, taking care to stay behind the trees as she went. It was hard to hear anything above the falling rain, which seemed to be getting heavier by the minute. She thought she saw a faint flash off to her right and began to move in that direction. A moment later, she *did* hear something. But it was coming from behind her. When she turned around, two shining eyes were looking back at her.

"Jesse?"

No answer. The eyes were joined by a second pair, and then a third. She knelt and swept the ground in front of her, not daring to look away. Her hand passed over a fallen branch and she picked it up.

"Jesse?"

Still no answer. Two of the eyes began to move toward her. Amanda reached back and threw the branch as hard as she could. The thing in front of her retreated. The word at the front of her mind was *woodchuck*. But that was absurd, of course. These were no more woodchucks than she was. Amanda knelt again, but before she could find something else to throw, the silence was broken by a long rising howl. The response was a chorus of them that seemed to be coming from all around her.

Amanda ran.

The pack maintained a safe distance, but it had now been joined by several more members, and the curiosity which had brought them was quickly turning to expectation as the smell of blood grew stronger.

When she rounded the tree and stumbled over the body, her first thought was that she had found the man who had shot at them. When she saw it was Jesse she let out a small cry of horror.

"Jesse?"

She put a hand to his face and brushed the hair out of his eyes. He didn't move and she could feel her own resolve shrinking. Then he opened his eyes.

"Mandy?" he croaked. "Mandy, is that you?"

"It's me. Jesse, we have to get out of here, now. Can you walk?"

He nodded. But when he tried to stand his legs buckled beneath him. She caught him before he fell, knelt down and raised him over her shoulder. It took all the strength she had to stand back up, but she got to her feet and placed one foot in front of her, took a step and then another. She carried him that way, mostly stepping and sometimes staggering, until she saw the dying embers of the fire up ahead. From there it was only another twenty yards to the cabin.

She heard a growl and looked back to see a wolf the size of a young bear reared down on its haunches not ten yards away. Amanda met its eyes and saw something in them that brought the naked truth of Darwin's Origin of Species home in a way two years of sociology never could. She lowered Jesse to the ground, turned around and let out a shriek so loud it made her vocal cords burn. When the wolf took a step back, she took one forward. It moved back further. Before she knew she was going to say anything, Amanda summoned all the volume she could muster and shouted, "Do I look like little red fucking riding hood to you? Do I!"

The wolf sprang back at the sound of her voice and disappeared. She had no way of knowing how final the retreat was, but she had no intention of waiting around to find out either. When she turned back to Jesse he was looking at her as if he'd never seen her before.

"Come on," she said. "We better get inside."

She laid him in front of the fireplace, stacked several logs into it and emptied the rest of the lighter fluid over them. Within a minute the fire was burning steadily. She pushed him as close as she dared and began to remove his clothes. She covered him with the blanket from the bed then sat down next to him and brushed the hair from his face. His eyes opened slightly and he tried to say something, but Amanda put a hand to his mouth and shook her head.

When she was satisfied that he was asleep and not unconscious, she stripped off her own wet clothes, crawled in under the blanket and pushed her body against his. Her mind was racing. If there was anyone else out here besides the man Jesse had just killed, they were done for.

She resolved to stay awake and keep watch.

It didn't work.

# CHAPTER 41

**Times Square, New York**
**Friday 21 July 2006**
**1140 EDT**

Mike got there twenty minutes early. The "something" had arrived by bicycle courier at his apartment just after nine. A plain white cardboard box with his name and address on the outside and a phone on the inside.

Mike walked over to a hot dog vendor outside the Foot Locker and ordered a Deli Dog with all the trimmings, only to find he had left his appetite on the subway. In the interest of keeping up appearances, he ate half of it and threw the other half in the nearest trashcan. He looked at his watch and saw it was only quarter to. Feeling too exposed on the sidewalk, he turned and walked into the Foot Locker.

He picked out a tracksuit, asked for directions to the changing rooms and was relieved to see they were actual rooms and not stalls. He chose the one furthest from the door and locked himself inside.

The phone was one of the cheap disposables you usually only saw on TV facilitating the tricky work of drug dealers. The man had said the number would be in the phonebook - which was a joke, considering there wasn't even a screen. He turned it over, thinking the number might be on the back. It wasn't. He was about to check the bag it had come in when it began to ring.

"Hello?" Mike said.

"You made it. That's good. Sorry about the phone. Slight change of plan."

"I really hope you know what you're doing," Mike said. "If someone's following me this is going to end badly."

"There are two people following you, not one. And neither of them followed you into the Foot Locker."

Mike suddenly felt very uncomfortable in the small room.

"Relax. They're strictly nickel-and-dime."

"That's very comforting," Mike said.

"Do what I tell you and you'll be fine."

"Where do I go?"

"Pay for the tracksuit and leave. Hang a left, walk to the end of the block and take another left onto West 44th Street. When you get to the Sondheim Theater, walk inside and wait for me to call."

When Mike got to the theater he made a beeline for the display stand at the back of the lobby, took a flier and pretended to read it. A moment later the phone rang again.

"I'm here," Mike said.

"So am I."

There were several people standing in the lobby, but none of them were on the phone. Mike looked outside and saw two yellow cabs at the curb. "Where?"

"Second cab. Jump in."

The driver was wearing a Yankees T-shirt, a baseball cap and a thick pair of black. He got in.

"Where to, sir?"

"What happened to the guys following me?" Mike said.

"One of them got careless and sprained his ankle walking off the curb, I think."

"And the other one?"

"Sunstroke. You wouldn't believe how common it actually is."

They joined the traffic, cutting off a delivery truck as they went, then sped forward and almost rear-ended the car in front.

"Got to keep up appearances," the driver said.

He made a right onto 6th Avenue and drove past Bryant Park then took a left onto East 40th Street and another right onto 3rd Avenue. Ten minutes later they were driving through the Queens Midtown Tunnel. By the time they emerged on the other end Mike was lost.

"Where are we going?" Mike asked.

"You'll know soon enough."

Francis pulled into the long-term parking lot at LaGuardia and took a ticket from the machine. He found an empty space between two vans and parked the cab.

"This is it. The end of the line."

Francis got out and walked to the edge of the parking lot. Mike joined him and they crossed a service road running along the shore of the man-made peninsula. When they reached the water Francis sat down on a boulder and beckoned for Mike to take a seat on a hollow tree trunk several feet away. An awkward moment passed in which neither man seemed to know where to begin.

"Tell me," Mike finally said. "What was in that safety deposit box that was so important you had to break into the Fed?"

"Ever heard of Operation Princip?" Francis asked.

When Mike only looked at him, Francis said, "No, of course not. Princip is the name of the Serbian who killed Archduke Ferdinand and inadvertently set off World War One. It's also the name of an assassination program financed by the CIA."

"And?" Mike said.

"And I was going to ask them to shut it down."

Mike pondered this for a moment. "If that's true, why would the CIA come after you, knowing what they know? It doesn't make any sense."

"Indeed it doesn't. But I'm afraid it's gotten a little more complicated. Or perhaps a lot more. I'm not sure."

"Meaning?" Mike said.

"Meaning the files I was looking for weren't there because Millennium Holdings no longer owns the box. In fact, it turns out Millennium Holdings no longer exists at all."

Mike's characteristic frown was back. "The CIA has the recording you made. They still wouldn't risk coming after you. Especially if they know you don't have their files."

Francis nodded. "True. But the CIA isn't the problem. Or at least not all of it. I took something from the vault. A hard drive. The people it belongs to are turning out to be both very determined to get it back and a lot more resourceful than I would have believed possible."

Mike looked incredulous. "Who?"

When Francis didn't answer Mike said, "Wow. You really don't have a clue who's after you, do you?"

"Oh, I have a couple of clues," Francis said. "I just don't know where they lead yet."

"To Vermont?" Mike suggested.

Francis shook his head. "The people sent to find Cynthia Ross had no idea what was going on."

"What *did* happen in Vermont?" Mike asked.

"Gerald was my partner, but I'm guessing you already figured that out. As for what happened in Vermont, I did. And in the nick of time."

"They were looking for *him*?" Mike asked.

"They were looking for *her*. They had already found *him*."

"Why?"

Francis walked to the edge of the water and stood looking out at the bay. Behind them a plane was spooling up its engines for takeoff. When the noise died down again Francis said, "She had the hard drive. Before I knew it had nothing to do with Princip I asked Gerald to get the files off it for me. When I realized what had happened Ross wasn't at home. I got him to call his wife and get her to leave the house with it."

Francis reached into his backpack and handed Mike the hard drive. Mike studied it for a moment. "It looks old."

"It is."

Mike handed it back. "The CIA obviously knows the box used to be theirs. They'll have put two and two together by now. You *do* realize that."

"Oh, I think they've done a lot more than put it together. But again, it's never quite as simple as it should be. Princip is run by a guy named Norton Weaver. He's what you might call the quintessential non-state-actor. Started off under Hoover with you boys, then moved to the CIA. He's now what the spooks call a free agent. And he's a nasty piece of work."

"What's your point?" Mike said.

"Norton knows what's going on. The cover-up in Vermont has his name written all over it."

"The terrorist plot?"

Francis chuckled. "Yeah. Gerald Ross wouldn't know a terrorist from a bull terrier, or anything else for that matter. As for his wife, you'd only need to talk to her shrink to know she spent most of her waking hours in a drug-induced fog. Nobody will, of course. When our star-spangled press hears the "H" word they all drop their pants, turn around and bend over. No, Norton knows what's going on and it suits him just fine because-"

"He knows that you know you've fucked up," Mike finished.

Francis nodded. "And he'll see this as an opportunity, believe me."

"How do you know all this?" Mike asked.

"I spoke to Director Fairchild."

Mike looked up in surprise. "You've spoken to Fairchild?"

"I had no choice. I had to warn him about Weaver. I also needed to find you."

Both men were silent for a moment. When he turned back to Francis, Mike said, "You say you don't know who the drive belongs to. Do you at least know what's on it?"

"Pictures mainly. And some technical drawings. Satellites, space probes, things like that. Nothing you can't pull off the internet. Oh, and an old Victor-class Russian sub, complete with someone's rather bizarre idea for turning it into a cargo ship."

"That's it?" Mike asked incredulously.

"Not quite," Francis said. "There are still some encrypted files on the drive that I haven't been able to open. And one of the drawings has the name Skyline Defense on it. Ever heard of them?"

"Sure," Mike said. "Their headquarters are right here in New York. Although I can't say I know much about them."

"I looked them up. They're a research and engineering company, dealing mainly with space-related technology. NASA and things like that. It's owned by some Swiss fund called the Ludvig Gustav Foundation. It's a-"

"Wait," Mike interrupted. "What did you say it was called?"

"I think it's called the Ludvig Gustav Foundation."

"You mean the *Karl* Gustav Foundation."

"Yeah, that's it. You've heard of it?"

"When they pulled the investigation out of the New York office, our director sent his White House liaison up from D.C., a man named Bruce Jessops. According to Jessops, he was there to supervise the handover. I admit it sounded like bullshit even at the time, but so did just about everything else that was going on. Jessops saw the file I had. I asked a friend in D.C. to pull his personnel record. Not because I suspected him of anything then, but because he annoyed the shit out of me and I'd never seen him before. I just wanted to know how the hell he'd ended up in D.C. I mean the guy looked about fifteen years old. Anyway, I didn't want to use my own terminal because everything is logged and it would have looked suspicious, especially under the circumstances, so I asked my colleague to do it."

Mike trailed off, as if trying to remember the rest.

"And?" Francis said.

"You have to know Mitch Rainey to understand – frankly I should have known better than to ask him – but he did a lot more than check his personnel record. It turns out Jessops is sitting on two million dollars, buried in some offshore account. And the money was coming from a company owned by the Karl Gustav Foundation. Jessops also made contact with the CIA station chief in Montpellier on Monday using a cell phone paid for by the bank that set up the account."

"He gave them the names," Francis said. It wasn't a question.

"So find Jessops, and you've..."

Francis was already shaking his head. "He won't know anything. These people are smart. He's a paid informant, nothing more. They used the list to find Gerald. He was never involved with the security system directly, but he knew everyone who was. His name would have come up too many times to ignore. We always assumed Gerald might be questioned, only by an official of the U.S. government, if you see what I mean."

Mike seemed to drift off again as Francis spoke. When his eyes returned to Francis, he said, "Has it occurred to you that what you did has gotten a lot of innocent people killed? Cynthia Ross, for one."

"You can believe what you want," Francis said. "But staying in the house would have gotten her killed for sure. By running, at least she had a chance."

"Did she?" Mike said.

"I had to get the drive back," Francis said. "I think the reason should be obvious enough."

"And if she had run without the drive?" Mike said. "You think they would have killed her then?"

"I think you still don't understand what's going on. If you think they would have spared her, you're in the wrong line of work, my friend."

"All right," Mike said, his temper rising. "I get it. They're crazy and you're innocent, because you didn't know who *they* were. Is that about it?"

"I don't claim to be innocent. But I sure as hell never intended any of this."

"Their blood is on *your* hands," Mike said defiantly.

Francis stood, leaned forward and poked a finger at Mike's chest. "You listen to me, you self-righteous son of a bitch! I've done things that would make you sick just listening to them, and the people that signed my paychecks were the same assholes that sign yours. It's taken me a long time to recover enough dignity to walk in the sun, and the last thing I need is a lesson in morality from a washed-up, half-ass bureaucrat. How many lives did you put on the line when you and your vanished friend started breaking the law and looking under stones best left unturned?"

Mike pushed the hand away and stood up. Both men faced each other, their noses almost touching. Mike's hand moved to the revolver under his jacket.

"Go on," Francis said. "I dare you. If you can kill me before I break your neck, I'll deserve it."

Mike looked at Francis and saw something in his face he didn't like. It occurred to him that he wouldn't be the first person to die looking into those eyes. He dropped his hand and sat back down. "All right, you win, pal."

"I'm not trying to *win* anything," Francis said. "We're dealing with something here that runs deeper than either of us understands. I've been playing this game for a long time. I know it sounds ridiculous, but there are rules, and the people after this drive are breaking all of them. I've done some things I'm not proud of, believe me. I thought I knew where the bottom was. Now I'm not so sure. "

"What do you mean?" Mike asked.

Francis sat back down and looked out at the water. He sat there staring for a long time before turning back, shaking his head and letting out a long sigh. "I killed a pregnant woman once."

Mike looked at him, frowning. He was about to say something, but Francis held up a hand. "She was a U.S. Citizen, guilty of nothing more than sleeping with a man she didn't know. The man turned out to be a Saudi prince. The order came from Weaver, but the request was made by a minister in the Saudi government. It's not something I'll ever be able to live with, but I'm telling you to make a point. I thought that was the end of the line. I broke into the Fed to put an end to it, nothing else."

"You were one of the operatives for Princip?" Mike asked.

Francis nodded. "You hear about conspiracies, and that one is as screwed up as they come. At least that's what I thought. Back-room politics, political assassinations, secret covenants between people who are supposed to hate each other, money and oil buying anything that can be bought. But these people don't fit the picture. You can bet the CIA has no idea what's on that drive or what this foundation does either."

"So you think the Karl Gustav Foundation is part of it?" Mike asked.

"A part, yes. But don't ask me how."

"What are you going to do?" Mike asked.

"I have an idea. But I need to know if you're on board first."

"On board? Me? I don't think you get it," Mike said. "I've got a family. My son is still in high school."

"I know," Francis said.

"Then you'll also know that they would be in serious danger if I did anything to piss these people off. Shit, you said it yourself, they're crazy."

"They're not in danger," Francis said.

"How the hell do *you* know?"

Francis looked up to the sky and closed his eyes. "Because they're no longer in Arizona."

Mike stepped back, drew his gun and pointed it at Francis. "What the fuck have you done? If you think you can blackmail me into going along with what you're planning, you're as insane as they are."

Francis didn't look at him. He picked up another stone and threw it into the water. "They were already being watched."

"What are you talking about? By who?"

"By men who weren't overweight ex-cops like the two back there in Times Square."

"How the hell can you *know* that?" Mike said, almost pleading now.

"Because I had both of them killed after I called you."

Mike brought both hands to his head and started pacing back and forth like a man hit with a sudden and painful migraine. "Oh, Christ. This isn't fucking happening. You had two men shot outside my goddamn house?"

"No," Francis said, still calm. "At the time they were in a hotel in downtown Phoenix. They were under orders to kill your wife and son if it came to it."

"Bullshit. This is all bullshit!"

"I had them interrogated before they were shot. Trust me, it's not bullshit."

"By who?" Mike said, his voice rising to a shout. "Who are these people? Who the fuck are *you*?"

"None of that matters," Francis said. "The point is you were being watched to see if you could keep your mouth shut. I don't know if Weaver was behind it or someone else, but the moment you stepped out of line, there would have been no warning, just a double funeral and a chance for you to reconsider your options. You're a high-ranking member of the FBI; killing you would lead to complications these people would rather avoid."

"And you don't think killing my family would have done that?"

"Killed is the wrong word," Francis said. "They would have died. A car accident or a house fire, most likely."

"You talk as if you know these fucking people," Mike said.

"I do know them. I was one of them, remember? It's the reason I'm still alive."

"You're a sick fuck, is what you are. I don't believe any of it."

"Then you need to open your eyes and take a good look around, my friend," Francis said. "Because nothing is what it looks like."

Mike walked to Francis and raised the gun. Tears were welling up in his eyes and his body had started shaking.

"You talked me into this fucking meeting! You got rid of the men tailing me! You set this whole thing up!"

"Put the gun down," Francis said.

Mike lowered it slightly but kept it pointed at Francis.

"Thank you," Francis said. "You're overlooking the point. I didn't talk you into anything. I may have given you a direction to walk in, but I think you'd be lying to both of us if you said you hadn't already decided to go *somewhere*. It wouldn't have had to be much. Even telling the FBI about Jessops might have been enough. Can you tell me that was never going to happen? Can you honestly say that when your friend's body washed up on the banks of the Potomac because he knew too much, you would let it lie?"

Mike slowly lowered the gun to his side and sat down on the ground. He wiped his nose with the sleeve of his jacket. "No. I can't. And I did consider my family before I came here. What do you make of that?"

"I think it makes you a bit of an asshole," Francis said.

Mike laughed, but there was no humor in it.

"I also think it says something about you that most people can't claim."

"What?" Mike said. "That I would sacrifice my wife and son?"

"No. I think it demonstrates a commitment to principle that few people have."

"Can you tell me where they are?" Mike said.

"I don't know myself, and that's the way it should be. Any man that claims he can hold on to a secret no matter what is a fool."

"But they're okay?"

"Yes," Francis said. "They're safe. The people looking after them are the best I know."

"So what do we do now?" Mike asked. All the fight had gone out of him. He suddenly felt like a leaf in a storm.

"We're going on a little vacation," Francis said.

Mike looked at Francis as if he were insane. "A vacation?"

"There's a man we need to see who just happens to live outside Orlando."

Francis held out his hand. Mike took it and Francis pulled him to his feet.

"What about the Foundation?" Mike asked.

"We leave that for now. I have a better plan in mind. We can always come back to it if things get desperate. "

"Get desperate?" Mike said.

Francis pulled a CD from his pocket and held it up. "I said Skyline was my only lead," Francis said. "But that's not quite true. *This* is what the whole thing comes down to. The key is in here somewhere. It *has* to be. And I know a man who can help us."

"In Florida," Mike said.

"Come on," Francis said. "We'll lay low for a few hours and catch the red-eye to Tampa."

Mike put his gun back in its holster.

"You might as well get rid of that now," Francis said.

Mike looked at the gun for a moment, then walked back to the edge of the water and threw it as far as he could. He stood for a moment watching the ripples it made then turned and followed Francis back to the road.

"My name is Francis, by the way," Francis said. "Although not for very long. You'll need a new name yourself. I was thinking you look like an Edwin."

"Tell me something," Mike said. "How did you get Fairchild to give you my name?"

"I told him I was going to send my video to the Motion Picture Academy if he didn't."

"Son of a bitch," Mike said.

"He might be," Francis said, "But I have a feeling he's going to be our son of a bitch from now on."

# CHAPTER 42

**Lake Commissaires, Quebec**
**Friday 21 July 2006**
**1300 EDT**

Jesse opened his eyes and scrambled out from under the blanket. Still half-asleep, he reached for the smallest log on the pile by the fireplace and prepared to swing it at the creature stirring at his feet. But when he looked down there was nothing there but the tattered remains of the waterproof jacket he had taken the night before. He noticed he was holding the log in his left hand and looked down to see a dark purple bulge halfway up his right arm. There was a distinct entry and exit wound on either side. His hands and forearms were covered in dried blood and something else he didn't even want to think about.

Ignoring the pain, he leaned over and prodded the jacket with the end of the log. When he was sure there was nothing alive hiding inside it, he reached down and picked it up. There was a small zipper just inside the lining. The cell phone inside it didn't look like any he had ever seen. It was a flat oblong shape and made of black brushed aluminum. There was a single line display on the front with a simple nine-digit keypad below it and five small LED lights above. There was no antenna or power button that he could see, and when he turned it over, there didn't appear to be a battery cover either. All five lights above the screen were red. On the green display the word *Contact* was flashing rapidly. He held the phone for a moment longer then put it down on the mantelpiece above the fireplace.

Amanda was still sleeping. Outside, the rain clouds had vanished to reveal a beautiful summer day. A thick beam of dusty light shone through both windows, creating two bright squares on the floor in front of him. Jesse knelt down beside Amanda and brushed her hair back from her face. Her skin was whiter than usual but not pale, and certainly not blue. Her lips were a healthy red and when he put one hand beneath the blanket and felt her thigh it was pleasantly warm, but not hot. He had no idea how long they had been asleep, but judging by his groaning stomach he thought it might have been ten hours at least.

Jesse removed three of the boards in the floor - they had only been pushed back down slightly - and rummaged inside for something to eat. He found a can of baked beans and a Swiss army knife. He had to put the knife between his teeth to pull out the can opener then squeeze the can between his legs to open it. He ate the beans cold by tipping the can into his mouth like a cup, then repeated the ritual again with a can of ravioli before letting out a long belch.

"How crude you are."

Amanda was sitting up on the blanket. When she saw his face she put a hand over her mouth. "My god Jesse, are you all right?"

Jesse considered the question and discovered to his own surprise that he was. In fact, he was more than all right, he felt strangely serene. He looked down at his bloodstained hands and smiled. "It's not mine."

"What happened?" Amanda said.

"I killed him," Jesse said.

The statement was casual, almost an afterthought. And yet there was no bravado or false modesty in it.

Jesse walked over to the bed. Underneath it were several gallon jugs of water and a large metal bowl. He poured half a jug into the bowl and began washing his hands. The cuts – there seemed to be about a thousand – stung like hell. He washed his right hand and arm, then tried using the right to do the left, but that was pointless. When he stood back up, Amanda was looking at him with wonder. He'd only seen that look once before. That had been behind the bleachers of Morisson Elementary School about a million years ago. It was a look of guarded admiration.

She stood up, letting the blanket fall to her feet, and only then did Jesse realize that he had been naked the entire time.

Something had happened to him that was difficult to understand and even harder to explain. It didn't exactly feel like a part of him had died - that half-baked poet's sentiment had nothing to do with it. It was more like something that had lain dormant until now had woken up. It made him feel about ten inches taller and ten pounds lighter. He hadn't killed the man because he deserved to die. He didn't think that would have been enough. He had killed him because Amanda deserved to live and she was his. Call it the coming of age, call it love or call it apple pie, all he knew and all he cared about was that she was alive, and the look on her face said she knew it.

He watched her cross the room, the ray of sunshine from the window moving up her stomach and across one pale breast. Their eyes locked. When she reached him she put her arms around his waist and pushed one side of her face against his chest. He felt a tear spill from her cheek onto his stomach and run down into his navel. His heart began to beat faster. When she looked up at him her eyes were wet, but she was smiling.

"Mandy, I've-" he began to say.

She put a finger to his lips and mouthed the words "I know," then gently pushed him back until his legs were touching the bed. She raised her hands to his shoulders and pushed him down onto the blanket.

"Lie down," she whispered.

The moment he felt her lips and the hot breath behind them on his ear he was overcome with an urgency he'd never known. She climbed on top of him and began kissing his wounded arm, moving up to his shoulder, his neck and finally his mouth. She reached down between his legs and slowly guided him into her with a soft moan, and for a while, everything that was wrong with the world was right.

When it was over they lay entangled beneath the blanket, lovers, deaf and blind to everything but each other, finding neither the will, nor the need, to ruin the moment with something as meaningless as words. Jesse thought he could have stayed there until the world crumbled to dust had it not been for the steady throbbing in his arm. When he let her go Amanda moaned in protest.

"You need to eat something," Jesse said.

"I'm not sure I can."

"How do you feel?" Jesse asked.

"Seriously, you're asking *me* that?"

"I just meant, you know, do you feel up to walking?"

Amanda smiled. "To the end of the earth and back."

"Good, because we can't stay here."

Jesse got up and went to the hole in the floor. He picked out several cans and lined them up on the board beside him. When he turned to her he saw Amanda was regarding him with a kind of puzzled reverence. He liked that look.

"We've got more beans and ravioli, hot dogs, peaches or rice pudding," Jesse said.

"Rice pudding sounds nice," Amanda said.

She got to her feet, pulling the blanket over herself, then swayed slightly. Jesse stepped forward to help her, but she held up a hand. "Just a little dizzy. It'll pass."

She walked across the room and stood looking at the embers in the fireplace. When she turned around her hand brushed the phone on the mantelpiece and it fell to the floor. She bent down and picked it up. "What's this?"

"Well it *was* my alarm clock, but I think it's a cell phone."

"Your alarm clock?" she said, looking puzzled.

"It started vibrating at my feet. I almost smashed it to pieces with a log, thinking it was a rat or something."

She turned it over in her hand and studied it for a moment. "It doesn't even have a brand name on it."

"I know. Weird, right?"

Amanda finished the can of rice pudding and looked that much better for it. Jesse had started gathering up supplies and packing them into a backpack he had found under the floorboards, along with an assortment of clothing and food. He also found a pistol, which he laid down beside the backpack.

They shared out the clothes, what little there were. When they were both dressed they surveyed each other. Jesse couldn't help laughing, even though it hurt his throat. To say they looked impoverished would have been a compliment. They looked like two homeless people who would give anything to be just poor. Jesse had the advantage of being male, but Amanda was both the wrong sex and several sizes too small. She had tied her jeans at the waist with a length of twine and folded up the hems several times. She wore a wool-lined red tartan work shirt with elbow patches that came almost to her knees. The only thing that fit her was her hiking boots, which had dried out by the fire. Jesse wore a pair of Wrangler jeans that were a decent fit, but the effect was offset by the brown corduroy jacket and boots that were at least two sizes too big. The most useful thing Jesse had found was two thousand dollars in small bills rolled into a rusty tin can.

Jesse remembered the satellite phone, but it wasn't anywhere in the cabin. When they were almost ready to go, he told Amanda he needed a piss and went outside. He walked back to where the woodpile had once been and stood surveying the carnage. There was a shallow, jagged crater where the entrance to the bunker had been. The butt of the M16 was sticking up out of the ground about halfway up the slope. A few feet away, beyond the edge of the crater, he saw the arm. It was bent at the elbow and two of the fingers were missing on the hand. He walked on, following what he guessed was the line of the tunnel, and found the exit. When he peered in, the first thing he noticed was the several inches of water that had built up in the bottom. He had been prepared to go in and look for the phone, but that seemed pointless now.

Halfway back to the cabin, he saw Amanda coming around the corner. She waved and walked over to meet him. When they were only ten yards apart she stopped and looked down. He looked down himself and saw the body. Amanda was holding a hand over her mouth. When Jesse reached her she raised her head slowly and the look she gave him sent a chill down his spine.

"My God," she said. "What happened?"

"Do you really want to know?"

She looked back down at the thing on the ground then shook her head. "No. I just want to get the hell out of here."

When they got back to the cabin Amanda took the strange cell phone from the mantelpiece and held it up. "I came out to ask you if you wanted to take this."

"Do you think we should?" Jesse asked.

"I don't know. It's creepy. Like the hard drive. And look where taking that got us."

Jesse took it from her and looked at it for a moment. The word *Contact* was still flashing on the screen. He dropped it onto the floor. "You're right.

It's a bit too much like déjà vu."

"All over again?" Amanda asked and they both laughed.

That phrase had been Bill Perry's all-time favorite for a whole year in high school. It got to a point where he would steer a conversation just to use it and it had driven Jesse and Amanda nuts.

"What do you think Bill's doing now?" Jesse asked.

"Probably trying to win over an Amish girl with some of his best Jesus jokes," Amanda said.

That made Jesse laugh again.

"I kind of wish he was here. Don't you?" Jesse said.

"I wouldn't wish this on anyone. Bill least of all."

"No. I guess not."

When they reached the lake they turned left and followed the beach. A few minutes later they found the boat. Jesse pulled the tarpaulin off and looked inside. The outboard was still there.

"I don't get it," Amanda said, "How did he leave without the boat?"

Jesse shrugged. "He probably had one of those James Bond fold-out helicopters stashed away somewhere out here."

"I'm being serious," Amanda said.

"So am I," Jesse said. "What do you think? Should we take it?"

"What's the alternative?" Amanda asked.

"A shitload of walking."

"I'll help you get it into the water."

They got the boat in, and Jesse mounted the small outboard. It started on the first attempt. They set off along the shore, keeping the boat no further than ten yards out. Amanda sat at the front with her face into the wind. It was a beautiful day. Above them, small cartoon clouds drifted carelessly through a baby-blue sky. Under any other circumstances it might have been cause for joy.

Jesse's arm had stopped throbbing and begun to howl. He strongly suspected he would need to get to a doctor sooner rather than later. When the lake narrowed he set a course for the other side. Not long after that they were pulling the boat back out of the water.

"I think the road is that way," Jesse said, pointing east.

"You think it's safe to hitch?" Amanda asked.

"Safer than starving to death out here."

"Ha ha, very funny. I meant people might be looking for us."

"People *are* looking for us," Jesse said. "But I don't see what else we can do. It took us hours to get up here by car. It would take a month to walk the same distance. And we'd still be in Canada."

"Where are we going, anyway?" Amanda asked.

"I don't know. But I think I need a doctor."

Amanda took one of his hands. "Your arm?"

"Hurts like hell."

"Fine," she said. "We get to the road and flag down the first car we see. It's settled."

They reached the road fifteen minutes later and just missed a truck going in the right direction.

"I think we should lose the gun," Amanda said. "Don't you?"

Jesse pulled the pistol out of his pocket and looked at it.

"I'd feel a lot safer if we didn't," he said.

"Can you even use it? I mean with your arm."

"Sure, I can shoot with my left."

Jesse thought Amanda might have persisted with the "old Jesse," but he was gone and she seemed to know it.

They reached the road, crossed it and set off at a lumbering pace in the direction of Three Rivers. Two cars passed them going the wrong direction in the first hour. About fifteen minutes later a truck came rumbling by and they both stuck out a thumb. It didn't slow down, but gave them a long honk on the horn and Amanda switched from thumb to bird.

"Patience," Jesse said, but he had started sweating and already felt a little feverish.

Ten minutes later a green pickup truck passed them and slowed down. At first it seemed the driver was only having a look, but then it pulled off the road and stopped. They started running. Halfway there Jesse stumbled and fell. Amanda came back and helped him up, then took the backpack in one hand and his arm in the other and urged him on. When they got to the truck they saw the driver was an old man.

"Three Rivers?" Amanda said. "Trois Rivers?"

She held up three fingers hoping it would help.

"Trois-Rivieres? No," the man said, shaking his head. "La Tuque."

Amanda shrugged and pointed at the truck bed.

"Okay?" she asked.

"Oui Oui," the man said.

An hour and a half later the trees began to give way to houses and small buildings. A quarter of an hour after that they were in La Tuque. The old man either didn't care where they wanted to get off or thought he already knew. He stopped outside the local bus station. They got out and Jesse almost fell again. People were already eyeing them. A few of the onlookers seemed amused, while others looked more disapproving. Amanda guessed there wasn't a big homeless problem around here if not even the bus station was safe from judging eyes. They stood on the curb looking lost and clueless.

"Wait here," Amanda said. "I'm going to see if there's a hospital or medical center around here."

Jesse watched her go with vacant eyes. The moment she walked through the door and out of sight he collapsed onto the pavement.

# CHAPTER 43

**Orlando, Florida**
**Friday 21 July 2006**
**2105 EDT**

The US Airways Airbus A320 touched down in Tampa shortly after nine and taxied to one of the many gates standing empty along the terminal building. Only twenty or so people were on the flight, most of them middle-aged men in cheap suits and comfortable shoes with a pack of cigarettes in one pocket and a lighter on stand-by in the other. In seats 32 A and B two men, Edwin Hollister and Charles Woodrow of Indiana, squeezed into the aisle, took their briefcases from the overhead locker and made their way to the front of the plane. They were both wearing off-the-rack Walmart specials, one navy blue, the other dark green, and cheap white sneakers. To a casual observer the phrase *scraping by* would probably have been about right.

The young male steward standing by the airlock put a hand over his mouth to stifle a yawn and wished them both a pleasant stay in Tampa. Charles, the younger of the two, gave him a wink.

"You be sure to get some sleep," he said, flicking his eyes down to the steward's crotch.

The steward smiled, gave him a quick once-over and turned to face the man walking up the aisle behind them. When they were in the main terminal building, Mike turned to Francis and chuckled. "Part of your disguise?" he asked, looking amused.

"The Sixties are over," Francis said. "Being gay these days is like being invisible. You should try it."

"I'm having enough trouble with the contacts," Mike said. "I'll leave the rough stuff to you."

"You can take them out as soon as we're in the car," Francis said.

When they reached the Hertz rental counter Francis handed his forged driver's license to the woman behind the counter. She flashed them both a well-practiced smile. "Welcome to Florida, Mr. Woodrow. Are you here on vacation?"

"Strictly business," Francis said.

She smiled again and handed him a set of keys. "The account's paid up so you just need to pick up the car. It's got a full tank. We ask you to fill it up before you drop it off. The shuttle leaves just outside the main door every ten minutes. Is there anything else I can do for you today?"

"No, I think we're all set," Francis said and offered her a tired smile in return.

The car was a white no-frills Chevy Cobalt. Francis opened the trunk, threw his briefcase inside and beckoned for Mike to do the same. When they were in Mike reached up, held his left eye open with one hand and pinched the contact lens out with the other. He did the same with the other eye and sat blinking for a moment.

"How the hell do people wear these things?" he asked.

"You get used to it."

"I don't think I want to."

There was almost no traffic and it took them only five minutes to get onto the 528 Bee Line Expressway. Francis stuck to the speed limit, keeping one eye on the rear-view mirror. Mike was looking out the window, lost in his own thoughts. Things had been happening so fast it was hard to get any real perspective on the situation. Four days ago he'd been sitting in his office contemplating the price of real estate with nothing but a rebellious son and a pissed-off wife to worry about. The man sitting next to him had changed all that. He wondered where Susan and Josh were and how they were coping with being kidnapped, because that's certainly how *she* would see it. He couldn't imagine what she had been told to get her out of the house, much less into a stranger's car with their teenage son. It occurred to him he might never see them again, but he brushed the thought from his mind.

Francis had been well prepared. When they had returned to the taxi at LaGuardia, the clothes, documents and briefcases had all been in the trunk. The picture on Mike's new license and passport had been taken from the FBI website and doctored somehow. His hair, naturally black, was light gray and his eyes had gone from brown to a dark blue. Before Mike could ask how that was going to work, Francis had produced the contact lenses and a bottle of hair dye. The result had been quite remarkable.

"Subtlety is the key," Francis had said. "Go overboard and you draw attention. The trick is to choose one or two prominent features and change only them. Short of reconstructive surgery, there's no better way to reinvent yourself."

To prove his point Francis had put on a pair of rimless glasses, then covered his hair in gel and combed a part along the side of his head. It was still clearly him, but someone asked to describe him was most likely to remember the glasses and the hair.

Edwin Hollister and Charles Woodrow worked for a small property developer in Terre Haute, Indiana and were in Florida scouting for a little slice of the vacation homes market, Francis had explained. The cover was strictly for conversational purposes, should they end up seated next to someone particularly social, or one of those nervous fliers who couldn't keep their mouths shut. That had turned out not to be necessary as the handful of passengers on the plane had been scattered throughout the cabin and the two of them had had several rows to themselves. To Mike, the experience had been nerve-racking, but Francis had slipped into character like a seasoned actor. Mike supposed a man who could kill an innocent woman - a pregnant woman - didn't get nervous too easily. The idea was almost too disturbing to believe, but Mike didn't think Francis had been lying about that. It made him both scared of the man and grateful to know he was in the company of someone who could handle things when the shit started hitting fans.

Francis stirred him from his thoughts by tapping him on the knee. "Almost there. I need you to wait in the car while I go inside. I shouldn't be long."

"Are you going to tell me who we're visiting?" Mike asked. "Or is it a secret?"

"It's not," Francis said. "But that's not why I haven't told you. Some people are quite touchy about who they do business with, and this guy is one of them. He'll tell you what he wants to. It's not for me to decide."

"An old colleague?"

"Something like that."

They left the toll road and turned onto State Road 520. Five minutes later Francis turned left onto a road called Denver Creek Road. They passed several large houses and a small lake. At the end of the road there was a single-story house barely visible in the moonlight where the grass gave way to a thick forest of slash pines. Francis stopped fifty yards from the house and turned off the engine.

"Don't get out," Francis said. "He'll know we're here, but not who we are. Until I've spoken to him it's best to be cautious. The law here isn't particularly kind to trespassers. Or fugitives, come to think of it."

Francis got out and walked down the road. When he was twenty yards from the house, he heard the soft clang of a rifle bolt.

"That's far enough," a voice said.

"I'm not looking for trouble," Francis said and held out his hands to show they were empty.

"Then you'd better turn around and head back to your car."

"I was hoping I might get a cup of coffee before I left."

"You won't be the first smart-ass I've buried," the man said. "Now get going."

Francis saw him. He was down on one knee at the corner of the house. The rifle was leveled in Francis's direction, the man's head hunched down to the scope.

"Who sent you?" the man asked when Francis didn't move.

"No one. I guess you could call me the Grinch that stole the Christmas of '98," Francis said.

There was a long pause. The man raised his head for a moment, then lowered it again.

"Nice try. I'm going to give you ten seconds; then I pull the trigger. Tell whoever sent you that I'm finding retirement every bit as pleasant as I thought I would."

"I still don't know why you blamed yourself when Marilyn lost the baby," Francis said and braced himself.

The man rose and started walking toward him, the rifle still pointed forward.

"You should have high-tailed it when you had the chance, asshole," he said.

The man's voice trembled with anger. When he was only a few feet away he stopped and pointed the barrel straight at Francis's head.

"You've got some fucking nerve-"

He stopped suddenly, his mouth dropping open in disbelief. "Francis Moore?"

Francis took off the glasses and smiled. "Hey, Colonel. You look good."

"I don't get it," the man said. "I signed the report myself."

"Did you see who wrote it?" Francis asked.

He considered the question. "Boomer. Was it Boomer?"

Francis nodded. "Yes. I didn't think you'd believe anyone else."

"Boomer hated you. Why would he cut you loose?"

"We made a deal," Francis said. "He stepped up and I walked. He only hated me because I was in his way."

"And I bought it," the man said, looking at Francis with wonder. "Boomer's dead, you know. Disappeared two months after you did."

"I know," Francis said. "I cut his throat myself."

"What?"

"You know as well as I do he was a maniac. He told me what you did after I - after I died."

"Threatened to do," he corrected. "If I had done it we wouldn't be having this conversation."

"I'm glad you didn't," Francis said. "Still, I'd have liked to see their faces if you had."

The man didn't answer. He was looking over Francis's shoulder to the car. "Who's your friend?"

"An esteemed member of the FBI field office in New York. Now unofficially retired."

"Do I even want to know what you've gotten yourself into?"

"I hope so," Francis said. "I could really use your help."

The man sighed and looked back toward the house. "Get the car into the garage and come inside."

As he walked back to the house, the man who had once been his trainer and operator turned back to Francis. "Francis Moore, back from the depths of hell. I should have known it was bullshit."

"How did it go?" Mike asked when Francis got back in the car.

"Not too bad."

One of the doors on the garage opened and Francis drove inside. There was a black 2006 model Ford Mustang GT parked in front of the other door with a double green stripe running from bumper to bumper. Their host was waiting for them in the doorway of the garage. Mike thought he looked at least sixty, perhaps a little older. Francis introduced Mike and the two men shook hands.

"Reginald Stiles. I'll let you know if I'm pleased to meet you once I've heard what you two are doing here."

Reginald led them into a large open-plan living room decorated in the style of a hunting lodge, complete with bear rug and trophy heads. There was a wide stone fireplace on one wall with several pictures on the mantelpiece of a much younger Reginald. In one of them he was seated in the front row of a group outside a sandbag bunker wearing green army fatigues. The plaque at the bottom of the frame said: A/75 LLRP - Quang Nam 1972. In another he was shaking the hand of Richard Nixon in the Oval Office dressed in the uniform of an army captain.

Reginald pointed to the sofa, and they both sat down. "Can I get you anything to drink?"

"I'll take that coffee now," Francis said.

"And your friend?" Reginald asked, looking at Mike.

"I'll have something a little stronger if you've got it," Mike said.

"What's your poison?"

"Single malt?"

"That I can do," Reginald said and left the room.

Mike noticed there was no television in the room. A bizarre turntable made of polished steel cylinders on a glass stand sat in one corner of the room next to a tall bookshelf filled from top to bottom with twelve-inch LP records. Small speakers were mounted in all four corners of the room. He was about to ask Francis a question when Reginald returned carrying a silver tray with two whiskey tumblers and a white coffee mug on it. He set the tray down, handed Francis the mug and offered Mike one of the tumblers. "Highland Park. I get it shipped over from the Orkney Isles."

Mike took the glass and sipped at it. It was clean and smooth, a far cry from anything he was used to. Reginald took a seat in one of two hand-carved rocking chairs that flanked the fireplace and picked up a pipe from the hearth. He peered into the bowl then used a long match to light it.

Reginald exhaled a large plume of blue smoke, took a sip from his glass and looked at his guests. "So, what exactly is it that I can do for you?" he said. "Bearing in mind I don't see the president very often these days."

Francis put down his mug. "Ever heard of Skyline Defense?"

"Sure. It's a research and engineering contractor. Belongs to some foundation in Austria or Switzerland. They do some stuff for the Pentagon, but they mostly work with NASA and the Europeans on satellite technology. I think they might have something to do with the shuttle program, but I'm not sure. Why?"

"Skyline is part of the Karl Gustav Foundation, and it's based in Zurich. Although I think it may be a front for something else, too."

"Every private foundation is a front for something else," Reginald said. "Usually greedy shareholders."

"I'm not talking about that. I'm sure the fund is what it appears to be, but I think it's also a base of operations for something a little more sinister."

"If it had anything to do with intel," Reginald said, "I can assure you I'd know something about it. I'm more curious to know what an employee of the FBI is doing in my living room."

Reginald nodded at Mike. "It's okay. Francis wouldn't have said anything if he didn't trust me to keep my mouth shut. So what *are* you doing here? I'm guessing you're not on vacation."

Mike, who had no idea who Reginald was, didn't know what to say. Francis shook his head to indicate he didn't need to say anything.

"He's become a target," Francis said. "So, incidentally, have I."

"A target for whom?" Reginald asked.

"That's what we're trying to find out."

Francis told him everything, starting with the break-in at the Fed and ending with the meeting between him and Mike in New York. It took almost an hour. By the time he was done Reginald's curiosity had turned to fascination. He had stopped Francis several times to ask questions and clarify details, and Mike was surprised to discover how many of the isolated events that formed the narrative Reginald already knew about. Mike, who had completely forgotten about the two missing kids in Vermont, listened with growing wonder as Francis described their trip across the border and into the Canadian wilderness. When Francis finished, Reginald stood. "Well, that explains the call from Weaver. Wait here."

Reginald offered no explanation, just walked out of the room.

"He looks worried," Mike said.

"Aren't you?" Francis asked.

"I mean he looks frightened."

"Men like him don't like mysteries," Francis said. "It comes from a lifetime of being the one behind them."

"So where did he go?" Mike asked.

"I don't know."

Reginald returned two minutes later with a laptop under his arm.

"You have a serious problem on your hands," he said and opened the laptop.

"Oh, Christ!" Francis said.

The page was an online newspaper article in the Burlington Free Press. Francis recognized the diner in the picture. The headline read: *Brutal Murder in Vermont Roadside Diner.*

"That's not all," Reginald said.

The second page was from the Trois-Rivieres News. The article was in French. The title read: *Local Park Warden Feared Missing.*

Francis got up and ran back to the car. He got his briefcase from the trunk and took out the satellite phone, then ran back through the house and out the front door. Mike followed him.

"Come on. Come on!" Francis said. "Hurry up."

A moment later the phone beeped twice and Francis dialed. He listened for a second, then ended the call. "Shit! I should never have taken them there! What the fuck was I thinking?"

"You were trying to protect them," Mike said.

"Not hard enough. I should have checked the papers myself long before now. All I've been thinking about is that damned hard drive."

"Isn't there someone you can call?" Mike asked.

"Yeah, he's dead."

"You need to get in here right away," Reginald said from the doorway.

The phone next to the front door began to ring as soon as they came back inside. Reginald picked it up and said, "What have you got?"

He listened for a moment, then said, "Okay. Where will they be taken?"

Reginald grabbed a pen and wrote something on the notepad next to the phone. "I need you to find out where they'll be moved and when. Call me back as soon as you know."

He put the phone down and turned to Francis. "They're alive. The Quebec State Police called it in a few hours ago. Jesse Corbin was admitted to Saint Joseph Hospital in" -he looked down at what he had written- "in La Tuque sometime this afternoon. The girl is with him."

Francis breathed a long sigh of relief. "Who else knows where they are?"

"The police called the U.S. Consulate in Quebec City, who called the FBI because they're both listed as missing."

"Shit!" Francis said. "Who do you know up there?"

Reginald thought about it and shook his head. "Nobody in that part of the world. Not anyone I'd trust with this."

Mike put up a hand. He looked like a schoolboy volunteering an answer. "I might be able to help."

Both men turned to him.

"If the boy can be moved," Mike said, "the State Department or the Bureau will charter a plane to the nearest airport and fly them both back to the U.S."

"They'll be dead or missing again before that happens," Francis said.

The room went quiet as each of them considered the problem. Mike spoke first. "I've got an idea. It's a little crazy, but it could work."

"Let's hear it," Francis said.

"Do either of you speak French?" Mike asked.

Five minutes later Francis put the phone down, closed his eyes and took a deep breath.

"Did they buy it?" Mike asked.

"I think so," Francis said, but he didn't sound very confident. "The police captain is going to call me as soon as they're on the road."

Reginald came back into the living room a moment later. "It's done. But it's not going to be cheap."

"That doesn't matter," Francis said. "How long will it take him to get there?"

"Four hours at least. He just left for the airport, but he's going to have to file an emergency flight plan and he wasn't too happy about the destination."

"This is really cutting it thin," Francis said. "Shit like this rarely works out the way you want it to."

"Get ready for the hard part," Reginald said.

"What do you mean?" Mike asked.

"Waiting."

# CHAPTER 44

**Lake Commissaires, Quebec**
**Friday 21 July 2006**
**2200 EDT**

The co-pilot signaled to Eugene by pointing a finger down and tapping the air. Eugene moved to the door and slid it open. A rush of cold air filled the cabin and the co-pilot almost lost the map spread out on the control panel in front of him. Eugene leaned out, using his left hand for support. In his right he held the GPS tracker. There was a small screen on it with a red dot in the middle that flashed every few seconds. He looked down and pointed it toward the shore. When he moved it to the left slightly, the dot grew larger and began to flash more rapidly. He signaled for the pilot to move closer.

When they were directly above the thin strip of pebble beach, Eugene held up his hand and the helicopter leveled off. He swung back into the cabin, grabbed a large cylindrical bundle hanging from a harness in the ceiling and pushed it toward the door. When it reached the doorway, the tracks it moved on extended out several feet into open air. Eugene pulled a cord on the bundle and it fell, unfolding into a rope ladder as it descended. He picked up the submachine gun lying on the seat behind him and climbed out.

He dropped the last five feet to the beach, pulled the tracking device out of his jacket and pointed it into the trees then set off at a slow run, adjusting his course as the dot grew larger or smaller. When it turned green and stopped flashing, he put it back into his jacket, unclipped a pair of thick goggles from his belt and put them on, then pulled the machine gun off his shoulder and pointed it straight ahead.

He reached the cabin five minutes later and stopped twenty yards away, scanning the area through the night-vision goggles. When he reached the door he pushed it open with the barrel of the machine gun, sprang forward into a roll and came up on his knees in the middle of the room. Spinning around on his heels, he stood up and spotted the red flashing light on the floor.

Eugene quickly found the tracks leading around the cabin and into the woods. When he reached the crater where the log pile had once stood he looked around for a moment, then walked over the lip and down the slope. He pulled the M16 out of the ground, examined it and threw it aside. At the top he stopped and looked down, then leaned over and prodded the arm lying next to the barrel of the machine gun. He found the rest of the body a minute later.

Eugene fell to his knees, picked up the remains of his dead brother and leaned back, cradling the body in his arms, then turned his head to the sky and let out a scream of rage that pierced the silence of the still night like a bolt of lightning. His whimpers gradually changed into a pleading whine as he rocked back and forth.

After a while he stood and picked the body up in both arms. He focused on the sound of the helicopter and followed it toward the beach. When he reached the water he put the body down gently and pulled a small hand-held radio from the breast pocket of his combat vest. A minute later the end of a climbing rope dropped to the ground a few yards behind him. Eugene tied it around his brother and began to climb.

The helicopter banked sharply and dipped its nose as it began to pick up speed. Neither of the pilots looked back or said a word. Eugene sat down on the floor next to the body and began to stroke the remaining arm like a lunatic repeating some senseless motion for reasons only he can understand. When his phone rang he ignored it. A minute later the pilot turned around and pointed at the headset hanging from a hook in the ceiling. Eugene stared at the man with empty eyes for a moment, then took the headset and put it on. As he listened, his eyes cleared. When the pilot switched the headset from radio back to the intercom Eugene reached forward and tapped him on the shoulder. "Turn around and land at the airport in La Tuque!"

The pilot shook his head and pointed at the fuel gauge. "We don't have enough fuel."

Before the pilot could say anything else Eugene turned and picked up the machine gun. He spun around, raising the steel butt and brought it crashing into the side of the pilot's head. The helicopter banked sharply and spun a hundred and eighty degrees. Eugene reached out and grabbed the pilot's seat to avoid falling back into the cabin. The co-pilot, who had been looking at his chart, grabbed the stick and pulled it up sharply, then reached down and dropped the torque just in time to avoid going into a spin. It took him a moment longer to get her level again. When he turned around he was looking down the barrel of a gun.

"Did you hear what I said?" Eugene asked.

The co-pilot nodded and reached for the map. He peered at it for a minute and pointed. Eugene looked down and nodded.

"We'll never get permission to land," the co-pilot said, now terrified.

"I don't care," Eugene said. "Just let me out and take off again."

The co-pilot glanced at the fuel gauge but said nothing. Much of the instrument panel was covered in blood and there was a growing pool of it spreading around his feet. He consulted the map one more time, then checked something on the instrument panel and sat back, not daring to turn around.

When they were less than two miles from La Tuque, the airport's traffic controller warned them in French not to approach. When he got no response he began to talk faster. The co-pilot turned to look at Eugene, who only shook his head. By the time the runway appeared beneath them the controller was shouting. He repeated the message over and over again, switching from French to English each time. "Unidentified chopper, this is La Tuque tower. We are TFR to unauthorized traffic. Abort your approach."

Eugene jumped out the moment the wheels touched the ground and the helicopter's twin turbines roared as the pilot applied maximum torque and rose back into the air. Two sets of headlights were rushing toward them. Eugene lowered the machine gun to the ground, stepped in front of it and put his hands up.

One of the vehicles was a fire truck, and it slowed to a stop as soon as the helicopter departed. The other was a police car, and it kept coming. They spotted him and stopped ten yards away. Two men got out, their weapons drawn. The one to Eugene's right was dressed in a police uniform, the other in a dark suit. Eugene saw the earpiece he wore reflected in the soft light coming from inside the car. The policeman said something in French. When Eugene didn't answer he looked at the other man.

"Identify yourself," the man said.

If there had been any doubt that the man was an FBI agent, the accent dispelled it. Eugene didn't reply.

The agent stepped around the door and took a few steps in Eugene's direction. After a moment of hesitation the policeman joined him. The agent saw the weapon behind Eugene's feet, but it was too late. Eugene dropped to one knee, picked up the machine gun and rolled to his right as both men opened fire. Their first salvo missed and Eugene put two rounds into the agent's neck before he could correct his aim. The policeman fired a shot that missed Eugene's head by an inch. Eugene rolled forward again and came up on his knees, machine gun raised. "Put the gun on the ground and step forward."

The cop, looking scared to death, did as he was told.

There was a black executive jet parked at the end of the runway under the floodlights outside the small terminal building. Eugene pointed to it. "Is that for the Americans?"

The cop nodded.

Eugene came forward, keeping the gun pointed at him and beckoned for the cop to get in the car, then walked to the other side and got in the back seat. "When will they be taken to the plane?"

"In about ten minutes," the man said in heavily accented English.

"Will they arrive in an ambulance?"

The cop nodded again.

"Turn off the lights and drive to the end of the runway," Eugene said.

When they reached the perimeter fence there was a burst of French from the police car's radio.

"Tell them there is nobody here, but you're checking the area to make sure," Eugene said.

"Zey are saying zey hear gunshots," the policeman said.

"Tell them the American fired at the helicopter. They'll believe that."

The cop picked up the microphone and spoke. There was a brief reply, then the cop said, "Zey believe it."

A minute later two sets of blue flashing lights arrived through the main gate and approached the plane. Eugene reached forward, grabbed the cop's head with both hands and broke his neck.

He drove toward the plane, keeping his speed down to twenty. When he got closer he saw two more men, clones of the one he had shot, standing near the foldout steps of the plane. They saw the police car, but only gave it a brief glance, more preoccupied with the ambulance. He watched it approach, followed by another police car. All three vehicles stopped only a few feet from each other. The back doors opened and a paramedic stepped out of the ambulance. Eugene waited for another ten seconds, then got out himself.

He ran to the ambulance and stopped behind it, shielding himself from everyone but the man in the police car. He rounded the corner and kicked the paramedic in the small of the back, sending the man flying forward onto the ground. The officer was half out of his car when Eugene shot him in the head and ran back to the other police car. He stepped around the trunk just in time to see both men outside the plane reach for their guns and run toward the ambulance. He shot them both twice in the back and returned to the ambulance.

Eugene flung open the back doors, pointed the machine gun at the figure on the gurney and pulled the trigger. He emptied the entire magazine into it, screaming at the top of his lungs. When the gun fell silent he jumped in and pulled off the sheet. There was nothing there but several stacks of folded white bed linen. Bellowing a scream of frustration, he jumped out and looked into the escorting police car. It was empty. He ran to the front of the ambulance and looked in but there was nobody there either, then spotted the paramedic trying to crawl beneath the ambulance. Eugen brought his boot down on the man's ankle, breaking it in two places.

"Where are the Americans?" he screamed.

The paramedic was too busy screaming himself to respond. Eugene grabbed him by his broken ankle and pulled him back out. He repeated the question several times before he noticed the paramedic had fainted. He looked over at the plane, then at the gate leading out of the airport, deliberated for a moment, then headed toward the plane.

One of the pilots was stepping out of the cabin door just as Eugene reached the steps. He saw Eugene, saw the machine gun in his hands and ran back inside. Eugene caught up with him just as he reached the cockpit. The co-pilot was busy trying to talk to the frantic air-traffic controller. When he saw Eugene he dropped the microphone.

"Take off!" Eugene said. Neither man replied. They began turning switches and dials while the panicked voice of the air-traffic controller went on asking questions and demanding answers. The pilot stood up and pointed behind Eugene.

"We can't start the engines while the door is open," he said, sounding both apologetic and scared.

Eugene stepped aside to let him through. As soon as the pilot came back and sat down, the engines began to spin up.

"The tower will alert the air force," the pilot said.

"Don't worry about that," Eugene said. "Just get this thing in the air."

The pilot shut the radio off and the frantic babbling stopped. A moment later the lights on the runway went out. Both pilots stopped what they were doing and looked up.

"I'm going to kill one of you if this plane doesn't take off in the next thirty seconds," Eugene said.

The pilots looked at each other, then the one who had closed the door put his hand on the throttle levers. They edged forward until the nose was pointing straight down the runway. He pushed the throttles all the way forward and the engines roared as the plane began to roll. Through the window the lines on the runway, illuminated only by the light on the landing gear, ticked past faster and faster until they became a solid white blur. Just as the pilot pulled back on the controls, the front wheels hit something, but only hard enough to send a shudder through the plane before it rose into the air.

# CHAPTER 45

**La Tuque, Quebec**
**Friday 21 July 2006**
**2200 EDT**

Amanda sat by the bed watching as the nurse pushed a cannula into Jesse's left arm and taped it down. Jesse was sitting up and watching the procedure with a distant, bleary-eyed curiosity.

When the doctor arrived, two uniformed police officers were with him. One of them was carrying the backpack Amanda had left in the ambulance. The doctor said something to the officers and they left. He examined the wound in Jesse's arm as well as the cuts on his face and his bruised neck. Satisfied, he directed the nurse to dress the arm and tend to the cuts, then left.

Amanda was on the verge of falling asleep herself when the door opened and a middle-aged man wearing a ceremonial police officer's uniform stepped inside. He closed the door gently and introduced himself as Captain Dupille, the local chief of police. He handed Amanda a printed sheet of paper with the logo of the US State Department on it. It was a picture of both her and Jesse. She recognized her own as one taken by her mother a few years earlier outside their home. The picture of Jesse looked like it might have come out of the high school yearbook. The captain spoke fairly decent English. He explained that arrangements were being made to fly them home as soon as Jesse could be moved. Amanda was too dumbstruck to say anything. When the doctor returned a minute later, the captain said something to him in French and he nodded.

"It's not really a good idea to move him so soon," the doctor said to Amanda. "But your people seem very determined to get you home. I read about what happened in Vermont in the papers, although it didn't explain what happened to the two of you."

"What happened in Vermont?" Amanda asked, as if she had no idea what he was talking about.

"You don't know?"

She shook her head.

"Then it's probably not my place to tell you," the doctor said.

"No. Tell me," Amanda insisted.

The doctor turned to the captain, who only shrugged.

"Several people were killed; a terrorist group, drug dealers. It's been all over the news. And a woman was murdered, too."

"And what are they saying about us?" Amanda asked.

"They say you made a call to the police on Monday night and nobody has seen you since. I have the paper downstairs if you want to read it."

Amanda's face had gone blank.

"Are you okay?" the doctor asked.

"I'm fine," Amanda said. "It's just coming as a bit of a shock."

"Of course."

"We just want to go home," Amanda said and gave him a smile that suggested the conversation was over.

"The main thing is that you're okay," the doctor said. "I've told the police you're free to go, but you'll need to keep the drip on him until the bag is empty. It'll take a few hours."

With that, both men left the room.

Amanda turned back to Jesse and saw he had been listening. The vacant look was gone and he was smiling at her.

"Some getaway, huh?" he said. The words came out a little slurred, but she could see he was lucid.

"They're flying us home," she said. "To Vermont."

Jesse shook his head slowly. "Not a good idea."

"Why not?"

"It wasn't safe there when we left. How do we know anything has changed?"

Amanda had no response to that. Jesse raised his left hand and stroked her face. She leaned her head forward and closed her eyes.

"Who do you think we were running from?" he asked. "And doesn't it strike you as strange that no one here has even asked us where we have been?"

She opened her eyes and looked at him, frowning. "You think these people are part of it?"

"I don't know," Jesse said. "But if the police were a safe bet, why did we run when we could have just gone to the sheriff's office?"

"Then what the hell are we supposed to do?" Amanda said.

Jesse looked down at the tube running into his arm. "I can't do anything. But you can."

The look on her face was a mixture of shock and anger. She shook her head. "If you think I'm going to leave you here, you've lost your mind, Jesse Corbin."

"We're not safe here," he said. "If they can find us in the middle of nowhere, don't you think they'll find us here?"

She stood up and turned away. When she turned back there were tears in her eyes. "Stop saying that! I don't want to fucking hear it. I'm not going anywhere and you can't make me."

Before Jesse could say anything else, the police captain returned. He saw Amanda and stopped. "I've arrived in a bad moment. Please excuse me. But I'm afraid we must go. Your plane is waiting."

Two more officers came into the room behind him. One was pushing a wheelchair, the other still had the backpack.

They helped Jesse out of the bed and into the chair. One of the officers pulled the IV bag off its hook, and Amanda stepped forward to take it. When they emerged from the building into the cool night air, the captain took one of his officers aside and spoke to him in guarded tones. The man nodded and walked to one of the two police cars parked next to an ambulance just outside the doors. The other officer put the backpack down and went back inside. He returned with a stack of folded sheets and walked to the back of the ambulance. The captain was talking to the paramedic by the driver's door. They seemed to be having a heated discussion about something. The captain raised his voice and shouted something at the paramedic, who turned around and got in behind the wheel. The officer with the sheets climbed into the back of the ambulance and began stacking them in bundles on the gurney. When he had spread them evenly he took the last one, unfolded it and spread it on top of the rest. Amanda and Jesse watched this bizarre chain of events unfold with puzzled amusement.

The officer who had done the trick with the sheets jumped out and closed the back doors, then pushed Jesse's wheelchair past the ambulance to the back door of the other police car. The captain joined them and opened it.

"We must go," he said. "I will explain on the way."

The two officers helped Jesse into the back of the car and Amanda climbed in next to him. The captain got in on the passenger's side.

Once they were on the road, the captain called someone on his cell phone and spoke to them briefly in French. A few minutes later, they passed the local airport and saw what looked like a helicopter hovering above the runway. The captain looked up and said something to the driver. Amanda couldn't understand the words but he sounded incredulous. She looked out the back window and watched as the helicopter rose into the air, then they rounded a corner and it disappeared from view.

"This is a precaution," the captain said, turning back to look at them. "The plane taking you home is at Trois-Rivieres, about two hours down this road. The one waiting for you here is, how do you say, a decoy?"

- - -

Jesse was asleep when they arrived. A security guard waved the car through the gate and they drove past the small terminal building straight onto the runway. A white executive jet sat at the end of it. As they got closer, they could hear the engines were already turning over.

A man was standing at the top of the airstair. He wore jeans, a blue denim shirt and a cowboy hat as white, and almost as big, as the plane. He descended the steps, took a cigar from his breast pocket and lit it with a Zippo lighter, turning it in his hand and sucking to get it going. The captain got out and the two men spoke for a moment, then the captain signaled for the driver to get out. The man in the hat stepped aside and let them carry Jesse up the steps. He took the cigar out of his mouth, spat a strand of tobacco onto the ground and winked at Amanda.

"How do, ma'am?" he asked in a thick Texas drawl.

"You're with the State Department?" she asked.

His eyes widened in mock surprise. "Hell, no!"

"Then who are you?"

"My instructions are to say that Maurice sent me. I don't know no Maurice, but I have it on good authority that he's the one paying the bill."

At the sound of that name Amanda felt a weight lift from her heart. She smiled and moved a step closer. "So what are you? Some kind of mercenary?"

He laughed and took a long drag on his cigar. "I've been called worse, but not by anyone quite as purty as yourself. Come on, time's a wastin' and this thing drinks fuel like a burning oil well."

He stubbed the cigar out on the heel of his boot and Amanda followed him up the steps.

"You got a name, Mister?" she asked.

"Name's George. But you can just call me Captain."

The inside of the plane was lavishly decorated in white and cream. There were several large chairs upholstered in tan leather that Amanda thought looked more comfortable than La-Z Boys. The police captain and his deputy had helped Jesse into one of them, but the junior man was stuck holding the IV bag. Amanda took it and the police captain shooed him out.

"I should be getting back," he said.

Amanda considered asking him who had ordered him to take them here, but didn't. She had a sneaking suspicion this man wasn't a collaborator at all, but someone who might very well be out of a job by the time the sun came up.

"Thank you for your help," she said.

"Not at all. It's my pleasure," he said and walked back to the door. "Perhaps you put in a good word for me, yes?"

She gave him a smile and a little wave. "I will."

"Bon voyage!"

George came out of the cockpit and pushed a button beside the door. A motor whirred and the door started closing. He looked over and saw Amanda's predicament.

"Just a sec," he said and disappeared back into the cockpit. He returned with two bungee cords and improvised a support for the IV bag above Jesse's head.

"Thanks," Jesse said. "Mandy tells me you're one of the good guys."

"Does she now? Well, that's very sweet of her." George said. "But you may want to save the ticker tape parade for the man who's footing the bill."

"Maurice?" Jesse asked.

"Yeah, Maurice. You guys must have been in a real jam."

"So you're a gun for hire." Jesse said.

"Son, I'm a pilot for hire. If you can find a gun on this plane you can shoot me with it. As a god-fearing man, I'm all for charitable deeds, but this is a thirty-five million dollar airplane and I've already broken the law twice getting here."

"Jesus," Jesse said.

"Nope. General Dynamics. But I reckon if Noah had been told to build an executive jet instead of an ark, it would have looked a lot like this one. Best damn plane I've ever flown. Now if you kids don't mind, I need to get us out of here before the Canuck air guard shows up."

They were airborne in less than five minutes. Jesse was asleep before the landing gear had retracted. Amanda found a towel in the small bathroom at the back of the plane and cleaned his face, then sat holding his hand and looking out into the darkness through the window. By the time they crossed the border into the United States she was asleep herself.

She woke to find George standing over her with a can of Coke in his hand. She looked up the aisle then down at the door of the cockpit.

"Auto-pilot," George said, "Don't worry, we're in good hands"

He handed her the can. "Thought you might be thirsty. I've also got food if you're hungry."

Amanda took the can. "Where are we going?"

"Merritt Island," George said as if that might actually mean anything to her.

"Okay. Which is?"

"It's about a stone's throw from Disney World."

"We're going to Florida?"

"That was the deal."

"Is Maurice there?"

"Little lady, I don't ask too many questions. I find the less I know, the better. But *someone* will be there. I ain't about to just drop you off and leave."

"How long will it take to get there?" she asked.

"Another three hours, give or take."

In the seat beside her, Jesse stirred and opened his eyes.

"Hey, mister sleepyhead," she said. "You'll never guess where we're going."

# CHAPTER 46

**Churchton, Maryland**
**Saturday 22 July 2006**
**0200 EDT**

Norton Weaver put the phone down and adjusted the blanket over his legs. Beyond the trees at the back of the garden the Chesapeake Bay sparkled beneath a cloudless, moonlit sky. The porch door opened and Edith, his wife of thirty-six years, dressed only in her bathrobe, walked out with a tray in her hands. She put it down on the table beside him. "Norton, you should come inside, dear. You'll catch a cold."

She put a hand on his shoulder and he covered it with his own.

"I won't be long," he said. "Go ahead. I'll be in in a minute."

When she was gone he took a sip of tea and looked back down at the paper in his lap.

The message had arrived just after midnight. It was a copy of a wire from the State Department containing an initial and sketchy outline of the events in La Tuque. The missing pieces weren't hard to fill in.

The Zimmerman brothers, two of the best operatives Norton had ever seen, were both dead. He didn't need the camera footage from the airport to know Baruch had been the one who crashed the party and hijacked the plane. The reason didn't require a great deal of deduction either. Although how things had gone so wrong so quickly beggared belief. The real bitch of it was, he needed them now more than ever. The loss of Princip had done little to moderate the appetite of the Whitehouse for an in-house laundry crew, willing and able to remove obstacles no one else could. And Norton had all but sold them on the idea of bringing his little side project in to meet the demand. Explaining what had happened was going to be hard enough without having to also renege on his promises.

When the phone began to ring, Norton signed and slowly reached for the receiver.

"Weaver."

"Sir, the plane is down."

"Good. We need to recover the bodies before the NTSB arrives. What about the helicopter?"

"No sign of it so far. We'll keep looking. There's something else."

"What?"

"The local police captain is claiming that Jesse Corbin and the Hinsdale girl weren't on the plane."

"What do you mean?"

"He says he received a call from the State Department asking him to take them to another airfield down the road in Three Rivers. Says he took them down there himself."

"What fucking plane?"

"We don't know. Air traffic control has no records of a flight to or from the area. Looks like it sneaked in under the ceiling."

"Jesus Christ," Weaver said. "Of all the fucking people on earth, why did it have to be the Canadians? Call whoever you need to. Just find that plane. And get someone out there to pick up the idiot who drove them down there."

"I'm on it, boss. What do you want to do about Fielding?"

"Find him. I want to know what was taken out of that vault."

"And Fairchild?"

"Don't worry about him. I'll deal with Fairchild."

Weaver set the phone back down and saw his wife standing behind the screen door.

"Is everything okay, darling?" she asked.

"Everything's fine. Go to bed. I'll be up in a minute."

# CHAPTER 47

**Orlando, Florida**
**Saturday 22 July 2006**
**0330 EDT**

Reginald put the phone down and looked at Mike and Francis. "Bird's in the air."

Francis breathed a sigh of relief and patted Mike on the back. "Looks like my two heads theory is working out."

"You mean three heads," Mike said, looking at Reginald.

"No, I mean two," Francis said. "It was your idea and Reginald here made it work."

Reginald wrote something down and handed the paper to Francis along with a folded Florida state road map. "They'll be landing at Merritt Island Airport. I've circled it. It's about an hour east of here. You need to use the freight entrance and show them this at the gate."

He handed Francis a white tag the size of a playing card. "Ask for directions to the maintenance hangar and park inside. If anyone asks what you're doing, hand them that and say nothing. The pilot's name is George. He'll taxi to the hangar. The tail number is on the paper. When you've got the kids, hand him this."

Reginald gave Francis a thick brown envelope.

"You know I'm good for this, right?" Francis said.

"I know. He won't count it. Tell him Bob sends his regards then get the hell out of there."

"Have I met George before?" Francis asked.

"No. He's not Ivy League. Strictly homegrown."

Francis picked up the keys from the coffee table and handed Mike the CD. "You guys may want to take a look at this while I'm gone."

Mike took the disc and felt a shiver run up his spine. It was hard to imagine that something so seemingly innocuous could be at the center of everything that had happened. Stored on that disc was a secret that at least ten people had already died for.

They watched through the window until the car disappeared from view. Reginald walked over to the fireplace and picked up his pipe. "Your family is safe."

"I want to believe that," Mike said. "But Francis also seemed to think those kids were safe."

"The kids were unprotected. Your wife and boy aren't. I can vouch for the people taking care of them."

"Where did you meet Francis?" Mike asked.

Reginald considered the question. He lit his pipe and gave Mike a long, thoughtful look. "In a bomb shelter in Lebanon."

"You were his boss, weren't you? He calls you 'Colonel'.""

"I recruited him. He was a second lieutenant back then, nineteen years old. His three best friends died in the embassy bombing."

"Recruited him into what?"

Reginald took a long drag on his pipe and sat down in the rocking chair. "A little side project over at the Pentagon."

"You assassinated people," Mike said.

Reginald looked at him in surprise. "He told you that?"

"He told me he killed a woman once," Mike said. "A pregnant woman."

Reginald raised his eyebrows and put the pipe down. "Did he mention he was told she was a left-wing radical plotting to kill a Supreme Court Justice?"

"No. He said she was innocent."

"She was. But he didn't know that until much later. It's why he left. One of the reasons, anyway. God knows there turned out to be plenty."

"I'm not surprised," Mike said. "You turned him into fucking Jason Bourne."

"If you're suggesting he was brain washed, I can assure you he wasn't. Well, not chemically anyway."

"So how did he get out?" Mike said. "It doesn't seem like the kind of job you just quit."

"He killed himself," Reginald said and shook his head in wonder.

Mike just looked at him, frowning.

"He staged his own death. Right here in Florida. Fooled us all."

"You thought he was dead when we showed up here?"

"As a doornail."

Mike laughed and turned his eyes up. "It makes me wonder if the Bureau really knows anything about what goes on in this country."

Reginald didn't answer. He stood up and held out his hand. "What do you say we take a look at that disc."

# CHAPTER 48

**Aurora**
**Saturday 22 July 2006**
**1100 EEST**

Mitch woke to the smell of frying bacon. He was lying on a king size bed in a lavishly decorated room that appeared to have been imported from the 1950s.

"Hello?" he said.

There was no answer.

He lifted the blanket and saw he was naked. On the chair beside the bed there was a pair of underwear and socks sitting on top of a neatly folded dark blue jumpsuit. He got out of bed and stood up, felt the world swim away, and sat back down. When the feeling passed he tried again.

To his surprise the jumpsuit was a perfect fit.

"Hello?" he said again.

The smell of bacon grew stronger as he neared the door. The hall outside ended on a large open-plan kitchen, every bit as Art Deco as the bedroom. A woman was standing at the stove with her back to him. Her long, blonde hair was tied into a ponytail that ran almost to her waist. She, too, was wearing a jumpsuit, but hers was white.

"Hello?"

"Good morning," she said cheerfully, turning to face him. "I thought you might be hungry."

"Where the hell am I?" Mitch asked.

She regarded him with a kind of eerie intensity, as if what she saw would have some bearing on the answer to his question. Then she smiled and said, "I'm not really supposed to answer that. I'm just here to make sure you're ready."

"Ready for what?"

"The chief wants to see you."

"The chief of what?"

She turned back to the stove without answering the question and scooped several slices of bacon onto a plate.

"Do you have a name?" Mitch asked.

The question seemed to make her blush. She closed her eyes and stood thinking for a moment as if trying to remember what it was. Then she walked up to him, put out her hand and said, "I'm Sarah, and I'm pleased to make your acquaintance."

To his amusement she then asked, "Was that proper?"

"It was fine. My name's-"

"You're Mitchell Stuart Rainey," she said proudly. "From Phoenix in Arizona."

Mitch was too bemused by this to know what to say.

When she offered him the plate, Mitch didn't think he would be able to eat. But that turned out not to be the case. Sarah sat watching him as if it were the first time she had seen anyone eat. When he was done she leaned her elbows on the table, put her chin in her hands and said, "You have the most beautiful eyes. They're so green."

Mitch almost choked on his orange juice and began to blush. This seemed to amuse her further. She twisted her head slightly and said, "What's it like? Arizona, I mean. Have you been to the Grand Canyon?"

"More times than I care to remember," Mitch said, "Where are *you* from?"

The question seemed to confuse her.

"From here," she said, as if this were obvious.

"Is this your place?" he asked.

"Of course not, silly. It's yours."

"Mine? I don't think so. For one, I would remember. And even if I didn't, I'm not that into the whole retro thing."

"Come see," she said.

She took his hand and led him to the front door. It opened onto a narrow white hallway. Directly across the hall there was an identical door with a brass plaque on it that said: 45 – Sarah. The sign on his own door said 46 – Mitch.

"This is yours," she said matter-of-factly. "And that's mine."

Mitch couldn't take his eyes off the plaque. His sanity seemed to be under assault from several different directions at once. Part of it was just disorientation, he knew. But it was also more than that. His conscious mind insisted it would pass, and it probably would have. But then the door at the end of the hall opened and in walked the chief.

The irrational conviction that stole over Mitch as the man approached them was that he, Mitch, had died and woken up on the set of Last Tango in Paris, so uncanny was the resemblance of the man to a middle-aged Marlon Brando.

The chief was roughly Mitch's height, but twice his size. His coveralls were olive drab, pressed to perfection. The toecaps of his boots had been polished into orbs of black glass and his graying hair was cut in a flattop so flat it looked like a stage prop. When he spoke, the accent was pure Louisiana drawl, the kind where "lion," "lying," and "line" all came out sounding exactly the same.

The chief acknowledged Sarah with a slight nod of the head and turned his attention to Mitch. "Mr. Rainey, come with me please."

Mitch looked at Sarah, who only offered him a sympathetic smile. Then he followed the chief, noting with some trepidation how the man walked with one thumb propped on the butt of the revolver at his waist.

"I'm Chief Lancaster," the chief said without turning to look at Mitch. "I might as well tell you now that you were brought here against my better judgment."

They walked up two flights of stairs and down another narrow hallway with several unmarked doors. When they reached the door at the end the chief took a blank plastic card from his pocket and held it to the plate just above the handle.

Mitch felt another one of those ripples in the fabric of reality as he stepped from the nondescript hall into the chief's office.

Like the apartment, the place had an unmistakable motif, although this room looked more like the Pentagon circa 1980 than 1950s Hollywood. The desk facing the door was at least eight feet wide and made of gray painted steel. With the exception of a black leather blotter and a Montblanc pen in a brass stand, it was empty. The walls on either side of the desk were a montage of picture frames in a variety of colors and sizes, but they all had one thing in common: each had a clear military undertone. Most were of people in uniform, either posing for the shot or shaking hands with the chief, who appeared to be in uniform in every single picture. Mitch thought he recognized one of these as the late Ho Chi Min.

The chief beckoned to one of the chairs in front of the desk. "Have a seat."

"I'd like to know where I am." Mitch said.

The chief pulled a flat silver tin from one of the drawers, snapped it open and took out a small cigar, then spent several seconds lighting it with an old brass Zippo. He sat back and regarded Mitch with eerie gray eyes. "Where you are is not important. Why you are here is. Do you know why you are here, Mr. Rainey?"

"I'm guessing it has something to do with Bruce Jessops?" Mitch said.

The chief was shaking his head. "Wrong. You were brought here because you broke the law. You were brought here because you violated your own code of conduct and went looking at things that didn't concern you."

"I'm pretty sure tapping the private phone line of a US Citizen is also against the law," Mitch said.

The chief took an ashtray from his desk and flicked the end of his cigar into it. "Son, I've been dealing with smart-asses all my life, so you can quit while you're ahead. One bad turn deserves another, Mr. Rainey. That was true long before Jesus felt the need to point it out. Whatever you think you're entitled to know, the fact remains that you broke the law. And in doing so, you have put us in a very awkward position."

"Us?" Mitch said.

The chief stood and stubbed out the cigar. "It has been decided that you will not be confined for the time you are here. Again, not my choice. However, if you venture out of your assigned quarters, it is to be in the company of either Miss Breland, who will continue to act as your host, or another member of staff. If these conditions are violated, I will see to it that you lose that privilege."

"I don't mean to sound ungrateful," Mitch said. "But I don't even know where *here* is. If it's not too much to ask, I think I'm at least entitled to know that much."

The chief turned to the wall behind his desk and pushed a button below a large watercolor painting depicting an enormous herd of buffalo racing across the great American plains. The picture began to rise inside the frame.

As Mitch approached the opening window, the confusion he had felt, the anger, all the questions, evaporated as his mouth fell open and his eyes grew wide.

"Welcome to Aurora," the chief said.

# CHAPTER 49

**Merritt Island, Florida**
**Saturday 22 July 2006**
**0600 EDT**

The plane landed at seven. Francis sat behind the wheel of the Cobalt and watched the sleek aircraft glide to a halt outside the hangar doors. When the airlock opened a man in jeans and a white cowboy hat stepped out. He said something to the waiting crewman, who nodded and left. Francis met him halfway and held out the envelope. "Bob sends his regards."

George took the envelope and tucked it under one arm, then removed the stub of a cigar from his breast pocket and lit it.

"Tell him it's been a pleasure," George said. "I mean that."

"How did you get on with the cargo?" Francis asked.

"Like a house on fire. Real sweet kids, those two. I don't even want to know what they've gotten themselves mixed up in."

"I take it you don't follow the news."

"Only Bloomberg. And the FT, if I'm desperate."

"You might not be able to avoid this one," Francis said. "It's going to make headlines."

George went back to the plane and emerged a minute later with two people Francis hardly recognized. Jesse looked pale and unsteady on his feet. There was a cannula in his left hand and he was holding an empty IV bag. Amanda looked much better, despite her attire and tangled hair. She smiled when she saw him and gave him a little wave. It filled him with an enormous sense of guilt. They came down the steps together, Jesse leaning on Amanda for support. When they reached the tarmac she surprised Francis by giving him a hug.

"I'm glad to see you, too," Francis said.

Jesse moved the IV bag to his right hand and held out his left.

"I think we owe you a thank you," he said.

Francis took his hand and squeezed it gently, shaking his head. "I'm the one who should be thanking *you*."

"I guess we did all right," Jesse said.

"I don't know *what* you did," Francis said. "But whatever it was, it was a hell of a lot more than all right. When you're up to it, I'd like to hear everything."

George came back down the steps holding their backpack and handed it to Francis, who slung it over his shoulder.

"Don't mean to be rude," George said. "But I need to refuel and be on my way."

Amanda turned around and gave him a hug. "You're an all right kind of guy, George."

They said their goodbyes; George walked back up the steps and vanished behind the closing door. A moment later the plane taxied away. Francis offered to help Jesse to the car, but he insisted on walking by himself. A smile crept onto Francis's face as he led them across the floor of the hangar. The boy was no longer a boy, and his pride had taken a compensatory leap.

They headed back along State Road 528. Jesse sat up front. Another point to be proven, Francis thought. When they passed the tollbooth Jesse said, "I don't think the man who came after us was human."

Francis looked at him with raised eyebrows, "What makes you say that?"

Jesse recounted the entire event. Francis looked at him a couple of times with something that was maybe astonishment and maybe even a little trepidation. When Jesse was finished Francis shook his head in wonder.

"And to think I told you not to touch the grenades," he said.

"I always thought of fear as something that paralyzes you," Jesse said. "But I felt the opposite. It was like my mind focused more sharply than ever and then I wasn't scared at all, just angry."

Francis knew exactly what he meant. One of the first things Reginald had taught him was that fear couldn't be eliminated, but it could be conquered and used. It had taken him over a year of training under some of the most grueling conditions imaginable to fully understand what that had actually meant. It made what Jesse had described all the more incredible.

They had sent one man to find them, and that man would have been expecting Francis, not the boy. He would also have been the best they had. The speed with which he'd discovered their whereabouts left no doubt of that in Francis's mind. Luck and surprise had played their part, but such things always did. Francis would have died many times over by now if he hadn't had plenty of both over the years. But while he, Francis, would have been able to make the best use of every advantage, Jesse had been acting on pure instinct in a state of near terror. He was both in awe of Jesse and a little ashamed for thinking of him in terms of his own experiences. The last thing he wanted was for Jesse to emulate him and become someone who could never quite give up the idea of killing a man as an entirely bad one. That road ended in a slow death of the conscience.

They arrived at the house to find Mike standing in the doorway smoking a cigarette. When the car was in the garage Francis led them into the living room and Mike came back inside. Francis introduced everyone and a rather awkward moment passed in which no one knew quite what to say.

Mike broke the silence. "Francis, I need to talk to you."

"Francis?" Jesse and Amanda said in perfect unison.

The moment was lost on Mike, but Francis held up his hands. "You got me."

"I think I like Eddie or Maurice better," Amanda said.

Mike was visibly impatient.

"Whatever it is, Mike, just go ahead and say it," Francis said. "We're all in this together."

"Reginald's been making a few calls. He's - I don't know - he's a little freaked out."

"Who's Reginald?" Amanda asked.

"A friend of mine," Francis said. "This is his house. He's been having a look at the stuff on the hard drive while we were gone."

Reginald appeared in the entrance to the hallway. "And here we are. Safe at last"

Another awkward silence fell over the room.

"Yep, here we are," Amanda said.

Again, it was Francis who stepped in. "This would probably be a great time to head up to SeaWorld and spend a few days getting to know each other. Because that's obviously out of the question, I suggest we all listen to what Reginald has to say. It's the reason we're here, after all."

Reginald picked up his pipe.

"Take a seat," he said, pointing at the couch.

They all sat down, Jesse next to Amanda on one side, and Francis and Mike on the other. When they all looked comfortable and suitably impatient, Reginald lit his pipe and sat down in the rocking chair. For a long moment he just sat there chewing the stub of the pipe and looking grim. When he looked at them all again he seemed unsure of how to proceed. "Okay. Feel free to pitch in at any time if you have questions. You all know about the hard drive and where it came from, so we'll ignore that for the moment. It contains mainly pictures and technical diagrams. Most of it appears to be random. A few satellites, a dock crane, and so on. There are also a few pictures of a Victor-class nuclear powered Russian submarine. Nothing you can't find on the Web, in other words. The schematic drawings are a little more specific. One of them is actually a highly detailed plan for the retrofitting of a Victor with a loading hatch. Don't ask me what that means, because I haven't got a clue. There is, however, a common denominator and that's Skyline Defense."

"What's that?" Jesse asked.

Reginald looked at Francis, who said, "Just run us through it briefly."

"All right. Skyline is an American company based in New York, although in reality it belongs to a Zurich-based foundation with very deep pockets. They design, consult on and provide engineering support in all fields of space-related technology. They work with NASA, The European Space Agency, The Russian Federal Space Agency and even the Chinese. During my time at the Pentagon there were even rumors that Skyline was lobbying to resurrect the Strategic Defense Initiative."

Amanda raised her hand like a pupil in a classroom and Jesse said, "It's a program Reagan began that was supposed to create a space-based defense shield against Russian nukes. Total waste of money."

Amanda smiled, squeezed his left hand, mouthing the words "thank you."

Reginald nodded. "That's right. Anyway, Skyline is a relatively minor player in the space game. I'm still waiting for a couple of people to get back to me, but what I've found out so far suggests they're more diverse than most people know. It has forty-three subsidiaries. A few of them are openly acknowledged, but the rest are hard to find. And if I found forty-three, you can bet there are more. Most of them are related to the company's primary activities, but a few aren't. They own a Finish maritime salvage and refit company based in Kotka on the Baltic Sea, which makes you wonder about the Victor drawings. They also own a Russian munitions manufacturer, a private university outside Sao Paolo in Brazil, and a small but highly successful company called Albion in California that manufactures water desalination systems. All four of these companies appear in the technical drawings on the drive."

Reginald sat back and re-lit his pipe.

"That's it?" Jesse asked.

"What about the encrypted files?" Francis said.

Reginald raised a finger. "I'm getting to that. I just wanted to get the things that make at least some shred of sense out of the way first."

Mike and Reginald shared a knowing look, while Francis, Jesse and Amanda just sat there looking perplexed.

"What are you talking about?" Jesse said.

"Come with me," Reginald said and stood up.

They followed him down the hall and into a spacious office lined on three sides with floor-to-ceiling mahogany bookshelves. Only one shelf in the entire room had any space left for more books. Against the remaining wall, below a large window looking out over a thick wood of slash pines, was an old writing desk with an enormous LCD computer monitor in the middle. Reginald sat down at the desk and they all gathered around.

"Ready for the weird part?" Reginald said.

No one answered.

"Okay, here we go. The hard drive Francis..."

Reginald hesitated and looked at Francis.

"Stole," Amanda said. "The hard drive Francis stole. I think we can dispense with the politeness under the circumstances, don't you guys? Or are we going to stand here and have a circle-jerk?"

She looked around, and smiled when she caught Francis's eye. There was no sarcasm or malevolence in it, just determination.

"Fine, I stole it," Francis said.

"Okay," Reginald continued. "So the hard drive Francis *stole* is old. It only has a capacity of just over three hundred megabytes, which by today's standards is nothing. The images and drawing files use just under half of it. The rest is taken up by four raw image files, each over thirty-five megabytes in size. The files are encrypted, which is why you couldn't open them. But the technology used to do it is even older than the drive, so breaking it was easy. I would have said they were digitally created because what they show can't be taken seriously, but they appear to be video stills. That doesn't mean they are real, but it does make you wonder. And the timing is a little too perfect to be a coincidence."

"Timing?" Francis said.

"You'll see what I mean in a moment."

Reginald moved the mouse cursor over the first of four files in the folder open on the screen and double-clicked.

It was a picture of a planet, its surface a marbled texture of rust reds, browns and grays.

"This is-"

"Jupiter," Jesse said. "It's Jupiter."

"That's right," Reginald said. "The most likely source of the image is Voyager II, the NASA space probe launched in 1977. It passed Jupiter in July 1979. Keep your eye on the top left hand corner."

Reginald maximized the folder and opened the second image.

It was the same picture, only in this one there as a small spec in the corner.

"Look like anything?" Reginald said.

Everyone shook their heads.

Reginald opened the third picture.

Now the spec looked more like a black line. "See it now?"

Everyone nodded. Jesse stepped closer and squinted at the screen. "Are we supposed to believe that's a – you know."

"Go on," Reginald said. "A what?"

"Okay, a spaceship. Are we supposed to believe that's a spaceship?"

Reginald didn't answer. He put his hand back on the mouse and zoomed in on the spot.

They stood looking at the screen for a long time, nobody saying a word. Mike and Reginald had already seen the picture, but they still looked just as dumbfounded as the others. A full minute went by before Jesse said, "Impossible. I mean, it's clearly meant to be a spaceship, I can see that. But it can't be real."

"I said exactly the same thing when I saw it," Mike said. "Then I remembered that several people had been killed by someone who wanted these pictures back. Can you explain that?"

"No, I can't," Jesse said. "I admit this whole thing is crazy. But I stopped believing in aliens when I was ten, and it's going to take more than that picture to change my mind."

"Mike?" Francis said.

Mike looked up from the screen and blinked like a man coming out of a trance. "What?"

"What's your take on it?"

Mike put a hand over his mouth, exhaled through his nose and shook his head slowly. "I don't know. I was ready for a lot of things, but this – I don't know. This is nuts."

"Reginald?" Francis said. "You got anything to say? Know anyone down at Groom Lake who might be able to give us a hand here?"

Reginald laughed. "No, actually. I don't."

"Groom Lake is another name for Area Fifty-One," Jesse said to Amanda.

She looked around at them. "Anyone care what I think?"

They all turned to her.

"I think that last week I was a junior at Penn State studying for a degree in sociology. I went home, went out for a drink, pulled over to help a woman who gave us a goddamned hard drive and a couple of hundred grand, got dragged out of bed in the middle of the night and whisked off to a cabin in Canada with fucking night vision cameras in the chimney. I was then shot at by a one-armed man, I hitchhiked to a town where the police chief handed us over to a cowboy with a jet airplane who flew us to Disney World. Right now, I'm prepared to believe Santa Claus was behind 9/11. And that thing, whatever it is, that's just a given. That's well within the norm at this point."

Nobody said anything for a long time, then Francis, Mike and Reginald all laughed, took one look at her face and stopped.

"Seriously, guys," she said. "We need to find someone who knows what they're talking about and show them that disc. If they say it's bullshit, fine, we're back where we started. Which appears to be nowhere."

Francis studied her with a clear sense of respect. "She's right. And what I suggest we do before we discuss where to go from here is get some sleep. I don't know about you guys, but I can hardly keep my eyes open."

Reginald put Jesse and Amanda in the spare bedroom and Mike in his own. When Francis suggested they stay up and discuss strategy for a while, Reginald handed him a blanket and pointed at the living room. "Tired men don't think straight. I'm sure we must have covered that at some point."

Francis considered arguing the point, took one look at his former boss, and grabbed the blanket. "Four hours, no more. Make sure you wake me up."

- - -

Everyone but Jesse was up by noon. They were sitting around the large table in Reginald's garden eating a cold lunch of ham sandwiches and potato chips. Jesse was still asleep in the guest bedroom. Reginald had gone off to make another phone call.

"I can't remember the last time I ate," Francis said as he piled another handful of chips onto his plate.

"I can," Mike said. "I had half a hot dog in Times Square that I was too nervous to eat."

Amanda was picking at her food and looking vacantly out at the pines beyond the garden fence.

"You okay?" Mike asked her.

"I keep thinking about my parents," she said. "They must be going out of their minds. I just wish there was some way I could let them know I'm okay."

Francis and Mike looked down at their plates, knowing there wasn't much they could say.

"I'd like to know where the hell we're going," Mike said.

Francis took another bite of his sandwich, chewed and said, "It's best to let him work it all out first. Reginald is a maniac when it comes to planning, trust me. When he's got it all figured out he'll give us a full mission briefing."

"I almost wish I'd brought my Marine fatigues," Mike said.

"You think you're kidding," Francis said. "Wait and see. The man's a detail Nazi."

"I don't see why we just don't put all that shit up on the Internet and let the world have at it," Amanda said. "Someone will figure it out faster than we can."

Mike looked at Francis. "She's got a point, you know."

Francis took a sip of ice water and nodded slowly. "Don't think I haven't considered it. There are two reasons I don't think it's a good idea. The first is incredulity. By which I mean, almost nobody will believe it. And the few who do won't be able to get anyone to believe *them*. Hell, *I* still don't believe it. Jesse made a good point about the Internet being full of stuff like that. It took almost two decades for people to get their heads around the truth behind the mess in Vietnam, and it wasn't for a lack of whistle-blowers. That's one reason, but not the main one."

"Go on," Amanda said.

"Let's suspend our disbelief for a moment and just assume that what we've seen is the truth. There's a spaceship out there. I hear myself say that and I want to check into Juniper Hill, but let's say it anyway. If the source Reginald suspects, the Voyager probe, is correct, it was taken 29 years ago. I don't know if Reginald told you, but there's a picture of that space probe on the disc."

"No, he didn't tell us that," Mike said.

"Well, now you know. But that's beside the point. What I'm trying to say is, I look at those pictures and I can't help but wonder what these people have been doing for the last three decades. Until we know, I think we should keep a low profile, as crazy as that may sound. Your suggestion, Amanda, that we find someone who knows what they're talking about, still sounds like the best plan to me."

She was about to say something when Reginald appeared in the doorway at the back of the house with Jesse beside him.

"Briefing in five," he said.

Mike turned to Francis and smiled. "Semper Fi?"

"Semper Fi," Francis agreed.

Amanda just shook her head and rolled her eyes.

Image captured by the Jupiter Eye

# CHAPTER 50

**Somewhere in Virginia**
**Saturday 22 July 2006**
**0800 EST**

Fairchild arrived just after eight in his own car and stopped by the side of the road. The sign nailed to a tree beside the closed gate said *Bushmoor Farm.* He got out and lit a cigarette, his first in several months, and stood looking down the road.

The van arrived a few minutes later. It was an old green model Ford, the fading red letters on the side reading *Fresh Produce - Delivered Daily.* It pulled up to the gate and the man in the passenger seat got out. He nodded at Fairchild and unlocked the gate.

Fairchild got back in his car and followed the van down the narrow gravel road. After about a quarter-mile the gravel ended on a small field. In one corner stood an old barn. It was intact, but barely. The roof was sagging heavily in several places and from the look of the grass surrounding it, it hadn't been used in years.

The van stopped by a side door and both occupants got out. Fairchild watched as they opened the back doors and led Weaver out. He had a cloth sack over his head, and his hands were tied behind his back, but there was no mistaking who it was. They led him inside and closed the door. Fairchild waited a few minutes then got out and went in.

The place was dark and smelled of rotting wood and old hay. Weaver was sitting in a chair in the middle of the empty barn. When the man cut the rope binding his hands, Weaver reached up, pulled off the sack and sat squinting at his surroundings. Fairchild stepped forward. The surprise on Weaver's face was almost comical.

"What's the matter, Norton?" Fairchild said. "Didn't think I had it in me?"

"You're way out of your depth, Dick. Do you have any idea who I am? You'll hang for this. You have my word on that."

"Will I? I'm not so sure. What do you think the White House is going to say when I tell them you ignored my warning and put the entire agency at risk?"

Weaver actually laughed. "My god, Dick. If I'd known you were this naïve, I never would have put your name forward for the job. What's the White House going to say? They're going to say what I tell them to say. That's how this works, Dick. Administrations come and go, I'm the guy who stays and makes sure democracy doesn't fuck everything up. I thought you were smart enough to know that."

"Bullshit."

Weaver shook his head and looked at the man and woman standing behind Fairchild. It took him a moment to recognize them. "What the hell is this?"

"Don't bother," Fairchild said. "They work for me now."

"Enough," Weaver said. "You guys know who I am. Let me go and I'll consider this a case of poor judgment. As for you, Dick, I suggest you start thinking of a plausible explanation for your resignation."

Neither of them moved.

"What's on the hard drive?" Fairchild asked. "Or haven't your friends at Skyline told you?"

Weaver looked genuinely surprised. "How did you..." he began to say then stopped. "He called you?"

When Fairchild didn't say anything Weaver said, "And you believed him? Jesus, Dick! Whose side are you on here?"

"My job is to safeguard this country," Fairchild said. "I'm on whatever side I need to be on to do that."

Weaver looked at him with the cynicism of a veteran detective regarding a young rookie cop, full of piss and vinegar and misguided ideals. "Dick, give it a rest. You don't know anything."

"I know enough. I want to know who your contact is at Skyline."

"We're done here," Weaver said. "If you two want to see this week out alive, you'll step aside and let me leave."

"The contact," Fairchild said. "Who is it?"

"Fuck you."

Fairchild stepped back and nodded. "I'll be outside."

# CHAPTER 51

**The Pride of Mumbai**
**Saturday 22 July 2006**
**1600 EDT**

Amanda needed the toilet.

"If someone doesn't let us out of here in the next sixty seconds I'm going to piss myself," she said.

Francis was standing by the doors, his ear pressed against the steel plate. "I think someone's coming."

They heard footsteps followed by the rattling of a chain. A moment later the door of the container swung open with a loud screech. An Indian man dressed in the uniform of a ship's captain smiled at them, revealing two rows of pristine white teeth. "I'm sorry it has taken me so long to get down here. We had some trouble with customs."

Francis was about to say something when Amanda brushed past him and said, "I need the toilet. Right now!"

The captain beckoned to a man standing several feet away. "Mohindar, please show this young woman to the water closet. We'll be in my cabin."

When they had left Francis said, "Thank you for this."

The captain raised a hand. "Thank me when we get there."

They followed him out of the cargo hold and up onto the deck. None of them were quite sure how long they had been at sea. At some point they had heard the engines start and the ISO container had begun to rock from side to side instead of front to back. They each had a single backpack, and Reginald had handed Francis a flashlight when they said their farewells at Port Canaveral. Then he had closed the door and locked the container.

The captain's name turned out to be Laxman, a name he informed them was Hindi and meant good luck. He had a spacious cabin aft of the pilothouse with a single window that offered a permanent view of the ship's wake.

"I'm afraid this is the best I can do," Laxman said. "We will be at sea for just over four hours, so at least you won't have time to get too uncomfortable."

"It's very kind of you," Francis said. "We'll keep out of your way."

Jesse was standing at the porthole looking out at the water. When Amanda returned she joined him and took his hand. Francis and Mike both looked at each other and shared a knowing smile.

"Feel free to look around," Laxman said. "I've asked my cook to prepare you something to eat. I hope you like Indian food."

"I meant to ask," Francis said. "How does an Indian freighter end up working in this part of the world?"

Laxman shrugged. "We're cheap."

- - -

Mike was standing in the pilothouse talking to the captain when the watchman called down to say they were within sight of land. He hurried back down to the cabin and walked in to find Jesse and Amanda kissing on the bed. He quickly closed the door again.

He found Francis in the armory talking to the master-at-arms. He was studying the barrel of a machine gun sitting in pieces on the bench in front of them.

"The problem is the oil you're using," Francis told the big Indian. "This stuff doesn't prevent rust. If you can't get hold of proper gun oil, use three-in-one or WD40."

When he saw Mike Francis said, "Hey, how are things topside?"

"Laxman says we'll be in port in twenty minutes."

The master-at-arms took the barrel and thanked Francis. They went back up and met Laxman in the hall in front of the cabin.

"Pilot's on his way," the captain said. "You're sure this man will be there to meet you? I only ask because arriving in Nassau without passports could get us all thrown in jail."

"He'll be there," Francis said.

They watched from the deck as the pilot's boat pulled alongside the freighter and a man in a white naval uniform climbed the rope ladder. Jesse and Amanda joined them a moment later. When Mike turned to look at them, they both flushed.

"Who's that?" Amanda asked.

"He's the harbor pilot," Francis said.

"Meaning?"

"He's here to help the captain into port," Jesse said. "If he's not familiar with these waters, the pilot will take command of the ship. Otherwise, he'll just supervise."

Francis and Mike looked at each other and nodded their appreciation. Amanda said, "Check you out, mister know-it-all."

"I watch a lot of Discovery Channel," Jesse said.

As soon as the lines were cast and the gangway in place, a blue Chevy pickup truck marked with the seal of the Nassau Customs Authority pulled up alongside the vessel and two black men in navy whites got out. One of them stopped at the bottom of the gangway while the other boarded the ship. A minute later Laxman arrived with the officer in tow. He looked no older than eighteen, and his uniform seemed at least two sizes too big. He approached Francis and said, "Your passports, please."

Francis looked at Laxman, who took a nervous step forward and was about to say something when the officer pointed at Francis's backpack. "Give me that, please."

Francis slid the bag off his shoulder. The officer took it, knelt and began to rummage through it. Mike looked at Francis, his eyes pleading, but Francis only shook his head. The man suddenly stood, pulled his hand out of the bag and held up four dark blue passports with the words Commonwealth of the Bahamas printed in large gold letters below the national crest.

"Here they are," he said and handed them to Francis with a wink.

"Follow me through Customs and wait outside the terminal," the officer said when they reached the gangway.

Laxman, who appeared to have been holding his breath, let out a long sigh and ran a sleeve across his forehead as he watched them leave.

The officer led them into the terminal building and made a show of checking each of their bags, then stamped the passports and handed them back.

"Five minutes," he said.

It took him ten. He was still driving a pickup, but this one was an aging Ford Bronco with at least one bad valve and a paint job that might once have been red, brown or terracotta orange. There was no way to tell.

The young man had changed out of his uniform and was wearing a pair of cutoff jeans, a faded yellow tank top and sandals. He introduced himself as Joe and offered to take Amanda's bag. Neither Mike nor Francis missed the look on Jesse's face. If Jesse hadn't recently killed a man it might have been amusing.

They drove inland through the densely populated neighborhoods that occupied most of the small island. The trip took less than twenty minutes. Joe pulled into the driveway of a large single-story house located right on the beach of the island's southern shore.

When Joe got out and disappeared into the house, Amanda said, "Do we know who this guy is? I mean, don't get me wrong, I'm all for a vacation in the Bahamas, but he seems a little too easygoing."

"Stay here," Francis said. "I'll be back in a minute."

When Francis came back out he approached Jesse and Amanda.

"I need to talk to you guys for a minute. Mike, do you mind?"

He led them around the side of the house and down to the beach. Down by the water line a group of kids were throwing a football back and forth across a small fire while the girls looked on, laughing and drinking canned beer. Francis sat down in the sand and bade them to join him.

"All right," Amanda said, "We're officially intrigued. Now what the hell is going on?"

"I want you guys to stay here," Francis said.

Jesse started to stand, but Francis put a hand on his shoulder. "Hear me out, will you? This is important."

Jesse sat back down reluctantly.

"This is Reginald's place," Francis said, looking back at the house. "You'll be safe here. And before you bring up what happened in Quebec, I'd like to point out that Reginald has people here who'll look out for you. I might also add that what happened in Quebec was that you came out on top."

Francis looked at Jesse as he said this. He knew it had been the right thing to say, especially in front of Amanda, when Jesse relaxed and began to actually pay attention.

"Getting us here was relatively easy," Francis continued. "Getting out of here won't be. The man I need to see is a thousand miles away. That means flying, and I don't think I need to tell you why that's not going to work if we stay together. It's safest if I go alone. It's also the quickest."

"What about Mike?" Jesse asked. "Is he going with you?"

Francis shook his head. "No. I'm sending Mike somewhere else. I can't tell you where, but he has a wife and son and that's where he needs to be. As soon as I know anything, I'll get word to you through Reginald. Joe will drop by the house when he can and make sure you're okay. And I'll leave you plenty of money. All I ask is that you keep a low profile. And whatever you do, don't try to get in touch with anyone you know. It's as dangerous for them as it is for you."

Francis waited as they took in what he was saying. Amanda leaned her head onto Jesse's shoulder and whispered something in his ear. He flushed suddenly and turned away for a moment.

"We'll stay," Amanda said. "I just wish there was something we could do to help."

"There is," Francis said. "Keep your heads down and stay safe. I got you into this mess and I mean to get you out of it. I just need a little more time."

"What are you going to do?" Jesse asked.

Francis shrugged. "What I always do. Move one step at a time until I find what I'm looking for."

"A spaceship?" Amanda asked.

They all laughed, but it was a nervous laughter.

"I'm trying not to think about that," Francis said.

Jesse nodded. "You and me both."

"Make that three of us," Amanda added. "And I think I can cast in Mike's vote while we're at it."

Francis stood up. "I'm going to talk to Mike. We'll come back down when we're done."

Francis found Mike standing in the kitchen with Joe. They were both looking at a copy of USA Today. When he saw Francis, Joe headed for the door and said, "I'll be outside."

"Have you seen this?" Mike asked, pointing at a picture of a burning piece of tail section. The headline read: *Plane Shot Down by US Air Defenses After Illegal Border Crossing.*

"I found a copy of the New York Times on the boat," Francis said. "Did you know any of the agents who were killed?"

"No," Mike said.

"You might not believe me," Francis said. "But I do know I'm responsible."

Mike shook his head. "No, you're not. That's bullshit and you know it."

"Do I?"

"You should. I know I said some pretty mean things back in New York, but that was before I really understood what was going on. These people are fucking nuts."

"I'm going to find them," Francis said.

"You? What happened to us?"

"You're not coming. There's somewhere else you need to be."

Mike had been looking out the window. Now he turned to Francis. "What the hell are you talking about?"

Francis reached into his bag, pulled out an airline ticket and handed it to Mike. Mike flipped the cover sheet over and said, "Panama? What the fuck am I going to do in Panama?"

"There's someone down there I think you'll want to meet. Two someones actually."

Mike was about to protest again when the penny dropped.

"They're in Panama?"

Francis nodded. "Not quite. The flight leaves at noon tomorrow. Joe will take you to the airport. Don't ask me exactly where they are because I don't know. There's a restaurant in the town of Nuevo Emperador called La Trona. Leave this on the bar."

Francis handed him a silver dollar with the Iwo Jima Memorial printed on one side.

"Go back at noon on the following day. Someone will be there to meet you. I also suggest you buy some local clothes, shave your head and leave the beard."

When Mike said nothing Francis raised his eyebrows. "What do you say, partner? Sound good?"

"No."

"No?"

"Tell me," Mike said. "What happens after that? Once I'm back with my family? We can't exactly head back to Phoenix or New York, can we?"

"No. Not for now."

"So what? We take up life in some rural farming community and pray that no one mistakes us for a group of Americans who have no business living there at all? Or do we live in the basement of some safe house and pray that word will arrive one day that everything is fine? And what if that word never arrives? What then?"

Francis nodded slowly. "I don't know, Mike. I promise I'll get word to you once this is over and it's safe for you to return home."

"Not good enough."

"What else can I do?"

"I'm coming with you."

Francis shook his head. "Out of the question. For one, you have a family. I don't know what I'm going to find in - where I'm going, but it's too risky."

"Really? That's what you're worried about? Not the fact that I might slow you down?"

"It's a factor. I've been doing this for a long time, Mike. I have no doubt that you're a good agent, but it's not the same."

"Bullshit. I don't buy it. I appreciate your concern for my health, it's very touching. But like you said, I'm a father and a husband. I don't want the people I love just living some hand-to-mouth existence. Not as long as there is something I can do about it."

"Is there anything I can say to make you change your mind?" Francis said.

"Yeah, you can tell me right now that the coast is clear and that I can take Susan and Josh home and not have to worry about anything. Can you say that?"

"You know I can't."

"Then it's settled. I'm coming with you."

Francis considered this in silence. When he finally looked up, it was with the faint trace of a smile. "Are you sure this isn't just a ploy because you'd miss me if I was gone?"

"Fuck off," Mike said, but he was smiling, too. "Besides, you're not exactly a spring chicken yourself. I have a feeling you might need someone to watch that prized behind of yours before this is over."

"Don't flatter yourself," Francis said.

"What did Mandy and Jess have to say?" Mike asked.

"They'll be fine. I plan to come back for them as soon as I can."

"When are we leaving?"

"In about fifteen minutes."

Mike nodded. "Come on then, we better go say goodbye."

# CHAPTER 52

**Aurora**
**Sunday 23 July 2006**
**0900 EEST**

Mitch was standing on a dock looking up at what had once been a Soviet nuclear submarine. She was over a hundred and twenty yards long and looked every bit as menacing as she had during her decade of service with the Baltic Fleet. Behind the conning tower two enormous hydraulic doors built into the top of the hull were slowly opening.

"I don't know what to say," Mitch said to the man standing next to him.

Aurora's dockmaster, a young man in his early twenties wearing a navy blue jumpsuit like his own, pointed to the far side of the small subterranean lake where a large oil tank stood on a concrete platform. "This side's for cargo; that one's for fuel. We use a lot of it here."

"Where the hell did you get it from?" Mitch asked, unable to take his eyes off the submarine.

"We bought it."

"You bought a nuclear submarine?"

"Not exactly. This is a first generation Victor-class, built in the late sixties. She was retired in '82 after running aground. The Russians stripped her and sold her for scrap to a company in Norway. We found her sitting in a port in Trondheim. The reactor and turbine had been removed, of course, along with almost everything else."

"And you rebuilt it?" Mitch asked. It was a stupid question, but the only one that came to his lips.

"From the ground up. I'm sure Captain Williams will let one of the crew show you around if you're interested."

Mitch was about to ask the next of a hundred questions he had when a man approached them and said, "Where do you want the generator, boss?"

Mitch watched as a large wooden box branded with the Caterpillar logo was pulled from the hold by a large crane on the dock and set down on the bed of a wide, and very futuristic looking, truck with a bubble-dome window. A hand tapped him on the shoulder and he turned around to see Sarah. She had changed out of her jumpsuit into jeans and a white blouse.

"Hey you!" she said.

"Hey yourself," Mitch said. "What happened to the boiler suit?"

"It's my day off. Well, it's supposed to be. I thought you might like to visit the museum."

"The museum?" Mitch asked.

"It should answer some of your questions," she said.

The access road to the dock snaked around an outcrop of rock onto a concrete platform surrounded by a narrow channel of water that ran all the way around the perimeter of the cave. Beyond the two small bridges connecting the platform with the rest of the facility the ground was covered in lush green grass and trees. Set into the high, steep walls were three stories of windows and balconies that made them look like apartment building chiseled out of rough stone.

They reached the intersection and turned right across one of the small bridges into what looked like a small New England fishing village. Mitch had seen it the day before, but the wonder he felt as they passed first a barber shop and then a small convenient store, was no less intense. The sight was so out of keeping with the rest of the place. It looked like a Hollywood film set built inside a giant indoor studio lot. There was a small cinema currently showing The Da Vinci Code and Disney Pixar's Cars, a clothing outlet and an English style pub called One Eyed Jack's. Several people waved at them as they passed. A woman who looked old enough to be Sarah's mother waived and Mitch found himself waving back, so surreal was the scene.

"Pinch me," Mitch said.

"Why?"

"Because I feel like Alice in Wonderland."

She smiled. "Wait until you see the museum."

Aurora

# CHAPTER 53

**New York, New York**
**Sunday 23 July 2006**
**0330 EDT**

"What the fuck am I looking at here, Jack?" Bosch said.

They were upstairs in the operations room. Marius had three news channels playing on three separate screens. On the first, a young female reporter was talking to the camera from the shore of a lake. Behind her in the distance the black tail fin of a large airplane was sticking out of the ground. A column of smoke rose from the wreckage, painting a sharp black line across the blue sky. The headline running across the bottom of the picture read: HIJACKED PLANE SHOT DOWN OVER US-CANADA BORDER.

The second screen was showing the chaotic scene on the edge of the runway in La Tuque. A motley and chaotic jumble of police cars, fire trucks and ambulances were scattered across the tarmac. The headline in this picture read: STATE DEPARTMENT PLANE HIJACKED IN QUEBEC.

On the third screen there was a picture of Amanda Hinsdale and Jesse Corbin above the words: MORISSON HOSTAGES STILL MISSING.

The three networks were shifting rapidly back and forth between the two stories.

"Jack?"

Jack seemed not to hear him. His eyes were fixed on the screen in the middle, where a Canadian police officer in a captain's uniform was making a statement behind a small podium in front of what looked like the town hall.

"Jack, can you please tell me what the hell is going on?" Bosch said.

Marius looked at Jack, his eyes pleading.

"Please tell me this has nothing to do with us," Bosch said.

Before he even knew he was going to do it, Jack had pulled his silenced nine-millimeter Beretta from under his left arm. Marius tried to scream but all that escaped his throat was a pathetic squeal. Jack pulled the trigger twice. Marius turned his head and stared in horror as Bosch sank to his knees and fell forward onto the floor.

"Help me move him downstairs," Jack said, putting the gun back in his shoulder holster.

Marius didn't move.

"We need to get him out of here," Jack said.

When Marius still didn't move Jack took his head in both hands. "Titov told me to do it. He wants the body out of here before he arrives."

That got Marius moving.

"Take his feet," Jack said and knelt to roll Bosch over onto his back.

They carried him to the elevator. Marius moved like a man paralyzed by a concoction of fear and bewilderment. When they were inside Jack dropped the body and pushed the button for the basement.

They dragged the body down a long corridor, past the boiler room and into a small loading bay to a white van sitting in the far corner. Jack opened the back doors. "Help me get him inside."

- - -

Ten minutes later, they were back upstairs.

"I need you to access the camera system and erase the footage from inside the elevator and the basement," Jack said.

Marius nodded and sat down in front of one of the computers. When he was done he said, "I still can't believe it. I mean, Carl? He worked for the director, didn't he?"

"For two years," Jack said. "It just goes to show you can never really know anyone."

"When is Titov getting here?" Marius asked.

Jack considered the question for a moment. "Did you erase the footage?"

"Yes."

There was a loud thump followed by a crash as the monitor in front of Marius slid off the end of the desk in front of him and fell to the floor. Jack put his gun down and lifted Marius's head off the keyboard. There was no exit wound but the face looked distorted somehow. One of his eyes seemed to have ruptured from the inside and turned red. A single line of blood ran from his nose to his upper lip and began to drip onto the keyboard. Jack set the head down and put the gun back in its holster.

He hurried downstairs to Bosch's office and opened the safe hidden behind an enlarged reproduction of van Gogh's Portrait of Doctor Gachet on the wall by the desk. He removed four bundles of hundred dollar bills, stuffed them into his pockets and replaced them with several sheets of paper, including a map of the Baltic Sea.

Twenty minutes later Jack was driving the van across the George Washington Bridge into New Jersey. On the seat beside him next to a German passport was a Delta Airlines economy class ticket to Zurich in the name of Dietmar Klein.

# CHAPTER 54

**Aurora**
**Sunday 23 July 2006**
**1000 EEST**

Mitch was standing in front of a large framed picture that Mike Banner would have recognized. But unlike the picture Mike had seen on Reginald's computer, this one contained two overlapping images. One was a close-up of the ship, the other a computer generated graphic depicting Origin in a detailed outline. At the bottom of the frame a small brass plaque said: Origin – Voyager II, July 1979.

Sarah was standing next to him but seemed more interested in looking at Mitch than in what would arguably be the most incredible discovery in the history of the human race, and clearly also the biggest joke.

"So what is this?" Mitch said. "Some kind of art project?"

According to the annotation in the picture, the ship was supposed to be over twelve miles long. That was the distance from Sky Harbor airport in Phoenix to his parent's house in Wedgwood Park, a trip that took twenty minutes in clear traffic and over an hour when it got busy. The idea that a manmade object - and there was a joke for you – could ever be that big just made the whole idea that much more ridiculous.

"What do you mean?" Sarah said.

"The picture of the giant spaceship," Mitch said. "It's an art project or something, right?"

She looked puzzled. "An art project?"

"Don't get me wrong, it's good. In fact it's very good. I used to know a guy back in college who did a lot of digital stuff like this. He got a job at Dreamworks."

Sarah was looking at him, practically staring him down. Mitch felt the start of another hot flush crawling up his neck and into his cheeks. People in the real world didn't stare at you like that because it was rude. To Sarah, who had apparently never lived in the real world, it was simply her way of showing him that he fascinated her. Or so he thought.

"Mitch," she said, "what do you think all this is? I mean, what do you think we're doing here?"

Mitch considered the question for a moment. "Well, I haven't seen anyone making Kool-Aid, so I'm ruling out mass suicide."

"Mitch, I'm being serious."

"Okay, I guess I'm assuming this is a research facility of some kind. Something run by Skyline Defense?"

"Oh my god!" she said. "What the hell did Brendan tell you?"

"You mean General Eisenhower?"

"Yes, the chief. Didn't he tell you *anything*?"

"Err...nope. Just that my being here wasn't his idea. Actually, I got the impression he'd be happier if I was locked up in the dungeon."

"What an asshole," she said. "Mitch, the spaceship is real. Origin is real."

As Mitch studied her face the smile on his own grew wider. "First of all," he said, "you're talking to a man who's done a fair bit of reading up on the subject of space travel. Nice try, though. I'm pretty sure the Saturn five was the biggest thing NASA ever built. I'm prepared to believe there are a few feasibility studies kicking around for making something bigger. Like the Russian orbit assembly idea for a manned scout to Mars. But-"

"Mitch," Sarah said, "we're not building a spaceship. Origin isn't a project. It's been there for hundreds, maybe even thousands of years. It's why we're here. It's why we've built all of this."

When she didn't return his smile, Mitch let out a sigh of exasperation. "I can't believe I'm actually having this argument, but fine. I've seen most of the project traffic at NASA. I'm not saying there aren't things going on there they don't want anyone to know about. There are. But assuming something like this was discovered, there is no way I wouldn't know about it. I probably shouldn't be telling you this, but I've actually seen some of the things our government is trying hard to keep out of the public domain. There's some pretty crazy shit, but on the subject of extraterrestrials it's mainly a lot of old men sitting around talking about how UFO sightings and stories about alien abductions have a way of turning into budget increases. What I mean is, there are no little green men out in Nevada, but no one will ever come out and flatly deny it because popular superstition is a hallmark of the American psyche and the basis for much of what goes on in our political system."

"Are you done?" Sarah said.

"Yeah, I'm done. I just-"

"Come with me," she said.

She led him outside and across the bridge onto the road that looped around the back of the cave. They passed the east corner where a crew of about a dozen men in yellow jumpsuits were busy burrowing two large holes. Mitch was mesmerized for a moment by the sight of a tractor that must have been electrical because it made no sound even as it moved forward and scooped up a bucket full of loose rock.

"Where are we going?" Mitch said.

"There's someone you need to meet," she said.

The glass panes opened automatically as they approached the doors on the platform at the other end of the road. Sarah led Mitch into a round tunnel about forty feet long that ended in another set of glass doors, although these were tinted almost black. The Roman numeral "VIII" had been etched into the wall above them.

"Wait here," she said. "I need to find him."

Mitch waited.

When a quarter of an hour had passed and he was still waiting, he stepped closer to the doors and was surprised to see them open.

The room was at least a hundred feet across and appeared to be a perfect circle rendered in smooth polished concrete. The ceiling was a conical shape that began about twenty feet above the floor and rose steeply, ending in a wide circular shaft that led up into darkness. Directly below the shaft a pole about ten feet high jutted out of the ground. It was roughly ten inches in diameter and appeared to be made of solid steel. It arched out at the top, making it look like a giant golf tee.

A thick concrete counter protruded from the wall and ran all the way around the room, broken only by the door behind him and an identical one on the opposite side of the room.

Mitch walked to the counter and examined one of the flat-screen monitors mounted to the wall above it. Below the monitor a pane of dark rectangular glass with a thin chrome frame was set into the counter itself. These workstations were duplicated at intervals all the way around the room. In fact the only things that didn't appear to be a permanent fixture were the strictly functional brushed aluminum chairs sitting in front of each terminal.

Mitch walked to the strange metal pole in the center and examined it for a moment. He reached out and touched it with his index finger. It was as smooth as glass.

"Hello?" Mitch said. "Anyone here?"

There was no reply.

He waited another minute or so, then, unable to help himself, he walked back to the computer terminal by the door and sat down in front of it. The monitor was both larger and thinner than any he had ever seen. At the bottom of the screen the letters TSI were etched into the white plastic frame. He found the same logo on the glass pane on the counter. Mitch, who prided himself on knowing just about everyone in the computer business, had never heard of TSI.

Convinced he had been forgotten, Mitch decided it would be best to find someone and let them know where he was before the chief or one of his guards walked in and found him in violation of his parole. As he stood up his hand brushed the glass plate on the counter and a keyboard suddenly appeared in crisp, bright lines and characters of neon blue. When he looked up a cursor was flashing in the top left-hand corner of the screen.

- - -

He had no idea how long he had been sitting at the terminal, only that what he was seeing so captivated him the rest of the world had all but ceased to exist. When someone spoke up behind him Mitch was so startled he almost fell off the chair.

"It's quite something, isn't it?"

Mitch turned to see a man standing next to the pole in the center of the room. He looked like he had just gotten out of bed and forgotten to brush his hair. Unlike everyone else Mitch had seen, he wasn't wearing a jumpsuit but a pair of gray tweed slacks and a green knitted cardigan.

"I was just admiring the keyboard," Mitch said. "I've never seen touch-screen technology that works this well before."

The man walked over and extended a hand. "I'm Heinz Gerber."

"Mitch Rainey," Mitch said.

"The man from Washington who found our missing satellite. Tell me, did you actually track it, or did Marius forget to secure the connection?"

"I used an index of signature values I created based on previous test readings," Mitch said.

"And if you don't mind my asking, how did you trace them to Darkstar?"

"The launch registry," Mitch said.

Heinz considered this for a moment and nodded. "Quite ingenious, I must admit."

"What is this place?" Mitch said.

"This is room eight, the home of my beloved Harriet," Heinz said.

"Harriet?"

"Our interface to the base-eight programming language used by Origin. I named it after my first dog because getting either of them to do what I wanted at first proved almost impossible."

"Used by Origin?" Mitch said. "The spaceship?"

Heinz laughed. "I know. When two grown men start using that word in a serious conversation you have to ask yourself what the world is coming to, right? But you get used to it, trust me."

"You're saying that programming language came from a spaceship?"

"Indeed," Heinz said. "From what I can gather, it's not unique to Origin either, but the base computer language of the entire civilization that built her. I'm speculating of course, but it seems like a fair assumption."

"I've never seen anything like it," Mitch said.

Heinz nodded. "That's hardly surprising when you consider the nearest computer using it is almost four hundred million miles away. The system uses eight characters because-"

"Because it's based on high-density multiple layer compression," Mitch finished. "I'm guessing something in the region of three or four thousand to one."

Heinz looked taken aback. "More like six thousand, actually. Sarah says you studied computer programming. May I ask where?"

"Arizona State. How fast is their system?"

"We don't actually know, but based on response times, we think somewhere in the region of one and a half terahertz."

"Christ," Mitch said. "How the hell do they do that?"

Heinz pointed at the pole in the middle of the room. "Probably by building systems out of that alloy. We pulled it out of the ice twenty miles from the North Pole. If it were made of steel it would weigh just under half a ton. Its actual weight is six point five seven tons. The alloy is one of four used in the ship's construction."

"You're telling me that thing is indestructible?" Mitch said.

"Hardly," Heinz said. "It would have been forged like any other metal. Although it's fair to say there isn't a foundry on this planet that would be able to get it much more than warm."

"What is it?" Mitch said.

"It's a probe. A kind of automated landing beacon, you might say. It has no propulsion or guidance systems, so whatever launched it was probably a lot closer to the planet than the ship is now. We think it was simply super-heated, aimed and fired like an arrow. It was buried in solid rock when we found it. The hardware is embedded in the top. It's a signal transmitter and receiver, an atmospheric measuring platform, a proximity sensor, and a link to the ship's main computer."

"You can actually use that thing to access the ship's own systems?" Mitch said.

"Not with that, no. Or at least, not directly. The probe has no user interface or input devices, and creating a physical bridge to our own system is out of the question. For one thing, we don't know enough about the hardware, so any attempt to deconstruct and reverse engineer it would almost certainly end in disaster. What we have had to do is intercept the incoming and outgoing signals and study them in order to create a crude emulator that can run base-eight code on a base-two system. I probably don't have to tell you, but that's like trying to render full-texture three dimensional video on a calculator."

"Is the transfer protocol at least similar to ours?" Mitch said.

"Not even close. Their system uses six separate data streams, each transmitted simultaneously at slight frequency variations within a very narrow band. The sixth stream is an encrypted merger algorithm needed to combine the other five. And it changes with every transmission. Once we put the files together, there are five levels of decompression. The main difficulty is that the merger algorithm is only valid for a single reply."

Mitch nodded. "You need more time than the system will give you."

"Correct. When you consider we have to not only decompress and assemble the files, but trans-code them too, and then reverse the entire process, we just don't have the power to return more than crude responses."

Mitch could barely keep up with his own racing mind. "Your emulator, what hardware does it use?"

"I'll show you," Heinz said.

Mitch followed him to the doors on the other side of the room and Heinz pushed a button mounted to the counter next to it. The doors parted to reveal a much thicker set of doors with a large rectangular view-port in each. Mitch stood looking in for a long time before he said, "What chips are the servers using?"

"Six hundred custom made eight-core processors using a chip-integrated liquid nitrogen cooling system."

"Clock speed?" Mitch asked.

"Sixty-three hundred Megahertz."

Mitch considered this and said, "You could get them to eight with helium. Seven and a half at the very least. How do you transmit the response if you can't use that thing?"

Heinz regarded Mitch with a kind of guarded reverence. "We don't actually intercept the incoming transmission here, only what the spike itself sends back. The atmospheric loss is too great for any of our ground receivers to pick up a clear enough signal. The amazing thing is that that thing can do it without a hitch. We still rely on the antenna array we put into orbit over a decade ago to see if the ship was sending anything at all. It's how we isolated the signal from Origin in the first place and also how we eventually located the spike. Our platform relays the signal to Darkstar, which passes it on."

Mitch turned and looked at the workstation he had been sitting at. "Is that their language?"

Heinz walked to the monitor. He pulled a pair of glasses from his pocket, put them on and knelt to look at the screen. The image contained a list of characters drawn from a simple matrix of symmetrical lines. Next to each was one or more letters from the English alphabet.

"Is it really that simple?" Mitch said.

Heinz stood and nodded. "They use forty-one letters, but the sounds they represent appear almost identical to those used in our own languages. Structurally, the language is remarkably similar to Hungarian, although the pronunciation is more Germanic."

For once, Mitch was lost for words. Heinz laughed and nodded. "That's right, the crew of Origin are as human as you or I. Or at least they were."

# CHAPTER 55

**London, Heathrow**
**Sunday 23 July 2006**
**1900 EDT**

Neither Jesse nor Amanda would have recognized the man who stepped into the arrivals hall at Heathrow International Airport that Saturday afternoon, but they would certainly have noticed him.

Gary Copeland was a punk of the old school variety, and the spikes of his Mohawk were colored green and red alternately to prove it. When he emerged from the bathroom he had added jet-black eyeliner and lipstick. There was a silver ring in his nose and several earrings in both ears. His faded black leather jacket had more studs than a Texas horse ranch. He'd also chosen a black t-shirt with the word "Pantera" printed across it in red letters made to look like dripping blood. To finish the look, he had even managed to squeeze into a pair of skintight dark gray drainpipe jeans that were held up needlessly with a black studded leather belt.

With only his backpack and no luggage to collect, he made his way to the underground tube station and took the first train to South Kensington, switched to the Circle line and got off at Victoria. He found a bathroom, washed the gel and dye out of his hair, then the makeup off his face and changed into a pair of jeans, a sweater and Converse All-Stars.

He took the Victoria line to Green Park and ran to the platform for the Jubilee Line just fast enough to know if he was being followed. He got off at London Bridge, then walked the last half-mile to the address Reginald had given him, arriving just after nine in the evening.

Francis crossed the street and stepped into the alley between two of the buildings. He waited for a full five minutes before crossing back over. Instead of ringing the bell, he waited until an elderly woman came out to walk her dog and slipped through the closing door behind her.

Inside he took a mobile phone from his pocket and called Mike, who, if all had gone according to plan, would be waiting in a bar just across the Thames. Ten minutes later, a black cab stopped two blocks down the road. The man who got out was bald, visibly overweight and dressed in a dark gray hand-me-down wool suit. He wore a pair of thick glasses held together in two places with dirty gauze tape.

Francis opened the door when Mike arrived. "You look good, Mike."

"Piss off. Can I take this stomach off now? It's beginning to make my back ache."

"Sure, but don't lose it. You'll need to put it back on when we leave."

They took the stairs to the fourth floor, emerging into a dimly lit, dusty hallway with a cracking stone floor and yellowing walls. 405 was the last door on the right.

Francis told Mike to stay back and stood at the door, listening. He was prepared to accept that nobody was home when he heard what might have been a pan drop onto the floor, followed by a quick round of cursing in a foreign language. Francis looked back down the hall, nodded at Mike and knocked on the door.

The man who opened it and peered out at Francis over the chain was sixty if he was a day. He was wearing a threadbare bathrobe and a pair of moccasins in no better shape. He looked like he hadn't shaved in a few days, but the face wasn't hostile or even suspicious, just curious. "Can I help you?"

He looked Francis up and down several times with no hint of a reaction.

"I was asked to give you this," Francis said and held out a brown paper envelope.

"Open it," the man said.

Francis tore off the end of the envelope and pulled out a stack of crisp British fifty-pound notes folded in a single sheet of lined notepaper.

"Here," the man said and held out his hand.

Francis handed him the envelope.

The man first counted the money then read the note. As he did, the creases on his forehead gave way to an amused narrowing of the eyes, and finally a smile. "I should send you back with an answer. But I'm guessing you didn't come from across the river."

He closed the door, released the chain and opened it again. "Come in. And please forgive my manners. When I moved here in '76, life was simpler. Now you never know what the hell people want when they start banging on your door."

Francis stepped inside and was immediately consumed by the unmistakable odor of books. It was a pleasant smell, not moldy exactly, but musty.

"I have a friend," Francis said. "Waiting outside."

"Then by all means, tell her to come inside."

"It's not-"

"I'm joking," the man said. "Ask him in. It's all here in the note."

When Mike joined them the man held out a hand to Francis and said, "My name is Maksym, but you should call me Max or I may not realize you're talking to me. It's been a long time since anyone used it."

"I'm Gary," Francis said.

"Ah, yes, Gary. Like Tom, Dick and Gary. Never mind, you don't have to tell me. You call me Max, I'll call you Gary and Tchaikovsky can write the music. It'll be great."

Francis laughed and stepped aside.

"I'm Mike," Mike said, and shrugged when Francis gave him a foreboding look.

"I'm pleased to meet you, Mike," Max said. "It's a good look for you, I think. You look like you sell shitty used cars to people like Gary here who can't afford anything else."

Both Mike and Francis found themselves laughing.

"I know, I'm hilarious," Max said. "My granddaughters think I look like that asshole on Coronation Street, you know the old man, Cole? No, of course you don't know. I don't really know either, but I can imagine. Most people on TV these days look like assholes."

Francis smiled, "Aren't you curious to know why we're here?"

"A little," Max said. "But I figure you're the one that came to see me, so you'll tell me or decide you don't want to, in which case I'd be an ass for asking."

"How do you know Reginald?" Francis asked.

"He's a bum," Max said and laughed. "I met him at the embassy in Vienna. The man can play poker, I'll give him that much."

"Where did you defect from?" Mike asked.

"The Ukraine. Although back then it was all just the USSR. Even today they call us Russians."

Max spat out the last word, as if it had left a bad taste in his mouth. "But enough about me. You have come a long way. I can tell by your accents. Are you Canadians or Americans?"

"Americans," Francis said. "I have something that might interest you. Do you have a computer?"

"Do bears shit in the woods?" Max said and walked down the hall.

They followed him into a spacious living room with an old oak writing desk at one end surrounded by several stacks of books. There was a tattered Chesterfield at the other end of the room in front of a large fireplace. Max sat down at the desk and flipped open the lid on his laptop. The desktop background was a grainy, sepia-tone picture of a group of young men in flight suits standing in front of an empty rocket launching site. Max saw both of them looking and said, "Baikonur in '72. I'm the handsome one."

Francis handed him the CD. "I should warn you now, it doesn't make a lot of sense."

"Like an American showing up at my door on a Sunday night to pay off a thirty year old gambling debt?"

When it was obvious Max was going to do things at his own pace and preferably in silence, Francis and Mike both took a seat on the couch and began leafing through old copies of National Geographic. Mike began to doze.

When he opened his eyes, he didn't know if he had fallen asleep or just nodded off for a few seconds, but when he turned around, both Francis and Max were gone. Mike was on his feet and moving across the room before he even noticed someone had taken off his shoes. He headed for the door, but saw the chain was still on. Then he heard a soft humming from somewhere in the house and followed it to the kitchen.

Max was standing by the sink pouring champagne into three tea mugs on a plastic tray. Francis was bent over at the other end of the kitchen with his head in the fridge. Max looked up when Mike came in with a grin that ended just below his earlobes. "My dear boy, I was just coming to wake you. I mean to propose a toast."

Francis looked on amused as Max picked up the tray and walked back into the living room.

"I'm not going to ask you where you got that disc," he began, "Because I think it might ruin the moment. But tell me, is it real?"

"It's real," Francis said. "I can-"

"Not another word," Max said. "That's all I wanted to know."

He handed them each a cup and raised his own. "Za vashe zdorovie!" he said and downed the mug in a single gulp.

They did their best to repeat the toast and followed his example. When he put his mug back down on the tray Francis said, "I'm glad we've made your day, I really am-"

"But you didn't come here to drink. I know. Forgive an old man his follies."

"Consider them forgiven," Francis said. "I just want to know-"

"If I've lost my mind or actually have something useful to tell you?" Max finished.

"Well, I wouldn't have put it that way, but yes."

"Have you ever been in space, Gary? Either of you. Mike?"

"Call me Francis, that's my real name. And no, we've never been in space. That's right, isn't it, Mike?"

"Very funny," Mike said.

"Okay," Max said, "then you'll have to use your imagination. Seeing the earth with the stars behind you changes a man. I don't mean it makes you crazy; that's just incidental in my case. Well, mine and a few others that I can think of. But anyway, I digress. Once you have been up there, you cannot look at the universe the same way again. It has a way of bringing the blind arrogance of those who believe we are unique to the universe into stark contrast with reality. The earth is not a grain of sand in the desert; it is a single molecule in one of those grains. When we talk of probability within the finite world of man on earth, we openly accept that as the numbers grow larger, the chances of variables increase. If we discover a rare bug on a tree or a flower in some remote rain forest, we conclude quite happily that the chances of finding another in all the thousands of acres that surround it are probably quite high. Only the bug or the flower, for whom such distances are unfathomable, and for whom their immediate surroundings are by necessity the world entire, would refute the possibility outright. The human observer accepts it as fact because he is on the outside looking in. To see the world from the outside, is to see that bug and marvel at its stupidity. The chances of there not being other intelligent life in the universe are so slim they don't bear thinking about. Do you follow me? Tell me if you don't; I know I'm rambling."

Francis nodded. Not out of politeness, but because he did understand. Or at least he thought he did.

"Everything on that disc is scientifically sound," Max said. "By which I mean, it fits together within the realms of possibility."

"Could you be a bit more specific?" Francis said.

"Sure. How about this? A professor at MIT, I forget his name…"

"Bershadsky," Francis said.

"Yes, him. He leads a team of software engineers to create a file compression program that NASA is going to test on board Voyager two. And why not? They have very limited bandwidth to begin with, so the smaller the files, the better. The Russian space program tried something similar at about the same time. You with me so far?"

"I think so," Francis said.

"Good. The timing checks out perfectly with the Voyager two launch and trajectory. The fact that NASA does not openly acknowledge it used such software means nothing. NASA, like any government organization, does not share everything it does with the public, especially the embarrassing things. And in this case, I'm tempted to think the reason is that the program didn't work. Or at least not at first. The question of how the pictures on that disc evaded all but a single person, and ended up in the hands of the man it did, may seem unlikely. But when you factor in certain circumstances unique to the period, it's easy to understand how it could happen. For one, the three decades preceding the '90s were the golden age of development and technology. That may be hard to appreciate when you look around and see how much sleeker and smaller things have become. But that's just the point. Almost every technology in use today, especially in electronics, is simply a scaled down or scaled up version of things that have been around for a long time. But in the late seventies and early eighties, things were moving too fast for any one person or organization to keep up with it all. Bear in mind also that reliability was a major issue at the time. Launching a rocket in those days, especially in the Soviet program, which was notoriously unreliable, was like playing Russian roulette, if you'll forgive the pun. Sometimes they took off and sometimes they just sat there and refused to go anywhere. More often, they blew up and killed a few people for good measure. And those that did make their way into orbit often stopped working when they got there. Sometimes they stopped and started again and sometimes they didn't. The point is, the cracks for such a discovery to fall through were everywhere. If you want to know what I think happened, NASA woke up one morning and found itself with a bunch of binary gibberish no one could make any sense of and realized the professor's program had decided to work. By then the software to decompress the files was probably gathering dust in a Massachusetts basement somewhere. So who do they call? Who else? And once he had the pictures and saw what they were, the conclusion is simple."

"It is?" Francis asked.

"Sure. Given the chance, I probably would have done the same. Although I doubt I would have been able to keep my mouth shut for quite as long. That is the truly astounding thing in my opinion."

"Reginald seemed to think they have done more than just keep it a secret."

Max nodded. "Indeed, quite a lot more. I was getting to that. The satellite in the images looks like a relatively conventional communications model, but the probes are not Russian, American or European. They must have been built in private. I would have said that was unlikely, but then I'm guessing you've already figured out that money doesn't seem to be an issue here."

Mike nodded, "The Karl Gustav Foundation."

"Right. So that just leaves the question of how they were launched. Building them is one thing. That could be done anywhere with enough resources. But launching something into space, even a relatively small object, is a major undertaking and not something that can be done unnoticed. My guess is the Chinese. They have been lifting cargo into orbit since '85, mainly for their own and the European programs."

"And what are these probes meant to do?" Francis asked.

"I have no idea. But judging by the unusually large number of antennas, I'd say they were probably designed to listen for signals coming from somewhere in the area of Jupiter."

"What about the submarine?" Mike said.

"An interesting idea, I have to admit. It's a first generation Victor-class boat. The hull may well have been available as scrap, but that's all it would have been. Everything else would have been stripped. It would have been an ambitious undertaking to get her seaworthy again, especially with those doors. Who knows."

Francis shook his head and sighed. "All that said, we're still no closer, are we?"

"To what?" Max said.

"To finding out who these people are."

"Aren't you?" Max said. "I would have thought that was the simplest riddle of all."

"What do you mean?" Francis asked.

Max sat down at the desk and opened a new window in the browser. He typed Professor Peter Bershadsky into the Google search bar and clicked on the images tab. A series of pictures appeared on the screen. He scrolled down to a black and white one and opened it.

"That's the professor at MIT in nineteen seventy-eight with his two daughters. Caroline, who is twelve, and Richelle, who is seven."

Max minimized the window, opened a new one and typed: Karl Gustav Foundation. Choosing the foundation's official website from the results, he clicked on a link marked Who We Are and a picture of a striking woman in her early forties dressed in a tan trouser suit appeared. She was standing casually outside the Fraumunster Church in Zurich. The title read: Caroline De Villepin, Chairman of the Karl Gustav Foundation and one of the city's most generous philanthropists.

"I checked the name," Max said, "De Villepin is their mother's maiden name. I'm guessing they changed it at some point to keep the name Bershadsky out of the limelight."

"Holy shit," Mike said.

"Sometimes the most obvious things are the easiest to miss," Max said. "Hitler had four million troops practically spilling over the Russian border in '41 and Uncle Joe still didn't believe there would be an invasion. Although that's probably not a very good analogy. But you know what I mean."

"So it's settled, then," Mike said. "Switzerland it is."

Francis nodded. "I guess so."

Max opened the disc slot on his laptop and handed Francis the CD. "You may need this."

Francis took it, hesitated, then handed it back. "I'd like to ask you for a favor. Would you mind...?"

"I've already copied it," Max said. "When should I expect a call?"

Francis smiled, "Give us forty-eight hours. If you haven't heard anything by then, go to the press."

This time is was Max who laughed. "My dear boy, taking this to the press would be like telling the pope you had a message from God."

"Then what do you suggest?" Francis said.

"The only way to go public with something like this is through people who would know what to make of it. Leave it to me. If I don't hear from you in the next two days, I think I can guarantee you a lot more than a back page story in the Sun."

# CHAPTER 56

**Pandora**
**Kattegat Sea, Denmark**
**Sunday 23 July 2006**
**2200 CEST**

Captain Almila was enjoying a plate of savusilli, a dish of smoked herring and new potatoes from his native Finland, when the call came through the galley loudspeakers that the Danish pilot was boarding the ship. He finished his meal and used the small elevator in the hall outside to make his way to the bridge. He got there before the pilot and was standing on the bridge when he arrived with the chief mate.

The ultra-modern bridge had long since ceased to be a novelty to the crew, but for the pilot who had never been on board a similar vessel, it was a unique experience.

Unlike most vessels her size, the Pandora was not directly powered by piston-driven engines, but used four of the largest and most powerful electric motors ever built to drive her propellers. Each motor was powered by a bank of three diesel generators. This made her both the most silent ship of her class, and arguably the least fuel-efficient.

A closer inspection of the ship would have raised more questions than answers even to a qualified engineer - chief among them, why an oceangoing research vessel would be built with a flat keel of three heavily reinforced steel layers.

The computer system that ran her left little for her crew to do - a fact reflected on the bridge, which contained only a narrow bank of dials and monitoring equipment. The bridge was rectangular in shape and situated at the top of a superstructure located behind the bow as opposed to at the stern. The tall curved viewing windows ran all the way across on both sides of the bridge, allowing the crew to see the deck of the ship and the sea ahead with equal clarity. In the center of the bridge, a chair that looked more like an upholstered throne was mounted on a revolving pivot that gave the occupier a three hundred and sixty degree range of motion.

Captain Almila greeted the pilot and pointed at the chair. "She's all yours, sir."

The pilot only looked at the chair and back to the captain. "Captain, I'm not sure..."

"Please," Almila said, "I assure you, it's quite straightforward."

The pilot stepped up and into the chair, clearly ill at ease with the alien nature of the controls, and sat down. Almila pushed a button on the armrest and a large screen descended from the ceiling, showing a map of the surrounding waterway. There was a joystick at the end of the armrest on the right-hand side. Almila took it and pushed the button on top with his thumb. The picture changed from the map to a video image of the ship from a camera mounted above the bridge.

"You can select any of the eighteen external cameras with this," Almila said.

When he pushed the stick gently to port the response from the ship was instant. She could be felt not turning so much as pivoting on a central axis.

"Amazing," the pilot said, still hesitant to take over the controls.

"Back and forth to regulate speed," Almila said. "She turns on a dime and the thrusters will bring her to a stop in less than a quarter of a mile. The button under your thumb will also select the fathometer if you push it to the right and radar to the left."

The pilot grabbed the joystick hesitantly and gave it an experimental nudge to starboard. "I've never seen anything like it. She handles better than my Volvo."

Almila laughed. "You're wondering what they pay me for, right? She's on autopilot at the moment, but please feel free to take control at any time. Now if you don't mind, there is something I need to attend to. The chief mate will assist you until I return. You have the con, sir."

Almila left the bridge and returned to his own quarters. The luxurious space looked more like a three-room suite at the Hilton than anything so humble as a cabin. He sat down at the large desk in one corner of the room and faced the computer. A moment later the face of Richelle de Villepin appeared on the screen. The image was striking, both for its clarity, and the beauty of the woman herself.

"We've entered the Kattegat," Almila said. "We should be in position in just under twelve hours, presuming we don't run into any problems."

"I'm glad to hear it, Captain. How did you get on with the pilot?"

"Oh, the usual. By the time we reach Bornholm, he won't want to leave. What's the status on RP One?"

"Still on course."

"Good," Almila said. "I'll contact you again when we reach Bornholm."

# CHAPTER 57

**Aurora**
**Monday 24 July 2006**
**1000 EEST**

Mitch and Heinz were sitting at a table on the veranda overlooking the harbor. Mitch had been listening in rapt fascination for almost half an hour as Heinz described both how the cave had been found and the enormous effort involved in turning it into a habitable structure.

The little harbor-front town – if you could call five buildings a town - had actually been the first thing built. According to Heinz, it was the indispensable representation of civilization without which life inside Aurora would be unbearable, if not impossible. The residents called it Amity, after the small town in the movie Jaws, although nobody seemed to know who had started it.

"I just can't get over it," Mitch said, "All these people living and working here in complete isolation."

Heinz took a sip of his coffee and greeted a man who sat down several tables away.

"That's Harold," Heinz said. "He's one of the programmers. If you want to know exactly how the emulator works, he's the man to speak to about it. The thing you have to understand is that this isn't just a random group of people, they're scientists, doctors, and engineers. And each and every one of them was thoroughly prepared for what they found here. We actually placed a question in one of the surveys we give to all potential candidates: 'do you accept the possibility that there may be other intelligent life in the universe?' It's one of a hundred and fifty other random questions, but it's the only answer we really look at. Anyone who says 'no' is out. Do you see what I mean?"

"That's actually quite clever," Mitch said.

"Anyway, my point is, you are the only person ever to set foot in this facility without a measure of preparation. I won't lie; there were some heated discussions about what should be done with you. It was Erik who finally convinced me that you should be treated no differently than anyone else who arrives here. I believe that conviction has been vindicated. In fact, were I a religious man, I might even say your coming here was providence. I'd like you to stay. I'd like you to join us, Mitch."

Mitch was silent for a long time. When he turned his eyes back to Heinz he said, "First tell me what happened to Mike."

"Agent Banner knows nothing that could compromise this facility or our work here. I assure you, he is safe and well."

"What about Bruce Jessops?"

"Jessops is what you might call a necessary evil. I'm afraid there is no way to legally elicit the help of a government official, and yet at times we have no choice - although I have a feeling your expertise might change that. Jessops is amply compensated for his efforts, as you well know. We are aware that Agent Banner could report him to his superiors. If that happens, we'll assist him and his family in any way we can. Remember, he was co-opted, not blackmailed. As for your own friendship with agent Banner, staying here would obviously mean you could have no further direct contact. I'm afraid that is a part of the choice I can't help you with."

Mitch nodded to say he understood this. "You still haven't explained what Jessops was doing in the first place. Unless you're telling me that you guys are behind what happened at the Fed."

Heinz held up his hands. "What happened in New York had nothing to do with us. We hold assets at the bank however, and Jessops was instructed to ascertain if it was safe to continue keeping them there. That is all."

"You had nothing to do with Vermont, the shootings, Gerald Ross?"

"I'm afraid I don't know anything about any shootings, or anyone named Gerald Ross. I'm the chief scientist; what happens at Skyline is Titov's business."

"Who?" Mitch said.

"Titov Kargin. It's his job to keep a lid on this place so we can get on with what we're doing. Unfortunately, both he and Richelle are away."

"Who's Richelle?" Mitch said.

"The boss," Heinz said smiling. "She's also Peter Bershadsky's daughter. She's a remarkable woman. She and her sister practically grew up inside these walls after he moved his family here."

"And her sister?" Mitch said.

"Caroline is the chairman of the Karl Gustav Foundation. The running joke is that Caroline makes the money and Richelle spends it. Although that's not entirely fair. So far Aurora has cost us over 50 million dollars. That's not counting the money we spend keeping the island free of visitors."

"How *do* you? Keep people away, I mean."

"Bribes, political contributions, a lot of sovereign debt purchases and a mole or two on the inside. The island's little more than a rock, really. The Soviets set up a testing facility here in the fifties and maintained a small garrison until '65. The soldiers called it the Isle of Dragons. After the fall of the communist block it became part of Estonia."

"So we're in the Baltic?" Mitch said.

Heinz nodded. "Thirty-four miles off the eastern tip of Hiiumaa, one of Estonia's two largest islands. One of our subsidiaries was hired to survey the place for traces of radiation after rumors surfaced that the Soviets had kept warheads here."

"Rumors that you started?" Mitch said, smiling.

"Oh, we may have had something to do with it. Needless to say, our results were quite disturbing. The outcome was a ban on all travel to the island and a three-mile exclusion zone. It's enforced by a private security firm based in Talin."

"Which you own," Mitch said.

"Which we own, yes."

"You have your fingers in a lot of pies," Mitch said.

"More than you might believe," Heinz said. "The world is a dangerous place, Mitch. You probably understand that better than most. Peter Bershadsky certainly did. He understood that Origin was not only the greatest discovery in the history of mankind, but that it might also be the most sensitive. And I can tell you, he's been more than vindicated on that account."

"What do you mean?" Mitch said.

Heinz hesitated. He looked at Mitch doubtfully for a moment, then seemed to make up his mind. "We have trouble transmitting to Origin, but we have no problem receiving. One of the reasons, perhaps the primary reason, their transfer protocol requires such high levels of compression is that they contain huge amounts of data. It took us a long time to understand why, but we now think it's because the nature of the media it's stored on makes it highly susceptible to degradation. The data, not the system. My personal guess is that the microscopic scale of their architecture is only achievable using the same high-density alloys the ship itself is made of. The problem is, the alloy has a very high level of resistance, making the transistors unstable. It's a trade-off, you might say."

"And they get around it by turning the whole system into a RAID array," Mitch said.

"Yes. Luckily for us, we've had more than enough time to decompress and trans-code a significant amount of it. And some of the things we've seen are truly incredible."

"Like what?" Mitch said. He looked like a boy on his way downstairs on Christmas morning.

"Origin arrived in its current location over two thousand years ago. To put it into perspective, that was the year Julius Caesar crossed the Rubicon with his Thirteenth Legion."

"Holy shit," Mitch said.

"Yes, I said the same thing. But what's truly fascinating about the ship, apart from its gargantuan size, is that she is one of a kind. Origin is a monumental achievement even by the standards of a race that is centuries, if not millennia ahead of our own. According to her own logs, she had been in transit for almost sixty-five years before she reached our solar system.

And from what we can tell, her sole purpose was finding it."

"She was looking for Earth?" Mitch said.

"Perhaps not Earth, but any life-sustaining planet they could find. The ship was built to travel distances in excess of anything else her makers were capable of achieving by other means. And when I say she is one of a kind, I mean Origin is truly unique, never to be duplicated. It took almost six decades to build her. My point is, if there is no one left on board, and frankly we don't see how there possibly could be-"

"She's the biggest insurance write-off in the history of the universe," Mitch finished.

Heinz laughed. "I wasn't going to put it quite that way, but yes, I guess you could say that."

"And there are probably things on that ship that could wipe us off the face of the earth, am I right?" Mitch said.

"There are things on board Origin that could wipe the earth off the face of the solar system," Heinz corrected. "Not that we haven't figured out how to do that ourselves already. In that respect, we are equals at least."

Mitch sat looking down at his coffee cup for a long time. To his amazement, the feeling that he had been swept into the Twilight Zone was passing rather than growing stronger. It was a testament to the adaptability of the human mind, if nothing else. When he spoke it was in a tone of resignation. "If this place ended up in the hands of the US government, we'd be as good as gone, wouldn't we?"

Heinz nodded. "Peter was a dear friend of mine. The first time he showed me what he had found we were sitting in a park in Warsaw. I admit I didn't believe him at first. Who would? But when I realized what I was seeing, I made a similar comment."

"And what did he say?"

"He was a lot more cynical than I was. He said the only possible outcome of exposing Origin was World War Three."

Mitch could find no answer to that.

"Of course, it won't come to that," Heinz said.

"How can you be so sure?" Mitch asked.

"I'm not," Heinz said, "but it's what I chose to believe. If I didn't, there would be no point in any of this."

They sat in silence for a long time, Mitch trying to imagine what might happen if someone really did find Aurora and Heinz looking at him in a way that suggested he understood exactly what he was going through. When their eyes met again, Mitch said, "What I can't quite believe is how you can know about this while nobody else does. I mean, if the picture in the museum is real, where did it come from?"

"The picture is one of four taken by Voyager two on the ninth of July nineteen seventy-nine," Heinz said. "And the story of how they evaded the people who run the program and landed in the hands of the professor is one that is both fascinating and a little too long for me to tell you here. Perhaps another time?"

"I'd love to hear it," Mitch said.

"Good," Heinz said and stood. "Now if you'll excuse me, I'm going to have to leave you. I'll let Sarah know you're here."

Mitch watched Heinz leave. The waiter, a young dark-skinned man in a white jumpsuit, cleared the table and asked Mitch if he would like anything else.

"I'm all right," Mitch said. "Well, that's probably being a little optimistic. I'm as all right as I can be."

The man only smiled, and Mitch realized his English was probably rudimentary at best. As he watched the man walk back inside, Mitch found himself thinking that things weren't so different here after all. The thought was both a slight relief and disturbing at the same time. The man who had sat down at the table a few yards away must have seen the expression on Mitch's face because he leaned over and said, "Guajas."

"Sorry?" Mitch said.

"They're Awa Guajas, an indigenous people from the Brazilian rainforest."

"That's not very reassuring," Mitch said.

The man laughed and stood up. He came over and introduced himself.

"I said the same thing when I first arrived," he said. "Rest assured, they're quite happy here. Most of them arrived before any of this was built. Kevin, that's the name of your waiter, is actually a foreman of construction. Come back tomorrow and you'll probably be served by someone with a PhD in metaphysics. We take it in turns. I'm on the booth at the theater this evening. And my wife will be serving the popcorn once her shift at the medical center is over. She's our resident pediatrician."

Mitch looked at him for a moment to make sure he wasn't pulling his leg. When he didn't smile, Mitch said, "Have you got a landscaping detail?"

To his surprise, Randolph nodded. "Sure do. If you want on board, you'll have to speak to Steve Dunphy. He's the chief electrician."

Mitch only shook his head. "This place is going to take some getting used to."

Randolph smiled and gave Mitch a pat on the back. "Welcome to the last outpost of true Marxist-Leninism."

# CHAPTER 58

**Zurich, Switzerland**
**Monday 24 July 2006**
**1100 EDT**

Francis ordered another cappuccino and picked up the newspaper on the table in front of him. From his seat to the left of the cafe door he had a clear view of the entrance to the building. In the hour he had been there only three people had entered, and only one had left. The Karl Gustav Foundation apparently did not have many visitors. He had noted four cameras monitoring the entrance, two above the glass double doors and two on the building across the street.

He called the waitress over and asked for the check. When it arrived he left fifteen Franks on the table, tucked the newspaper under one arm and crossed the street. As he reached the curb on the other side, Mike rounded the corner and took up his seat outside the cafe. He watched Francis stroll by the entrance to the building, take one casual glance inside, and carry on down the street.

As soon as Francis came back around the corner Mike paid for his coffee and set off alongside the building in the other direction. They met up again ten minutes later in the lobby of Zurich's central train station.

"It's a goddamn fortress," Francis said.

"It is?"

"All the adjacent buildings have cameras pointed across the street. Even at the back where there is no entrance. Don't you think that's overkill for an office building?"

"It's not just any office building though, is it?" Mike said.

"No, it isn't. The waiter at the cafe was also watching us."

"He was?"

"Trust me."

"So what the hell do we do?" Mike asked.

"We switch to Plan C."

"Okay. What was Plan B, just out of curiosity?"

"Doesn't matter. It won't work."

"And Plan C will?"

"It might. Ideally I'd like to get eyes on the place for a day or so but it's too risky."

Francis pulled an envelope out of his backpack and handed it to Mike. Written on it in cursive letters were the words *Caroline de Villepin.*

"You see that guy over there by the door?" Francis said.

"The one in the suit?"

"Yeah. Now look over there, the guy sitting at the table."

"In the Lycra shorts?"

"Yes. He's a bike messenger."

Francis handed Mike a ten and a hundred Frank note. "Give the guy in the suit the letter and the money. Then tell him he can keep the ten if he gives the hundred and the letter to the biker and asks him to deliver it to number 53 Bahnhofstrasse. Can you remember all that?"

"Sure, 53 Bahnhofstrasse, I got it."

"As soon as suit man stands up and walks, you head out the door. Go."

Francis watched with some trepidation as Mike approached the man in the suit. The man listened then took the ten Frank note and put it in his pocket. When he got up and walked away Mike made a beeline for the door and was outside before he reached the biker. At first Francis didn't think the biker was going to do it. The younger man looked skeptically at the envelope and shook his head. The man in the suit reached into his pocket and handed him the note. The biker took the money and put it in his pocket then stuffed the envelope into the shoulder pouch next to his chair and the two men parted company.

Francis waited until the messenger finished eating then followed him outside where Mike was waiting. They watched as he unlocked his bike and rode off.

"Suit man gave him the ten," Francis said.

"You're fucking joking!"

"Nope. He tried to get him to do it for nothing. When that didn't work he gave him the ten."

"Son of a bitch."

"Makes no difference to us," Francis said.

"So now what?"

"If she's there you're going to meet her in an hour on the Munster Bridge."

"You don't actually think she'll come, do you?"

"No. But someone will."

"Great, so you're using me as bait. And if the someone who comes isn't happy about it? Then what?"

"I doubt they would try anything stupid in broad daylight."

"You doubt? Are we talking about the same people? I seem to remember a speech you gave me once in which you made it very clear that these people don't play by the rules."

"If they pull up in a car and you think they might make a grab for you, jump."

Mike's face was stunned. "Into the fucking water?"

"It's not a very high bridge. I checked."

"Yeah, that's not the point-"

"You said you wanted into the spy game; well, here it is. We kill people, we try not to get killed ourselves, and sometimes when we have no other choice we jump off bridges."

"All right. And if they just want to talk?"

"Then you talk. Keep them occupied. The longer, the better."

"And where do you come into Plan C?" Mike said. "You going to be sitting on a nearby rooftop with a sniper rifle?"

"Not exactly. She won't come to the bridge, but I'm betting she'll be there. She'll want to see you herself."

"What makes you so sure?"

"Because you're a friend of her father's."

"I am?"

"An old colleague. You've come to tell her something important, but you need to do it in person. You would have gone to the office but you think someone may be watching you. A regular mystery sandwich, as they say. Gets 'em every time."

"And while she's watching me you're watching her, is that it?"

Francis nodded and handed Mike several one-hundred Frank notes. "If they ask you to go with them you refuse and you make your way back here. There's a police station around the corner from here in that direction. Wait outside and I'll get back here as soon as I can."

"And if I end up in the river?"

"Then you swim."

# CHAPTER 59

**Aurora**
**Monday 24 July 2006**
**1200 EEST**

Mitch saw Sarah walking up the street as he stepped out of One Eyed Jack's.

"So, what do you think of Heinz?" she asked.

"He seems like a nice guy," Mitch said.

"He was the first person the director ever told about Origin. My father says they would never have found the signal without him. But I guess he told you that."

"No, he didn't actually."

"I can't believe he brought you here. I don't think I've ever seen him do anything but work. He must like you."

Mitch wasn't listening. He was looking up at the roof of the cave. "He said we're on an island."

Sarah raised her eyebrows. "He did?"

"Yes. In the Baltic."

"That's right," she said. "Although-"

"He wasn't supposed to tell me that, I know. He also asked me to stay."

Her face lit up. "Well if Heinz wants you here, you can stop worrying about the chief."

"What's his deal, anyway? The chief, I mean."

"Brendan has always been that way. He was Peter Bershadsky's personal bodyguard until he died. My dad calls him the 'cold warrior' when he's annoyed with him. He said Peter met him in Berlin when Brendan was still in the army. He might be a pain in the butt sometimes, but he's also one of Richelle's most loyal friends. And he takes his job very seriously. Maybe a little too seriously."

"I don't know about that," Mitch said. "From what I've just heard, I don't think that's even possible. I just hope he doesn't go on hating me, especially if I'm going to be sticking around."

"He doesn't hate you," Sarah said. "He just doesn't know you. Don't worry, he'll come around."

To his surprise, she took his hand and led him down the side walk, "If you know where we are, I guess we might as well go up and have a look around."

"Up?" Mitch said.

"To the surface. You didn't think we were all stuck down here, did you?"

# CHAPTER 60

**Zurich, Switzerland**
**Monday 24 July 2006**
**1300 EDT**

Francis cursed and lowered the binoculars. If Caroline was here, he couldn't see her.

They had arrived early. Not one, but two men, approaching from opposite ends of the bridge. One of them had stayed on the other side as his partner first passed Mike then turned back and leaned on the railing several feet away. They had been talking for almost two minutes, and Francis didn't think Mike would be able to keep them there much longer with the little he knew.

"Come on. Where are you, Caroline?" Francis said.

Francis picked up the binoculars again and trained them on the man on the other side of the bridge, then swept back to Mike. The man standing next to him raised his foot and gave the railing a light tap with the toe of his shoe. Francis moved back to the man on the other side, who saw the signal and took out his phone.

"Go on, you son of a bitch. Show me where she is," Francis said.

The glance was subtle but Francis was looking for it. The man's head turned towards the east bank for a moment. There were two lines of cars parked there in front of the church on the street below him. Francis scanned them. In the middle of the row nearest the church there was a yellow GT3 Porsche with tinted windows. He was about to turn away when he saw her head come up briefly and then disappear again.

"Got you!"

He threw the binoculars into his backpack and ran across the roof to the top of the stairs. Halfway down he almost collided with a cleaning woman coming the other way. He emerged from a side door and walked to the edge of the building where he could just make out the rear spoiler of the Porsche behind a black Mercedes. Throwing his backpack over one shoulder, he lowered the sun visor of his baseball cap and rounded the corner. As he passed the car he turned and saw her hunkered down in the driver's seat.

Francis reached into his pocket and put his hand around the butt of the small revolver there. He walked to the end of the line of cars and knelt, pretending to tie his shoe. When he glanced over at the bridge, Mike was gone.

"Take your hand out of your pocket and stand up."

Francis turned. It was the man who had been covering the meeting on the bridge.

"Excuse me?" Francis said. "Do I know-"

"Your hand, take it out of your pocket."

Francis did.

"Good. Now stand up and walk toward the bridge."

Francis began to stand then crouched back down and sprang into the gap between the two cars on his right. He landed on his hands, rolled forward and darted around the front of a blue Saab. The man shouted something in German and the engine of the Porsche suddenly came to life. The rear wheels began to spin and send up clouds of smoke as the driver floored the accelerator and reversed out. Francis raised his head above the hood of the Saab and saw the man crouch from view, gun held out at arm's length.

Francis broke cover and ran just as the Porsche drove away toward the bridge. For a split second, he caught a glimpse of her wide, terrified eyes. She swerved towards him and almost succeeded in running him over. Francis jumped and felt the wing mirror break off as it hit the heel of his shoe. She turned onto the bridge, tires screeching and gunned the four hundred horsepower engine. Francis ran after her.

As he reached the bridge the man behind him fired two shots. One of the bullets hit the metal railing and ricocheted past Francis's head. The Porsche reached the end of the bridge and had to stop behind a van. Francis ran faster. He had almost reached the car when the van pulled out and the Porsche swerved past it and turned left along the bank of the river. He turned and saw the man who had shot at him was now running toward him.

A white Volkswagen Golf turned onto the bridge in front of him and Francis ran into the middle of the road and held up both hands. The driver stopped and rolled down his window. Before he could say anything Francis was pulling him out by the collar of his jacket and getting in behind the wheel.

The man running after him fired two more shots. One shattered the rear window, the other went through the passenger seat and lodged in the dashboard. Francis reversed straight out into the traffic behind him, forcing a large truck to swerve and mount the curb to avoid a collision. The Porsche was already several hundred yards ahead of him now.

Francis had been expecting little from the small German car, but when he put it in gear and stepped on the gas, it accelerated quickly. Ahead he could see the Porsche trying to nudge its way between two other cars, but the gap was too narrow for the wide sports car. He was only fifty yards behind her when the traffic began to move again and she turned left across the next bridge, quickly opening the gap between them. Somewhere in the distance he could hear approaching sirens. Francis hit the steering wheel with both palms and cursed.

He caught up to her again just as the road veered around to the left. She swerved into the oncoming traffic and accelerated through the red light into the intersection. Francis followed her and almost ran straight into the side of a bus. He was too intent on keeping up with the faster car to notice the black Mercedes that had been parked next to her join the chase. The first he knew of it was when it rammed him from behind as he slowed down to make a sharp right turn. The force of the impact almost sent the Golf into a spin that he just managed to bring back under control.

When he checked his rear view mirror he saw that the headlights of the Mercedes were blinking alternately, as were the blue ones behind the grill.

"Just what we fucking need," Francis said.

Up ahead, the Porsche turned again and crossed a small bridge before flying through another red light and into a narrow street between two tall buildings. The brake lights suddenly came on and Francis saw she was trapped. A van had stopped halfway down the street, blocking the road. Francis slammed on the brakes and came to a stop in the middle of the intersection. Behind him, the Mercedes was closing in fast. When he saw her get out of the car, he backed up and blocked the road, then got out himself and ran after her.

She saw him. But instead of running, she ducked behind the front of her car. There was a loud crash behind him and Francis turned to see the Golf roll onto its roof in the middle of the intersection. A moment later the Mercedes, its grill now gone and the hood buckled, swerved past it and drove into the road behind him.

Francis didn't see the car that pulled up behind the van. When he turned back, two men were running past the Porsche in his direction. The Mercedes screeched to a halt only twenty yards away. Both men in front of him were armed and shouting something in German. It wasn't exactly hard to guess what they were saying. Francis weighed the odds and considered making a run for it back to the intersection. But when both doors of the Mercedes opened and two more armed men stepped out – one of them holding a large caliber machine gun – he realized the game was up.

Francis dropped the gun and raised both hands. "I'm not armed."

They approached him cautiously, weapons raised and clearly prepared to shoot at the first sign of any trouble. They stopped several yards short and one of them – Francis thought he recognized him as the man who had spoken to Mike on the bridge – shouted something in the direction of the van blocking the road. Francis turned and saw Caroline stand up. She looked hesitant, but the man said something else to her and she started walking in their direction. Francis noticed several people standing on the balconies above watching them.

Caroline stopped between the two men in front of Francis. "Who are you?"

"Where's my friend?" Francis said, ignoring the question.

"He's unharmed. How long that remains the case is up to you."

Francis looked around. "If he and I aren't released immediately everything on the drive goes public. You know what that means? It means you fucking people are going to burn."

The threat didn't produce the reaction he had expected. In fact, it produced none at all.

"Take him," Caroline said.

One of the men stepped forward and took out a set of handcuffs.

"You think I'm joking?" Francis said. "If I go down, Skyline goes with me. You hear me?"

Caroline was already walking away. The man put the cuffs on Francis and nudged him toward the waiting Mercedes. Francis turned and shouted after her. "Are you really going to throw away everything your father has done? His precious fucking spaceship?"

Caroline stopped. "What did you say?"

"I said the world will know about the ship and everything you've done to try and hide it."

For a long moment she said nothing. Francis watched her, trying to read her eyes.

"Who the hell are you?" she finally said. "And where did you hear about-"

One of the men stepped forward and said something to her. Caroline shook her head. When he repeated himself she looked at Francis, bewildered. "Take the cuffs off him."

"Miss de Villepin," the man said in heavily accented English, "we have to take him in."

She ignored him. "Why did you come here?"

"I want your people to back off. I'm willing to return the drive, but not the copies. They will be kept safe as long as you hold up your end of the deal. Try anything stupid and I send a copy to every newspaper and intelligence agency I can think of."

"Drive?" Caroline said. "What are you talking about?"

Francis held out his hand for his backpack. Caroline nodded and one of the men inspected it briefly and handed it over. Francis took out the hard drive and handed it to Caroline. "This one."

She took it. The surprise he saw on her face was genuine.

"Where did you get this?" she asked.

"Like you don't know. I would have thought-"

A sudden wave of hot air swept past them, knocking Caroline to the ground along with the two men behind her. A split second later the explosion reached their ears. Through the heat haze Francis saw the

Porsche leave the ground, rise at least eight feet into the air and fall back to the street on its side. Everything around it was engulfed in flame. The force of the blast had knocked the van onto its side and Francis saw a man run out of the building on the right, his clothes on fire.

One of the men behind him pulled Francis back by the collar of his shirt while the other ran forward to help Caroline. The man was saying something, but every car alarm in the street had gone off and Francis couldn't make out a word of it. Caroline got to her feet and shouted something at the two men behind her. One of them ran forward, the other limped toward the sidewalk. A sliver of yellow metal was lodged in his leg just below the knee.

Suddenly Francis was being picked up and dragged toward the Mercedes. When one of the men opened the trunk, Francis was both horrified and relieved to see Mike inside. His hands were tied behind his back and his mouth had been covered with a wide strip of duct tape, but otherwise he seemed unharmed. They lifted Francis off his feet and pushed him inside. He got a final glimpse of the intersection, where a police car had stopped next to the overturned Volkswagen, then the trunk closed and the world went dark.

# CHAPTER 61

**The Callisto**
**Monday 24 July 2006**
**1430 CEST**

Captain Williams stepped into the doorway and waved the smoke out of his face.

"What the hell happened?" he asked his engineer, who was kneeling at the base of the diesel generator.

"Someone knocked out one of the oil seals," the engineer said. "The fucking thing looks like it's seized up completely."

"What do you mean, *someone*?"

"I mean someone knocked it out."

The engineer reached down and picked up a small metal disk. The floor under his feet was covered in oil. He held it up and pointed at a dent in the lip of the seal. "It was pried out with something. Probably a screwdriver or a small crowbar. Doesn't really fucking matter which it was, because we're stuck here either way."

Williams took the seal and inspected it. "You're saying someone deliberately sabotaged the generator?"

"That's exactly what I'm saying."

Williams turned to one of the men behind him, "Get me the Master at Arms down here right away."

He turned back to his engineer, "Can it be fixed?"

"No idea. If any of the piston rods are bent, there's no way I'll get her going again. I'll have to remove the head and take a look."

"Get it done," Williams said. "Use as many men as you need. I'm going to contact Aurora."

The captain left the engine room and ran back to his cabin. Titov Kargin, the organization's unofficial chief of security and all-around mister fix-it, was sitting on the captain's bunk reading a book. At two inches shy of seven feet, the Russian was too big to use the desk.

"What's the problem?" Titov said when he saw Williams.

"Engine trouble," Williams said and closed the door behind him. "We also have a saboteur on board."

Titov raised an eyebrow. "We do?"

"Someone pulled one of the oil seals out of the generator."

There was a knock on the door. It was the communications officer. "Sir, we've lost the link to Darkstar."

Williams and Titov shared a foreboding look.

"Can it be fixed?" Williams asked.

"I'm not sure, sir."

"Go back and try. I'll be there in a minute. And tell the master-at-arms to get his ass in here!"

"I don't like this," Titov said. "You're sure the generator was disabled deliberately?"

"Ben is. That's good enough for me."

"Then we need to find out who did it before he destroys anything else."

"You mean like the comm link?"

Williams opened the door and shouted, "Where the fuck is Shane?"

A boy of about eighteen ran up to him and said, "Sir, the Master at Arms isn't in his cabin."

Williams looked back at Titov, who stood up - crouched might be a more accurate description - and said, "Come on, let's go."

They made their way to the bridge where the comms officer was busy trying to reconnect to the satellite.

"Sasha, what's wrong with it?" Williams asked.

"I'm not getting anything back from Darkstar, sir."

Just then the Master at Arms arrived. He was still fastening his belt.

"Where the fuck have you been?" Williams said, then looked down at the newspaper in the man's hand and went on, "Never mind. We have a situation. Go get the chief up here."

The Master at Arms returned a minute later with the chief engineer in tow.

"Is it possible the seal was removed before we left?" Williams asked him.

"No."

"What if it was pushed back in?" Titov said. "Not all the way, but far enough to get us here before falling out."

The chief considered this and nodded. "It's possible. I only started the generator after we surfaced, so yes, maybe."

"All right," Williams said. "Get back down there and do what you can."

Williams turned to Sasha. "Anything?"

Sasha shook his head. "Nothing, sir."

"Fuck!" Williams shouted. "When I find the son of a bitch behind this I'm going to hang him. I want every man we can fit in the engine room down there helping the chief. We need to get this boat back on the move as fast as possible."

"And if it can't be fixed?" Titov asked.

"Then it looks like someone is going for a very fucking unpleasant swim."

# CHAPTER 62

**Zurich, Switzerland**
**Monday 24 July 2006**
**1500 EDT**

It took them ten minutes, but Francis eventually managed to get his hands close enough to pull the tape off Mike's mouth. However, before he could ask Mike anything the car stopped. They heard a door being rolled shut and then two of the doors on the car opened. Caroline was saying something to one of the men in German. It sounded like the two were arguing. A moment later the trunk opened and they found themselves looking up at the stern face of Caroline de Villepin. Her hair was a mess and the navy blue trouser suit she was wearing was done for, but she seemed unharmed.

"We need to talk," Francis said.

"Who sent you?" Caroline asked.

"No one. And I didn't blow up your car, if that's what you're thinking."

"Why should I believe you?"

"I'll tell you what," Francis said, "you arrange it so my friend here can get his knee out of my balls and I'll do my best to explain it to you."

Five minutes later Francis and Mike were seated on opposite sides of a steel beam protruding from the floor. Their hands were tied behind their backs and their feet were bound together with thick plastic wire ties.

"This isn't exactly what I had in mind," Francis said. "What about you, Mike? Is this what you had in mind?"

"I had my heart set on a couch, actually," Mike said.

The man guarding them didn't respond. He just stood there, stone-faced, looking straight ahead. He had an MP5 submachine gun slung over one shoulder.

"What happened to you, anyway?" Francis asked. "I told you to jump if they tried anything."

"I was never a very good swimmer," Mike said.

A door opened at one end of the empty warehouse and Caroline walked in through a dusty beam of bright sunshine. She was talking to someone on the phone and sounded agitated.

"Then find him, god damn it," she said. "I want him on the phone in the next hour."

"Things not going well?" Francis said when she put the phone down.

"I'm going to ask you one more time," Caroline said. "Who sent you?"

"And I'm going to tell you one more time," Francis said. "No one sent us. We're here alone."

"Where did you get this?" she said, holding up the hard drive.

"I stole it from the Federal Reserve Bank of New York," Francis said. "I thought it belonged to the CIA."

She clearly didn't believe him, but evidently decided to humor him all the same. "And how did you know it was being kept there?"

"I just told you, I didn't. I had no idea what was on it until you assholes started killing people."

"Killing who?"

"Are we really going to do this?" Francis asked.

Caroline only looked at him.

"All right," Francis said, "Gerald and Cynthia Ross, for starters. Valerie Tremblay and the cook out on I-91, for another. Any of this sounding familiar yet? Several FBI agents in La Tuque? No?"

The bitch of it was, she really didn't seem to know what he was talking about. It wasn't in her face or the eyes - those things were easy enough to control with a little training - but in the way she was getting annoyed. Not because he was telling her things she already knew, but because she clearly thought he was just buying time.

"I'm running out of patience," Caroline said. "I want to know who sent you and who gave you this drive. If you're not going to tell me freely, then it will have to be under duress."

Her choice of words and the way she said them made the threat sound pathetic somehow. Francis didn't think the idea of torturing anyone had ever crossed her mind before.

"Mike," Francis said, "if you've got any ideas, now might be a good time to share."

"We know about Bruce Jessops," Mike said. "Why don't you call and ask him how we got the drive?"

Again, the name seemed to mean nothing to her. Before Mike could say anything else the man beside Caroline spoke. The only word they recognized was Jessops. Caroline frowned and asked him something else. When he answered she said, "How do you know about Jessops?"

"I met him at the FBI field office in New York," Mike said. "You may not believe it, but the Fed was broken into, and this is the guy who did it. I know because I was one of the investigating officers."

"You're an agent of the FBI," Caroline said. It wasn't a question, but her way of saying she didn't believe him.

"Yes, I am. Or was. Jessops was sent from Washington to supervise the handover of the investigation, which is how he got-"

Caroline's phone began to ring and she answered it.

"Where the hell are you?" she said.

She listened for a moment and said, "Carl? Are you sure?"

She listened again and said, "All right, I'll leave right away. Call me when you find him."

She hung up and said something to the man beside her, who nodded and pulled back the cocking handle on his MP5. Caroline was halfway to the door when he turned it toward Mike and offered him a humorless grin.

"We know where the submarine goes!" Francis shouted after her.

She stopped but didn't turn around. The man holding the gun on Mike lowered it and looked at her. Francis saw real worry on his face.

"If we go missing, half the US Navy is going to show up on your doorstep," Francis said. "Might be a bit awkward, don't you think?"

Somewhere outside, a turbine engine fired up, followed by the sound of rotors beginning to pick up speed. Caroline seemed to be in two minds about what to do.

Francis and Mike had no idea what the man with the MP5 said to her, but whatever it was, it seemed to make up her mind. She said something and walked out the door. A moment later the man Francis thought of as bridge guy number one came back in. He untied them as MP5 guy stood back. They were led out of the warehouse, which wasn't a warehouse at all, but a hangar, and out into a farmhouse courtyard. They saw the helicopter about fifty yards beyond the low stone wall sitting in the middle of an open field. Its rotors were now a blur and the wind caught them as soon as they walked through the rusty steel gate.

Francis recognized it as a Kazan Mi-172, a converted version of the Mi-17 Russian transport helicopter. It was painted a dark blue and appeared to have only two windows toward the front of the fuselage. Caroline stood aside as they were ushered up the steps into a luxuriously decorated interior. Bridge guy number one walked to the end of the cabin and opened a narrow door. MP5 guy told them to get inside.

When the door was closed and locked they were back in the dark. Francis felt around and was relieved to find a cushioned seat running along both sides.

"We know where the submarine goes?" Mike said.

"Hey, it worked, didn't it? I don't know if you were keeping up with current events back there, but we almost bought the farm."

"I don't think she has a fucking clue what we were talking about," Mike said.

"I think you're right," Francis agreed. "I'd say we were dealing with one of two possibilities. Either they take a very laid-back approach to management, or someone has broken ranks and set out on their own. I'm inclined to believe the latter."

"Why would their own people want to cover up the missing drive?" Mike asked.

"I don't know," Francis said. "But we better convince them that that's exactly what's going on, because I don't have any more aces up my sleeve. The old submarine trick was the last one."

# CHAPTER 63

**The Callisto**
**Somewhere on the Baltic Sea**
**Monday 24 July 2006**
**1600 CEST**

Titov and Captain Williams were sitting in the officer's mess looking over a map when a member of the crew came in.

"Sir," he said, "The chief asked me to tell you that he can fix the generator, but it will take him another three hours."

"Good. Tell him I'll be right down."

Williams took the plotting compass and held it between their position and the town of Utska on the Polish coast. "One hundred and eighty miles. There's no point turning back to Aurora without the comms link. If we're moving again by 1900, we could be there by 0330 at a stretch."

Titov nodded. "What choice do we have?"

"None. I'm going down to the engine room to see if I can speed things up."

# CHAPTER 64

**Utska, Poland**
**Monday 24 July 2006**
**1930 CEST**

The three men seated around the table all looked up at the guard as he came in.

"Contact Aurora and tell them we've lost contact with the Callisto." Richelle told him

The man left in a hurry. Richelle looked down at the map in the middle of the table where a large circle had been drawn to indicate the position of the Pandora, now anchored halfway between Klaipeda on the Polish coast and the Swedish island of Morbylanga. "I fucking knew something like this would happen," she said. "God damn it!"

A moment later the head of the security team appeared in the doorway.

"What is it, Gary?" Richelle said.

"Ma'am, there's a helicopter approaching. It's using the correct authentication codes."

Richelle stood. "Keep trying. I want Captain Williams on the line by the time I get back."

As they walked out into the back garden another guard came running out of the house behind them.

"Who the hell is that?" Richelle asked.

"I don't know, ma'am," the security chief said.

"Is it ours?"

Before he could answer the helicopter turned on its landing light and they were both temporarily blinded. Richelle moved back, covering her eyes.

"Move back and be prepared to shoot anyone that gets out," she said.

Both men cocked their machine guns and knelt down behind the low hedgerow running along the back of the house. The helicopter turned as it descended and Richelle saw that it *was* one of theirs. It touched down gently on the grass and the pilot immediately switched off the turbines. The blades were still spinning when the door opened and Caroline stepped out.

"What the hell are you doing here?" Richelle said when Caroline reached them.

"Has Jack Fielding called?" Caroline said.

"No, he hasn't. Are you going to answer my question?"

Caroline turned back toward the helicopter and signaled. "We have a serious problem. I thought Jack would have called to let you know we were coming. It was his idea."

Richelle watched as Mike and Francis were led down the steps and across the lawn. When they stopped Francis winked at Richelle and said, "Evening, ma'am."

"Who the fuck are these people, Caroline? And why would you bring them here, of all the god damn places on earth?"

"Someone tried to kill me, Richelle."

"What?"

"Someone planted a bomb under my car. I would have been on my way to Frankfurt at the time, but these two showed up..."

Caroline's voice trailed off and went silent, as if this fact had eluded her until now.

"Someone better start making sense," Richelle said.

"Richelle," Francis said. "May I call you Richelle?"

"No you may not! Who the hell are you?"

"Okay, Ms. de Villepin, then. My name is Francis Moore. I admit we came to Zurich to find your sister, but we had nothing to do with the bomb. If you can just accept that in good faith for the time being, perhaps you'll let me explain why we are here. From what I have seen, it may be more important to you than it is to us."

Richelle studied Francis for a moment. "What are you doing here?"

"To cut a long story short, I used to kill people for the Pentagon. Ten days ago I broke into the Federal Reserve Bank in New York with the help of a man named Gerald Ross. A man your people killed. I did it to get my hands on something I needed to blackmail my former employer into shutting down the program I used to work for. The safety deposit box I found your drive in once belonged to the CIA. If I'd known that was no longer the case, I would never have taken it."

Caroline handed the drive to Richelle. "He found this at the bank."

Richelle studied the drive for a moment. "You found this in a vault in New York?"

"Yes," Francis said. "We came to Zurich to return it. And to tell you we have no interest in what's on it as long as you call your people off."

Richelle looked almost too stunned to speak. She turned to Caroline. "Is this true?"

"I - I don't know. He had the drive. I called Jack from Zurich to ask if he knew anything about it."

"And what did he say?" Richelle asked.

"He said Carl had a safety deposit box at the Fed, but didn't know anything about the drive."

"I should think not," Richelle said. "These were all supposed to have been destroyed. And Jack told you to come here?"

"Yes," Caroline said, "until he could find out what was going on."

"We had nothing to do with the bomb under your car," Mike said.

"And *you* are?" Richelle asked.

"Michael Banner. I'm an agent with the FBI field office in New York. I was assigned to the investigation before it was taken over."

"Jesus, Caroline," Richelle said. "You brought him *here*? What the hell were you thinking?"

When Caroline didn't answer Richelle said, "Never mind. It doesn't matter now. Gary, take them downstairs and lock them up."

"Jesus, lady," Francis said. "Did you hear what I just said? If you don't know anything about this, then you've got a traitor on your hands. They tried to kill your sister. If they know where she is, what makes you think they won't try again?"

Richelle's hands became a blur. One moment her left was down at her side, the next it was gripping Francis by the throat. With her right she had drawn a pistol and put the barrel to his temple. "Listen, I don't know who you are or what the hell you're doing here. If you ask me, your story sounds like pure bullshit. Until I get a call telling me otherwise, you two are the only people I'm suspecting of anything. Clear?"

"Crystal," Francis said. "But you're making a big mis-"

Richelle took her hand off his throat and brought the elbow of her right arm crashing into his temple. Francis looked at her, his eyes suddenly dull. He stumbled to one side and fell to his knees. When he spoke the words were slurred. "That all you…?"

Then he fainted.

Mike stepped forward and the man behind him pulled him back. "You people are insane! I hope whoever is taking you up the ass from the inside does a good job of it."

Richelle was already walking inside. "Take them downstairs."

# CHAPTER 65

**The Pandora**
**The Baltic Sea**
**Monday 24 July 2006**
**2000 CEST**

Captain Almila watched the screen on the bridge as the divers checked their equipment and walked to the ladder on the edge of the launch deck. Both were wearing military spec Aqualung rebreather systems.

"You're clear," the chief officer said into his radio. "Proceed to position one."

Both divers gave the camera a thumbs-up. When they were in the water a crewman passed one of them an underwater camera. As soon as they were submerged, the chief switched the camera feed and they watched as the divers descended several yards and began swimming toward the bottom of the hull.

The divers reached the stern and turned toward the port side of the ship. The camera panned past one of the screws and moved forward until they reached a round steel hatch about two yards across.

"We've reached position one, sir. Ready when you are."

The chief pushed the first of six green numbered buttons lined up on the console in front of him. The hatch didn't open, but blew out, followed by a wash of air bubbles. The camera followed the heavy steel cover as if flipped over like a coin dropped into a fountain and quickly disappeared into the depths below.

"Cover is clear," the diver said. "You're good to go."

The chief turned the switch below the first button. Both divers moved back as the end of a thick, hollow steel tube emerged from the open shaft. The tube kept coming until all ten yards of it was free. When it finally cleared the cylinder and stopped, the jolt reverberated all the way up to the bridge.

"Number one is clear, sir. It looks good."

"Drop it," Almila said.

The chief turned the switch another forty-five degrees. The tube suddenly began to drop, trailing a thick metal cable behind it. Less than thirty seconds later the cable stopped as the pylon hit the seabed.

"Okay. Proceed to number two," the chief said. "Let's get this done quickly. We've got weather on the way. I want you boys back on board as soon as possible."

"Roger that, sir."

It took just over an hour to drop all six. By the time the divers were back on board, the ship had begun to roll visibly. The chief saw the worry on the captain's face and said, "We should be all right, sir. All the reports have this passing by 0200."

"I hope you're right," Almila said. "I don't even want to think about what might happen if it doesn't."

# CHAPTER 66

**Aurora**
**Monday 24 July 2006**
**2230 EEST**

Mitch was sitting in his living room toying with the touch screen remote that controlled the apartment's wide range of gadgetry. The one that fascinated him the most was the windows. Although it was buried inside a block of solid granite like everything else at Aurora, the apartment had six windows, the largest of which was in the living room. The remote controlled the view using some kind of high definition LCD display which created a remarkably clear and realistic image of just about anything you wanted, from the New York skyline at night to a remote location in the Bavarian Alps. Mitch had just changed the picture again to a view of earth from outer space when Sarah arrived.

"Hey, you," she said and sat down on one of the highchairs at the breakfast bar. "You like the windows?"

"I've never seen a resolution this high on a digital display," Mitch said.

"They put them in last year," Sarah said. "We own part of the company in Germany that makes them."

"TSI?" Mitch asked.

"Yes. You've heard of it?"

"Not until yesterday," Mitch said. "You guys seem to have your fingers in a lot of pies."

Sarah laughed. "What a stupid expression."

"Oh, I'm full of them," Mitch said. "So what's on the agenda for today?"

"Actually," she said, "I thought you might take me to the movies."

Mitch looked up from the remote in his hand with wide eyes, then looked away again as the color in his cheeks began to rise. "Ah…sure. We can go to the movies. If you like."

"Great," she said. "Peter and Julia are going to be there. Although I think Julia is only going to see Brandon Routh."

"Who?"

"You don't know him? He's the new Superman."

"Oh, yeah. Of course. Brandon Routh. Sure, I know him."

"So it's a date?" she asked.

At the sound of that word something in the pit of Mitch's stomach leaped into his throat and all he managed was a grunt in the affirmative.

"You okay?" Sarah asked.

"Sure. I'm fine."

"Then I'll pick you up in an hour?"

Mitch nodded. "Sounds good to me."

She sprang from the chair and walked to the door, then turned around and gave him a little wave before stepping out. Mitch walked straight to the bathroom where he filled the sink with cold water, splashed his face several times and stood looking at himself in the mirror.

"All right, Mitch, take it easy. You can do this. Beautiful women ask nerds out all the time. You just don't hear about it very often because society is too shallow to admit it."

He walked to the small computer terminal in the bedroom and sat down. Mitch had already spent several hours at the desk examining Aurora's internal information and communications system and had been surprised to see how easy it was to hack. Although he supposed it made sense when you considered the threat of an internal security breach was probably not something anyone took very seriously around here.

He found the location on the server that stored personnel records and pulled up Sarah's. Unlike the records of those who had been recruited, hers contained very little information beyond her age, blood type and the small entry that had been made by what Mitch assumed was the resident doctor at the time of her birth. She was only three months older than Mitch and had been born by C-section after her mother went into early labor, according to the notes. But what Mitch was interested in was the photo of her. He opened it on the screen and sat looking at it for a long time. It had clearly been taken several years earlier. In it she was smiling serenely; a young girl born and raised inside a cave, and as oblivious to what that meant as an ant might be to the hill it lives in. He spent several minutes restructuring various lines of code, then went back to the living room. Where the image of Earth had been, Sarah's face now occupied every window in the room.

He sat looking at her for a long time, thinking about his own family. His mother had died several years ago from ovarian cancer and his father less than a year later in an accident that had been far too unlikely to be just bad luck. That left an older brother in Colorado that he hadn't seen since their father's funeral and a few scattered aunts and uncles, most of whose names he couldn't even remember.

Mitch made a decision.

In many ways he guessed he had already made it. But what had drawn him to this place before now was simple logic. This was different. He thought he might actually be able to make a life here, strange as it would be. And not just because he had so little to go back to. It just felt right. *She* felt right.

# CHAPTER 67

**Utska, Poland**
**Monday 24 July 2006**
**2300 CEST**

"I'd tell you how bad this headache is," Francis said, "but I don't have the vocabulary."

They were sitting in a small room furnished only with a trestle table and two chairs. The walls were bare concrete and the riveted steel door had neither a handle nor a keyhole in it. A single dim light bulb hung from the ceiling in a wire frame.

"Well, we're still alive," Mike said. "That's something. I think she's just spooked, myself. It's not like the facts aren't staring them in the face."

"I'll tell you something about the truth that might surprise you," Francis said. "To people who don't want to listen, it's not worth two flying fucks in a snow storm."

"Don't forget," Mike said, "I've spent over a decade in the service of the United States government. I know how it works."

"Then you'll know-"

The door suddenly swung open and Richelle entered. The man behind her stopped in the doorway and raised the barrel of his submachine gun. She made no effort to acknowledge them, just stepped to the table and put a picture down in front of them. "Do you know this man?"

They looked at the picture, shared a puzzled glance and shook their heads. She snapped the picture back up and put another down.

They both leaned forward to look at it.

"Never seen him before," Francis said.

"Nor have I," Mike said.

"What about this one?" she said.

"That's Bruce Jessops," Mike said. "But I think you already know that."

She picked the photos back up. "You're lying."

"If you think we're lying," Francis said, "you're not only a fucking lousy judge of character, you're also blind."

The man behind her took a step forward but Richelle shook her head and he moved back.

"And what is it exactly that I'm not seeing?" she asked.

"The bigger picture," Francis said.

"Which is?"

"That someone in your organization is acting without your knowledge to cover up what I did."

"And tell me, Mr. Moore, why would someone do that?"

"Well now, that's the million dollar question, isn't it? Aside from the little we've managed to learn from your hard drive, I have no idea what it is you people are doing or why. I suggest you start with whoever knew about the box at the Fed, then ask yourself why that person might not want anyone to know it went missing."

"And I would," Richelle said, "But for some reason, we don't seem to be able to get hold of him."

"You think *we* had something to do with that?" Mike said incredulously.

"I *know* you did. The only question is, are you going to tell me the truth, or will I have to beat it out of you? Unlike my sister, I know what's on that drive, so you can spare me the bullshit."

Francis shook his head slowly but didn't look up.

"Who hired you to kill my sister?" Richelle asked. "I want a name. Was it Bruce Jessops? Give me a name and I'll think about-"

Richelle didn't get to finish the sentence. In the time it took the man behind her to look down the hall and back again, Francis was on his feet and swinging the chair. It flew across the room, narrowly missing Richelle's head and caught her companion square in the middle of the face. The gun fell from his hands as he stumbled out the door. Richelle was fast but this time Francis knew it. She was kneeling to pick up the rifle as he jumped over the table. He landed on both feet and pushed her aside with a shoulder barge. He picked up the weapon and had it pointed at her before she was back on her feet. Mike hadn't moved. He looked like a dumbstruck member of the audience at a magic show.

"You'll never get out of here alive," Richelle said in a tone that betrayed her fury.

"Actually, If I wanted to, I could," Francis said and held out the machine gun to her. "Go on, take it. Call it a peace offering."

She reached out and grabbed the butt. Francis held on for another couple of seconds then let go. For a moment they only stood there looking at each other.

"I'm getting a little tired of the mind games," Francis said, "so I'm going to say this one last time. We did not try to kill your sister. We came to Zurich to call her out and put an end to the bloodshed. That's all."

Something in Francis's look made her drop her eyes. She looked down at the weapon in her hand then at the doorway where the man who had come to protect her now lay unconscious. For a moment Francis thought she was going to shoot them both anyway, then she set the weapon down on the table. "The box was leased by one of our staff in New York. We're looking for him as we speak."

"Go on," Francis said.

"I'm afraid I can't do any better than that."

"I'm not saying I can help you," Francis said. "But under the circumstances, I'd be willing to try. For my own sake, as much as yours."

Richelle looked at Mike, who offered her an innocent grin.

"Tell me," she said. "How the hell did *you* get caught up in this?"

Mike looked at Francis, who nodded.

"How much time have you got?" Mike asked.

"Actually, not very much," Richelle said.

"Then I'll make it quick," Mike said.

He ran her through events, beginning with his own arrival at the Fed, and ending with their meeting in London and the decision to find Caroline. When he finished, the suspicion on Richelle's face had been replaced by the clear signs of worry.

# CHAPTER 68

**The Callisto**
**Somewhere on the Baltic Sea**
**Tuesday 25 July 2006**
**0100 CEST**

Captain Williams reached into the cupboard in the corner of his cabin and pulled out a double-barreled shotgun.

"That's it?" Titov said.

"Not quite."

Williams reached back inside and handed Titov a .357 revolver. It was black with a white rubber grip. Titov took it and checked the cylinder. "Do you have any more ammunition?"

"There's a box of shells for the shotgun in my safe, but that's it for the revolver. This isn't exactly a pirate ship."

Titov stuffed the gun into the front of his pants and pulled his shirt over it.

"You sure that's a good idea?" Williams said. "I don't want you blowing your balls off."

Titov laughed. "With this I'd be lucky to hit them even from here. That thing's not a lot better."

Williams held up the shotgun and pointed it at the door. "Oh, I don't know."

Titov put out his hand and Williams handed him the shotgun. He broke it and thumbed out both shells. The red plastic cases were faded and one of the brass heads had started to rust.

"I really hope we don't run into any trouble ashore," Titov said. "Because if we do, we're fucked."

# CHAPTER 69

**Aurora**
**Tuesday 25 July 2006**
**0200 EEST**

Brendan was lighting another cigar when the guard entered his office and handed him a small sheet of folded paper. "Chief, we found this in his apartment."

Both Heinz and Erik were seated in the chairs in front of the chief's desk.

"Show me that," Heinz said.

The guard looked at the chief who nodded. "Give it to him."

Heinz unfolded it and looked at it for only a moment. "It's the password to the Darkstar control interface."

"Find Rainey," the chief said to the guard. "I want him in his quarters and under guard."

When the guard had left Erik said, "Listen, Brendan, I honestly - we honestly didn't-"

"I'm going to stop you there, Erik," the chief said, holding up a hand. "What either of you think when it comes to the security of this facility is irrelevant. If it wasn't true before that little shit arrived, it certainly is now."

The chief took the piece of paper from Heinz and said, "You said he had unsupervised access to the system. Could he have shut down the link to Darkstar knowing this password?"

Heinz nodded, but didn't look up. "Yes."

The chief stood and leaned forward with both hands spread out on his desk. "It didn't occur to you that that might be a really fucking bad idea? That maybe that's the reason he's here?"

When Heinz only kept looking down the chief turned to Erik. "It's my ass on the line, Erik. Although I'd really appreciate it if you make it clear to Richelle just how adamant you were that he be given the run of the place. Now if you don't mind, I've got a clusterfuck to attend to. I suggest you get busy re-establishing the link to Darkstar, Heinz."

Both men stood and left the room. A moment later the radio on the chief's hip squalled. "Sir, we've got him. Miss Breland is asking to see you."

"Not now," the chief said. "I'll be down in a minute."

# CHAPTER 70

**The Pandora**
**The Baltic Sea**
**Tuesday 25 July 2006**
**0250 CEST**

They were standing on the observation platform above the bridge. Five men and two women, each looking up, transfixed, into the black cloudless sky. In another setting they might have resembled a clan of superstitious Neanderthals gaping in fear, or wonder, or both, at the mystery of the heavens.

Captain Almila studied the people around him with a growing sense of detachment, recounting the events that had led them all to this surreal moment. He had been the first officer on board a Finish navy patrol cruiser less than four years ago. Recently divorced, childless and increasingly disillusioned with life, he had accepted the offer of a job abroad, not so much as a career move but as an opportunity to put the past behind him.

His first encounter with the Pandora had been in the Korean shipyard at Busan, where her hull was still under construction, and her purpose as much a mystery as the reason he had been selected to captain her.

His mind skipped ahead to his first day at Aurora, meeting the beautiful young woman who was now both his friend and superior. Like so many before him, the truth of what he was involved in arrived in stages between intermittent bouts of disbelief and incredulity. Unlike Mitch Rainey, he had at least been warned to expect the unbelievable. Yet for all the wonder of that subterranean paradise and the progress on the Pandora, whose design and construction became increasingly shrouded in secrecy as her true purpose was revealed, none of it could really prepare a person for this.

"Sir, we've lost the link to Darkstar."

Almila turned to see his chief officer standing behind him.

"It's probably just temporary interference," Almila said. "Try again in a minute. I'm going to stay up here a little longer."

# CHAPTER 71

**Utska, Poland**
**Tuesday 25 July 2006**
**0230 CEST**

Caroline put the phone down and looked around at the faces in the room.

"Well? What did she say?" Richelle asked.

"Carl left her a note saying he had to fly to California," Caroline said. "But she says she hasn't booked a flight and doesn't know anything about it."

"So where the hell is Jack?"

"She doesn't know."

"Has she asked Marius? He'll know where they are."

Caroline shook her head. "She hasn't seen Marius since yesterday."

"Who's Marius?" Francis asked.

"He runs all our security systems out there," Richelle said.

Caroline looked close to tears.

"What is it?" Richelle asked.

"What the hell is going on?" Caroline said. "I don't understand. Everyone's missing. Jack should have called by now."

Francis sat turning over a pen in his hand. He seemed to be concentrating on the top row of one of the bookshelves in the small library.

"I don't want to panic anyone," Francis said, "but you should prepare yourselves for the worst."

Caroline only looked at Richelle. "What does he mean?"

"Nothing. It's okay."

"How well do you know Jack?" Francis asked.

"Jack's been with us for over ten years," Richelle said, clearly annoyed at the implication. "I trust him with my life."

"Hey, I'm just ask-"

Francis suddenly cocked his head to one side and held up a hand.

"What is it?" Richelle asked.

Francis stood and walked to the balcony overlooking the long slope of woodland that ran from the end of the front garden to the coast less than half a mile away. He leaned down until his head was below the stone railing and listened.

"Are you expecting company?" he asked.

Richelle shook her head. "No. Why?"

Before he could answer her one of the guards ran into the room. "Ma'am, the perimeters sensor array is down. I can't reach any of the-"

There was a sudden burst of gunfire from somewhere outside.

"Everyone get down!" Francis shouted.

There were several more shots, followed by an explosion that shook the whole building and shattered several of the glass panes in the balcony doors.

"Get her out of here," Francis said to Mike, pointing to Caroline. To the guard he said, "How many men do you have in the building?"

The man looked at Richelle.

"Tell him," she said.

"Six. They were on their way out to replace the patrols but I called them back."

"Good. Get them all up here now. If you have surplus weapons, have them bring whatever they can carry with them and as much ammunition as possible. And if you have any grenades, we need them all."

The man ran back out.

"What's going on?" Richelle asked.

"I think we're about to find out," Francis said. "Are you as good with the barrel of a gun as you are with the butt?"

"Better."

"Good."

There was another burst of gunfire, much closer to the house this time. Francis heard footsteps running up the stairs, but the sound was cut off by another volley of gunfire. Then the front doors downstairs burst open.

"Move!" Francis shouted at Richelle, but it was too late. One of the heavy oak doors of the library flew off its hinges and passed a foot above her head before crashing into the bookshelf behind her. Richelle was knocked off her feet by the blast. One of the guards staggered in through the open doorway. When he sank to his knees and turned to look back, Francis saw the back of his head was gone. He dropped face-first onto the floor.

Francis ran forward, rolled the body over with the heel of his shoe and picked up the man's weapon. It was a 7.62mm HK 417 battle rifle. Francis recognized the man as the one he had assaulted himself less than an hour ago. Richelle was back on her feet and kneeling behind the table, her eyes wild, but not hysterical. Francis held a finger to his lips and moved toward the door.

He listened.

Several people were coming up the stairs. They were moving cautiously now that it was quiet again. As they reached the landing Francis moved his head to peer through the crack of the door still on its frame.

There were three of them. They had stopped at the top of the stairs and were looking around. Two of them had PP-2000 compact submachine guns. The third man carried a Dragunov SVU sniper rifle. They were dressed in black and all three wore balaclavas.

Francis turned to Richelle who had moved out of sight behind a chair. He held up three fingers and pointed toward the door, then walked two of them across his palm and held up his hand to indicate they should wait.

She nodded.

The group split up. Two of the men walked away toward the door at the other end of the landing while the other passed the door to the library and followed the bannister. Francis slipped off his shoes and moved slowly across the polished hardwood floor, checking each step for a weak board before moving on. When he was in front of the doorway he moved onto his stomach. The men emerged from the room at the other end of the landing together. One of them saw Francis, but his attempt to raise the alarm was cut off by the first shot, which opened a hole in his throat big enough to look through. The second shot hit the man beside him just above the chin, shattering his top teeth before exiting at the base of his neck. Francis adjusted his position and waited for the third man to return, but when he pulled the trigger again, it produced nothing but a soft dry click. The man heard it and raised his own weapon. As the man pulled the trigger, a book – Francis thought it must have been the Oxford unabridged dictionary judging by the size of it – hit him in the right shoulder and sent the shot wild. The man stumbled back, readjusted his aim and fired again. Only this time there was no muzzle flash, and instead of finding his own brains splattered across the library floor, Francis watched the man twist and fall to the floor.

"Mike?" Francis said.

"Did I get him?" Mike shouted.

Francis stood up and looked around the corner. "Oh Christ, Mike."

Mike was sitting with his back against the wall below the window at the end of the landing. Half his face was covered in blood. But what caught Francis's eye was the blood flowing from beneath the hand on his right hip. The carpet was already soaked with it.

"You got him, Mike," Francis said. "But someone got you first, buddy. Don't move."

"Grenade fragment," Mike said.

"And don't talk either."

Francis moved his hand and saw that Mike was at least partially right. A splinter of wood the size of a stick of dynamite was protruding from the left side of his groin.

"Is he okay?"

Francis turned and saw Caroline standing in the doorway. She was bleeding herself, but the cuts were small and she seemed not to even notice.

"Not for long," Francis said. "I need you to find me a towel."

Caroline didn't move. Francis stood and pushed past her into the room. He found several towels stacked on the granite counter of the on-suite bathroom. When he came back out Richelle was standing over Mike. She had taken the weapons from all three of the dead men and was looking around nervously. Francis called to Caroline again and when she still didn't move he reached out and pinched her earlobe. "Hey, eyes on me."

He tore one of the towels into three strips, then rolled and twisted one of them and coiled it around itself to form what looked a bit like a large doughnut.

"Whatever you do, don't try to pull it out," he said, and pushed the makeshift compress around the splinter. He took Caroline's hand and placed it over the towel. "I need you to push down on this as hard as you can. Use both hands and put your weight behind it. If he screams you just keep pushing. Got it?"

Caroline nodded.

"Good. I have to go."

Francis stood and Richelle handed him the sniper rifle.

"Let's go," she said.

"You need to stay-" Francis began.

"I'm not staying," Richelle said. "Now are you coming, or not?"

One look at her face told him they would all be dead by the time he changed her mind.

When they reached the bottom of the stairs Richelle knelt beside the body of one of her guards and pulled a grenade from his hand. She threw it to Francis, who caught it.

"They'll have come in from the beach," Francis said. "Any idea how they shut down the security system?"

Richelle considered this for a moment and pointed at the doors leading into the east wing of the house. "There's a tunnel that runs a few hundred yards into the woods between here and the sea. It comes out in the emergency generator room."

"Lead the way," Francis said.

They moved along the ground floor and through the kitchen to a door leading out into the courtyard. Richelle pointed to a small stone annex about twenty yards from the house. "It's in there."

She began to walk but Francis grabbed her arm and pulled her back. He put a hand on her shoulder and forced her to kneel beside him.

"Look," he said, pointing to the right of the small building.

Two men had emerged from the tree line and were running across the open lawn toward the front door of the house. Still kneeling, Francis raised the rifle and bent his head to the scope. He focused the crosshairs on the lead man, then moved it slightly ahead of him and raised it a notch before pulling the trigger. The man behind him ran straight into the back of his colleague just as the top of his head exploded.

"Go on, hit the deck, idiot," Francis murmured under his breath.

But the man didn't. Instead he turned toward the sound of the shot and ran, weaving to the left and right every few paces.

"All right, I take it back. You're not an idiot," Francis said.

When the man was only twenty yards away Francis told Richelle to get up. The man saw her and stopped weaving. He began to raise his rifle, but Francis shot him twice in the chest before he had a chance to aim.

"I make that five," Francis said. "If they knew what they would find here we should expect at least double that, maybe a dozen at most."

He followed her inside the generator building and down a short flight of steps to where a large diesel generator sat mounted on two steel beams. The control panel had been unscrewed and several of the wires inside cut. She led them around the generator to a thick steel plate that had been pushed aside to reveal a flight of narrow steps.

"I'm going down," Francis said. "I need you to cover this end. Push the cover back and take up position behind the door. If anyone comes in let them get to the bottom of the steps before you open fire."

"Who *are* these people?" Richelle asked.

"Russians," Francis said.

He was gone before she could reply.

He covered the distance in a series of sprints, cupping the small flashlight in his palm so that it illuminated only a few feet of the floor ahead of him and stopping every twenty yards or so to listen. There was a steel ladder at the end of the tunnel leading up about fifteen feet to a manhole cover. He reached the top, listened for a moment, then pushed it aside and emerged into a small clearing. Through the trees he could see the moon reflected off the surface of the sea in the distance.

On the simple reasoning that the men he shot had come from the east, Francis moved west on a course parallel to the shore. He had gone about three hundred yards when another burst of machine gun fire erupted from somewhere near the house. Spurred on by the sudden fear that he was too late, he broke into a sprint.

Francis saw them first but lost the advantage when his shoulder hit a tree and he dropped the rifle. He counted four men spaced several yards apart on the edge of the lawn. One of them shouted something in Russian. Francis turned back, intending to pick up the rifle, but had to sidestep it to avoid a hail of bullets that peppered the ground at his feet.

Francis changed course, nearly ran face-first into a tree and lost his balance as he swerved to avoid it. He risked a quick look back and saw they had spread out and were quickly catching up. One of them fired an unsteady three-round burst and almost got lucky. Francis heard one of the bullets hit a tree not three feet from him.

There was a time in his life when Francis might have been able to keep up the pace almost indefinitely, and it was squarely in the past. Already his legs were beginning to feel heavy and his lungs had started to protest at the lack of oxygen in his blood. His eyes, never great at the best of times – if Francis had a superpower it had always been his hearing – began to blur in and out of focus.

But with no other option available he had no choice but to keep running, first parallel to the shore, then toward the water. He ran until the muscles in his legs felt as if they were slowly petrifying and his throat burned.

Francis barely saw the man he ran into. Only to his ebbing consciousness it wasn't a man at all, but a troll. One moment he was moving forward, the next he was falling back onto the ground. A lively exchange of shouts gave way to an even livelier exchange of gunfire. Francis found himself crawling forward, muzzle flashes exploding all around him. He felt a sharp sting in his right calf and then another in his buttock. A moment later a hand gripped each of his ankles and he was being first dragged, then turned onto his back.

Francis opened his eyes, closed them in defiance of what he saw and tried again. The man standing over him was huge, and nothing in his face or body language suggested he was going to let Francis live much longer.

"Who are you?" the man asked in a heavy Russian accent.

By the time the answer reached Francis's tongue the man had been joined by another. Neither of them took their eyes off him.

"Is he one of them?" the giant said.

The man next to him shook his head. "I don't think so."

"Who are you?" the giant repeated.

But Francis was no longer conscious.

# CHAPTER 72

**Zurich, Switzerland**
**Tuesday 25 July 2006**
**0405 EDT**

Jack Fielding stepped off the plane just after four in the morning and joined the other passengers as they made their way to Immigration. He tried his best to look casual as two armed policemen passed him on the stairs. Neither of them so much as looked at him, but it did little to steady his nerves, which felt like they were now wired to a high-voltage battery.

By the time he reached the back of the line in front of passport control he had started to sweat. The woman in front of him was doing her best to keep her two young children from running off in different directions. She offered him a sympathetic smile.

As the line grew shorter he was relieved to see the Immigration officer in their booth was a woman. She was smiling openly at the passengers as they filtered through and appeared not to be checking anyone's passport. When it was his turn Jack stepped forward, put his bag down beside him and handed her his passport. She opened it and looked up at him.

"Not a fan of flying, I see, Mr. Klein," she said.

He thought she was commenting on the lack of stamps in his passport then realized what she meant. "No. I'm not much better in a car, I'm afraid."

"Where are you headed?"

"Romanshorn. I'm attending a conference."

"Perhaps you should take the train," She said.

"I intend to."

She passed the passport beneath the scanner on the counter, looked at him again and handed it back. "Have a pleasant stay."

"Thank you."

Jack was too intent on getting out of there to notice that she didn't call the next person forward. When he was gone she took a sheet of paper from beneath the counter with six faces printed on it in color and looked up at Jack's face on the monitor. When she raised her hand the officer in the booth next door stood and came over. He took one look at the screen and left. When he returned to his own booth, he asked the young man waiting there to step back into the line and picked up the phone. "We have a match on the wanted list for Jack Fielding. The name on the passport is Klein.

# CHAPTER 73

**Utska, Poland**
**Tuesday 25 July 2006**
**0430 CEST**

Francis opened his eyes and tried to raise his head. He was lying in an enormous four-poster bed. Something about the room was familiar but it took him a moment to put his finger on it. It was the room he had taken the towels from. That made him think of Mike. He turned to the open door and saw the large bloodstain on the carpet. When he tried to sit up a bolt of pain ran from his ankle and up the back of his leg to his right buttock. The events of the night before began coming back in patches: the attack, moving through the tunnel, running.

"Good morning."

Francis turned to see Richelle standing in the doorway. She had changed into jeans and a chambray work shirt and looked as if she was preparing to go on a hike.

"Good morning to you, too."

"Titov says you ran into some trouble in the woods. You're lucky he found you."

"Would Titov be a troll by any chance?"

She laughed. "Oh I think that's a bit harsh. He's more like a giant teddy bear once you get to know him."

"He's your man?"

She nodded. "We lost contact with them shortly after you arrived. They came ashore and were on their way up to the house when you ran into them. Literally, from what I'm told."

"What happened?"

"They killed the men who were chasing you. We lost all twelve of our guards and both pilots."

Francis gritted his teeth in anticipation of the pain and twisted his legs out of the bed. His calf had been crudely bandaged and someone had put a towel under him to stop the bleeding in his buttock.

"Titov says you'll be fine," Richelle said. "No bullets to take out."

"Where's Mike?" Francis asked.

She looked down at the floor. "He's in bad shape. We've taken him to the hospital at Slupsk. Caroline is with him."

"Will he make it?"

"We don't know yet."

Francis stood up and winced at the pain in his ankle. "You know the people who attacked this place were Russian, don't you?"

Richelle nodded. "If you can walk, there is something I'd like you to see."

Francis tried a step, moved his right ankle to see if it was going to cooperate and took another. He followed her at a hobble out the door and down what remained of the stairs.

"I closed the hatch after you left and moved to the stairs," Richelle said. "He came in a couple of minutes after you left. I was going to kill him but he put his weapon down to move the hatch and I settled for shooting him in the leg."

"Who are we talking about exactly?" Francis asked.

She opened the door. "Him."

The man was sitting on a chair in the middle of the kitchen. His hands were bound behind his back and someone had wrapped a towel around his bleeding leg. Titov was standing behind him with a rolling pin in one hand. The other man Francis had seen in the woods was standing by the counter inspecting a mobile phone.

"This is Titov Kargin," Richelle said. "And David Williams."

Both men nodded at him and Francis returned the gesture.

"And this," Richelle said pointing at the man in the chair, "is Captain Salnikov."

Salnikov raised his head and Francis could see that the man hadn't exactly volunteered his name. His lip was split in two places and one of his eyes was swollen shut.

"Who is he?" Francis asked.

"A retired captain in the tenth Independent Spetsnaz Brigade of the Russian Southern Military District," Titov said. "Now working for a man named Victor Manin."

"*General* Manin?" Francis asked.

Titov raised his eyebrows. "You know him?"

"Sure. He retired after the Soviets threw in the towel and set up a security firm in Moscow. He was sued by the Russian government for recruiting directly from the army. Does this guy know who hired him?"

"Carl Bosch," Richelle said. "Jack was right. Bosch was trying to kill us both."

"Why?" Francis asked.

"We don't know."

Francis studied Salnikov for a moment and said, "How did he know the name of the client?"

"He met Carl in New York a week ago," Titov said. "He says he was sent there to collect something, but that Carl didn't have it."

"The drive?" Francis asked.

"He doesn't know," Titov said.

"Have you got a picture of him?" Francis asked. "A picture of Carl

Bosch or one with him in it?"

Richelle thought about it. "Perhaps. Why?"

"Bring it here."

Richelle looked at Titov. When he nodded, she shrugged and left the room. She returned a minute later with a picture in a silver frame. In the shot at least a dozen men and women were standing on the front lawn of a house, all of them smiling. Francis recognized both sisters and Titov.

"Ask him to point out Carl," Francis said.

Titov showed the picture to Salnikov and said something in Russian. Salnikov studied the picture for a moment and pointed.

Titov frowned. "Him?"

"No," Salnikov said. "The one in the white jacket at the end. He's the man I met."

"You're sure?" Titov asked.

"Why would I lie?" Salnikov said. "I met him at a construction site in Queens. He said he didn't have the package. That he would give it to Manin himself when he arrived in Zurich."

Titov handed the picture back to Richelle, "That's Jack," he said.

Before Richelle could respond, Francis approached Salnikov and said, "Does Manin know you failed?"

Salnikov shook his head. "He'll figure it out. I was supposed to call."

Williams held up the phone in his hand. "This is his."

"You're going to call him now," Francis said. "Tell him the operation was successful, but you've been compromised and can't return to the beach. Tell him you've decided to bury your equipment and split up."

"He'll know something is wrong," Salnikov said. "I'm supposed to send him a picture."

"A picture of what?" Richelle said.

"You," Salnikov said. "Dead."

Both Francis and Titov turned to look at Richelle.

"You guys are sick," she said. "I won't do it."

But she did.

# CHAPTER 74

**Aurora**
**Tuesday 25 July 2006**
**0500 EEST**

Mitch sat up when he heard footsteps approaching the door. It swung open and the chief stepped inside.

"Look," Mitch said, "There's been some kind of mix-up. I-"

But the chief was in no mood to talk. He crossed the room in three long strides and had a hand around his neck before Mitch could say anything else. "Who sent you here?"

Mitch tried to say something but all that escaped his throat was a dry croak. He found himself hanging on with both hands to one heavily muscled forearm as the chief lifted him off the couch.

"You're going to tell me why you disabled the comm link."

One of the guards in the doorway stepped inside and held up his radio. "Sir, it's Heinz. He says the comm link is back up."

The chief let go of Mitch who fell back onto the couch holding his throat.

"You better pray that everything is all right," the chief said. "In the meantime, I suggest you consider how you want this to go. Just know that I'll find out what I want one way or the other."

# CHAPTER 75

**Utska, Poland**
**Tuesday 25 July 2006**
**0700 CEST**

Francis ended the call and turned to Titov. "You said Jack was recruited in Germany?"

Titov nodded. "Yes. In '93. We had him change his name before he was moved to New York."

"Why?" Francis said.

"He was our informant inside the German Federal Police for several years," Richelle said. "We thought it was best."

"And he reports to Carl Bosch?" Francis said.

"No," Titov said. "He reports to me. As the CEO of Skyline, Bosch is his nominal superior, but most of what Jack does is coordinated directly through our offices in Zurich. "

"And you've never had reason to suspect him?"

They both shook their heads.

"Jack has been one of our most reliable people," Titov said. "He ran the security detail here for a while before we moved him to Skyline."

"He and Richelle were..." Titov began, then trailed off.

"We were engaged for a while," Richelle said and offered Titov a stern look. "Not that I see what that has to do with anything."

"I can tell you from experience," Francis said, "that treachery is never as simple as you want it to be, nor is it always logical. But if Jack was involved in what happened here, he wasn't alone. You said the satellite link couldn't be shut down from here. Would Jack have been able to do it from wherever he is?"

Richelle shook her head. "No."

They heard the sound of an approaching car and walked out onto the balcony to see a black Jeep Cherokee pull up in front of the house. Caroline got out.

"How is he?" Richelle asked.

"He's going to make it."

Caroline joined them in the library a minute later and stopped when she saw the looks on their faces. "What is it?"

"Jack Fielding was behind the attack," Richelle said. "I think we can assume he's also responsible for the bomb under your car."

"Jack?" Caroline said. "How do you know?"

"I don't have time to explain," Richelle said. "We need to find him. And we all need to get the hell out of here. Titov is going to take the two of you back to Zurich and leave for New York right away."

Caroline took a newspaper from under her arm and threw it on the table. It was a copy of USA Today. She opened it and pointed at an article titled *FBI Employee Killed in Burglary Attempt*. Above the article was a picture of Bruce Jessops standing outside a large house with his wife and two children.

"You're right," Francis said. "Now would be a good time to leave."

# CHAPTER 76

**Aurora**
**Tuesday 25 July 2006**
**0730 EEST**

Mitch had been practicing what he was going to say the next time the chief, or anyone else, decided to pay him a visit. But when the door opened it was Sarah.

"Come on," she said. "We need to go."

"What-"

Mitch saw the man lying on the floor in the hall behind her.

"Don't worry," she said. "He's not dead. Now let's go before someone else comes."

She took him by the hand and began walking down the hall.

"Are you going to tell me what the hell is going on?" Mitch asked.

She led him through the door at the end and down several flights of stairs. Beneath the last one, a narrower set of steps led down to a door that didn't look like it had been opened in years. Sarah fished in her pocket and brought out a key.

"Is this a good idea?" Mitch asked.

"You have a better one?"

Mitch didn't.

Sarah handed him a small flashlight and Mitch went in. Beyond the door another flight of steps led down into a dank, narrow tunnel with a rusty metal conduit running along one wall. When Sarah joined him she took the flashlight and pointed it in both directions, then began walking. "This way."

The tunnel ended in a small round chamber that forked off in three directions. Sarah studied the fading red letters above each of the arched entrances and pointed to the one on their right. "This leads to the old generator room. You'll be safe there."

"Safe from who?" Mitch asked.

"I don't know," she said. "They've..."

She began to cry then and Mitch put his arms around her. "Hey, it's okay."

"It's not," she said. "My father said you were sent here to cut us off from the outside world. I know that isn't true."

"It's not," Mitch said. "Did he tell you why?"

"He doesn't know. Brendan is furious because Brendan's the one who said you should have been locked up."

"Did your father give you the key to the door?" Mitch said. "I'm only asking because he could get in trouble."

She shook her head. "No, I took it. None of this makes any sense."

"That's true," Mitch said. "But then around here, what does?"

In the beam of the flashlight her face looked pale. "Come on, we need to get you to the generator room."

They reached another fork in the tunnel and turned left. The passage began to slope gently down. By the time it leveled off again they were knee-deep in water.

"What *is* this place?" Mitch asked.

"The old tunnels. Before they stopped using them there were pumps to keep the water out. I haven't been down here since I was a child."

"If it gets any deeper we'll be swimming," Mitch said.

"There," Sarah said. "That's the door to the generator room."

The rusting steel door was at the top of a flight of steps that rose several feet out of the water. When Sarah tried to move the lever holding it closed, nothing happened.

"Let me try," Mitch said.

Mitch put both hands on the lever and pulled. It moved less than an inch. He knelt down and positioned his shoulder beneath his cupped hands and used his legs to push up. It moved another few inches. He pushed until he felt lightheaded and let go. "Jesus, when was the last time anyone opened this?"

"I don't think anyone's been down here in years," Sarah said.

Mitch took a moment to get his breath back and tried again. It took him three more attempts. By the third he was seeing stars on the edges of his peripheral vision. For all the effort it had taken to move the handle, the door itself opened easily. The air inside was stale and smelled of sulfur. Mitch took the flashlight and went in first. He was running the beam over the ancient diesel generator in the middle of the room when Sarah closed the door behind him.

"Make sure you lock this when I leave," she said. "I doubt anyone will find you down here, but it's best to be safe. I'll be back as soon as I can."

"I wish you wouldn't," Mitch said. "Has it occurred to you that maybe this is the reason I'm here? To take the fall? Because it has to me. Think about it. It makes sense."

"That's crazy," she said.

"No crazier than anything else that's happened in the last week. What if it's not safe for you to go back out there? When they find me gone, you'll be one of the first people they suspect. You do see that, don't you?"

Sarah nodded. "Maybe. But I don't care."

"I do," Mitch said.

She touched his face and smiled. "I know. I'll be fine, I promise."

Mitch watched her open the door and walk back down the steps. When she was gone he closed it and pushed the internal locking handle down. He sat looking around the room with the flashlight for a moment, then turned it off, leaned back and closed his eyes.

# CHAPTER 77

**Utska, Poland**
**Tuesday 25 July 2006**
**0800 CEST**

"Will Mike be safe where he is?" Francis asked.

"I've arranged to have him transferred to Berlin as soon as he is stable enough," Caroline said.

Richelle put a hand on Francis's arm. "We own the hospital. He'll be safe there."

When they stepped out into the courtyard Francis was surprised to see a number of men in navy blue overalls busily scurrying about under the direction of Captain Williams. Two of them were carrying the body of one of the attackers into a stable at the end of the yard. Another two came walking around the corner carrying what looked like a metal steamer trunk.

They walked past the spot where only a few hours ago Francis had killed two of the intruders. Titov came out of the house behind them pushing a bound and blindfolded Salnikov in front of him.

"Where the hell did *they* come from?" Francis asked.

"All in good time," Richelle said.

Captain Williams stopped the men carrying the trunk and said, "Is that the last of them?"

One of the men nodded. "Yes, sir."

"Good. Let's get it down to the dock. We leave in half an hour."

When Williams saw Francis he frowned at Richelle. "You really think it's a good idea to take him with us?"

"We don't have a choice," Richelle said. "Besides, I think we owe him-"

She was interrupted by another of the jumpsuit-clad men who seemed to have appeared like elves from the trees. "The comm link is back up. I have Brendan on the line."

Richelle walked back into the house. When she was gone Francis approached Titov and gestured at his captive. "What are you planning to do with him?"

"He'll be joining us for the flight back to Zurich," Titov said. "Although I plan to drop him off before we get there."

Francis laughed.

Titov didn't.

"You disapprove?" Titov said.

Francis shook his head. "No. It's probably what I would do."

"I know," Titov said. And this time he *did* smile. "Perhaps you'd like the honor?"

"That's okay," Francis said. "I'm getting a little tired of killing people whether they deserve it or not."

"Well, wish me luck," Titov said. "My pilot's license expired two years ago."

"I'd tell you it was like riding a bike," Francis said, "but I highly doubt it."

Titov laughed. "We'll know soon enough. Myself, I would run to Zurich if it means getting my hands on that son of a bitch."

"Be careful," Francis said. "He may not come alone. If he's been colluding with the likes of Norton Weaver and Manin, you can bet one or both of the old assholes is keeping an eye on him."

Francis saw Richelle. She was walking towards them with Williams and the two seemed to be having a heated debate about something.

"What's going on?" Titov said.

"I leave for a week and everything goes to shit," Richelle said. "That's what's going on. Did you know anything about this new arrival? The so-called 'security breach'?"

"Of course," Titov said. "You ordered him transferred yourself, didn't you?"

Richelle looked incredulous. "I ordered him transferred? Really? Do you all think I'm a complete fucking idiot? Go on, I'd like to know. You think my father left me in charge because he was soft in the head? For your information, I begged him not to. But I'm beginning to see why he insisted."

"Richelle," Titov said. "Calm down. I saw the transfer order. Your signature was on it."

"First of all, don't tell me to calm down. There are too many calm people around here as it is. And so we're perfectly clear, I signed no transfer order for anyone. Now if we're done playing stupid, I'd like to get out of here."

She walked away, leaving the three of them standing there.

"What the hell was that about?" Francis said.

"She's under a lot of pressure," Titov said. "She'll be fine. I better go before she comes back."

Williams set of in the direction of the generator house. "Come on," he said to Francis. We better not keep her waiting."

They walked down the tunnel in single file, Williams at the front and Francis taking up the rear. Once outside they set off through the trees toward the shore.

The tree line ended about a hundred yards from the beach. The vessel at the end of the wooden pier looked like an upmarket diving boat, not quite big enough to be called a yacht, but larger than any Francis had ever seen. The low, flat stern was covered by a canopy and had enough seating to carry at least two dozen people. The name painted in gold leaf across the stern was *Helen* and he saw the boat was registered in Stockholm. Several of the men in blue began to bring the metal containers they had carried from the house onto the boat.

Francis stepped onto the deck and helped Richelle down. Someone started the engine and Francis reached for the rail behind him as the boat pushed forward.

Less than five minutes after setting off the boat slowed and began to drift. There was a sudden flurry of activity as the crew began to prepare.

"What's going on?" Francis asked Richelle.

"Just watch."

The small boat listed gently to port as twelve thousand tons of titanium and steel broke the surface less than twenty yards away.

"She's quite something, isn't she?" Richelle said, smiling at the look on his face.

"I've seen the drawings," Francis said. "But I don't think I ever really believed they were anything but a crazy idea."

"Crazy ideas are what we specialize in," Richelle said. "They come with the territory."

"Your very own milk cow," Francis said, unable to take his eyes off the giant submarine.

"What?"

"The Germans called their resupply U-boats milk cows. I mean it's basically a submersible freighter, right?"

"Something like that, yeah. I'm sure Captain Williams will tell you all about it if you want to know. He supervised the refit."

Half a dozen crew had emerged from the conning tower as soon as the submarine surfaced. They were now casting lines to the boat and pulling them in. When they were close enough two men unhooked a gangplank hanging on the side of the boat and pushed it across to the hull of the Callisto. Captain Williams stepped off the bridge and began shouting orders.

Francis and Richelle were the last to board. Two of the crew had changed into fisherman's slicks and were staying with the boat.

"Are they going back?" Francis asked.

"No," Richelle said. "They're taking her back to Sweden."

"And if someone finds the house and the bodies?"

"They won't."

"How can you be so sure?"

"We pay a lot of people to mind their own business. Let's leave it at that."

The boat turned away and sailed off as soon as they were on the deck. Francis climbed the ladder to the top of the conning tower behind Richelle where Williams stood scanning the water around them through a pair of binoculars.

"We've got company," he said. "Let's get the hell out of here."

Francis reached the top and stepped onto the observation platform as Richelle climbed down into the hatch. He took a quick glance around and saw a small shape on the horizon but couldn't make out what it was. He followed Richelle down and moved back as Williams shut the hatch and shouted, "Get this fucking boat below the surface before we're spotted."

# CHAPTER 78

**Zurich, Switzerland**
**Tuesday 25 July 2006**
**1500 EDT**

Jack Fielding was on the verge of falling asleep when someone tapped on the passenger window. He turned to see Manin standing there. Jack lowered the window and said, "Get in."

They drove out of the hotel parking lot and joined the afternoon traffic. "Salnikov lost two men," Manin said. "He says your estimate of the number of guards was inaccurate."

Jack shrugged. "I haven't been there for years. I told you that. Is she dead?"

Manin took a picture from his pocket and handed it to Jack. In it Richelle was lying on the floor of the downstairs landing. One of her legs appeared to be broken and her face was covered in blood.

"And the other one?" Jack said.

"Don't you read the newspapers?" Manin asked.

"I've been a little busy."

Manin took the picture back. "I've held up my end of the bargain. Now where is the drive?"

"Somewhere safe," Jack said. "You didn't think I'd have it here, did you?"

"Where are we going?" Manin said.

"You'll see."

They left the city and headed toward Basel along highway 2. When they reached the outskirts of Baden Jack turned off. A few minutes later they were driving through a small industrial park. The road wound around several small factory buildings, then turned east along a dirt road into thick woodland. It ended in a small clearing beside a single-story building that looked like a public utilities station of some kind.

"Wait here," Jack said and got out.

Jack walked around the corner of the building and out of sight. He reappeared a moment later carrying a hiker's backpack over one shoulder. When Manin got out of the car Jack put the backpack down in front of him.

"It's all there," Jack said. "Have a look."

Manin leaned down and undid the straps of the top flap. As soon as he pulled it open Jack thumbed back the hammer on his own pistol. "Stand up slowly."

Manin did.

"Walk toward the back of the building," Jack said.

Jack followed him past the door and around the side of the building. Manin saw the open body bag on the ground and stopped.

"Go on," Jack said. "Don't be shy."

"It's ironic," Manin said. "Don't you think?"

"What is?"

"That we've both been instructed to kill each other. I'm assuming the order came from *him*, did it?"

"Yours might have," Jack said.

"Then why?" Manin said.

"Let's just say I've changed my mind. And if you were really ordered to kill me, not a moment too soon, it seems."

Manin studied him for a moment. "You don't have it, do you? You still don't have the drive. What the hell happened, Jack?"

"Never fucking mind what happened. Stand by the bag."

Manin moved to the edge of the bag. "I suppose a deal between you and I is out of the question?"

"You don't have any idea what this is all about, do you?" Jack said. "Has he even told you why he needed you? It's just that you seem to think you had some role to play in his plans for the future and if you knew him, you would also know that could never happen."

"I know about the island," Manin said.

Jack looked surprised. "He told you about the island?"

They both heard the distant sound of a helicopter coming from somewhere in the direction of the city. The difference was that Jack looked up and Manin didn't.

Manin dropped to his knees and grabbed a small rock. He threw it just as Jack fired. The shot went wide and Jack stumbled back, tripped on something and fell. Above them the sound of the helicopter was getting closer. Manin was on his feet and running by the time Jack got back to his. Jack fired again as Manin rounded the corner of the building and looked up just as the helicopter appeared overhead and turned on its searchlight, momentarily blinding him.

Jack turned and ran. The beam followed him as he headed for the trees. A German voice boomed from the loudspeaker above him, ordering him to stop. Jack ignored it.

He ran another hundred yards, stumbling several times and getting back up. The voice commanding him to stop was growing impatient. The trees suddenly ended as he reached a firebreak and he tripped again. When Jack looked up the helicopter was hovering just above the trees. A man was leaning out of the open side-door with a scoped rifle. Jack shielded his eyes from the light with one hand and fired several shots into the air. Then something hit him in the chest hard enough to throw him back to the ground. When he tried to take another breath it came not through his mouth, but through a hole just above his heart. The first shot was followed by another that caught him in the right shoulder. His last coherent, if not exactly pertinent, thought was that this is what an amputee must feel like. Then his head sank slowly back onto the soft grass and he thought no more.

- - -

As soon as Jack ran, Manin had sprinted for the car and set off back down the road. But he didn't get far. Where the dirt track ended on the edge of the industrial complex there were now three cars blocking the entrance. Manin stopped, intending to go back, but saw at least a dozen armed police officers emerging from the trees on either side. He took a final look around, then rolled down his window and stuck both hands out.

The first officer to reach the car pulled the door open and several of his colleagues pulled Manin out and piled onto him. When he had been searched and cuffed, they raised him to his feet. As he was half dragged, half carried, toward the cars at the end of the road, a black Mercedes pulled in behind them and a man in a smart three-piece suit got out of the back. A heated exchange ensued between the newcomer and one of the police officers. It was settled a minute later with a phone call, after which the police officer seemed to relent. Manin was taken to the Mercedes and put in the back seat. A moment later, the man in the suit joined him. He nodded to the driver and the car quickly left the scene.

When they were back on the motorway, the man turned to Manin and said, "You were supposed to kill him."

Manin regarded him for a moment and said, "He sent you?"

The man nodded. "We can't exactly have our star general talking to the Swiss police, now can we? Did he give you the drive?"

Manin shook his head. "He didn't have it. He also seemed quite sure my own days were numbered."

The man laughed. "Did he now?"

"He did."

"Jack was an incompetent fool. I'm more interested in hearing how you got on at Utska. Have you taken care of our problem?"

Manin reached into his pocket and produced the picture of Richelle.

"Good," the man said. "Very good."

# CHAPTER 79

**The Callisto**
**Somewhere on the Baltic Sea**
**Wednesday 26 July 2006**
**0200 CEST**

Richelle handed the mic back to the communications officer and turned to Williams. "Jack's dead. He arrived in Zurich yesterday morning. We also have Victor Manin."

They returned to Williams's cabin where Francis was waiting.

"Has Manin talked?" Francis asked.

"He didn't so much talk as sing," Richelle said.

"Oh?" Francis said.

"The general is currently the guest of honor at my sister's house in Zurich. Although he doesn't know that."

Francis regarded her with a wry smile. "He thinks he's been sprung by his own people?"

Richelle nodded. "By his contact inside our organization, yes. Although he has no idea who it is. His instructions arrive through a drop at the central train station in Moscow."

"And the drive?" Francis asked.

"We already know Jack was supposed to give it to Salnikov in New York, and why that didn't happen. According to Manin, he had been told Jack would bring it to Zurich. He had been promised proof of the claims being made about our organization before he committed himself to the task of helping to take it down."

"I guess if you knew what it was all supposed to mean, that makes sense," Francis said.

"He also says Jack tried to kill him before the police arrived."

"Because he still didn't have it," Francis said.

"It looks that way," Richelle said. "And if Manin had no idea what happened in New York, I think it's safe to assume that his contact doesn't either."

Francis considered this for a moment and said, "Titov seemed convinced that this person, the one your security chief says shut down the communications system, arrived on your orders."

"I knew nothing about it," Richelle said.

"No. But the question is, who would have been able to make it look like you did?"

"I've thought about that," Richelle said. "Jack would have been able to originate the transfer request in New York, although it's hard to believe

Marius wouldn't have noticed. The problem is, we can't get a hold of Marius, or Carl Bosch for that matter."

"I think you should prepare yourself for the very real possibility that they're both dead," Francis said. "The behavior of your friend Jack since he lost the drive has had desperation written all over it, including his partnership with Norton Weaver. Although knowing Weaver, he wouldn't have been given a choice. That old bastard would have been as desperate as Jack to find the drive. It's just the kind of asshole he is. I'm not a betting man, but if I were, I would put my chips on your insider as the man who arranged for this guy to show up just in time to take the heat. Do we even know where he came from?"

"I didn't have time to ask," Richelle said. "But I intend to."

"You need to be careful," Francis said. "The person you're looking for will panic if they know you're still alive. They may try to run."

Richelle and Williams shared a knowing look.

"What?" Francis said.

"They can't run," Richelle said. "I don't have time to explain why, and you might not believe me if I did, so just take my word for it."

Francis ignored this cryptic comment and went on. "Fine. But to be on the safe side, who actually knows you're on board?"

"Just my security chief."

"Then I suggest you keep it that way," Francis said. "Do you trust him, your security chief?"

Richelle laughed. "Brendan? It'll probably take all three of us just to keep him from turning the place into a concentration camp until we find who we're looking for. He was my father's personal bodyguard for ten years."

"Fine," Francis said. "If it was up to me, I'd bring him on board as soon as we arrive, brief him and send him back to try and root out your traitor. Although if you think he's going to go off half-cocked, maybe it's better to send Captain Williams."

"He'll be fine," Richelle said. "Once he understands the situation."

They were interrupted by a knock on the door.

"Come in," Williams said.

"Sir, we've arrived," the crewman said.

"I'll be right up," Williams said.

Williams walked to the door and turned around. "What's the plan, then?"

Richelle hesitated for a moment then looked at Francis and said, "Bring Brendan on board. Don't tell anyone else I'm here and make sure the crew doesn't either. In fact, have them come back inside once we've docked."

# CHAPTER 80

**Aurora**
**Wednesday 26 July 2006**
**0230 EEST**

They were sitting in the galley of the Callisto. Richelle, Francis and Williams on one side of the table, the chief on the other. When Richelle finished speaking he shook his head and said, "My god. And Jack Fielding, of all people."

"You knew him?" Francis said.

The chief looked uncertainly at Richelle.

"It's okay, he's fine," she said.

"Not exactly," the chief said. "I met him a few times at Utska when he was running the security team there. Never would have taken him for a traitor, though."

"Join the club," Richelle said.

"And I would have bet my right arm that Rainey was behind what happened to Darkstar," the chief said.

"What did you say his name was?" Francis said.

The chief looked at Richelle again, clearly uncomfortable answering questions from this newcomer.

"Tell him," Richelle said.

"His name is Mitch Rainey."

"He wasn't an employee of the FBI in DC by any chance, was he?" Francis said.

The chief looked startled. "Yes, he was. How the hell do you know that?"

"Jesus," Francis said. "Mitch Rainey was the guy who helped Mike on the Fed investigation. Mike said one of their calls had been tapped and that he hadn't heard from him since."

"Where is he now?" Richelle said.

The chief lowered his head and said, "Actually, he's missing."

"What do you mean, he's missing?" Richelle said.

"We believe Sarah Breland helped him get away."

"Erik's daughter?" Richelle said.

"Yes. She was...err...she was rather taken with him, I think."

Richelle was shaking her head. "Christ, Brendan. What the hell is going on around here?"

"He was being held in his quarters. She left one of my guards unconscious. I guess it's hardly surprising if she knew he was..."

The chief suddenly stopped. He seemed troubled. When he looked back up at Richelle he said, "There is something else. I think Heinz may be involved."

"Heinz?" Richelle said. "Why would you say that?"

"He's the only person here with open access to the system. He could easily have shut down the comm link and forged the transfer order."

"So could you," Richelle said. "That hardly makes you a suspect."

"He was taken with Rainey," the chief said. "Ask Erik. He invited him to stay. He also let him access the system unsupervised."

Richelle looked stunned. The chief reached into the breast pocket of his coveralls and brought out a folded sheet of paper. "I didn't want to show you this in front of anyone else. I had Heinz's room searched before you arrived and found this in a box under his bed."

The chief pushed the paper across the table. It was a photograph of her taken at Aurora several years earlier. In it she was standing next to her father. Both of them were smiling. But there was nothing sweet about the photograph now. It was covered in obscenities of every kind, both words and sketches. A crudely drawn axe was buried in her father's head with the words *born in sin* written on the handle. There was a collar around Richelle's neck and a leash running to her father's hand. The words *daddy's little cunt* had been written across her face. As she looked at it, her face went pale.

"Enough," Francis said taking the picture. "Where is this Heinz?"

"Waiting outside," the chief said.

"I'll go," Williams said. "You stay here."

"No," Richelle said. "*I'll* go."

"I'm not sure that's such a great idea," the chief said.

"I don't give a fuck what you're sure of," Richelle said. "This is my job, and if that son of a bitch doesn't like it, he can say it to my face."

# CHAPTER 81

**Berlin**
**Wednesday 26 July 2006**
**0300 CET**

Mike Banner had no idea how close he had come to reliving the nightmare of his friend Mitch when he regained consciousness briefly and saw the stars through the cockpit of the helicopter. Unlike Mitch, however, no one needed to put him back down. The morphine in his system took care of that.

When he woke up again he was in a private hospital room. A nurse was adjusting the roller on his drip and was about to leave when Mike moved his right arm and knocked something off the bed.

She turned and offered him a sympathetic smile. "Welcome back, Mr. Stipe. How are you feeling?"

Mike tried to speak but his tongue seemed stuck to the bottom of his mouth. She saw he was struggling and walked to the sink to pour him a glass of water. "Easy now, just a little bit."

None of it seemed to reach his throat. It was like pouring water on hot sand. He had drunk half the glass before he regained the use of his tongue. When he spoke, the words came out in a drunken slur. "Where am I?"

"You're at the Karl Gustav Clinic in Berlin, Mr. Stipe. You were flown in late last night."

He tried to ask her what had happened to him but the few words he had managed seemed to have drained him of all his strength. She smiled again and said, "It's best if you rest for now. I'll let the doctor know you're awake."

She left the room and Mike found himself alone, unless the incoherent jumble of thoughts and half-memories in his head could be called company. The thought that kept coming back to him was of Susan coming to New York for the weekend. Although how they were going to go house hunting if he was in a hospital bed was anyone's guess.

He tried to move his arm again but it was too heavy. He managed to twist his head to the right just far enough to see a bouquet of flowers and a card standing next to them on the edge of the table. When he tried to focus on the writing his vision blurred, turning the letters into little more than black swirls. He closed his eyes and opened them again. This time he could read the name.

Not *Susan*, but *Caroline*. The name meant nothing to him. He closed his eyes and fell back down into sleep, the two names swirling around in his head.

Susan.
Caroline.

# CHAPTER 82

**Aurora**
**Wednesday 26 July 2006**
**0330 EEST**

"Christ, I've known him all my life," Richelle said. "My father trusted him above anyone else."

She was standing in front of the window in the chief's office looking out at the harbor below. From here, no one would know anything had happened. To the staff of Aurora it was just another day at the office.

The chief approached her and put a hand on her shoulder. "If I've learned anything over the years, it's that you can never truly know anyone."

"But why not admit it? That's what I don't get. Why not at least have the dignity to own up?"

"I don't think he can," the chief said. "But it's all here. I even had Harold look into his communications logs. He's been deleting his external calls from the main index, but Harold found the backups."

"I still can't believe it," Richelle said. "And what the hell am I supposed to do about RP One? Heinz practically ran the program by himself. Without him the risks are too high. We could lose RP One *and* the Pandora. The last ten years down the fucking drain."

She sat down and buried her head in her hands. "I could kill the old fuck. You know that? I really could."

"What about Rainey?" the chief said.

"What *about* him?"

"Heinz seemed to think he was practically a genius. According to Erik, he understood more about Origin in twenty minutes than some of our brightest people have figured out in years. Heinz may have been lying about a lot of things, but I don't think he was lying about that. If you think about it, it makes sense. He would have needed someone to help him if was going to take over."

"He's been here for what, a week?" Richelle said. "I'm sure he's smart, but not that smart. According to Heinz, the margin for error on the landing is less than three percent. And I don't think he was lying about that either."

"Still," the chief said. "It wouldn't hurt to speak to him yourself. Sarah was hiding him in the old generator room. They've gone topside to get some fresh air. You could probably use some yourself."

"I don't know," Richelle said. "I don't know what the hell to do, Brendan. Everything that's happened, it's all too much. Maybe Heinz was right. Maybe I'm not up to this."

"Don't say that," the chief said. "Your father chose you because he knew you had what it takes. For what it's worth, I agree with him."

"Fine," she said. "I'll speak to him. If nothing else, I guess I owe him an apology."

"We all do," the chief said. "Come, I'll go with you."

# CHAPTER 83

**The Callisto**
**Wednesday 26 July 2006**
**0400 EEST**

Francis was waiting in the galley when Williams returned.

"How did it go?" Francis asked.

"It wasn't pretty."

"It never is."

"Brendan had one of Heinz's staff check his external communications records. It looks like he's been in touch with both Jack and Manin on a regular basis."

"We should be grateful things went as smoothly as they did," Francis said. "In my experience things like this rarely end without casualties."

"Come on," Williams said. "I think it's time you got a look at the eighth wonder of the world."

If Mitch had been surprised to see Aurora for the first time, Francis outdid him by a margin of two to one. He stood on the observation deck looking out at the facility for over a minute as Williams watched in amusement.

"I've seen some crazy things in my time," Francis finally said. "But this tops them all."

"If it's any consolation," Williams said. "I still get goose bumps every time I see it again. It's a shame Peter Bershadsky never got to see it like this. You could say this place is the culmination of his life's work."

"I wish Jesse could have seen this," Francis said.

"Who?"

"It's a long story. Perhaps I'll tell it to you sometime. Preferably over cold beers."

"It's a deal," Williams said. "Now if you're done being amazed, I thought you might like something to eat."

"Lead the way."

They left the dock and walked toward the houses on the waterfront. Francis stopped when they reached them.

"I think this is the most surreal moment of my life," Francis said.

"We call it Amity. After the-"

"Jaws," Francis finished. "I can see why."

When they reached the small movie theater with its classic round ticket booth below the canopy Francis stopped and stood looking at a poster in the window advertising an upcoming rerun of A Few Good Men.

"You seen it?" Williams asked.

Francis didn't seem to hear him. He was transfixed by the poster. When he turned to Williams he said, "The security chief is ex-military, am I right?"

"Yeah," Williams said. "He was a lieutenant general in the army."

"I need to see him."

"What, now?" Williams asked.

"Yes, right now."

"Sure, okay. Any particular reason?"

"I'll tell you when we get there."

When they reached the chief's office there was no one there and the door was locked.

"He's probably in Richelle's office," Williams said. "Come on, it's on the top floor."

Francis began to follow Williams, then suddenly turned and ran back toward the door. He hit it dead center with his right shoulder and it flew open, hit the wall and almost returned the favor on the rebound.

"What the hell are you doing?" Williams said, looking astonished.

Francis ignored him. He walked straight across the office to the chief's desk and began opening the drawers. When he found one that was locked he kicked it twice and pulled it out with both hands.

"Would you mind telling me what the hell you're doing?" Williams said.

"Looking for something?"

"What?"

"This," Francis said and pulled a small book from the drawer.

It was a diary. Francis reached into his pocket and brought out the picture the chief had shown Richelle. He flipped through the diary until he found a page with several lines of writing and laid it down beside the picture. "I knew I'd seen it somewhere before."

"Seen what?"

"That," Francis said pointing at an arrowhead scribbled below Richelle's left foot in the picture.

"What is it?" Williams said.

"You see the way the inside lines curve back up?" Francis said, "The only other place I've seen an arrow drawn like that is on the crest of the US Army Special Operations Command. Are you telling me a German scientist would just draw that? And look at the lines of the writing. Look at the S's and the R's."

"Oh my god," Williams said. "It's Brendan's writing."

"We need to find him right now," Francis said.

# CHAPTER 84

**Aurora**
**Wednesday 26 July 2006**
**0420 EEST**

The chief waited until Richelle was out of the elevator before turning the key in the panel and putting it back in his pocket. They approached the double steel doors at the other end of the small room and Richelle pressed the green button beside the door. The two heavy steel doors parted on a narrow dirt path weaving around several large trees into much denser woodland a few yards away. The glow given off by the dim lights that marked the boundaries of the path every few feet was just enough to see by.

"Where are they?" Richelle said.

"Probably over by the lookout."

They set off along the path. It ran through a thick pine forest for a hundred yards or so before bending sharply to the left. The wind began to pick up as they rounded the corner. The path sloped down onto to a semicircular platform surrounded on one side by a low, stone wall. Beyond the wall the ground ended in a sheer cliff face that ran down to the sea. Even this far up, the waves could be heard crashing against the rocks below in a steady procession.

"I thought you said..."

Richelle stopped when she saw the gun in the chief's hand.

"Brendan, what the hell-"

"Shut up!"

"I don't-"

"I said, shut your fucking mouth. If I have to listen to any more of your bitching and whining, I honestly don't think I'll be able to stop myself from shooting you."

She looked at him, her eyes wide with surprise. "Brendan, I don't know what you-"

He stepped forward and slapped her across the face with his left hand. The force knocked her off her feet.

"You have no idea how long I've been wanting to do that," he said. "Now get up. We're going to the launch."

She got to her feet slowly and took several steps back toward the wall.

"Go on," the chief said. "Try it. I dare you. I run five miles a day up here. It would be fitting when you consider I spend most of that time wishing you were in front of me."

When she didn't move, he said, "I'll even give you a head start. I wouldn't want you to think I was taking advantage of a helpless little bitch with nowhere to go."

"You're fucking insane," Richelle said. "You'll never get out of here alive."

The chief nodded toward the path leading down the slope along the cliff edge. "You seem to forget that I'm the one who decides what does and what doesn't leave this island. But then you always were a cocky little bitch. Move it."

Richelle seemed to consider her options one final time, then did as he said.

The path moved gradually closer to the cliff edge for another two dozen yards, ending at the top of a set of steps carved from the rock with a thin metal railing along the outer edge.

"Down you go," the chief said. "Try anything stupid, and I'll throw you over the side."

"What are you going to do?" Richelle said.

"The first thing I'm going to do is finish what that idiot Manin was clearly incapable of. After that I guess I'll have to improvise, now that your boyfriend has thrown a wrench in the works. It's just as well Jack is dead. I don't think he would have approved."

"You're a twisted old fuck," Richelle said. "You know that?"

The chief laughed. "Perhaps. I spent fifteen years listening to your father and his naïve ideas. Frankly, I don't know how I didn't kill him sooner."

Richelle stopped. When she turned around, the look in her eyes was pure poison.

"That's right," the chief said. "I killed your father. It wasn't hard. I mean, he was practically dead already. I smothered him with his own-"

Richelle let out a scream of rage and charged up the steps. The chief swung the butt of his gun at her face but she ducked and brought all her weight into his midsection. He stumbled back and had to let go of the gun to grab the railing. She let out another scream and pushed with all her strength. For just a moment it seemed he might actually go over. But then he grabbed her neck with both hands and pushed her head away.

"You shouldn't have done that," the chief said.

He tilted his head back and lifted her off the steps. Still holding her by the neck, he brought his forehead crashing into the bridge of her nose. Her wide, vacant eyes looked at him for a moment longer, then they rolled up and she went limp. The chief picked her up as if she were a child and slung her over his shoulder.

He carried on down the steps, taking them three and four at a time. As he rounded the final corner the boathouse came into view. It was a large, shoddy, wooden structure built on the shallow rocks at the bottom of the cliff and accessed by a narrow pontoon gangway. As he neared the bottom, a light came on in one of the windows. A moment later the door opened and a man stepped out.

He was dressed in the uniform of the Estonian coast guard and appeared to have been asleep. When he saw who was coming down the steps he turned back and shouted something, then came running forward across the gangway. "Chief? Is everything all right?"

"It's Richelle," the chief said. "She's hurt. We need to get her inside."

The chief laid her down on the bottom of the bunk bed at the back of the small room, then turned to the other man who was wearing the same uniform and gestured toward the cupboard by the door. "Get me the first aid kit."

The man who had come outside knelt beside the chief to get a closer look at Richelle. "Jesus, chief. What happened?"

The chief leaned down, pulled the revolver from the guard's holster and shot him in the back of the head. The other guard turned at the sound of the shot and went crashing back against the wall as two bullets caught him in the chest.

Richelle's eyes fluttered open briefly as the chief dragged her from the bed and through the inner door. A 40-foot twin-engine patrol boat marked in the colors of the coast guard and flying the Estonian flag sat bobbing in the swell.

He bound her hands and feet and cuffed her to the bulkhead in one of the small storage compartments below deck. As soon as he entered the wheelhouse he heard Captain Williams's voice on the boat's radio. "Paul? Roger? Are you there? Pick up. If you can hear me, do not let the chief leave the island. He has-"

The chief took the gun from his pocket and fired the three remaining shells directly into the radio. There was a burst of static followed by a shower of sparks.

"Eat my shit, you nosy bastard," the chief said as he started the engines and eased the throttles forward. The boat bumped up against the barn doors of the boathouse and rebounded. He let the boat drift back, then opened both throttles all the way. The engines let out an almighty roar and the stern sank into the water as the boat bounded forward. This time the doors burst open in a shower of splinters. The hull scraped against one of the rocks in the shallow water with a high-pitched screech, then it was clear of the boathouse and picking up speed.

A few minutes later the island was little more than a silhouette against the backdrop of the rising sun.

Isle of Dragons

# CHAPTER 85

**Aurora**
**Wednesday 26 July 2006**
**0445 EEST**

Williams slammed the mic down on the table. "He's taken the goddamn launch!"

"The what?" Francis said.

"We keep a patrol boat on the eastern side of the island to ward off anyone who gets too close," one of the guards said. "It's the only boat we have."

"What about the Callisto?" Francis said.

Williams shook his head. "Too slow. We'll have to take the helicopter."

"I'll get Yoshi," Erik said. "He'll meet you top side."

Francis followed Williams out of the radio room and back down the hall to the stairs. A door at the top led to another hall that ended in a set of elevator doors. Williams took a small set of keys from his pocket and inserted one of them into the lock at the bottom of the panel. When he pushed the call button nothing happened.

"He's locked it," Williams said and pounded on the doors with both fists. "God damn it!"

Erik came running up the hall a moment later. "What's going on?"

"He's locked down the elevator," Williams said

Erik pointed at a door several yards up the hall. "You'll have to use the access shaft."

The room was little more than a broom closet with a ladder at the back disappearing into a round hole in the ceiling.

"It's a long way up," Erik said. "The cover at the top is probably a little rusty, so you'll have to give it a good push. I'll send Yoshi up when he gets here."

Francis went up first. By the time he reached the top he was sweating so badly he lost his grip on the ladder several times and almost went flying back down. When he finally did reach the top the cover turned out to be more than just a little rusty. He had to lean back and rest his shoulders on the opposite side of the shaft to free up both hands. Even then it took three attempts to get it open.

"Everything all right up there?" Williams shouted.

"Fine," Francis said. "Come on up."

If Francis looked tired, Williams seemed on the verge of fainting as he climbed out of the hole into the small room and sat down to catch his breath. "I'm going to kill him. You watch me."

"We're going to need to catch him first," Francis said. "I hope this pilot of yours knows what he's doing."

"Yoshi knows what he's doing. He used to be a rig pilot."

"How many miles to land?" Francis said.

"Thirty-four," Williams said.

"Then we better get a move on."

They followed the path to the lookout and turned right instead of left toward the boathouse. The path in this direction went uphill and Francis found himself having to slow down to let Williams catch up. As they neared a large clearing Francis could just about make out the round, oblong shape of the hanger on the far side. The entire area was suddenly flooded in bright light and Francis found himself instinctively running for cover.

"It's okay," Williams said between gasps for air. "Erik will have turned them on from the control room."

They heard footsteps and turned to see a short Asian man running up the path toward them. He was wearing a black flight suit with shower slippers on his feet.

"Captain, is this shit for real?" he said. "Erik said the chief's gone mad."

"It's for real, all right," Williams said. "And he has Richelle. He tried to kill her at Utska. And Caroline."

"What?"

Francis headed toward the hangar. "The explanations are going to have to wait. How soon can you have the chopper in the air?"

Yoshi looked at Williams, bewildered. "Who's he?"

"Never mind," Williams said. "It's a long story."

The helicopter was a British-made Westland Lynx. Like the patrol boat, it was white and bore the markings of the Estonian coast guard.

"We're not going anywhere in that," Yoshi said.

"What do you mean?" Williams said.

Yoshi pointed at an open panel in the side of the helicopter. Below it on the floor there was a small puddle of oil. He pulled out the end of a split hose. "Oil feed. Looks like the chief got here first. Luckily, I'm a sentimental fool."

"What the hell is that supposed to mean?" Williams said.

Yoshi pointed to the back of the hangar where something big had been covered by an old dusty tarpaulin.

"What is it?" Francis said.

"The old Bell 47," Yoshi said. "I was supposed to fly it to the Gustav after this thing arrived, but things just keep coming up, if you know what I mean. Help me get the cover off."

The three of them pulled off the tarpaulin. Francis stood looking at the small bubble-dome cockpit with a sense of growing dread. "Will it fly?"

"Oh, she'll fly all right," Yoshi said. "If she starts, that is."

"If she starts?" Francis said.

"Relax. I'm joking. Just help me wheel her out."

They pushed the small helicopter out of the hangar and out into the clearing. Francis couldn't help but notice the thick coat of dust on the narrow seats and the enormous cobweb running from one of the control sticks to the instrument panel.

"Stand back," Yoshi said. "She's going to smoke a little."

She smoked a lot.

By the time the engine finally began to turn over it looked like the small helicopter was on fire. Yoshi raised the thumb of one hand and Williams stepped forward.

"Hold on," Francis said. "There's only room for two on that thing."

"Yeah," Williams said. "And I'm one of them."

"Listen," Francis said. "Don't take this personally, but this isn't going to be easy. Assuming we even find them, it might not end well for any of us."

"I don't care," Williams said.

"Maybe not. But I do. Enough to know that if you catch up to him, he'll kill you before you know what's happening. And I think you know I'm right."

Williams ignored him and stepped forward. Francis reached out and put a hand on his shoulder. "Captain? I'm serious."

Williams hesitated for a moment then looked down and nodded slowly. "Fine."

"All right," Francis said. "Now get back down there and do what you can. If I can't stop him you're going to have to do it some other way. I suggest you and Erik get busy figuring that part out."

Francis turned and ran toward the helicopter.

"If you find that son of a bitch, you kill him," Williams shouted. "You hear me? You kill him."

But Francis didn't hear him. Yoshi had the engine at near full throttle. As soon as Francis jumped in the helicopter began to rise.

"Head straight for land," Francis shouted.

The pilot nodded. "I'm Yoshi by the way."

"Francis."

"Nice to meet you, Francis. Have you ever jumped out of a helicopter before?"

"Actually, I have. Just not onto a moving boat."

Yoshi smiled and banked sharply to the left. When they were over the water he tapped Francis on the shoulder and pointed at one of the gauges.

"What is it?" Francis said.

"Fuel tank's almost empty. There's enough to get us to the coast, but not back. I guess we'll both be jumping."

If this fact bothered Yoshi, he didn't let on. If anything, it seemed to amuse him. He tapped the gauge several times with one finger to see if maybe it wasn't just stuck, then shook his head and shrugged.

Five minutes later Yoshi pointed down at the water ahead. It took Francis a moment to make out the small shape rushing across the water about half a mile in front of them. Judging from the size of the wake the boat was moving fast. By the time Yoshi dipped the nose and began to descend, the first signs of land appeared over the horizon.

"I'm going to get as low as I can," Yoshi said. "That thing is a lot louder than we are. If we're lucky he won't see us until we're on top of him."

Francis nodded and reached for the handle. He had to use both hands to get the flimsy plastic door open. When they were only about twenty yards from the stern of the boat Francis saw the back of the chief's head through the window of the wheelhouse. He wedged his foot into the gap of the open door and braced himself. The helicopter suddenly misfired and dropped several feet and Francis saw the chief turn around.

Under less precarious circumstances the look on the chief's face might have been cause for laughter. Francis saw the gap widen as the helicopter began to misfire repeatedly.

He jumped.

His first thought was that he was going to end up in the water if he was lucky, and being churned into mince by the propellers if he wasn't. But he reached out and managed to grab the railing with both hands. Out of the corner of his eye he saw the helicopter rise and bank away. Francis managed to get one foot on the deck and was pulling himself up when he saw the chief.

He was moving far too quickly for a man of his size and age, Francis thought. One moment he was bounding over the rail of the wheelhouse onto the rear deck, the next he was practically on top of him. Francis managed to avoid being pushed into the wake of the speeding boat by pure chance. The chief tripped over a steel plate on the deck and landed hands-down a few feet from the rail.

Francis leaped over it and rushed forward, intending to seize the advantage while the chief was down. He brought back his foot and aimed the toe of his boot at the chief's ribcage. But what should have been soft tissue and weak bones, felt more like a slab of solid granite. The chief hardly seemed to notice. He got to his feet, the grin on his face not so much amused as insane.

"You shouldn't have done that," the chief said. "Now you've made me angry."

"That's funny," Francis said. "I was just thinking the same thing."

For a moment both men stood, each trying to read the intentions of the other. Francis glanced toward the wheelhouse and saw the chief's grin widen.

"Go on," the chief said. "Try it."

Francis turned and darted to his right. He made it to the wheelhouse and jumped for the rail. He was half way up when a hand seized his left ankle and pulled him back down. Francis hit the deck on his right shoulder and tried to roll away, but the chief was too quick. He grabbed Francis's ankle with both hands and began to pull him across the deck toward the rail. Francis kicked out with his free foot, stunned at the sheer strength of the man.

When they reached the rail, the chief let go with one hand and bent down to grab Francis's other foot. Francis pulled it back, planted both hands on the deck and brought the heel of his boot into the side of the chief's face. He had to do it three times before the hand around his ankle let go and the chief stood up to avoid the next kick. He put a hand to his ear and looked down at the tips of his fingers. Francis saw the top of his ear had split open.

The chief let out a howl of rage and sprang forward. Francis found himself scrambling back across the deck on all fours. The chief reached down to grab his neck but Francis ducked and the chief got a handful of his jacket instead. The chief pulled back hard, but Francis managed to get his arms out and climb back to his feet.

Francis ran for the wheelhouse and this time he made it. He closed the rolling door behind him and latched it shut. The chief came bounding over the rail a second later and ran for the open door on the other side. The moment he stepped into the doorway Francis pushed the left throttle back and spun the wheel. The chief stumbled back and disappeared over the rail of the wheelhouse as the boat listed heavily to starboard and began to turn.

Francis shut off the engine and scrambled for something he could use as a weapon. All he found was a small gutting knife on top of a pile of maps in one of the drawers below the broken radio. He pushed it into his boot and slowly approached the open door. "Hey big guy, why don't you try that again?"

There was no reply. Francis approached the rail and looked down. There was no sign of the chief. He scanned the sky briefly looking for the helicopter, but that too seemed to have disappeared. Not quite daring to believe the chief had fallen overboard, Francis circled the wheelhouse, slowly scanning the deck for any sign of movement. "What's the matter, chief? You decide you're not-"

Francis caught a flicker of movement out of the corner of his eye. A moment later something clattered to the deck below him and rolled to a stop. He flung himself to the deck and covered the back of his head with both hands. When nothing happened, he slowly raised his head to look around, and that was when he saw him.

The chief was standing behind the twin machine guns mounted to the deck toward the front of the boat with both hands on the grips. Francis barely had time to get to his knees before both barrels erupted in a burst of flame. Francis was showered in broken glass as he scrambled to reach the back of the wheelhouse. One of the bullets ricocheted off the window frame and passed so close to the back of his head it shaved the hair off in a neat little line. Another grazed the back of his calf, and a third tore off the heel of his left boot.

The chief was shouting something Francis couldn't make out. He crawled beneath the rail and lowered himself down to the deck. Several bubbles appeared in the thin steel bulkhead of the wheelhouse as the rounds hit the back of the wall inside. A moment later they began to smoke as the paint around them melted.

Francis ran for the back of the boat, climbed over the rail and jumped into the icy water. He made his way along the side of the hull intending to reach the bow, but when he looked up he saw the chief lean over the rail and spot him. He had removed one of the machine guns from the mount and was swinging the heavy weapon over the side. Francis drew in a deep breath and dived. He heard the muffled sound of the gun as several bullets hit the water behind him, leaving little streams of bubbles in their wake. Francis stayed where he was until the firing stopped then resurfaced where he had been. He heard the chief running across the deck to the other side and carried on toward the front of the boat. He could feel his limbs stiffen as his extremities began to shut down from the drop in temperature.

The bow curved up sharply, making it impossible for the chief to see him, much less lean over and shoot him. But the advantage was moot.

"Checkmate!" the chief shouted. "Looks like your luck finally ran out, you meddling shit."

The chief was standing somewhere above him on the bow, clearly as aware of Francis's predicament as *he* was.

"Show yourself and I'll make it dignified," the chief said. "It's the least I can do for a fellow soldier."

Francis tried to say something but found he was shivering too much to do anything but stutter.

"Perhaps you'd like your little bitch in there with you," the chief said, clearly amused by the situation. "But you'll have to make up your mind soon. I have a feeling your new friends might be on their way."

Francis had decided his only chance would be to return to the stern and try to get back on board when the motor suddenly roared to life and the boat began to move forward. He reached up to grab the steel ring welded to the hull above him, but his fingers slipped and he found himself being pushed aside as the boat began to accelerate. When he was halfway to the stern he managed to grab a length of rope hanging over the side. He prepared to let go and dive as soon as he saw the chief lean over the rail, but there was no sign of him.

There was a sudden burst of fire again and Francis raised his head above the edge of the deck just in time to see Richelle duck behind the exhaust vent on the stern deck. Her hands were bound behind her back. The chief was standing outside the wheelhouse firing down at the deck in a wide arc. Richelle spotted Francis and her eyes widened. Francis held up a hand and patted the air to tell her to stay where she was. The chief bounded over the rail and landed on both feet, the heavy machine gun still in his hands.

As the chief passed him, Francis lowered himself down into the water. The boat was now moving at full speed again and he found himself skimming along the surface, barely able to hold on. A quick glance back told him they were now headed back out to sea. When he raised his head over the deck again the chief was standing in front of Richelle. Francis pulled himself up over the rail and untied the end of the rope. He wound a short length of it around both hands and stepped forward.

Francis didn't know if it was something the chief saw in her eyes, or just his intuition, but he suddenly spun around and raised the barrel of the machine gun. Richelle tried to rush him from behind. Without even looking around, the chief reached back with his free hand and pushed her so hard she went flying into the rail and almost over it. The chief nodded his head to the side, motioning for Francis to join her. "Well isn't this nice? The two of you reunited one last time. I had intended to use her to weed out her bitch of a sister, but I've changed my mind."

Francis helped Richelle to her feet.

"I'm sorry," he said.

But Richelle didn't seem to hear him. She was looking at the chief.

"You're a dead man, Brendan. Even if you make it ashore, Titov will find you and tear every limb from your body."

The chief threw back his head and laughed. "You put too much faith in that Russian lapdog of yours. I look forward to meeting him again. If I'm lucky, he'll put up more of a fight than this sorry excuse."

Francis was visibly shaking now.

"Look at him," the chief said. "He's half the man *you* are, Richelle."

"Stop talking and get it over with, you fucking spineless piece of shit," Richelle said.

She was too preoccupied with her own rage to notice Francis reach over and put an arm around her waist. The chief raised the machine gun then stopped, frowning.

Francis was clutching the rail behind him and looking over the chief's shoulder. The chief turned just in time to see the Callisto break the surface dead ahead of them. Francis pulled Richelle over the rail and into the water only seconds before the patrol boat slammed into the hull of the submarine. The chief darted for the side of the boat, but it was too late. The smaller vessel practically disintegrated on impact. The chief was thrown into the wall of the wheelhouse like a Louisville Slugger at a fastball. His dying scream was drowned out in a cacophony of twisting metal and splintering wood.

By the time Francis and Richelle surfaced, what little remained of the boat was already sinking beneath the waves in a smoking ruin. They saw Williams raise his head above the edge of the observation platform and mouth what could only have been a series of incredulous obscenities to someone behind him. Francis raised a hand and waived. A moment later he saw Williams climbing down the side of the conning tower with several men in tow. As they neared the submarine, Francis saw that one of them was Yoshi.

Two of the crew lowered a rope ladder down to the water. Francis helped Richelle up first. When he reached the top himself Williams extended a hand and raised him to his feet.

"I've got to give it to you," Francis said, his teeth clattering. "Your timing couldn't have been better."

"Thank him," Williams said, nodding at Yoshi. "It was his harebrained idea. I thought he was going to get you both killed."

Francis turned to Richelle, who was now shivering too. "We've got to stop doing this."

# CHAPTER 86

**Aurora**
**Friday 28 July 2006**
**1600 EEST**

For Francis, the next two days passed in a kind of euphoric haze. Part of it was almost certainly the absence of something to run from, but mostly it was the place itself.

Both Mitch and Sarah had been waiting for them on the dock when the Callisto arrived. What impressed Francis most about the young computer whiz from DC was the way he appeared to be taking the whole affair in his stride, as if being kidnapped and brought to the island sanctuary of a secret organization was an everyday occurrence. That Mitch had apparently also found the time to strike up a relationship with a beautiful young woman made it that much more spectacular.

Mitch and Sarah had shown him to his quarters, a modern and spacious apartment down the hall from Mitch's own that had apparently never been occupied. Despite his absolute conviction that sleep under the circumstances would be impossible, Francis managed an uninterrupted twelve hours, and probably could have slept for another six if his chaperones hadn't called to say they would be by to take him to dinner as soon as he was showered and dressed.

And so Francis had found himself enjoying a beautifully prepared meal of steak and chips on the outside veranda of One Eyed Jack's. Sarah had listened in polite silence as Mitch and Francis compared notes on their respective roles in the debacle that had started with a not-so-simple misunderstanding and ended in the deaths of over two dozen people, if the raiding party at Utska was added to the tally.

Erik had arrived as they were getting up to leave and informed them that Richelle was on her way back with Titov and would arrive the next day. In the meantime, perhaps Francis would like to see the museum or take in a movie.

Sitting down to watch a film when you were essentially living one, struck Francis as both odd and strangely unappealing. But he *had* agreed to see the museum and had been as stupefied as Mitch to learn that Origin was real.

While Mitch had interpreted the ship's size in terms of a rush hour commute through his home town, Francis found himself thinking of his early soldiering days and the twelve-mile marches they had been required to complete twice a year in under three hours. The idea that an object could be constructed on such a scale was mind-boggling.

That had been yesterday. Now, standing in the kitchen of the apartment

(Sarah had insisted it was his, but Francis couldn't quite bring himself to see it that way), he found himself turning to the long-term future for the first time he could remember.

The idea of staying made him uneasy. But Francis thought that had more to do with his mindset than anything else. Eight years of living in the shadows under a myriad of assumed names had simply made the idea of staying *anywhere* for too long both impractical and dangerous.

But this place was different, of course. Here everyone was living in the shadows. If you really thought about it, it was almost too good to be true. But unlike Mitch, for whom the question of staying hadn't really been a question at all, with or without the added attraction of Sarah, Francis was a different animal altogether. To a man like Francis Moore, even something as incredible as Origin and all it implied had surprisingly little impact on his view of the world, which in many ways was more similar to the late chief's than those of Richelle and her colleagues. A lot of it came down to his own experience with the way the world actually turned and the deep sense of cynicism this had cast over his once guileless ideals. But he also understood something that he suspected few of the people who had dedicated their lives to Aurora and its mission did; namely that much of what they wanted to fix was broken for a reason and it had little to do with resources or technology.

His thoughts were interrupted by a knock on the door. It was Mitch.

"Hey, Francis."

"Hey, yourself. What's up?"

"Can I come in?" Mitch asked.

"Of course."

Mitch stood looking over the apartment for a moment and nodded appreciatively, "Nice digs. Want to trade up? I got the nineteen twenties suite. Not really my bag."

"I'll pass, thanks," Francis said. "Besides, I kind of got the impression you might not be living alone for long."

Mitch smiled. "She told you?"

"Actually, it was her father who told me. He'll probably never bring himself to say it, but Erik thinks the sun shines out of your ass."

"Really? You think so?"

"I know so. Although I can't for the life of me figure out why."

"Ha ha, very funny," Mitch said. "She's one hell of a girl, you know."

"It's nice to see you've landed on your feet here, Mitch. I'm happy for you."

Mitch nodded absentmindedly at this, then took a deep breath, steeled himself and said, "You should stay."

"I should?"

"I know you and I aren't in the same boat, despite appearances. I also know that if our roles had been reversed, I'd be dead now and you - well, who knows. My point is, this place might not be your version of heaven, but you have to admit it has a lot more to offer than whatever might be waiting for you out there."

Francis nodded, "I suppose."

"So?" Mitch asked.

"So I'm just… " Francis began, then trailed off.

"Worried something like this might happen again?" Mitch suggested. "That someone will find this place and come charging in, guns blazing? Don't you see, that's just it? That's why we need you here. Tell me, you think you could escape the fallout if something like that really did happen? I probably don't need to tell you this, but if this place fell into the hands of our government, or the Russians or Chinese, we can all kiss our asses goodbye. Could you live with yourself knowing you might have been able to help prevent it?"

Francis said nothing for a long time. When he finally raised his head to look at Mitch there was no humor on his face. "Is Titov back?"

"Yes. He and Richelle arrived about an hour ago."

"Have you talked to him?" Francis asked.

"Yeah, we had a little chat. Why?"

"What happened with Fairchild?"

"Exactly what you said would happen. He agreed to the terms."

"And Weaver?" Francis asked.

"Weaver's dead," Mitch said.

Francis looked taken aback. "He is?"

"Fairchild's no idiot," Mitch said. "If anything, I'd say he was probably grateful. His views on Princip couldn't have been that different from yours if he was willing to get rid of Weaver."

Francis considered this for a moment and said, "And the people in New York?"

"Dead," Mitch said. "Titov found the van Jack took using the on-board GPS tracker."

Francis nodded thoughtfully and said, "I want to ask you something, Mitch. And this is deadly serious."

"Go on," Mitch said.

"Do you think these people realize what would have happened if Brendan had succeeded? I mean, do you think they've really thought it through?"

Instead of answering, Mitch held up the small book he had been holding, opened it and began to read. "If I am certain of anything, it is that this discovery must never be exposed to anyone whose motives are not altruistic beyond question. To allow it would be to open the gates of hell itself and invite upon the world a future in which all that is good, all that is decent and worth living for, would eventually burn at the hands of those who see power and control as the only virtues, and hold all else in contempt. I do not know if what must be done can be achieved against such odds, only that I must try. For what other hope is there?"

Mitch closed the book and looked at Francis. "This is the diary Peter Bershadsky kept until the day he was killed. He wrote that in a hotel room in Stockholm in 1985. At that time he was the only living person aware of Origin. I think that answers the question, don't you?"

"I guess," Francis said.

"And I'll tell you something that no one else around here will," Mitch said. "These guys need you more than you need them. Titov might talk tough, and I have no doubt he's as loyal as they come, and Richelle is clearly too proud to beg, but that's the truth. And I think you know it."

"I do?"

"Come on, Francis, who are we kidding? These guys may have the money, and I have no doubt they have the best of intentions, but you didn't ask me if I thought they understood the implications of what they're doing here because you thought they were dumb, did you?"

"I didn't say I think they're dumb," Francis said. "I just think they're-"

"Naive?" Mitch said.

"Maybe."

"And who better to pull the wool from their eyes than a man who knows what they're getting into?"

"I think you're overstating my value," Francis said. "I haven't got a clue what they're getting into. And I'm sure they don't either. That's what scares me."

"And I think you're *understating* your value," Mitch said. "No one can know exactly what will happen, but you're a hell of a lot better suited to dealing with the unexpected than anyone else around here. Besides, you know the old Chinese proverb don't you? I'm pretty sure it applies here. You owe it - we owe it - to these people to help them."

Francis went into the kitchen, poured himself a glass of water and stood looking at it, his eyes distant. When he came back into the living room he sat down in front of Mitch, looked at him for a moment longer, then said, "All right. I'll stay. Now get out of my apartment before I change my mind."

Mitch stood and held out a fist. "Put it there, brother."

Francis sighed and bumped the fist with his own. "Go on, off with you. Take that girl of yours to dinner. I need a little time to arrange my thoughts."

When Francis opened the door Richelle was standing in front of it, one hand raised to knock. Both her eyes were black and she had a small Band-Aid over the bridge of her nose.

"Bad time?" she asked.

"Not at all," Francis said. "Mitch was just leaving."

When he passed her Mitch gave Richelle a little thumbs-up and got a wink in return.

When he was gone, Richelle said, "Everything okay?"

"Five by five," Francis said. "And you?"

"I'm just glad this is all over," she said. "Did Mitch tell you about Fairchild?"

"He did."

"Did he say anything else?"

Francis smiled at her but said nothing.

"What?" She said.

"Richelle, I may have been born at night, but it wasn't last night. I know a double act when I see one."

For a moment she was at a loss for words. "It was that obvious?"

"It's okay," Francis said. "I understand why you did it. Mitch is quite a character, isn't he?"

"He certainly is," she said.

"If you ask me, I'd say he is going to be a lot more useful around here than me."

She regarded him for a moment with a stern gaze. "We need people like you as well, Francis. And everything that's happened has only made that more obvious than ever. You see that, right?"

"Sure," Francis said. "I guess I just don't see where I fit in exactly. I'm no science major. And I sure as hell don't know anything about space. Now Mitch, he's all of that and probably more. I have one skill, and I'm not sure it's what you're really looking for."

"Killing people?" she said.

Francis nodded. "Yeah. Killing people."

She shook her head. "You're being a little hard on yourself, don't you think? Can I ask you something?"

"Sure."

"What were you going to do? Once you succeeded in shutting down your program? What were you going to do then?"

Francis considered the question and said, "The truth? I don't really know. I spent so long getting to that day, I guess I never thought beyond it."

"You want to know what I think?" Richelle said.

"Why do I get the feeling you're going to tell me anyway?"

She smiled. "I think you did what you did because you recognize that there are things in this world that can't be allowed to exist. And whatever part *you* may once have played in that, you've more than atoned for it, believe me. I'm not talking about getting the CIA to shut down some assassination program. I'm talking about this. You said it yourself, Brendan wasn't trying to shut this place down, or simply replace me as the person in charge. He-"

"He was going to try and use it as a weapon," Francis said.

"Yes."

"And could he?" Francis asked. "Use it as a weapon?"

"I don't mean to sound overly melodramatic," Richelle said. "But Heinz assures me that there are technologies on board Origin that would make nuclear weapons look like swear words. So when I say, you've atoned for whatever you've done, I'm talking about what might have happened, no, what *would* have happened, if you hadn't come along when you did."

"All right," Francis said. "And now that I have. What next? What exactly is the plan?"

She looked at him as if the question was self-explanatory. "We use what we know to do what we can. We employ the technologies we find as a force for good. I don't know if you've noticed, but assassinations are the least of the world's problems. My father was always clear about his intentions. He wanted to use whatever we found to do something about it."

"So you're going to save the world?" Francis said.

Richelle looked offended. "Well you don't have to make it sound so fucking naïve."

She saw he was smiling and said, "What?"

"I'm sorry. I didn't mean - maybe I just needed to hear you say it."

"Say what?"

"That this wasn't all just some..."

"What?" Richelle said. "The fucking Umbrella Corporation?"

"The what?"

"Never mind. Although I'd like to think you've seen enough to understand we're not a bunch of screwballs."

Francis held up his hands. "You're right. And I'm sorry. Look, it's all happening a bit fast, that's all. I mean, there's an alien spaceship up there for god's sake. The problem is, I don't actually believe in aliens. It's a bit like meeting Gandhi in a strip club. You know it can't be him, and you know he can't be there, and yet there he is."

Her features softened as he spoke. When he was done, she chuckled and said. "Gandhi in a strip club?"

"Yeah, it happened to me in a dream once. Weird, right?"

This time she really laughed. "You're not all there, are you?"

"What, here? Inside the island stronghold of the new alien revolution? No, I'm not sure that I am."

Richelle struggled to stop herself from breaking into a fresh bout of laughter. A moment later Francis began himself.

In all the years that lay before them and all the trials and triumphs yet to come, that moment would be one they both remembered as among the best. Perhaps because none of it had happened then, and perhaps because on some level they both knew things would never be that simple or easy to laugh at again.

# CONCLUSION

## I

Mike finished reading the four-page document and handed it back.

He was sitting up in his hospital bed still hooked up to a plethora of machines and sensors. The man who had come to see him, a career CIA attaché from the embassy named Frank, reached into his jacket pocket and handed Mike a pen. Mike took it but didn't sign the document.

"Agent Banner," Frank said, "I'm not authorized to discuss the matter with you any further. If you have questions, you'll have to take them up with Director Fairchild when you get back."

"I'm not signing this until I know Susan and Josh are safe," Mike said.

Frank sighed and closed the door. "Your wife and son arrived in Phoenix this morning. That's all I can tell you. I fully understand your concern, and I can't tell you how sorry we are about what's happened, but that's *all* I can tell you. The director assures me every effort will be made to compensate you and your family. But we need to know that we can rely on your discretion in this. If you sign the document, I'll see what I can do about arranging a phone call home."

"So you're blackmailing me," Mike said.

Frank shook his head and was about to reply when Mike said, "It's all right. I'll sign it. Just tell Fairchild I expect him to clear this up with the Bureau before I come back."

"I'll be sure to pass it on," Frank said.

Mike signed the paper and handed it over. "Can I ask you a question?"

"Sure," Frank said. "Just don't expect an answer."

"Has Norton Weaver seen that?"

Frank folded the paper and put it back in his pocket. "I'll be back a little later. In the meantime, you should get some sleep, Agent Banner."

Mike laughed and shook his head. "You guys crack me up, you know that?"

Frank didn't answer. Mike watched him leave and laid his head back down on the pillow.

"Francis," he said to himself, "you crafty son of a bitch."

## II

Joe pulled the rusty old Bronco to the side of the road and looked at Jesse and Amanda in the rear-view mirror. "You guys going to be all right? We don't have to do it today if you don't want."

Amanda shook her head. "If we put it off for another day I'm going to lose my nerve completely."

She took Jesse's hand. "You ready?"

"As ready as I'll ever be."

Joe got out and opened the door on Amanda's side. She stepped out onto the gravel and gave him a long hug. "Thanks, Joe."

When Jesse joined them the two men shook hands.

"You take care of her," Joe said, winking at Amanda.

Jesse reached into his pocket and handed Joe an envelope. "Could you give this to Reginald when you see him?"

Joe took the letter. "Of course. There's a bus stop about half a mile up the road. It will take you into town. If you ask the driver he'll be able to give you directions to the consulate."

They watched Joe get back in the truck and waved after him as he turned and headed back the way they had come.

"Do you think we'll ever see Francis or Mike again?" Amanda said as the truck disappeared from view in a cloud of dust.

"I don't know. Maybe."

Jesse took her hand and they began to walk. "Come on, let's get this over with before we forget what the hell we're supposed to say."

She grinned at him and slapped him on the backside. "You just want your Warhol moment. Admit it."

## III

"And you're not going to tell me where we're going?" Francis asked.

"No," Richelle said. "You'll understand why when we get there."

They were sitting in the galley on board the Callisto. On this particular day Francis was experiencing another first in a seemingly unending line of them. Although it wasn't really a first because Francis had had plenty of hangovers, just not on this side of the new millennium.

"I hear you enjoyed yourself last night," she said with a knowing smile. "Did no one warn you about drinking with Titov?"

"As a matter of fact, no. And I'm not sure it would have done any good. We share a deep mutual passion for vodka and table dancing."

Richelle laughed and said, "Yes, I heard about that, too. It must be an army thing."

"Where were you?" Francis asked. "I get the impression you're the only one that Titov would have listened to last night. You might have been able to do us all a favor."

"Like I said, all will be revealed soon enough. In the meantime, you might want to ask the chef for something to take the edge off your hangover. You look like shit."

By the time the Callisto surfaced and the commotion began in earnest,

Francis was fast asleep in the small bunk he had crawled into after drinking what he still suspected had been a mixture of dog shit and human vomit. That said, it had done the trick. He still didn't feel like a million dollars, but he felt a lot better.

He dressed quickly and made his way up to the bridge where Williams was busy shouting orders without pausing for breath. When he saw Francis, Williams pointed at the ladder leading up to the hatch and said, "Better hurry up, party's starting."

Francis waited for him to elaborate, but Williams had turned to help two of his crew, who appeared to be mounting a large video camera to the eyepiece of the periscope.

Francis's first impression as he stepped onto the observation deck was that they hadn't gone anywhere at all. Then he realized that what he had first taken for the dock inside Aurora was in fact the hull of a small vessel. Neither boat was showing any lights. When he looked up he saw there were no stars out. The wind was blowing an ice-cold draft off the water that made him shiver in the thin coveralls.

"You'll want to get down here and across quickly," someone said from below. "We're leaving."

Francis looked down and saw a crewman standing at the bottom of the ladder leading down onto the hull. He was shining a dim red beam of light up to indicate where the ladder was and Francis climbed down.

"Gangway's over there," the man said when Francis was down. He pointed the beam at a set of steps suspended by a small crane from the boat.

"Where are we?" Francis asked.

"The Karl Gustav. Although if you don't get moving you'll be in Davy Jones's locker in about sixty seconds."

The man ushered Francis toward the steps and he scrambled up just as they began to rise. As he stepped onto the deck of the Karl Gustav, Francis almost walked straight into a short, stocky man with a battered old captain's cap covering a thick tangle of red hair.

"I was just coming to see where you were," the man said in a thick Scottish accent. "I'm Captain MacDonald. Francis Moore, I presume?"

"That's me," Francis said.

"A good name, that," the captain said. "Welcome aboard. I'm afraid Richelle neglected to tell me we had a guest until I ordered the gangway raised. Things have taken an unexpected turn for the worse and as you can see we're all shitting bricks."

Francis wasn't sure if the man was joking or just crazy; he was smiling as he said it.

"What the hell is going on?" Francis asked.

"We're about to witness a miracle," the captain said. "Although if the weather gets any worse it may be a short-lived one. Come, follow me."

Francis, no closer to getting an intelligible answer to his question, followed the captain across the deck and through a small door at the bottom of the superstructure. It had started to rain by the time they got inside. As soon as the door closed, a light came on in the ceiling and he saw they were in a narrow hallway leading to a set of steps.

"When I get a hold of the arseholes at the weather station who promised us clear skies and smooth seas for tonight I'm going to castrate them with my bare hands," MacDonald said as he led Francis down the hall. "Up you go. Straight through the door at the end. I've got to get back outside."

Francis watched the captain run back to the door and disappear. He stood there for a moment feeling the ship rock gently and thanked the cook on board the Callisto, he of the dog-shit cocktail, for his uncanny foresight. Had he still been feeling like death warmed up, Francis thought he would have had to race the captain back to the door and onto the nearest rail for a spot of projectile vomiting. What he did instead was take a deep breath and climb the steps.

When he walked through the door at the end of the passage onto the bridge, what greeted him was pandemonium. There were at least a dozen people present. Francis recognized only Richelle and Heinz. Most of the crew were gathered around the communications console where several of the panels below the control interface had been removed. Someone had climbed inside and was buried to his waste in a jumble of wires and cables.

Francis walked over to Richelle. "What's going on?"

It was Heinz who answered. "The transponder for the remote piloting system has shorted out."

"Okay," Francis said. "In English?"

Before Heinz could answer the door flew open and Captain MacDonald and one of his crew came stumbling in carrying a large red steel box. Both men were drenched and panting heavily. As soon as they set the box down two of the crew began removing the lid. When the man below the console extracted himself and stood up, Francis saw it was Mitch.

"Hey, double-O-seven," Mitch said. "I was wondering when you'd show up."

"I feel a bit like a fifth wheel around here," Francis said.

Mitch cocked a thumb back at the hole he had just climbed out of. "So was I until things started falling apart."

As soon as the lid was off the box Mitch reached inside and pulled out a long narrow circuit board. He crawled back to the hole beneath the console and began pulling out wires. "Charlie, these things aren't going to connect themselves."

A young man – Francis thought he looked no older than seventeen -

handed Mitch a small butane soldering iron. They all watched as he began stripping the wires and attaching them to the board. When he was done, Mitch tucked everything back inside and said, "All right boss, try that."

Heinz was standing below a monitor mounted to the ceiling of the bridge. It displayed two identical outlines of a ship's hull against a dark graph background. One was white and centered on the screen, while the one in red was several centimeters to its right and at a slight angle. He typed something on the keyboard below the screen and stood back. The bridge was silent for almost a minute as they all watched. When the distance between the two outlines began to decrease Heinz breathed a long sigh of relief and said, "She's back online."

A cheer went up among the crew. Several of them slapped Mitch on the back. Everyone was celebrating but Francis, who remained clueless as to what was happening.

Heinz raised his hands and said, "That's all very well, people. But we still have a job to do here and we're not out of the woods yet by any stretch. Jonas, get her back into position. And someone contact Captain Almila and let him know."

Richelle walked over to Francis and pointed to a ladder at the back of the bridge, "Come on, let's go up. We'll get a better view from there."

"Better view of what?" Francis said.

"You'll see."

When he emerged from the hatch at the top of the ladder, Francis saw they were on a large helipad. Where the helicopter was supposed to be, however, there was now a row of large video cameras mounted to the deck on heavy-duty tripods. To Francis they looked like the cameras used to shoot movies or record television programs. Richelle joined him, spoke briefly to one of the people operating the cameras then came back.

"All right," Francis said. "I'm officially dying of curiosity. What are we doing here?"

Richelle smiled. "I'm sorry. I had intended to bring you up to speed on events when you arrived. But as you can see, things weren't going so well."

"Okay," Francis said, "And now?"

"Much better."

"So?"

Richelle looked at Francis the way a teacher might look at a pupil when deciding how best to explain a particularly complicated idea. When she appeared to have made up her mind, she pointed at the camera nearest them and said, "Come. Have a look."

When the man operating it stepped aside, Francis saw it was a night vision camera. Although unlike the ones he had used many times himself, this one was clearly state-of-the-art. The screen still had a slight green tint to it, but the image wasn't grainy at all. What he saw was a large ship with its superstructure in the bow.

"That's the Pandora," Richelle said. "She was commissioned at Busan eighteen months ago. In reality, she isn't so much a ship as a landing platform for what we've been calling RP One."

"RP One?" Francis said.

"It stands for reconnaissance platform. It's a small scout module used to survey the surface of a planet in preparation for a mass landing. RP One left Origin six days ago. Until we actually sent the launch signal, we had no idea it was even going to work. It's also the reason Brendan made his move when he did."

Francis was looking at her as if she were making him the butt of an intriguing but ridiculous joke. Only if it was a joke, the three people now standing next to him must have been in on it, because none of them looked remotely amused.

"Let me get this right," Francis said. "We're waiting for a spaceship to land? *On* that ship?"

"Now you understand why I didn't bother trying to explain it before. But yes, that's exactly what we're doing. Although it's not really a spaceship. It was launched from Origin by catapult. If Heinz is right, and he has been about everything else so far, it uses some kind of ion converter engine in the upper atmosphere to slow down as it descends because it has no propulsion of its own."

"Onto that?" Francis said pointing at the screen.

"That's the theory," Richelle said. "The Pandora is being controlled from here. Which is why she began to drift out of position when the transponder failed."

"You're saying there is nobody on that ship?"

Richelle shook her head. "If the calculations are right, RP One will be about three hundred and fifty degrees Celsius when it touches down. Not only that, but the electric charge it will be putting out would probably fry anyone on board. And that's not the worst of it. Because of the alloy it's made of it's extremely heavy for its size. The Pandora was built with all these things in mind, but the truth is, we're really not sure how accurate any of our predictions are."

"And if you're wrong?" Francis said.

"I'd rather not think-"

She was interrupted by one of the others who pointed at the sky and said, "There," before running back to his camera and pointing it upwards.

Francis looked up and saw what looked like a bright star, a sight that was only peculiar because there were no others. A moment later Heinz's voice came over the radio in Richelle's pocket. He sounded almost delirious with excitement. "Richelle, are you seeing this?"

"I see it."

"I can't believe it," Heinz said.

"Well, if *you* can't," Richelle said, "where does that leave *us*?"

Francis thought it was a very good question. Heinz replied with a burst of nervous laughter.

As they watched, the light grew steadily brighter and began to take on a pale orange tint. To Francis's mind, struggling now for dear life to bring what it was seeing into line with what it could accept, the thing up there was not a spaceship, but a giant meteor, hurdling to earth with promises of Armageddon. As if to confirm this, the spot began to glow brighter and grow in length.

A moment later they heard it. It began as a low humming, like the sound of overhead power lines or a low note on an amplified bass guitar, then quickly increased in tone until it was almost a screech. Francis felt Richelle's hand first brush his own then curl around it in a death grip as the thing appeared to pick up speed.

"Jesus Christ," Francis said, "It's going to crash!"

Richelle didn't reply, but the look on her face suggested she was thinking the same thing.

That's when it exploded.

Or so it seemed.

Francis saw the Pandora, looking tiny and insignificant as the fireball descended like the wrath of God himself. When it seemed only a few hundred yards above the ship it erupted in a flash of blinding brilliance. Bolts of lightning began to shoot out in all directions, some touching down on the surface of the water, others arching around and finding the ship. The high-pitched whine grew louder for a moment, then suddenly turned into the roar of a thousand afterburners spinning up for takeoff. Francis felt his ears pop. He closed his eyes, convinced that the next thing they would see was either a mushroom cloud or a wave several stories high rushing at them across the water. But when he opened them again, what he saw was nothing. Other than the ringing in his ears and the bright spot in the center of his vision, the night had returned as quickly as it had been interrupted.

Richelle looked at him, then down at her hand, which was still clutching his. She let go and said, "What the hell just happened?"

The way she said it and the expression on her face made her look twelve years old. Francis, who had no idea what the hell had just happened, only reciprocated the look. When he turned to the camera crew he saw they were no better off. Richelle raised the radio in her right hand and said, "Heinz? You there?"

"Hold on a moment," Heinz said, "We've got a visual, but it looks like the sensor readouts are...no wait, I think we're getting something."

"Heinz," Richelle said, "never mind the fucking readouts, have we lost the Pandora?"

There was a pause. When he answered, Heinz sounded both elated and a little annoyed. “Lost the Pandora? No, of course not.”

“And RP One?”

“Well, we’re still waiting for a response from the-”

“Heinz, just tell me if RP One is on board that ship.”

“Yes.”

Richelle let the radio fall from her hand, then sank to her knees and looked up at the sky. Francis thought she had started to cry, but when she looked at him he saw only relief in her eyes. A moment later Heinz appeared in the hatch behind them and climbed out onto the landing pad. Richelle got to her feet. When Heinz extended his hand she ignored it and put her arms around him instead.

“We did it,” she said.

“We did,” Heinz said. “We really did. And if we don’t get out of here we’ll probably all be in jail by this time tomorrow.”

She let go of him and stepped back, the smile on her face widening as she turned to Francis. “Never one to waste time on sentiment is our chief scientist.”

“What?” Heinz said, “I’m serious. We can’t-”

“I know you are,” Richelle said, “Go on, off you go. Get us out of here. I’d give you a week off when we get back, but I don’t see the point in making you miserable after all you’ve done.”

Heinz hesitated for a moment, apparently unsure if the conversation was over, then he lifted his radio and said, “Get the Pandora out of there. I want full thrust on all motors. She’s going to struggle to pick up speed with the extra weight.”

The Karl Gustav began to vibrate as her engines were pushed to full throttle. Richelle and Francis stood looking out at the sea where the first glow of the coming dawn was just breaking over the horizon. In the distance, the silhouette of the Pandora painted both a majestic and somehow ominous picture, a silent promise of things to come.

## THE END

Nathaniel Dean James
April 2012 – January 2014

Arrival of RP One

# DEAR READER

Now that you have finished this book, perhaps you would consider leaving a review. Reviews are a great way for readers for discover new books, as well as for authors to discover new readers. Provided you have an account at Amazon, leaving a review is quick and easy. It would be greatly appreciated.

# AFTERWORD

Although I have never been a particularly big fan of Science Fiction, I have always subscribed to the belief that in all the billions of galaxies that make up the known universe, we cannot possibly be the only intelligent life. This is not so much a religious or scientific conviction as a simple acknowledgement of the law of probability. In so far as any author will inevitably imbue one or more of his or her characters with some trait or aspect of themselves, my own views on this are clearly echoed in the words of our friend Maxim, the retired cosmonaut who Mike and Francis meet in London on their way to Zurich, with whom I otherwise have little in common.

As for the likelihood of our ever encountering such intelligence? I believe it is highly improbable. And for the same reason that I'm convinced it must surely exist; the sheer size of the universe. Luckily for you and I, we need not concern ourselves too much in these pages with such trifling things as likelihood.

In sitting down to begin work on this manuscript one fine Spring day in 2012, I asked myself just two questions; what if there really *was* a spaceship sitting out there? And what if one man came into possession of that fact to the exclusion of all others? The first presumption aside, I think the second is not as farfetched as it may seem. Everything that followed on the heels of these two "givens" was born in the writing. The only challenge I set myself was to ensure that the "fantastic" did not impinge too heavily on the story itself, the characters and the pace of events. By this I mean the temptation to allow technology to become a deus ex machina to the men and women of Aurora, whose hopes rest so heavily on the potential of their discoveries to set things right.

But as Francis Moore understands only too well, the problems that face humanity cannot be solved by technology alone.

Having already completed much of the second book in this series, I have remained loyal to this premise. For while Origin and its many secrets continue to play a part, that part is necessarily limited. As we rejoin Richelle and her team, still reeling from the impact of recent events, and faced with the challenges presented by the arrival of RP One, it is not to the stars that we must turn for answers, but to that powder keg between the 48$^{th}$ parallel and the Yalu River known as the Democratic People's Republic of Korea, where, even as we speak, sinister forces are conspiring to bring the world to the edge of imminent peril.

Origin – Season Two, is scheduled for publication in November 2014.

ACKNOWLEDGEMENTS

As any author knows, writing a book and actually publishing one are two very different kettles of fish. Not only in terms of personal effort, but also that of the many people essential to making such a venture a successful one. I would therefore like to take this opportunity to offer my undying gratitude and deepest respect to the following people:

To my dear mother, whose loving support always has been and always will be indispensable. To my father, for pointing out the viability of this work at a time when I was anything but sure of it myself, and for providing the help and enthusiasm to take it forward. To the patron saints, Eddie Wheeler and Alasdair "Mac" MacDonald, who, aside from remaining true and loyal friends, also provided the roof under which most of this book was written and the cash to bring it all together. To Sarah Cohen, Leigh Bowles, Pete Cable and William Tucker, who have each read the manuscript in one or more of its many incarnations and provided invaluable feedback. To Kay, for teaching me one of the hardest and most valuable lessons along the way. To the editors, Mel Hughes and Indy Zoeller, who saw enough promise in the project to provide top-dollar work at rock-bottom prices (keep those rain checks in a safe place!). To BB eBooks for their passion and devotion to detail. To Professor Edwin V Bell of the Goddard Space Flight Center, without whose valuable insights many of the tenets in this book would have been wholly ridiculous, rather than just highly unlikely. To the hard working men and women of the Wikimedia Foundation, who continue to reside over one of the most open, comprehensive and useful sources of information available. And last, but not least, to you, the reader, for taking a chance on this book. If you enjoyed reading it half as much as I enjoyed writing it, we should be all square.

# ABOUT THE AUTHOR

Nathaniel Dean James is the pseudonym of author Jonathan Ronnquist.

Born in the town of Cuckfield in West Sussex, Jonathan spent much of his early life on the road, moving first to Stockholm and Copenhagen, and later to Clearwater, Florida, where he soon developed a passion for sailing. After an extended stay in Mexico City, recently ravaged by the devastating 1985 earthquake, he left school in the United States and headed for the Caribbean, where he became a radar operator on board a cruise-liner sailing out of Curacao in the Netherlands Antilles.

Jonathan returned to the United Kingdom the following year, but was soon off again, this time to Eastern Europe, where the post-communist era was only just beginning to reshape the region following several decades of political and economic deprivation. Despite having completed little formal education, he obtained his teaching credentials from the University of Cambridge and spent the next several years teaching English in both Hungary and the Czech Republic.

On his return to the United Kingdom at the turn of the millennium, Jonathan enrolled in the British Army, first as an infantryman in the Parachute Regiment, and later as a member of the Royal Military Police, where he completed a tour of the former Yugoslavia as part of operation Palatine.

Having never attended, much less graduated, high school, Jonathan turned to books at an early age to fill the gap. And it was only after his honourable discharge from the military that he turned his attention to the prospect of writing, an ambition fuelled both by his love of reading and three decades of exposure to the many people and varied cultures of his wide travels.

Jonathan now lives with his wife and their two children in West Sussex.

Origin is his debut novel.

29401757R00195

Made in the USA
Charleston, SC
12 May 2014